HEARTSTONE

THE RED VELD

by

NICHOLAS RINTH

www.nrinth.wordpress.com

Cover Art, Design, and Illustrations by Fabian Rensch
www.fabianrensch.com

ISBN 978-0-9988216-2-7 (Print)
ISBN 978-0-9988216-3-4 (Ebook)

PRINTED IN THE UNITED STATES OF AMERICA

FIRST EDITION

To Gabriel,
*for all of the nonsense we've shared throughout the years;
amidst waves of darkness, you are a shaft of unfailing light.*

FERUS
TERRIA

Pit

Tor

Hermit's
Hovel

PULKA
RUINS

Purine

Narrow
Marsh

ON

Rotten
Woods

Yorn

Ice Crown
Mountains

Spier

Tearwood

PLAINS

Eirinne Mountains

ERIAM

Thyme

Cheryll's
Cottage

ZEXIN SEA

Drowned
Tower

rbug
Mire

Pernelia's
Temple

N

W   O

S

CANTICLE OF THE LOST

The world laments your departure,
Cries of parting for another farewell,
Amidst the wails of torment, darkness runs deep,
Shadows are cast by the fading light,
In your ears ring the echoes of silence,
And nothing remains,

The life you breathe is no more,
Weep not, for tears are wasted,
Grieve no longer, for cries are needless,
In shackles you were wrought,
But to chains you shall ne'er return,
For they await, for they await,

The First Zenith, timeless and enduring,
Their pine for you is eternal, their compassion overflowing,
Comfort and forgiveness, they offer freely,
Pain, you shall know no longer,
Your sorrows shall be erased,
In death, you are freed from the burdens of existence,

With open arms of elemental lore, they beckon,
With voices of exultation, they sing,
"Come, for our reach is boundless,
In our arms lie rest,"

On the eve of morrow's gloom,
Their song shall pierce the stillness,
Where you shall once more find light.

1

He felt something crawl along his skin.

Hazy tendrils crept over his arms, sucking the flesh from his bones like vacuums of personal torture. Painful. That's what it was. Absolutely painful.

Suffocating. Overpowering. Maddening.

The world was silent. His heart stopped for an endless age. It felt like a lifetime stretched into a handful of seconds. Time, however, waited for no one. Let alone a mortal. So, the moment passed, and he lost the chance to brace himself. His heart throbbed with newfound ferocity. Its frantic beat was the only sound that rang in his ears. It thrashed like a monster that banged on the doors of his subconscious, peeking through the floorboards, and telling him to get out of his cowardly crouch to grant it entrance. And here he was, actually considering the idea.

But this was reality. A different kind of hell. At times, a worse one. He didn't have the luxury of focusing on the demons that haunted his mind. Because he was in the company of real monsters. Live ones that existed in the physical world. They had finely crafted masks and tuned personalities. Tweaked humans that showed only the most valued of faces.

Terror lingered in the air. The stench of fear was so potent that he crinkled his nose in distaste. Around him, the men and women in their fine suits and their pretty dresses screamed for their lives. Their voices sounded strangely muffled to his ears. Distant. Like they'd been submerged in water. And, he realized, with an almost stone cold sort of calm that, so was he.

Wait.

He inhaled sharply.

No.

No, he wasn't. He could breathe. He could feel the rise and fall of his chest. He could hear the clink of his shackles. Even as shaky rasps of desperate prayers unintentionally dripped like honey from his lips.

A woman fell, involuntarily kneeling before him with her mouth open in a silent scream. Her hair was so wrecked it looked as if a bird had somehow found its way inside and built a home. Tears raced down her cheeks and her body was wracked with sobs of panic. Her peers were on the ground behind her; their robes stained black with blood. The ones left standing, however, bore expressions of anger. Or was it fear? He no longer knew. Those emotions were all birthed from the same passion.

What he did know was that they were clinging to life, as if they were irreplaceable existences in the elaborate web of fate. As if any of them were worth more than a sack of gold and a few sleepless nights.

Like their lives have meaning, he thought bitterly, then scoffed. It came out as a guttural rasp, but he didn't care. They were nothing but fools that made all of the wrong choices in a futile attempt to find purpose; to maintain their standing; to rise in the social circles of the Institute. *Always complaining. Never satisfied. Why do they even want to carry on?*

He knew the significance of life. It was a precious thing... or so everyone claimed. But what he didn't understand was why they bothered. Their lifespans were limited. Morality was humanity's number one shared trait. He'd met many that justified their selfish actions by claiming that they were simply making the most out of their time. As if that made things better.

They wanted to leave behind their mark of existence. But that was such a laughable notion. Society was dynamic, and like all unstable things, it was every bit as doomed as they were. Sooner or later, their legacies would fade. They'd be replaced by better people with even grander tales, until the only mementoes left were embellished whispers rarely talked about in third-rate taverns. They were clinging to a moment of fame.

Fools, he decided long ago, *the lot of them.*

They were dying, and all he felt was numb, calm, and just a little too happy. How long had he waited for them to disappear and leave him be? Five years? Ten? Twenty? Long enough.

He sighed in relief, before his breath hitched.

All of the pain he'd felt abruptly ceased, and then turned inward. His insides burned. The agony spread like a candle set to rivers of oil. He doubled over, somehow managing to balance himself on all fours. Heat bubbled in his chest, before something wet, sticky, and unbearably hot needled its way up his esophagus. He felt it scorch everything it passed, and it wasn't long before he was coughing, gasping for breath between each terrible fit, until it came out. When it did, he wasn't at all surprised by what he saw.

Red.

It was everywhere.

A glob of blood stained not only the floor, but also his hands, his mouth, even his teeth. As if his situation wasn't bad enough, now even his illness was catching up with him. Impeccable timing as always. Why in the world would whatever deity out there plant the seed of disease in him, further destroying his already doomed mechanism? He didn't doubt that the Creator hated him. But what did he do to deserve it?

From the beginning, he'd been cast into a life of unfinished sentences and undisclosed potential. He was forced to drown in the realization that he'd never truly be able to accomplish anything with the hand he'd been dealt. Sure, he could've played his cards a bit better or he could've cheated every now and again. But even those on the brink of desperation couldn't utilize skills that had never been in their arsenal to begin with.

Unlike him, the Creator was all powerful—or so he always heard from the well-dressed priests that were tasked to preach his greatness. Many claimed that the Creator was the giver and taker of life. Birth and death all wrapped into one encompassing package. The Creator lingered in the wind, the trees, the sea foam. Nature's spirit given a name. A being that's sole purpose was to make sure everyone had an equal chance at life.

Equal, he thought with no small amount of disdain. The word alone made him gnash his teeth in fury. *The Creator had one job. Just one job.*

Did he find humor in his suffering? Did his woes provide entertainment or some sick form of pleasure? A priest had once told him that the illness that wrecked his insides and forced him to cough pools of blood on a daily basis was the Creator's will. That everything that had passed and everything that had yet to come was already predetermined for some higher cause and they were simply left to construe.

How stupid.

He found no solace in an incorporeal presence guiding his life. He'd been told on more than one occasion that he should be grateful for being born to begin with, and he'd say the same thing each time: "So, I could know nothing but hardship?"

There were an optimistic few that told him to look on the bright side of things. To reflect until he found that silver lining he didn't believe existed. They were a positive, yet annoying bunch. While he wasn't against their hopeful outlook, he did have a problem with their flawed sense of reasoning, and how they always seemed to shove those rosy ideals down his throat. They argued that because of adversity, he knew compassion. Because of hate, he could appreciate warmth. Because of poverty, he learned how to treasure the little he did own.

As if a slave owned anything. He didn't even own the links between his wrists. *Fools and their worthless drivel,* he judged darkly. Fool wasn't enough. *Incorrigible human scum.*

They were nice words, to be sure, and he knew they were only trying to comfort him, but it didn't change the fact that to him, the Creator was nothing more than beautified hokum. An abstract spirit created by those that wanted to claim some false support from something larger than any single person could explain. But of course he couldn't say that. Lest he receive another whipping. So, he was forced to brush away his thoughts and add his name to the ever-growing list of people that were dealt a less than stellar hand. He was forced to play the part of ardent advocate; forced to believe that a brighter future awaited him in a tidy, bow-topped bundle outside of death's door.

He hated it.

So much so that he couldn't even verbally express his own animosity. At this point, thinking about it hardly even enraged him. His hatred had cooled, and was now a solid piece of iron-cold coal left in the pit of his stomach. There was an indescribable heaviness to it that trailed after him like a shadow.

His mind was his only solace. It was a safe place, where he could speak without ever truly doing so. He was free to believe whatever he wished there. And, in the sanctity of his thoughts, he wasn't having *any* of it. The only thing he'd ever sought in life was to change the world. No. *His* world was more accurate.

He wanted to change *his* world.

It was a simple idea to think about, but actually carrying out the necessary steps was more daunting than anything he'd ever known. He wasn't ignorant enough to not realize that all of his actions altered his life in some way, but to change it so much that it yielded discernible results took more time. Decades more than what he had. It was a long and drawn-out process. Exhausting didn't even begin to describe it. But it was still better than doing what everyone expected of him. It was better than sitting back, praying, and quietly accepting his fate.

He wouldn't settle. He rejected that idea. He wasn't buying it. The Creator needed better sales pitches because he held only loathing for Ferus Terria's so-called god.

His fingers twitched, casting ripples in the puddle of blood before him. He didn't want to see this. So, his brown eyes darted around the hall, searching for a distraction. They rolled in frantic circles all around his sockets. He wasn't tired. Not really. He'd been on the brink of exhaustion many times before, and he knew for a fact that, right now, he wasn't even close.

And yet, he felt sluggish somehow.

The world moved in slow motion. The rich shades that the pigs around him donned blended into one blur. Just out of focus enough to give him a sleepy kind of headache. He felt the onset of it wash over him in the form of half-numbed pangs of pain that stemmed from his temples, then rippled out across his forehead.

He closed his eyes. They felt useless now.

Don't you dare close your eyes.

They immediately snapped open at the order, then further widened in shock when an echo of the words resounded inside of his mind. It bounced like a sharp cry of steel hitting stone. But, more importantly, it made his headache disappear. He bit his tongue to keep verses of gratitude from escaping his lips.

His body felt light. The fatigue that blanketed him abruptly retreated. Even his violent coughing stopped. He felt better than he had in years. Like the world—the entire future—was at his fingertips. All he had to do was grasp.

But, right now, his hands shook, and he trembled at the sight of all the blood. He would've grimaced had he been able to wipe the shock off of his face. That was impossible though.

His eyes widened when noise became disturbingly lucid. The cries he thought distant were suddenly so near, so vulgar, and oh, so important. It scared him more than he cared to admit, but it intrigued him, too. Had he been hearing muffled tones all of his life? It certainly seemed like it. The world had always been a buzz of orders. His only real companion was the ringing in his ears. Until now.

Thelarius Merve, a dreadfully sweet voice called.

It was the first time his name bobbed around inside of him. Drawn out in such a way that even he thought it belonged to someone important. That voice reminded him of the bedtime stories his dead brother used to tell. It had the power to both soothe and excite all of the nerves in his body. Tantalizing him in every possible way.

A pair of dainty feet bathed themselves in his blood. Black haze rose from underneath the stranger's toes, enveloping all she stepped on. He watched faces form as the smoke floated upward. They spoke in a language that sounded like birds feasting, before they vanished into an aura of dark mist.

Are they cursing me? he pondered, knowing it was likely. He had the worst luck.

Don't look away.

Thelarius startled again, failing to brush aside his anxieties.

Wiping his mouth with the back of his hand, he looked up, and for one insane instant, he wondered if this was the Creator. Here to personally punish him for his blasphemous thoughts.

The Creator was prettier than he expected—and a woman to boot—with a full head of luminous hair, alabaster skin, and glowing beauty, she made even the best he'd seen seem unsightly in comparison. Thelarius was captivated by the bright glow of her gray eyes. They were completely limpid. Otherworldly was the only word he could use to describe them.

Is she here to send me off?

If she was actually the Creator, then he had a lot to say to her. But he was too enraptured by her form to speak. Despite knowing that the beauty of a god was strictly a matter of course, her mere appearance was enough to still his tongue and take his breath away. His jaw slackened in wonder. Thoughts chased each other in his mind, but he couldn't organize them enough to speak. So, he didn't try. His voice was already gone from him anyway, waddling off like a boggled duck.

Is this how men die? Thelarius mused. *Asphyxiated by beauty?*

She casually pushed aside the dead woman on her knees—he'd forgotten that she was there—and placed a hand on his chin, smirking all the while. As if she could hear his thoughts. As if she knew all of his intimate secrets.

Thelarius didn't doubt it.

Is it power you seek? she whispered.

He shuddered. The feel of her breath gliding across his face assured him that she was, indeed, real. Not just a hopeful figment of his overactive imagination. Not just a hallucination from the lack of blood. It would've been better if she was. The Mentalists always sent those with one too many cracks in their heads away.

Answer me, she urged.

Thelarius gave her a grim smile, flashing bloody teeth. He sought something far worse.

"I seek life."

She smiled, and he trembled.

Her beauty was astounding and terrifying and just so utterly beyond belief that all he could do was wonder how she could be real. Her eyes were more striking than anything he'd ever known. Granted, he saw very few beautiful things in his life. But even he could discern divinity from the mundane attractions of every day. Yet, why was it that all he could think about as he gaped up at her was blood and screaming?

You shall have it.

Her words broke him in ways she could never comprehend.

A searing pain erupted from his fingertips and spread like burning poison across his body. His skin boiled. He felt like his entire body was being branded. His throat, although hoarse, was still somehow able to produce sound, and he screamed at the sensation. His mouth frothed over with saliva. Thelarius' shouts were loud enough to even surprise the goddess before him, but he abruptly paused when the spit exiting his gullet turned into fresh blood. It caught in his throat and made him gurgle.

The pain didn't numb as time passed. Each instant felt hotter than the last, until the few shreds of his sanity slipped away from him. Everything was replaced by pain.

Yet, he didn't die.

For all intents, this kind of burning torture should've killed him, or at the very least, knocked him into oblivion. Thelarius endured it, however, in consciousness. Perhaps he was forced to.

Don't entertain any false notions of escape.

Without warning, the pain stopped. Thelarius' voice died with it. He collapsed at its absence. So abrupt as to be missed. His breaths came out short and harsh. Every exhale made his shoulders quake, and they showed no signs of easing anytime soon. He needed to calm down, but every pant was wetter than the last. Thelarius could taste the iron tang of gore on his tongue. He knew that he wasn't about to get over this just because he willed it. Nothing was ever that easy. Especially not for him.

Thelarius shook his head, trying to clear it enough to wrap his mind around what just happened. Around what was *still* happening.

You're not getting away.

He keeled over to vomit a mouthful of bile. There was no food in his stomach to release. It left a rancid taste in his mouth that easily overpowered the copper. Thelarius remained there for a long time, uncaring for the way his hands and knees quivered in protest. He stared at his reflection against the puddle of spittle and blood. *His* blood. Thelarius squinted at the face that looked back at him, unsure if what he saw was real.

Then, despite the rawness of his throat, he screamed once more at the sight of his eyes.

They were stained crimson.

You're mine.

A flood of power coursed through his veins, followed by another wave of incessant pain. But this time, he didn't cry out. Because, despite the perpetual ache that rocked his very bones, he felt good. Better than he had in a long time. The contrast was a strange one, and he didn't know how to reconcile the gap in his mind, so he didn't try. All he focused on now was how clearly he could breathe and how his fatigue slowly, but surely ebbed away like steam lost to the sky.

Thelarius couldn't help the grin that stretched his lips then. A cerise smile. Manic, hurting, and more pleased than he had any right to be. It was the most satisfying feeling in the world.

This is it, Thelarius thought. He knew, without a sliver of doubt, that this was what he'd been seeking.

The beginning of his new world.

***

Jack opened his eyes.

They burned with the sun.

Flinching, he waited a good minute, before risking another peek. Jack blinked in incomprehension when he found himself settled against a rock along an unending stretch of emptiness. Grass filled his vision, followed by the pale flash of the open sky. For a moment, Jack was muddled by his surroundings, but then his half-awake brain caught up with him, and he... sighed.

The Yovakine Plains, he thought without affection. *Right.*

Weeks of travel, and they had yet to reach the Red Veld. His feet were sore and his head pounded with a vengeance as the last vestiges of his dream—a memory of the past, he suspected— faded into the faraway edges of his mind. He'd been having a lot of those lately, and each was stranger than the last. Jack tried to recall the already blurry details, but a sudden noise disrupted his thoughts, making it slip away completely.

He turned toward the foreign sound. Surprise chased naked relief across his face at the warm glow of orange eyes. Though the familiar robes had been concealed by a common cloak, he easily recognized the distinctly pale features. Not even the sun stood a chance against flesh whitened under the Zexin Sea.

"Syl," Jack called hoarsely.

His tongue flicked out, wetting sandpaper, as he caught the waterskin she threw him. It was running dry. With no civilization as far as the eye could see, he could only hope for rain. But after a particularly long night that ended in ruin and both of them essentially homeless, he had a special revulsion for the rain. Jack supposed he could freeze something and suck on the icy frost left by his magic instead, but he wasn't that desperate. Not yet.

"Where'd you go?" he asked once he drank his fill.

Sylvie eyed him then. Half of his face darkened by receding shadows and the other half lit brilliantly by the sun. Yet his eyes were brighter than even the rays of fire above them somehow.

Jack stretched, ignoring her stare, as lines of smooth and less than pleased *Íarre* slipped from his tongue like a spell that warmed her from head to toe. Sylvie failed to translate the words fast enough. Although Jack spent most of his time teaching her, *Íarre* was a difficult language to learn. There were too many slight nuances that she couldn't fully grasp. But it didn't stop her from trying, nor him from teaching.

Twenty three days, she thought, *since the Drowned Tower fell.*

"Your mind is late as usual," Jack said in the trade tongue, startling her from her stupor. His voice held all of the aggravation she associated with his usual mood. Plus a hint of amusement for flavor. "Don't tell me you wandered off like this."

"I was trying to find the Red Veld," she finally answered.

"And?"

"I found it. A speck in the distance, but it's there. Its walls were clear."

"An Institute locked in yearlong winter. A city filled with gold. Flourishing towns. Lava-filled landscapes. Even old ruins!" Jack ticked each one off on his fingers, while internally hoping that they ran into an Amorph. He briefly recalled the horrid affair with his mother back in the Eirinne Mountains, before groaning in frustration. "So many options, and my mother chooses to leave us in the middle of the Yova Plains with little more than a shrug and a wave in the right direction."

It made him want to burn something.

Instead, he was painfully reminded that fire was no longer in his skill set. An Elementalist with only one element. Jack scoffed in self-deprecation. He might've given them up willingly, but even he thought the resulting situation was idiotic. Perhaps it would've been better if his eyes shifted, too, but he doubted it. Such a drastic change would've shocked him straight into denial.

Jack's gaze trailed away from the rising sun and to the west.

The supposedly poor lands of the south were more beautiful than he thought they'd be. There were no seedy urchins or emaciated drifters wandering about. There weren't even any half-dead men splayed across the grass. Just emptiness. Vast and encompassing. Jack closed his eyes and took a deep, satisfying breath.

He felt free.

Well, almost. The shackles branded onto his legs were sore reminders otherwise. He shook each one out self-consciously, then brushed his fingers against the Orive crystal entrenched along the side of his head out of habit.

"Bad dream?" Sylvie asked, then drew an imaginary line on the side of her head. "You always rub here when you're agitated. Do you want to talk about it?"

He'd rather set himself on fire.

Jack forced his hand down. "Thelarius help me if even you're able to read me now."

"Maybe *she*'s giving me the power of insight."

"I'm glad I'm not the only one that thought you needed it."

Jack laughed when she glared.

That voice within the Heartstone had become something of a running joke between them. Though they felt *her* presence, and even saw the darkness within, *she* hadn't spoken to them since they left Cheryll's cottage in the Eirinne Mountains. Jack knew that *she* was waiting—for what exactly, he wasn't certain—but he wasn't going to force *her* to speak. That thing would talk when it wanted to. *She* seemed smart enough to do so. Right now, he was reveling in the lack of power offers and unreasonable orders.

Besides, they had their own problems to deal with. Like their fellow practitioners from the Drowned Tower slowly turning into refugees. Some were even hunted down by the Vanguard Circle for attacking Nebbin. Whenever they found a band of travelers headed their way, all they seemed to talk about were the happenings in the east. Not one word concerning the Alps left their mouths, which was a feat in itself.

"Well, *I* had a strange dream," Sylvie said, dragging him

from his thoughts, as they began the mundane task of walking.

"And?" Jack prompted, disinterestedly placing one foot in front of the other. It was a chore just to move. He could handle rough conditions, but that didn't stop him from wishing for a roof over his head. Maybe even a soft bed.

"I saw Thelarius Merve."

Jack lurched to a stop.

Sylvie looked back at him, one eyebrow raised in question at his wide eyes.

"You're joking," he said.

"Why would I joke about something like that?"

"That's what I'm trying to figure out."

Jack stepped back when she put her hands on her hips in offense. He gripped his sleeves when she even went so far as to describe her dream in vivid detail. How she could remember such things were beyond him. But the picture she painted was familiar enough to stir his own memory.

"Wonderful. So, *she's* invading both of our dreams," Jack said. "The least *she* could do is spare one of us. *She* hasn't spoken in, what, three weeks? If this continues, then I'd rather *she* talk to us directly. I can't be sleep-deprived on top of everything else."

"*She* was with Thelarius," Sylvie murmured in concern.

"Does it really matter who *she* was with? We still don't know what *she* wants. It's best to focus on what mother wan—no, what we want to do."

Sylvie hesitated, before conceding. "You're right."

He grinned at that. Roguish, even for him. Sylvie didn't trust that look. It spelled nothing but trouble. Jack didn't seem to notice her dismay because he surged forward with renewed enthusiasm. Not even something as disturbing as sharing a dream could put him down. Though she knew him well enough by now to know that he tucked the thought away for more in-depth scrutiny later tonight when he could brood over it without her reading his every expression. Sylvie commended him for that. But only because it was also a reminder that they had more pressing things to do than consider questions they didn't have answers to.

Jack had wanted to leave the Drowned Tower for so long. So, even if his feet ached with every step, he was damn well going to enjoy it. The Institute crumbling had been the loss of a lifetime. Still, a better gain. He wasn't going to let anything temper his drive. Especially not some vague dream.

"Come on." Jack turned, momentarily recoiling from the sun's glare. He arched his eyebrows at her in expectance, then flashed her the most vibrant grin he could muster. "Pick up the pace. We've got a long walk ahead of us."

The disgruntled look she threw him only made him laugh.

Reed,

It's been almost a month since you passed, and I still find myself writing to you. It's... therapeutic. I never understood why you'd jot things down in your tome, turning it into a journal—I remember Master Cephas yelling at you for that on multiple occasions—but I see now how calming it is. Still, I hope I'll get over this soon. (I doubt it.) The company I'm keeping at the moment isn't exactly the most comforting. Jack's a man of extremes. His personality can be tiring or rejuvenating depending on his mood.

I've gotten to know him fairly well these past few weeks. There isn't much to do but talk out here. We get along about as much as you'd expect. Though sometimes he looks at me as if he's contemplating ramming his head against a wall in annoyance... oh, and did I mention his conceit? It's physically draining. But there are some days when I see him looking down at his hands, and I remember that he's just as lost as me. It makes me wish you were still here. We could use someone to balance us when we're being too stubborn to admit our wrongs.

Every day it seems as if we're getting into more and more scrapes—with Nebbin, with mercenaries, with each other. I should've listened more when you taught me how to properly care for my wounds. The bandages I tie aren't exactly pristine. My sterilization skills could use some work, too. I actually miss that scented soap that Master Cephas used to give away. The pink one with the burgundy spots.

We've been roaming the Yovakine Plains for a while. It's large and filled with miles of nothing. The cities are but promising specks in the distance. Villages are far enough from each other that passing out from walking is an actual problem. I don't know if you would love or hate it. The sky looks so big. The Drowned Tower seems so far away. It's been twenty-three days since we left you alone under the Zexin Sea, and we've yet to really do anything with our lives or our so-called freedom.

I miss home.

I have to go now. Jack calls. I don't trust the energy in his grin.

I'll write again soon.

Sylvie Sirx 11.27.CA

2

Merchants, and those modest enough to ignore their worn shoes and hooded faces, were invaluable sources of information. Oddly enough, those that travelled in small groups were the most welcoming. Jack would think they'd be more cautious because of their numbers—or lack of—but those they passed had always been kind, happy, and terribly gullible. How they managed to survive was anybody's guess. Jack knew many that would happily mug them. Even he played with the idea on more than one occasion.

Maybe there was something about them that he was missing. A sign of sorts. He did recall seeing a certain symbol adorning their wares—a manacle stitched over cloaks of fine red. It was a vicious-looking emblem, but he knew better than to ask its meaning. It didn't take much to put two-and-two together anyway. Once he saw the word: 'Fetters' branded upon their caravans, he had an inkling about the type of wares they dealt with. Nevertheless, Jack kept his mouth shut and maintained his persona of naïve country boy because they had better things to do than worry about empty wagons and smiling salesman.

Today, however, he wasn't feeling so tolerable. Maybe it was the lingering thought of his and Sylvie's shared dream or maybe it was how one of the men, with his crooked nose and his rotten teeth, grinned slimily at them. It could've even been the way the man placed a hand upon the hilt of his sword. An action filled with such malice that Jack couldn't help the sudden narrowing of his eyes.

Jack couldn't say for certain which of these threw him over the edge—perhaps all of them—but his good mood had evaporated in an instant and what was left of his already thin patience had disappeared along with his smirk.

Before Jack could second-guess himself, he was already sprinting, his hands were glowing, and magic was leaping from his fingertips. Jack was just as shocked as the merchants when a spray of frost spread out and enveloped their feet. He'd wanted to frighten them by pushing them back with a spray of sharp gravel, not still their movements with ice. But he supposed that this worked just as well.

The more mindful of the two drew his sword once Jack drew near. But his magic was faster. It crept upward in the span of a breath, encasing the slaver in a layer of ice four inches thick. His companion screamed in horror, no doubt traumatized by the sight. But it wasn't long before he, too, was silenced.

While Jack froze the nameless man's body numb, Sylvie picked out what they could use from the dead men's meager supply. It wasn't much. Drapery, linens, a few bruised potatoes. The clothes looked—and likely felt—expensive. They'd fetch a high price in the right market, but they were also numerous and heavy. It was far too much for them to carry.

Jack watched her stuff what she could into her sack. He doubted she'd be able to close it, deluged as it was, but he didn't bother telling her. Jack merely dusted himself off. Ice fell from his clothes, tinkling, before evaporating into nothing above the soil.

"We can sell these," Sylvie said once he caught up with her.

She shoved a pile of badly folded silk linens in his hands. If Sylvie was concerned about his sudden bout of violence, then she didn't show it. The realization that they needed to find proper shelter before night came and brought the winds with it took precedence over his ever-changing mood.

During their first days of travel, they both quickly learned just how volatile the weather of the Yovakine Plains was. Biting nights and sudden storms were common. There was never any adequate shelter either. Although several settlements were scattered across the Plains, it took an age to get anywhere near them. It didn't help that Jack insisted that they remain on foot to avoid any unwanted attention. Sylvie hadn't disagreed with him at the time. But at the end of the day, when her aching legs could no longer carry her weight, she thought that perhaps the extra attention might be worth it. She was tired of going to sleep with stinging calves.

"Finally," Jack muttered, then pointed at a shack in the distance. It was as shabby as the dozen beyond it.

Jack drew an old map from his pack. Notes were scribbled along the edge of each city's name in a mixture of *Íarre* and the trade tongue. Between them were rough sketches of family symbols piled on top of each other in an untidy system that only he could make out.

Sylvie looked away from her futile hunt for supplies to where he was pointing. She was immensely pleased to find a village that even her sore feet could walk to. It was a blessedly short distance away from the Red Veld, too.

"What village is that?" Sylvie asked.

"A new one."

"What makes you say that?"

"It isn't on the map. I can see why, too. It's not exactly worth noting. But it's our only option right now. You ready?"

"As I'll ever be. I just hope they let us pass."

"Why wouldn't they?"

Sylvie gestured meaningfully to his hood, and his mouth opened in belated understanding. Jack quickly tried to adjust it in a way that still covered his eyes. But it was a wasted attempt that ended with his hair in his face.

"Does this look less suspicious?" he asked.

"No," Sylvie answered, then swiftly walked past him in a poor attempt to hide her growing smile.

"At least I tried!" Jack called out.

Their petty concerns, however, were for naught. Entering the village was easier than either of them expected. Too easy. There were no guards at the gate. Just one lone lookout. Asleep, drunk, and far too plump to be of any real use.

The village was full of poor, backwater folk that openly stared as they passed, though none made a move to stop them. Most slept between dirty hovels. Perhaps they found it preferable to actually being in one. Bony urchins strolled aimlessly about, already tired of begging. Even the stalls were empty, save for one or two ears of overpriced corn.

It came as no surprise that seeds were in short supply. Few used the Yovakine Plains' soil for farming; an effect of the sudden rekindling of slavery, no doubt. The people were afraid, and it showed. The practitioners that hid themselves away in the Veld didn't seem keen on helping them either.

A ratty woman quietly approached the pair. She flashed them a smile filled with holes. Her features spoke of childhood beauty, but that had long been smothered by poverty.

With desperate eyes, she scrutinized them in a mixture of plea and envy. Though the woman spoke fluent *Yövín*, the words came out too thick for anyone to understand. Sylvie thought her tongue numb. Still, the woman persisted. Her tone was rough and desperate like she was expelling an ancient curse.

Sylvie could guess well enough her words. The look in her eyes said more than her failing tongue ever could—she sought alms. But just as Sylvie grabbed one of the lavish linens they'd gathered to sell, bruising fingers yanked her back.

A dirty urchin skidded his way between them and the woman. Sylvie swallowed a yelp, as Jack kept his hands firmly locked on her shoulders. The urchin paused to glare briefly at the cloth in Sylvie's hands, debating whether or not to run back and try again. But Jack's glare was dark enough to make the boy endure his hunger for another day.

The woman, however, wasn't so quick to flee. With strength neither of them expected, she swiped the silk from Sylvie's fingers, dirtying it beyond reprieve, before she scurried off into a small shack flanked by a group of red-faced drunks.

Then, silence.

Broken only by Jack's sudden, annoyed exhale.

"Lovely." Sylvie brushed him away and walked ahead, her stride brisker than before. "I was going to give it to her anyway."

"Which was stupid of you," Jack said. He shrugged when Sylvie wrinkled her nose at him. "The Veld may be the largest of the four Institutes, but it's not the wealthiest. I doubt they help the people here like what the Tower did for those on Eriam."

"Clearly."

"Just be sure to watch yourself," Jack advised. "Desperation breeds fools."

Sylvie nodded. It seemed fate still had a few surprises for her. She'd thought the fall of the east enough to sate it for a while. She was wrong of course. Sylvie just hoped that the next thing she lost wouldn't be too close to her heart.

Without thinking, she gripped the Heartstone, as if it could grant her wish. Perhaps it could. She didn't dare underestimate the silent presence hidden beneath its surface. Sylvie snuck a peek at its glow. It shone like it always did. But today, it seemed a tad brighter against their rotten surroundings. Soon, the presence within would speak. She knew it would. All she had to do was wait.

Sylvie shivered at the thought. Feelings of anticipation and foreboding flittered across her heart, before it was replaced by immense relief as she looked across the town to find the lofty walls of the Red Veld, which stood proud, despite the consequences of age. It was an impressive sight to behold, and though it looked as if it needed a thorough cleaning, it didn't make the sight any less remarkable. But neither did it do wonders for the smell. As soon as the scent of grime reached their noses, they scrunched their faces and turned away in distaste.

The stench alone was formidable. Even more so than the circular wall that surrounded it. The wall was made from broad, connected panels. Each one was so high that Sylvie suspected they would be little more than specks should she ever reach its peak. Engraved fortifications ran along the enclosure, pulsing blue with each passing second. Should a Nebbin look upon it, they'd find that the fort had only a singular chained entrance that had been kept closed for decades, but they knew better.

Old tales told of an ancient passage beneath the wall's overgrowth that sported Silas' mark, where a burst of magic could be used to move what many falsely believed to be unyielding stone. In this case, the stories rang true, as it was proven time and time again by visiting practitioners. All they had to do was find it.

Watchtowers were positioned along key points to protect the Institute from unwelcome Amorphs. Few, however, were foolish enough to come to the Red Veld uninvited. There was no point. There was little left to steal, and what did remain, was protected fiercely by a long line of impertinent Arch Potens that gained fame for their tenacity—to the point where even their apprentices became a running joke amongst the other branches. Hailing from the south meant poor social standing and even poorer discipline. Few willingly dealt with ticking time bombs. So, the Veld was avoided. Now that slavery and riots had once again become common over the years, the entirety of the south became a haven for deserters that wanted to remain lost. Although only a handful actually managed to succeed in that regard. Hunters were nothing, if not efficient.

But such unstable conditions held no appeal for common merchants. Which led to the formation of mercenary bands and other unsavory groups that found opportunity in the Yovakine Plains' growing underworld. Cities sprang up one after another under their protection. Though only a handful strived. Barely. The dilapidated town they were in was a fine example of that.

"Talk about intimidating," Sylvie commented, as she craned her neck to an impossible degree.

"It's an Institute," Jack reasoned. "What did you expect?"

"More sunlight? People? Something more welcoming than enchanted stone and... gray."

"Something different from the Drowned Tower, you mean?" Jack asked, getting right to the heart of her problem.

Twenty five days, she thought, grimacing.

"Endless drear is a trademark of all the Institutes," he continued, ignoring the look on her face. "Everyone knows how disturbing constant supervision can be, but I think they've gotten numb to the sensation over the years. I'm not looking forward to being under someone's watch again."

"Do you think they'll let us in?"

"I'm sure the Arch Poten could use a few more lions in her den. My concern is if they'll let us *stay.* The Veld's dirt poor. That's no secret. I'm willing to bet that more than a few refugees have come along already."

"A chance at having a roof over our heads is better than none at all."

"Personally, I'd rather continue sleeping on the cold ground than chance sharing a room with half a dozen senile men."

"You're impossible," Sylvie said. Jack smirked at the remark. "Is that man, the Arch Poten's husband I mean—"

"Vidal Verne," Jack supplied.

"—yes, Vidal. How do we know he's even here?"

"There's only one way to find out."

***

They left the following day, just before dawn painted the sky with new light. Most were fast asleep. Those that weren't scurried off to hide like rats, escaping punishment for their misdeeds. They only peeked their heads out once the pair had finally left the outskirts of the nameless village. No doubt to spread baseless rumors, then continue on with their dull lives.

Sylvie didn't care. The only thing that troubled her now was the sun and its lethargic ascent. Because when the sun was lazy, everyone's body clocks seemed to copy its behavior. They, of course, weren't exempt from that, and moving their booted feet through the shrubbery was a chore in itself. One that they didn't want to do. But responsibility waited for no one. Thankfully, the Red Veld was a short distance away. With recovered strength and a lot of backhanded encouragement thrown at each other, they settled on something like a pace. It wasn't long before they found themselves enveloped by the Institute's shade.

Their eyes roamed its greatness, searching for Silas' mark— a six-pointed sun—and hoping that it wasn't hidden somewhere too far above to see; guarded perhaps by the murder of cawing crows that warned them away. But they couldn't leave. They still had things to do. Things that didn't allow them the influence of exhaustion and fear. But duty didn't stop their hesitance when an especially nasty bird swooped down, perching itself on one of the vines along the wall to better glare at them. Its eyes were as black as tar. Coupled with the shade of the Institute, they couldn't tell if the crow was an Amorph or just another bird. Both, perhaps, their enemies.

"I doubt he'll show us the way," Jack muttered, glaring back.

"Then we move on."

Hours passed, and by their ninth circle around the Veld, the sun had ascended completely. It outshone the clouds. They physically felt its burn on their backs, despite the kindness of shadow. Layers of cloth were shed and the little that remained clung indecently to pale skin. It seemed even their smalls were acting out against their purpose.

"There's no special entrance," Jack declared, before falling gracelessly to the ground. He wasn't patient to begin with, and his sour mood was only amplified by his sore neck. It didn't help that he was starting to become conscious about the lines on his forehead. Getting into situations that made him constantly crease his brows certainly wasn't doing him any favors.

"There is," Sylvie insisted.

"Where then?"

"That's what I'm trying to find out. Get up and help me."

Jack ran a hand through his hair in preference, then grimaced at its greasiness. He sorely wished for his old powers back. It would be a simple thing to conjure up a storm and fling them inside. A few broken bones and a brush with death was better than circling this fortress again.

"Point it out when you find it," Jack said, leaning back on his palms. "I'm taking a break."

"Really, Jack? Come on."

"Look, if you find it, then I'll gladly walk there with you on my back. How does that sound?"

"Awful," she deadpanned. "We'd find it faster if you just stopped your complaining."

"We've been here for hours, Syl. Do you want to know what I've learned during that time? The only unsealed entrance to this hellhole is up." Jack pointed at the sky for emphasis. "And unless you're secretly an Amorph, then it'll take us a week and a half to get there. Maybe longer. I'm not the best climber."

"Let's walk around one more time."

Jack made a face.

In the time of Silas and his pyre, a voiced crooned without warning. It startled them both into standing. Together, they looked upon the Heartstone to find it glowing as brightly as it always did. *The Red Veld was once a haven for all travelers, welcoming practitioners and Nebbin alike from the furthest reaches of Ferus Terria. By day, all men here stood as equals.*

"You're back." Jack tried to ignore the cold beads of sweat that slipped down his spine. "Fantastic."

By night, she continued, disregarding him, *the practitioners of old would chant spells of fortitude, raising the impenetrable walls that would one day give the Red Veld its title of, Citadel of the South. A worthy name. One it has lived up to, and one it has held even now, as the sun continues to reach its zenith.*

"I'm not here for a history lesson."

What then, do you seek? she whispered the question he hated so. As if he had any right to the power *she* promised. Jack knew better. *She* was toying with him, and he wouldn't have it.

"If you have something to say, then say it. I have enough

voices in my head. I don't need your worthless whispers."

"Jack," Sylvie rebuked, grabbing him before he could swipe the Heartstone from her neck in his haste to be rid of the thing.

His eyes widened at the heat of her touch. At the sleeping fury underneath. Jack breathed to steady his emotions.

"What?" he bit out. Ice sparked in his hands.

"Temper yourself."

He shrugged her off. Embers flew from her hands as they dropped. They flickered across the dry grass, but fizzled out soon after. Jack watched them vanish, knowing that their passing was as much Sylvie's doing as their spark. When he spoke again, it was only to the unseen presence before them.

"I seek the entrance to the Red Veld."

Sylvie followed with her own affirmation.

Then, because they both said it, lullabies slipped through the cawing murder above them, ringing familiarly in their ears. That voice in their heads joined it.

The sun is high. Walls are but an illusion to those blind to Silas' light.

As if on cue, a wave of raw magic pulsed from the Institute. Bluer and brighter than anything they'd ever be able to produce. It circled a deep line that ran across the entire wall. Like a stroke from a madman's paintbrush, it spread upward, moving toward the burning six-pointed sun.

Silas' mark didn't sit upon any one wall. It remained so long as the sun was up, settling only once dawn turned to dusk and Nebbin were no longer permitted inside of the Red Veld.

Rubbing her hands together, Sylvie made her way past the overgrowth. Her eyes strode past lines of detailed spells. Some kept tiny, barely readable scrawls along the sides. Not part of any enchantment. But not close enough to interfere with the ancient fortifications either. It was fairly thought out work. Forgotten mementoes slowly washed away by time. They were carved by practitioners, she knew. Skilled ones at that. Because only they could engrave something so close to such a grand source of raw magic without being flung aside before they could finish. This wasn't the time to carve promises on age old fortresses however.

Her hands settled upon the great wall. It lit as brilliantly as any magic, blinding them both. Stone shifted, creaking, until she was forced to move away. Dust and dirt fell around them like rain, drenching them in the scent of filth finally disturbed.

They heard shouts from beyond. Sylvie stepped forward boldly. Jack objected when she did, but didn't hesitate to follow. His hands settled on her shoulders once the light died down enough for them to see past the layers of grime. He was fully prepared to shove her to the side if need be.

They were surrounded by twenty odd practitioners.

The hour was early enough that their greeters weren't quite dressed, though late enough for them to be more than half awake and armed with weapons. One held a spear pointed disturbingly close to Sylvie's jugular. As she looked upon him, she couldn't help but think that he'd been handsome once. His hair had thinned, his strong jaw was hammered down by wrinkles, and the blue eyes that met her own were dimmed by age. Still, the look on his face was captivating. He wore a black robe that would've been worthless had it not been for the silver lines running parallel with his lapels' stitching. One look at his scarred hands told her that he wasn't one to be trifled with.

Behind them, the stone panel fell back into place.

A younger practitioner fueled the wall with a fresh burst of magic, commanding it down into submission. Three more moved behind him, chanting incantations meant to steady the wall and ward it against foreign energy so that such an incident wouldn't happen again. As far as Sylvie was concerned, it shouldn't have happened at all. But she couldn't blame them for their negligence. The entrance was hardly evident. They just happened to have an age old being guiding them. Though they certainly didn't need to know that. Not now and not in the foreseeable future.

Sylvie eyed the practitioners around her. A fair few of them were scared witless. Those that weren't, pointed their weapons at her. An array of bows, swords, and spears that made her hands spark blue out of reflex. Jack's own slowly slid away from her, until he held them both low above his shoulders in surrender.

"Relax," Jack said in a tone unbefitting his usually impatient demeanor. "My name is Jacques Dace, son of Leonas Dace, Elder of the Zenith Council."

Doubtful whispers erupted among them.

"Leonas Dace..." Spear Holder muttered, warily lowering his weapon from Sylvie's neck. "What's the son of one of the leaders of the Vanguard Circle doing here?"

"I'm escorting the Drowned Tower's new Arch Poten to the north." Jack inclined his head toward Sylvie. "We were passing through the Plains and decided to visit your leader."

"We've already received the Zenith Council's invitation. Arch Poten Verne wants nothing to do with the Summit."

"This isn't about the Summit," Jack said

"Then what is it about?"

Jack rolled his eyes. He stepped closer and fearlessly grabbed the man's weapon. It froze quickly in his hands. So fast that Spear Holder barely had time to drop it. He fell gracelessly to the floor, staggered by the suddenness. The speed of Jack's magic didn't impress all of them however. And it wasn't long before they found themselves once more on the receiving end of pointed swords and drawn bows.

Why are all of them armed? Jack wondered. *Is weapon's training mandatory here?*

"If she isn't available, then her husband works, too," Jack said after a moment. "But preferably one or the other."

"No." Spear Holder glowered from the floor. He was confident for someone that had yet to gather his bearings. "If you want to meet with them, then you need to get through me first."

"Flaming stubborn." Jack rolled his eyes. "Have you always been this way or did you hone it over the years?"

"Why you—"

"Look, I get why you're skeptic," Jack smoothly interrupted.

"But we didn't travel all this way to be told no by a peon like you. Who are you to tell me that your leaders can't spare us a few short minutes?"

"Delicacy, Jack," Sylvie chastised, wondering where his patient tone had disappeared to.

"I don't do delicacy."

"Try," she urged.

Jack shot her a dirty look, but quieted down nevertheless. The crowd around them breathed a collective sigh of relief when his magic dissipated.

"Sorry, Syl," Jack suddenly whispered. The mere act of him apologizing was bizarre enough to startle her into facing him. "Let's try this my way for a bit."

Before Sylvie could question him, she felt a blow against her neck. Distantly, she noted the terrible taste of salt settling like burning tea in her mouth, then the ground tipped up to meet her and she thought nothing at all.

Partner,

Sylvie is going to kill me. Slowly. Painfully.
(A sluggish roast, I suspect.)
I honestly don't want to write this. But I'm waiting for someone and it's intolerably quiet. I can physically feel my boredom. That's how bad it is. I need to do something. Anything at this point. Which is why I'm writing this if that wasn't obvious already.
Sylvie's... indisposed for the moment. I can already imagine all of the furious curses and clipped sentences (that somehow manage to sound more degrading than a full-on lecture) waiting for me when she wakes. It won't be pretty. She's going to make my ears ring, I tell you. I don't think they'll be able to handle it. I abuse them enough as it is. Her adding to it might actually give me constant tinnitus.
In short, evisceration is nigh, partner. This is as much a record as it is a way to appease her. Appease us both. She's been pestering me for the past few days to write something.
'A letter,' she says, 'it's okay even if you don't send it.'
How ridiculous is that? What's the point if I don't send it? Senile firecracker. Like we have all of the ink in the world to waste.
Anyway, I'm writing this because maybe, just maybe if I show it to her, then she'd let up a little... or something like that anyway. Ugh. Whatever. As if I know what I should even be saying on this thrice-damned piece of paper. Words are so disgustingly lacking, and I've rambled long enough already. But I'll try to express my feelings about these past few weeks. For my sake, if not for hers.
Ready, partner? Here goes: Things haven't been going well.
Good enough?

Jack 14.27.CA

3

Jack scowled at the guards.

They were the only things that stood between him and Arch Poten Monet Verne's office. The slimmer, doe-eyed one flinched at the look on his face, but otherwise held his ground. His eyes were orange and unsure. His companion, on the other hand, was beefier and gruffer than most. He snarled as soon as he saw him, then raised one eyebrow in challenge.

Jack almost rose up to it. Almost.

He crossed his arms in preference. Jack's eyes may have told otherwise, but he only had one element at his disposal. If he engaged, he didn't think he'd be able to get away without revealing that particular secret. He was still sore about it, and some days he didn't even accept the fact. But he didn't regret his decision back then either.

Looking across the square, Jack found the mob of practitioners discussing whether or not to move Sylvie, then pausing whenever they reached a consensus. They threw him curious glances, as if he'd explode should they so much as lay a finger on her. He might. At this point, even he wasn't sure. Winging it seemed to be the best option. It was certainly getting him places.

After surprising them with his sudden actions, Jack reasoned with a Dace specialty called: steady, unrelenting forcefulness. He employed a tone he'd seen his father use numerous times as a child. Coupled with his mother's glare, his words commanded attention. Jack coerced them with his name, Sylvie's title, and the fact that he couldn't hold Sylvie up any longer on his own—a bad attempt to appeal to their kinder nature. But it seemed to work because they took her from his hands, albeit reluctantly, and laid her on a short flight of stone steps, where cots had been set up for the injured. Then they simply stared, not quite sure what to make of their two blue-blooded intruders.

"I'll leave her in your care," Jack had said, before an elderly man clasped his shoulder from behind and led him to a nearby pew. It was placed peculiarly in the middle of a central walkway that was flanked by altars. Sisters clucked about like headless chickens around him in preparation for the evening sermon.

"Wait here," the man had said, brisk but not unkind. "I'll inform Arch Poten Verne of your arrival."

That had been three hours ago.

Jack was tired of waiting, and he certainly didn't want to bend over in prayer. The only litany that would ever leave his lips was the invective sort.

That dreadful voice in his head laughed at his thoughts, and the sound was sudden enough to startle him into yelping. The noise caught the attention of more than a few people that he avoided all eye contact with.

Pinching himself, Jack focused again on the two guards.

"Is this how the Veld treats all of its guests?" Jack asked in a tone he knew would piss the bigger one off. He sighed, before purposely meeting his eyes. "I've been waiting for hours. Sylvie's going to wake soon, and if I've gotten nowhere, she's going to bristle and yell and burn things. Do you fancy your walls? She's got this terrible reputation for melting entrances."

"Arch Poten Verne isn't taking visitors," he said obstinately. His voice was grittier than Jack expected.

Then why am I waiting here? Jack thought, though what he said was much different. "Have a heart." His tone was more argumentative than pleading. "Syl might really kill me if I don't at least get five minutes."

"Not my problem."

Jack clicked his tongue, silently reveling when the man's eye twitched. He was touchy for a Healer. "The Veld really is full of savages," he drawled. "Haven't you ever heard of compassion? You're a Healer, aren't y—"

The man made a swipe for him, before the words fully left his mouth. Having expected it, Jack took an immediate step back. The Healer's fist was followed with a brutal lunge that definitely would've broken something had Jack not twisted out of the way.

The others across the square were looking at them in full now. Jack felt like he was stuck in a ring with a Mozolisk—tough, violent creatures with little regard for anything, including their own kin. They hunted for food, but more often for sport. He'd come across one in the Alps once when he was a child. It was the only time Jack saw his father burn something without restraint.

Red eyes darted in every direction, carefully regarding the unamused faces of those around him to see if they'd jump into the fray. None of them looked too keen on doing so. Save for one group in the corner with their arms crossed and their expressions fixed like stone. Jack was certain they'd attack him if he so much as lifted a finger against their comrade. Fatal or not. He'd have to keep an eye on them.

"Stop running!" the Healer roared, chasing him with renewed vigor.

As if he'd do that.

Jack only had his reflexes to thank when he narrowly dodged another punch. It was thrown with such force that he didn't doubt its ability to twist his nose a sickening angle. He was fast for someone so large.

How is that fair? he thought.

The next punch, however, hit home.

Jack stumbled back, staggered by the taste of iron and the sound of cheers. His cheek felt like it had just been pommelled with an iron-plated hilt. He spat a glob of red, then wiped his lips with the back of his hand. Jack lifted his chin to face the Healer. His blue eyes egged him on in ways that Jack couldn't adequately describe, but it was beyond frustrating.

"What?" the Healer jeered, looking smugger than any single person had any right to be. "Never been hit before? Come on!"

So, the Red Veld really did have a few time bombs. Curious, how they only acted now. From the rumors, he'd expected more than half of them to clock him in the jaw just for breathing. They had so many teenage practitioners, he could only wonder where all of the older ones had gone. He just hoped they weren't as wimpy as this Healer's companion.

Jack grinned in excitement. Where were the rest of these guys? He would be sorely disappointed if this man was it.

"You hit hard for a Healer." Jack rubbed his abused cheek. His fingers twitched in anticipation. He had to consciously keep them from glowing blue.

"For a Healer?" the man scoffed, his mood darkened along with his expression. "You hang around too many puffs, pretty boy. I'll show you just how hard Healers can hit."

"Come on then, man cow," Jack taunted with a wry quirk of his lips. "I'll rip your throat out."

The Healer's face took a turn for the frightening. It wasn't long before he charged. There was no time to sidestep, and Jack knew he wasn't strong enough to take him on directly.

Without pausing, Jack dropped to his haunches and covered the floor in a thin sheet of frost only the Healer's companion seemed to notice. The young Conjurer shouted a warning, but the Healer was already slipping forward. He flew right past Jack, who righted himself and grinned all too triumphantly when he crashed into a group of unsuspecting practitioners down the hall. Jack chortled when the barrels they carried burst open and buried the Healer in potatoes. Although Jack didn't make good on his threat, this was a far better alternative.

"You cheating bastard!" the Healer shouted, indignant. "I can't believe you used magic!"

"Rules? In a fight?" Jack flashed him a smile so mocking that the Healer's upper lip curled at the mere sight of it.

"This is about fighting man-to-man."

"When have men ever played fair?" he waved, before making for the Arch Poten's door. The Conjurer didn't even get in his way, too busy fretting over his companion. "Let's play again later, Spud. I've got better things to do."

Before he could grab the rusted handle however, the door flew open to reveal a woman grown heavy with age. Silence descended around them, as she blew a stream of hot air in his face. It reeked with the scent of alcohol and rotten eggs. Jack's lips twisted in disgust, but he didn't dare bring his hand up to save his nose. It would be a futile attempt, and a delicacy he didn't care to show. For a moment, he was caught by the sight of her dreadful smile. Both of her front teeth were missing, and from how scarred the rest of her was, he knew that she didn't lose them in a cooking accident.

"Having fun?" she asked in a rich, smoky voice that made shivers crawl up his spine.

The woman passed him, before he could retort. She lifted her eyebrows at the throng of practitioners that quickly turned away. They all pretended to be doing something infinitely more important, so as to avoid her attention. Some had even taken to looking at the sky and loudly counting the clouds. Like she was a witch that would curse them if they blinked at her the wrong way. She certainly looked the part.

A younger woman followed her out. She had dark skin and dreamy eyes that lingered on him. There was a coquettish simper on her face that told Jack that she was curious about his appearance. From what he could tell of her features however, she was from Sicin. They were notorious for being interested in everyone. He noticed her clothes more than anything else. She was dressed in garb befitting an ambassador. All silk and fine trims. Expensive enough to impress even the Drakone family. How no one had robbed her yet was a mystery greater than the legend of Pulka's ancient wizard.

The crowd behind him welcomed her with open arms and

quiet whispers. They led her to Sylvie's cot, while filling her in on what he'd done. When Jack saw the woman's hand glow and her lips form the words of a curing spell he was all too familiar with, he kept his gaze firmly in front of him. He didn't dare look back now. Sylvie was going to kill him if she caught his eye.

In the room proper, Jack found Arch Poten Verne leaning on her desk and scrutinizing his form. He knew it was her simply because of the aura she exuded. There was such authority in her movements. Jack noticed the distinct orange of her eyes and the dual scars that lined her chin, giving her a severe look. She wasn't fashioned in robes, but in a suit of mid-weight armor that had been polished to a shine. A sword rested on her hip. He knew little about blades, but even he could tell the difference between mass produced work and utter magnificence. The scabbard alone told tales of unholy expense, never mind the hilt.

"Are you the reason for all of this commotion?" she asked, lifting a knowing brow. Her accent was thicker than his head. "Tell me what you want, so you can be on your way. I have better things to do than deal with Cheryll Dace's son."

"You know my mother?" Jack asked, before he could catch himself.

"Enough to know she sent you," Monet retorted. Her frown deepened. "I already told her *no*. I'm far too busy to campaign for her husband in the Summit, and how does she respond? By sending her son to convince me. Insufferable woman."

She was badmouthing his mother, but all Jack could do was smirk at their unexpected similarity. "Funny," he said, "she said something similar about you."

Monet grimaced, but she didn't look at all staggered by the revelation. "So, what do you want?"

"Officially? I want nothing."

"You're lying."

"I don't lie," he reflexively replied, then shrugged off her perplexed expression. "I'm just escorting the Tower's Arch Poten to the Alps on my mother's behalf. She had no Hunters to spare."

"I heard you struck the poor girl unconscious. You're not a very good escort, are you?"

"She was tired. I helped."

"And so here we are." She shook her head in amusement. "But for the Tower's newly crowned Arch Poten to leave so quickly after its fall... just what happened there?"

"I'm not here to talk about the east," Jack said evasively.

"Then what are you here for?" she asked, sardonic and harsh all at once. Her voice counted among the most severe he'd ever heard. "A free meal? A warm bed? We're scarce enough as it is."

"Like I said, officially, I'm just going along with my Arch Poten's wishes. I remember Sylvie saying something about going through your archives before she fell asleep though. I'm sure she wouldn't be opposed to helping you with anything she possibly could in exchange for that privilege."

"What makes you think I need help?"

"I've heard the Veld has been having problems lately. The sort that requires your presence here and not in other places like, say... the Diamond Alps."

Her eyes thinned in distrust. "Where did you hear that?"

"My mother. Chatty barkeeps. Your practitioners." Jack pointed a thumb over his shoulder at the closed door. "I wouldn't be opposed to helping either, so long as you remember that it was our families that helped you—Dace and Sirx. But if my mother asks, mostly Dace."

Monet's eyebrow ticked in irritation, but he didn't miss how her fingers bounced on the table. She was considering his offer, whether she admitted it or not.

"And unofficially?" she asked after a moment.

"The Tower's practitioners scattered after it fell. I doubt my mother has enough time on her hands to find them all. Most probably don't even want to return to that cursed place."

"You think they're here?"

"Aren't they?"

"A few."

"How much is a few?"

"More than we know what to do with."

Her exasperation rang clearly in her voice, if not in her eyes. But Jack was glad that she didn't sound like she'd be throwing them out on the streets to be cajoled by sleazy merchants and mercenaries looking for gullible fighters. It seemed his fear was for naught. Jack didn't know if she was noble or foolish for helping them.

"We're going to return them to the Tower," she went on. "Not now though. We've got civilian riots to deal with, slavers that need to be wiped out, and a thousand more urgent problems to wrap up. We can't spare the men."

Jack raised an eyebrow at her reasoning. That cursed Demar Spell immediately sprang to mind. He hated it, but he couldn't deny its effectiveness. "Why can't they go on their own? Cast a tracking spell and let them leave."

"Have you seen them?" she retorted. "Have you seen their faces? They're like frightened children! They flinch before the sun and peer cautiously into the shadows. Most don't even want to leave. They just stay holed up in their rooms."

Jack stilled in realization. "The Tower isn't like the Veld. Most practitioners weren't even allowed outside."

"Which is why I half expected them to be jumping for joy! My men trained the willing ones, but the rest sit in their quarters and mope like they're the only ones that have experienced loss. I wanted to take them back to the Tower when I heard news of its reconstruction, but sending them out there without escorts is just asking for something terrible to happen. The Yovakine Plains has witnessed enough tragedies."

Jack couldn't agree more.

"So," he met her gaze head on, "what would it take for you to avoid another?"

"What?"

"You want more men. My mother wants your support up north. Sylvie wants access to your archives. And we all want to bring everyone that doesn't belong here back to the Tower. *Safely.* The solution seems simple to me—we take care of one of your bigger problems, so your men are freed from the burden, and then you order them to escort my peers back to the Eriam."

"Do you really think it's that simple?"

"Isn't it? Oh, and dump a particularly big worry on us, would you? Something that'll give even you some spare time, so you can head up north to support my father."

She bristled at his words. "Are you really so arrogant as to believe that you can single-handedly take care of problems that I've been trying for years to?"

"I have people on my side that you don't."

"Let me make this clear: I don't need your help, and I certainly don't *want* it."

"Then tell me who does," he said, finally understanding why his mother wanted him to go to Vidal instead. But where was he?

"You talk like her." Monet scowled. She looked at him like she was fighting the urge to unsheathe her sword and cleave him in two just to escape his mouth.

Jack knew that she was referring to his mother again. The remark was disconcerting—as he always believed himself to be more like his father—but not unwelcome. Not now.

"I know."

Before she could fire off another smart response, the door flew open and a man stumbled inside, startling them both. With his hands on his knees and air barely filling his lungs, his wild eyes circled the room, as if he didn't know where he was. But then he gathered himself, and what he uttered had Monet rushing to the front gate with Jack hot on her heels.

"Refugees, my lady. From the east."

***

When the stone panel drifted upward and Healers crowded around the spill of newcomers, Jack was struck by their numbers.

But in no time at all, they were herded away from Silas'

magic door, where the Veld's more combative practitioners had picked up newly oiled weapons to make sure no other unwanted guests slipped inside while they had their backs turned. Even the birds that circled the sky descended a little lower, cawing loudly in warning at half a dozen curious men a distance away. They were too far for Jack to tell if they were Nebbin, but close enough for him to see their starved appearances.

In front of him, Arch Poten Verne regarded the state of her Institute. Her eyes darted back and forth, counting heads and looking every bit like someone ticking things off of a mental check list. He'd seen the Masters back in the Tower do it plenty of times. Jack ceased his mindless following when two willowy, but important looking practitioners flanked her. They spoke quickly about ordering provisions and growing riots in a neighboring city.

Jack jumped on top of an ill-placed pile of concrete blocks, so he could look over the masses of Veld practitioners and at the newly arrived refugees. They were dirty and crying. Others more than most. From the lack of clucking Healers, he knew instantly that most of them were unscathed. But those that were had fatal injuries, indeed. Jack angled his head back to see a small child, covered in blood. An older man sat beside him. His wrinkled hands were clasped in front of his chest, as he recited something that looked a lot like a prayer. By the end of it, the old man covered the child with a blanket, masking both injury and gender from Jack's gaze.

The mob of Healers that had initially come down were already returning to wherever it was they'd holed themselves up in until now. Some even had the audacity to drag their feet and complain about the lack of emergency. Just what were they doing that was so important that checking for any injured took a back seat? Were they treating more refugees?

Jack swiftly examined the abundance of doors around him. He'd have to check or, better yet, ask Arch Poten Verne directly. But she was busy now, and he knew from experience that it was better not to get in the way of someone barking orders.

Finding himself at a loss, Jack walked reluctantly over to the sobbing mob. Most recognized him. He could tell from the way their mouths hung agape, opening and closing in wonder at his presence. The only ones that didn't were the younger children, and even then, only a few. Jack surmised that they were likely a part of the new additions to the Tower; the class brought in just before it fell. They had horrible luck.

He, on the other hand, knew none of them.

Their faces were as unfamiliar to him as the ones in every other Institute across Ferus Terria. But they were once part of the east—or so they claimed—and from the weary eyes of the Veld's residents, he knew that their presence wasn't exactly welcome. It was just another obligation to add to the long list they already had. They didn't dare say anything though. Not even a whisper escaped their lips. Jack's respect for Arch Poten Verne rose a bit more at that. Her practitioners simply opened their gates and ushered them inside, despite their lack of supplies. They were certainly a giving bunch. Jack wondered how they could be so when just one look at their halls made their hardships apparent.

Jack's gaze ventured off to the side, where holy sisters knelt with clasped hands, invoking the blessing of one of the First Zenith—likely Maurice.

"What happened?" Jack asked, startling the teen beside him. His hair was long and hay-like. It covered everything from the tips of his ears to the worn leather guards over his shoulders. The boy pointed at himself, then looked side to side, as if he couldn't believe he'd been spoken to. Jack raised his eyebrows at that.

"Yes, *you*," he went on. "Who else would I be talking to?"

The boy swallowed, then hunkered in on himself. He fiddled with his fingers in a way that reminded Jack of a scolded child.

"Well," he began, head bowing forward and spilling bundles of hair in front of his face. "*I—we* were…"

"Hauled off," a woman interrupted, then scowled darkly at Jack like it was his fault that the boy was so jittery. "Tower went ta hell, yea? We got done in by the blast like the rest a' the sorry loons that weren't fast enough ta make it topside. Ya wouldn't happen ta know anythin' about that, would ya, Dace?"

Jack's eyes narrowed, but he kept his silence. When she saw that he wasn't going to rise to her words, she continued, her tone harsher than the lines around her face. "Driftin' in the far waves, holdin' each other's hands an' tryin' ta find the shore one fraction, then the next we're suddenly in cramped wagons an' carted off ta underground lots as goods across the Plains! Can ya imagine what that's like? No, of course not!"

She spat at his feet.

Jack returned her fury with quiet contemplation, though he wasn't able to keep his hands from shaking at the thought. How many more were out there? How many more could the Red Veld take? Would they be able to return them all to the Tower? He didn't know, but he needed to ask. Or make a solution himself.

"How'd you escape?" he asked.

"Reached an auction house in Yorn," she hissed, but her eyes softened at the memory. "Man was there. Tall, spindly thing, yea? Practitioner. Spoke fluent *Yövín*. He unclasped us an' promised haven in the Veld. Didn't believe him. He was a stuffy twat. Liked ta brag, sayin' how he had friends in high an' low places. But his name made those Amorphs flyin' up there listen. The Arch Poten hasn't rounded us up yet neither, so can't deny that his name really was worth a few sacks."

"This man," Jack muttered, thinking. "What was his name?"

"Hell if I know. I wasn't in my right mind then, yea? Ya can't expect me ta remember every single name I happen across."

"You don't remember? *Really*? I thought he saved you."

"He did!" she protested loudly, before saying in a softer voice, "Look, all I remember is that it was some northerner name, okay? V... somethin'. Short. Hard ta pronounce with this tongue. Had a steady ring ta it though. Vlad? Valdin? Veneer?"

"Vidal?" Jack offered. "Vidal Verne?"

"That! That's the one!" she exclaimed, snapping her fingers. "How'd ya know?"

"And the auction house," Jack continued, ignoring her question. "Do you remember what it was called? How to find it?"

"Why do you care?" she asked. Her face scrunched up into a sneer as her mood took another turn for the sour. "You've been livin' good 'ere. Must be nice ta come from a well-off family. Bet they took ya in right away, huh? So, what, you pay 'em ta live 'ere or somethin'?"

Jack's eyes narrowed dangerously in response and from the way she shrunk away, he knew she saw the black tendrils in his depths. His fingers jerked and the woman stared, entranced, as frost crept from the tips of his nails to coat up his wrist. The ice glinted like pearls under the light. He barely noticed it. His eyes were only on the obstinate look on her face that was just itching for an excuse to yell at someone.

Clenching his fists and forcing his powers back beneath his skin, he said through gritted teeth, "The only one that got inside these walls with another's name was you." The woman opened her mouth to argue, but he beat her to it. "Spare me your complaints. I'll be leaving soon enough. I have business with Vidal. The sort that might help you and others from the east."

There was a pregnant pause, where the woman pursed her lips stubbornly at him. But when he didn't make a move to leave, she looked away and sighed. She pointed reluctantly at the meek boy beside him.

"This one 'ere was our escort," she told him. "Don't know what that big-head was thinkin' sendin' us off with this snivelin' mess, but he ain't all bad I s'pose. He got us 'ere alright."

Jack faced the nervous boy. "*You?*" he asked in disbelief.

"Me." He tentatively raised a hand. When he finally moved his hair away, Jack's mouth dropped at the brown eyes that peered back at him. "I work for Vidal Verne as a runner at the House of Silver Strings in Yorn. It's a pleasure to meet you."

"You're… Nebbin?" Jack asked dumbly. He stared like a fool as the boy nodded.

"Rhouess. But everyone calls me, Rus, sir," he introduced,

extending his hand. "I can take you there now if you're ready. I need to be heading back out soon anyway. Sir Verne needs me back as soon as possible."

"Jack," he responded, limply shaking his hand. Why would a practitioner willingly hire a Nebbin? And such a scrawny one at that. Ease of travel? Safety purposes? He'd have to ask. "I have pressing business with your boss. Also, *good god, yes*. I'm ready to go. You're the first person that's shown any sense of urgency since I arrived. Let me just wake someo—"

"Are you insane?"

Jack stiffened.

"Never mind," he muttered, just loud enough for Rus to hear. Jack put on his best fake grin, before whirling around to find Sylvie standing there with her arms crossed. She was donning the most unattractive scowl he'd ever seen. He resisted the urge to distance himself when her fingers trembled and familiar angry sparks fell to the ground.

"Good morning," Jack greeted, voice dead of all inflection. "Sleep well?"

"You did not knock me out just for the sake of surprising them and getting your way," Sylvie said, challenge in her eyes and in her voice. "Tell me you didn't."

"No," he corrected. "I did. It worked, too."

"*Jack.*"

"I'm not sorry, Syl."

"Of course you aren't," she said, glaring heatedly at him. He didn't look away, and the longer they regarded each other, the more he had to physically keep himself from speaking out about her awful cot hair. The sight was beyond dreadful.

Jack bit his tongue. He was walking on a very thin line right now. *Careful*, he thought to himself. *Be very careful.*

"I met the Arch Poten," Jack said, trying to quell her rising annoyance. "Mother was right. She's a stubborn woman, but a fair one. She's been having problems with a few local slavers apparently. I figured if we got rid of them, then she'll help us in return. But we'll have to speak to Vidal. He'd likely be more open to cutting the particulars of that whole Summit support deal."

"There are limits to what you can and can't do," she chided, ignoring his attempt at distraction.

Jack rolled his eyes. "A lecture, Syl? Really?"

Sylvie stared at him like he should've expected it, and really, he did. He'd even anticipated a shouting match and a few giant fireballs blown his way in anger. But his plan *did* work. As they usually did. Although a part—a tiny, insignificant part—of him felt guilty about his actions, he'd be damned if he admitted it. Jack pointed an emphatic finger at Rus in a final endeavor to show her the fruit of his brilliant work.

"Meet Rus," Jack presented, before she could get another word in. "Our *guide* to Yorn. He knows where Vidal is."

Sylvie's glare hardened and she crossed her arms, before raising an eyebrow at him in doubt. He relished the defiant lift of her chin, as she challenged him in a manner that he was all too familiar with. He wasn't about to get away with his ego intact or his motives left unquestioned.

Fine then. Neither was she.

***

From across the yard, Monet observed the two blue-bloods argue in a manner completely unbefitting their station—publicly, that is. She'd expected them to work out their problems behind closed doors, while shooting meaningful stares at each other the entire time. Not in the middle of the Red Veld's square. Damn whoever claimed that only her practitioners lacked basic manners. Cheryll would've been appalled by her son's behavior.

Their voices were quiet, but steadily growing louder. A pack of curious onlookers had even gathered around them—herself, included—though neither of them seemed to notice. Their hands sparked blue and the Dace boy was already red in the face, but they didn't dare use their magic. They weren't that stupid.

Most of the refugees ignored them, as if fights like these were a common occurrence once upon a time. They were more pre-occupied with drinking their weight in water. That Nebbin her husband loved to abuse with work, however, was shaking in his boots. He raised his hands, only to stop them mid-ascent, as he lost himself in a timid debate of whether or not he should touch their shoulders to catch their attention.

He called out to them instead.

"Excuse me," he said softly. But his words were lost.

They continued to slip snide remarks to each other about things either too low for her to hear or too personal for her to understand. They mentioned something about old punishment chambers, past grievances, and a nameless woman that when mentioned, was apparently horrifying enough to thrust them both into a spell's silence.

Are they talking about Cheryll? Monet deliberated. She wouldn't be surprised. The woman was a menace.

After a good ten minutes passed, the crowd finally began to disperse. Again, they failed to notice.

"They're leaving," someone from beside her stated. Monet turned to find her adviser, Wilhelm, staring at the pair. His shoulders bore an invisible weight that was only noticeable to those that knew him well.

"I know," Monet muttered.

"Shall I send someone to follow them?"

"What for? If they want to go on a suicide mission, then let them. My men don't babysit."

"But Mistress, they're important—"

"To who?" she scoffed. "The Zenith Council? The Tower's Assembly? The Vanguard Circle? They *are* children. Nothing more, everything less. How can you expect me to fuss over arrogant kids when I have an entire Institute to run? If they want to run off and get themselves killed, then they're free to do so. Let them learn for themselves how harsh the world is."

"And if they succeed?"

Monet looked at him like he was demented. Maybe he was.

His hair had gone from patchy grey to pure white in a disturbingly short amount of time.

"Are you suggesting they have a chance?" Monet asked.

"That depends."

"On what?"

"What they want from us."

Her eyes thinned. Monet looked back at the quarreling pair. They'd taken to silently scowling at each other now. That Nebbin she could never remember the name of shifted awkwardly between them. Children, indeed. Complete with broody faces and wild gestures. But Cheryll must've sent them for a reason other than her bidding, and from what she could see, neither looked the type to go above and beyond for orders that already required an incessant amount of effort. In fact, both seemed rather upset at the thought of more travel.

From desperation stems persistence, Monet thought in the voice of her ever wise husband. *But why are they so desperate?*

They were clearly hiding something. It was obvious why the Dace boy would want her support in the upcoming Summit, but why did they need access to the Veld's archives? Monet doubted it was for a beginner's guide on running an Institute. There was advice for that everywhere. Most of it, unwarranted.

As much as she loathed to admit it, the Red Veld had little information regarding... anything. They'd been robbed so much throughout the ages that their archives were more like a storage closet of backwards literature than a grand library of timeless secrets. It didn't help that they were short on skilled restorers. Whole volumes were unreadable, if not missing entirely, and more than a few covers had been encrusted with colorful molds. So, unless they were looking for one or two historical anecdotes, then the Veld had very little to offer.

Is it an excuse to learn here? Monet wondered. The Drowned Tower's new Arch Poten was a Conjurer after all. *But then why go through so much trouble?*

Monet would've agreed to the occasional lesson had the Sirx

girl simply asked. Or did she believe they kept hidden spells specifically tailored for Conjurers stashed in their archives? That was optimistic. Even for a child.

An Arch Poten teaching one from another branch, she thought. It was unheard of. Candidates were always groomed by each Institute's respective Potentate Union. But the Tower had always been different from the rest. Their way of governing was proof of that. Monet scoffed at that.

Little good it did them.

She watched the trio slip out just before the walls fell for the final time that day. It wouldn't be opening for the next week, if she had anything to say about it. Their departure was noticed by everyone, despite their attempts at being sneaky. But if Wilhelm could place even an ounce of confidence in them, perhaps they were worth a bit after all. A smidgeon, if little else. But if Vidal saw something, too, then they might actually be able to rid her lands of a few unwanted slavers that were growing bolder than they had any right being. It would certainly help. Not that she'd ever tell them that outright.

If they succeeded, she'd assist them in any way they wanted, so long as they filled her in on the details of their research while they were at it. But for now, Monet had better things to do. She could already see a crowd of stern-faced men gathered behind a large window on one of the Red Veld's higher floors. They stared down at her in disapproval.

It seemed her Potentate Union wanted a meeting.

Vidal,

The Drowned Tower's residual sprog are coming to Yorn. You can thank that worker of yours for that. Entertain them if it pleases you, but they don't look the type to be easily amused.

And for the love of the First Zenith, leave the Veld's affairs out of it. I won't have my men running around for another one of your inane plays. Didn't that insufferable master of yours tell you—on more than one occasion—that you needed to contain your games?

Recall his words, if you won't listen to mine. In fact, I'd prefer it. I'm certain a previous Vanguard Circle Head would've said it in a way that even you wouldn't dare to ignore.

Watch yourself out there.

Monet Verne née Thareen 14.27.CA
Arch Poten, Red Veld

4

When Khale awoke that morning, head pounding and joints aching, he knew that the day ahead would be far from kind. Ferus Terria seemed to be conspiring against his delicate senses because everything irritated him. The sun burned too brightly, while the winds were icy in contrast. Khale swore they were more brutal than the throwing knives Pom kept tucked under his pillow. It didn't help that his robes did absolutely nothing to ward against the weather. He didn't even have a hood to cover his forehead from the sun's rays, so he was forced to suffer constant tans.

He'd gotten so much darker since being forced to leave his home. It was enough to startle him whenever he peered at his reflection. Just as he was about to complain about it, Khale paused to sniff the air.

He looked up. It would rain soon.

Just what I need, Khale thought bitterly. *Why's it always rainin' in the Surbug Mire anyway? Can't there be one good day?*

But the cherry on top of this already horrid morning was the trail of hooves their ragged group found. Well, they weren't so ragged anymore. They were twenty strong and growing. Every one of them were armed with weapons and magic within the bog they claimed as their own for the past few weeks. Hunters had opted to leave them alone for the time being, granting them some semblance of peace.

The Hunters always trudged past their settlement to assist Cheryll Dace with the rebuilding of the Tower, leaving with nothing more than a promise that they'd be back to relocate them. Khale could care less about their words. So long as the kids were well under Olivia's—shockingly gentle—care and full from their hunts, then that was all that mattered. But even he knew that they couldn't keep living like this. Sooner or later, they'd have to move back to Eriam... or Pom would drag him away. Which, if he was being honest, was a far more likely outcome.

His partner, energetic rogue that he was, had been antsy for weeks. Ever since the Tower's unfortunate demise, Pom could be found shifting on the balls of his feet. Eager to move; eager to leave. Tiv's sudden disappearance only fueled that desire. Pom wanted to search for their missing friend, unwilling to let another person slip through his fingers.

He wanted to go, and he wanted to go *now*.

They were hardly in a position to do so however. Although it was easy to remind him of that fact, Khale knew he couldn't leash Pom forever. They were partners. He wasn't his Master or his guardian, and he certainly wasn't in any position to order Pom to do anything.

The one that could, Khale thought, drifting off, as he examined his partner worriedly. He clenched his fists. *No, I can't think about that. Orpha's gone.*

Pom vented his frustration rather unhealthily. He violently attacked all of those foolish enough to cross the mire. But Khale supposed there were poorer ways to vent. At least this helped them. Somewhat.

Quieting his steps, Khale followed Pom behind a dense line of trees. The scent of blood was so strong he could taste it. Khale quickly found its source. Three men stood a ways before them in light armor meant for quick travel. Their leathers looked worn, but even from where he stood, he could tell that they were sturdy. Three horses neighed in the corner, digging their hooves into the soggy ground beneath them, while their riders bent to inspect the dozens of unmoving bodies sprawled across the mire.

Their eyes indicated Nebbin.

Khale's gaze met Pom's for a tick. His partner waggled his eyebrows in unmasked delight and offered little more than a suggestive shoulder shimmy. Pom brandished his dagger against bark, etching thin lines into the wood. Knowing what he was going to do, Khale reached out to stop him... only for his fingers to grasp air as Pom transformed into a hawk.

With a feral squawk, Pom clawed out the eye of the nearest Nebbin. He got another good slash across his jugular, before his companions snapped into action.

A burly man unsheathed a sword twice his size and swung effortlessly in Pom's direction. But Pom was faster. He flew upward to rest on a tree, morphing into an owl in order to blink... owlishly at them. Khale would've laughed at the thought had his fingers not clamped over his lips. It wouldn't do for him to give away his position. Not yet.

The other drew a sword as unwieldy as his companion's, and Khale noticed the burning eye emblazoned over their prideful backs. It stared right at him. Unblemished and pure. It was a sign that they rarely turned away from an enemy. He could respect that. Respect more that they were a part of the Hellion, a renowned mercenary band in the Yovakine Plains. Khale had seen their crews cross the mire now and again, killing smugglers from the Crystal Cartel. He knew all of their crests well enough by now. Though they weren't as great as the Tipping's—a group that consisted of highly trained merchants of death—Khale still admired their skill.

"Why are you here?" Pom asked, easing himself over the branch. His black eyes were fixated on them.

"A practitioner, huh?" one muttered. His grip tightened over the hilt of his blade. "We have no quarrel with you. Only the dead at our feet."

"You've got to be kidding me!" His companion whirled around to pin him with a glare. His jaw sawed back and forth in anger. "He killed Brev!"

"Quiet, Floren."

The man settled at the severity of his tone, but not without a scathing glance at Pom. It was obvious who their leader was.

"The name's Jorn," he introduced. His grip slackened, as his posture eased into something more natural. "We weren't ordered to hurt anyone. Well, except these two," he gestured crudely at the bodies, "they stole from us after we gave them a warm fire and a fluffy pillow for the night. I'm sure you can understand our actions."

"Jorn," Floren hissed, enunciating every syllable.

"What?"

"What do you mean *what*? He killed Brev!"

"I heard you the first time." Jorn grabbed Floren by the arm. "And we're intruding upon their territory. Remember what the boss told us. Stay low and don't invite trouble."

Floren clamped his mouth shut.

Pom watched them with huge, unblinking eyes, clearly not expecting such a controlled reaction. He leaned forward to re-examine them because surely, he'd missed something during his initial assessment. Khale didn't blame Pom for his sudden curiosity. He was interested in what they'd do next, too. Because from the long list of possible responses to a comrade being slaughtered, Khale had never before counted keeping a level-head among them. Their group leader—Jorn—either didn't care for their comrade as much as his lackey believed or had an incredible poker face. Perhaps both. Regardless, they'd obviously underestimated just how ruthless the members of the Hellion could be. To simply blink while their companion gurgled at their feet wasn't just heartless, it was downright cruel.

Khale remained in the shadows, concealing himself should they decide to reclaim common sense and pick up their blades. Pom had a way of taunting even the most stoic of men. It was a trait most primary apprentices shared. Khale could attest to that.

"Sorry about that," Jorn apologized with a grin. He ignored how Floren huffed beside him. "He's touchy, but he doesn't mean any harm. None. I swear it. Imp's honor."

"Honor?" Pom questioned, raising a skeptical brow. "From a hired sword?"

Jorn remained unaffected. Floren, on the other hand, was thoroughly insulted by the implication. Jorn had to grab him by the collar to keep him from attacking.

Pom, tickled by the reaction, smirked, further taunting the already incensed Nebbin until he was shouting a steady stream of curses that might've hurt had his ego been less resilient.

"Why, I have plenty!" Jorn insisted merrily. His smile was a bright thing. The light in his eyes, even brighter. "Honor, that is. And I've at least one good eye, too. I don't suppose you've ever thought of joining a group of hired swords for extra coin, have you? I know our boss wouldn't mind having another set of stable hands on his side."

"Jorn!" Floren hissed.

"What now?" Jorn asked, feigning ignorance.

"This question again? This filthy morph killed—"

"—Brev," he finished. "Yes, you so *helpfully* told me that. Hell, I even saw it, too. A crying shame really. But even you have to admit that the man wasn't exactly the brightest stone on the road. Plus, boss *hated* him. But this one..." Jorn faced Pom with shining eyes. "Boss would *love* him. We could always use another deserter. Especially one that doesn't whine and scream Cephas every bleeding moment."

Floren opened his mouth to retort, but Pom smoothly interrupted. "Cephas?" he said, as impartial as his burning curiosity allowed. "You don't mean, Columbus Cephas?"

"That's the one!" Jorn exclaimed. "Does everyone know the sod? Don't take this the wrong way, but I'm not a fan of his name. It's incredibly irritating when screamed enough times. Is he some kind of divine being amongst you practitioners?"

"No," Pom said, not missing a beat.

"Well, these runaways kept shouting for him, talking about how he saved them from the Drowned Tower. It's a shame what happened there, but I doubt apologizing to a dead man would do them any good. Unless, of course, they *wanted* to damage their vocal cords because that's definitely one way to do it."

Pom's stomach churned at the meaningful look on Jorn's face. He was trying to get a rise out of him. But Pom wasn't falling for it. Not yet anyway. Pom swallowed thickly, and as he put a lid over his emotions, Khale finally deemed it necessary to step from the cover of the bushes in all of his pale-skinned glory. He didn't even bother to transform. Khale simply placed his hands on his hips and grinned madly at their blood-spattered gathering.

Floren and Jorn's hands dropped to the hilts of their swords out of instinct, but they otherwise remained still. As if—like any predator of the wild—they expected Khale to lash out at them if they made any sudden movements. A foolish notion.

If anything, Pom would be the first to strike.

Khale spread his arms out before him. More for the sake of presenting his liveliness than to show his empty palms, so they could ease back into more comfortable stances. His eyes met Pom's for the briefest of seconds. Silent understanding connected them, as swift and as passing as the final flicker of dying flames, before they focused on the mercenaries once more. They had an entire night's worth of conversation in that one moment. The sort of age-long discussion that could only be conveyed between the eyes of two people who knew each other as much as they did their own faults. It was a talk of future plans, of present actions, and of snappy decisions still untempered by time.

Just as Khale feared, his partner's desire had finally been unleashed. It was either leave with him now or stay behind with Olivia and the rest. There was no more time to decide. Pom wouldn't allow him more. They had a duty to protect the younger practitioners and hand them safely over to Cheryll Dace once a proper settlement on Eriam was established. But they also had a duty to their lost friend, to find him and bring him home.

Pom had already made his choice.

As the sun continued to burn down upon them, Khale knew then that he'd already made his as well. He'd made it long ago.

He was selfish, and had no qualms about admitting such. His personal goals always sat at the forefront of his mind. That was just another one of the many traits most primary apprentices seemed to share. Perhaps it was due to the fact that they were continuously pitted against each other to obtain their position. But right now, Khale couldn't find any fault in that. Not if it meant getting closer to Tiv—the one who rallied them to rise against the Assembly. He might not have predicted all that would happen when he did, but that didn't change the fact that, ultimately, Tiv had saved hundreds of lives that day. By bringing the practitioners out of their rooms, they stood a far better chance of escaping. Some qualities were necessary, despite how vile others made them out to be.

"So," Khale cleared his throat, "one of you hires mentioned somethin' 'bout employment, yea?"

The two Imps blinked numbly back.

"Reckon yer boss'll accept two birdmen?" Khale continued, undeterred. He purposely eyed Floren. "Cause yer friend 'ere seems ta think we're nothin' more than murderous varmints without a home an' proper chains."

"Accepting so easily?" Jorn smiled once he gathered his wits. "This might be a trap, you know? You did kill our friend."

"I'm willin' ta risk it, but I guarantee you'll lose more than a few limbs if it is. Us Amorphs don't go down easily."

"Fair enough." Jorn held out a hand. "All tykes, terrors, and scamps have a place in the Hellion."

Khale regarded the proffered appendage like a foreign object, before looking at Pom for confirmation that he easily gave. Pom twirled his dagger around like a man who had absolutely nothing to do with the situation. Khale's eyes drifted back to Jorn's wiggling fingers. It took him a moment, but eventually, he grasped his arm up to the elbow in solid, confident consent.

"When rain starts ta fall, don't regret those words, Nebbin," Khale warned. "Bad things happen in the rain."

"Let the farmers worry about the weather," Jorn replied,

backing away just enough to pat him twice on both shoulders. Not in any assessment of strength, but as if he were a young boy that had just done his father proud. Khale doubted joining a band of killers for hire would make any father proud—not a sane one anyway—but he knew nothing of where they were going or the trials that lay ahead of them, so he didn't pull away.

The more friends they had, the better.

"You two are Imps now," Jorn said, addressing them both with a smile as real as the sweat beading down their backs. "May dawn's breath always smile upon you, friends."

***

As it happened, the Hellion kept a den in the port city of Brantine. The city overlooked Lake Kloren, where Silas' temple stood in perfect tranquility, undisturbed by the happenings of the rest of the world. And as most things did these days, it reminded them of the Tower's demise. Pernelia's sanctuary had remained silent throughout that dreadful night, and long after it was over. The sisters within did nothing but pray... or so the more optimistic ones liked to believe. For all they knew, they could've closed their eyes, shut their ears, and ignored them entirely. No litanies, no songs—nothing.

Just the thought was enough to make Khale's blood boil. So, he shook his head and turned away from the shadow of Silas' temple. He kept his gaze firmly fixed on their destination instead. The Hellion's den wasn't close by any means, but with the help of horses and magic, they arrived in half a day. It gave them both ample time to brood over leaving Olivia behind, as well as speak to Jorn about the hierarchy within their newfound allegiance. It wasn't complicated. Like all syndicates, there were leaders, their collection of confidantes, special right-hand men, and grunts. Or Imps, as they liked to call them. The title fit Pom well, though if his partner fancied it, he didn't show it.

"We're stuck doing the legwork then?" Khale heaved a heavy sigh, already regretting his decision.

"You're practitioners," Jorn assured. "Amorphs at that. Good trackers, even better scouts. You'll move up quickly. Just smile, say the right things, and if you have to step on somebody's toes make sure to crush them real good. You don't want angry men racing after you."

"Sounds like a plan."

"Truth be told, we don't get many of your kind in our ranks. All the talent ups and joins the Tippings as soon as they get the chance. More gold, they say. Better protection, too, apparently."

"Smart of 'em then," Khale said. "Hunters are no joke."

"So I hear."

"You can't believe everything you hear," Pom cut in.

"Solid advice. You've got a good head on you." Jorn nodded, as he stroked the stubble on his chin in a way that he liked to think made him look wiser. It didn't. "Maybe they're being offered something more than gold and protection then. Who knows? I certainly don't. I can only go on what I do."

"Yea?" Khale asked. "An' what's that?"

"Clean clothes, leather bags, cheap soapy smell," he listed. "You two definitely aren't after gold. You don't look like the type, and you certainly don't look like you're being hunted."

"That intuition or experience talkin'?"

"A little of both."

"Are you sure you want to rely on observation?" Pom asked. "What if we've got a big, bad, red-eyed Elementalist on our tails and we're using you as cover?"

Jorn didn't believe him for a second. Stopping, he pointed two fingers at Pom's eyes. Pom immediately stepped back and bared his teeth ferociously.

"You've got bite, kid," Jorn complimented. "But your eyes don't scream desperation. Caution, though… they're full of that. Right, Floren?"

Jorn nudged Floren, who only grunted in agreement, before looking up at the darkling sky and trying his best to ignore them. Floren was still reluctant to speak. Not that either of them were particularly bothered by it. In fact, Jorn was the one that seemed most torn up about his behavior. But when Floren had tried, Jorn had scolded him for not being polite enough.

Floren was aggravated by the whole situation. And who wouldn't be? They did kill one of their so-called friends. Violence never made for a good first impression. But they weren't exactly looking for an invitation into their band of ruffians at the time.

"This way," Jorn said, making a sharp turn left.

Brantine was small, but as they led them through dozens of back alleys and one too many overly crowded side streets, they realized that it held much more than they'd ever be able to explore in one day—or five for that matter. It was a bustling world of storm lanterns and wood. When the lumber began to wear, they were replaced by more. Caravans came and left. Their riders were followed by prancing children, even as they announced their departure. Trade happened all around them. It was enough for the scent of old coins to become a permanent fixture in the air.

This city was one of few in the Yovakine Plains that actually strived, due in large part to its location. Shops were scattered across every walkway, more hidden in some areas than others. Although the food dealers set up their stalls far from the main squares and closer to the weathered gray wood of the docks, the stink of fish remained. It spared nothing. Not even the people.

Pom and Khale couldn't help but notice how much better off they were compared to the stories they'd heard about the south. Barely any urchins wandered about, and the ones that did were given coin. The older ones, however, were cast aside. No compassion to be found for children over twelve with hands deemed steady enough for work. Still, it was better than seeing an entire village worth of starving men like they'd expected.

Jorn was kind enough to wait for them to finish gawking.

"Welcome to the Chattering Crow," he said, stopping in front of a plain wooden door masked in a shady corner street.

The door was round at the top with a rusted black knob. There were no nearby signs or lamps. It could've easily been mistaken for someone's house. The curved walls that flanked the entrance blessed the passage with some semblance of privacy. Enough that it was worth suffering through the echoes from the main street bouncing like noisy beetles all around them. The building's few windows were shielded by wooden planks, so the only visible light came from a hole at the bottom for the door and a flickering oil lantern just outside of the bend, badly in need of a refill. It made the shadows dance around them in a way that was decidedly ominous.

"Getting cold feet?" Jorn ribbed. "Don't worry. I promise you'll fit right in. We aren't as powerful as the Tippings, but we've got influence."

Pom rolled his shoulders in an attempt to ease them, as he lifted one eyebrow in unmasked skepticism. "When you try so hard to sell yourself it makes me think the exact opposite."

Khale smacked him. "Be nice, yea?"

Jorn laughed at the display, garnering the attention of a few curious onlookers and a grouchy merchant with an awful snarl. "The Plains are divided under two leaders," he began. "Drage's in charge of Tarsin and Pigmy. Redmount, too, if that hellish place even counts. He's a sensible man, despite his... habits."

"Let me guess," Pom said, "he's the one we're meeting."

Jorn nodded.

"A big fish already." Khale beamed. "We're movin' up."

"Not quite," Jorn said. "But I'll let you decide for yourself."

He opened the door, unveiling the faint lights and alcohol dazed men within. They were all armed to the teeth, and neither of them could help the tingle of magic that responded beneath their fingertips. Khale caught sight of a man with blue eyes seated by another with the same color. Their eyebrows scrunched in interest at their entrance.

Their group's appearance brought dirty looks and silence. Chatter died with each step they took closer to a man leaning heavily against the tavern's counter. He was rogue-like and handsome by anyone's standards. He seemed to know it, too, because there was an air of confidence about him that gave them pause. Despite the fresh stubble and shaggy hair, he looked clean. Although Khale blamed it on the seedy backdrop. The man simultaneously stood out and fit in perfectly with the bar. He even nursed a drink in his hand. It was so potent that Khale's nose wrinkled at the scent, despite his distance. Enhanced senses were as much a curse as they were a blessing.

Twice, they were stopped by towering brutes that were quickly waved off by Jorn, before the shaggy-haired man looked away from his drink long enough to realize that they wanted to speak with him. He stepped forward to greet them, before offering a grin that didn't quite reach his eyes.

"Boss," Jorn acknowledged.

Drage's lips tilted up into a smirk that spoke only of trouble, before he squared his shoulders like he was preparing for a fight. Two guards were at his back in an instant. Both women. The one closest to him had sharp eyes, but untried hands. She held her sword the way someone with too much pride and not enough skill did. They'd seen enough of her kind to know that she wasn't a threat, despite the snarl on her face. The other, however, was at once appraising and unconcerned. She had a heavy bow on her back and a set of daggers at her hips. Long, flesh-colored scars ran along both of her arms.

Gotta watch out for that one, Khale thought.

"Jorn," Drage drawled in a silken accent that undoubtedly made women swoon. "Back so soon?"

"Here to curry favor," the woman with the daggers said, her tone was sharper than any blade. She breathed self-confidence and flaunted tension, carrying herself with all of the traits that made seduction what it was—and she knew it. "Just look at that walk," she laughed freely. "All pride and far too smug. He must be compensating for something."

"You would know, wouldn't you, Celina?"

"The size of his," Celina trailed off, purposely looking down and laughing unabashedly. "Have class, Drage. I would never."

"You have standards," he said, scandalized, making the woman leer. They stared at each other, before Celina jutted out a saucy hip and tilted her head meaningfully at Khale and Pom, who remained silent behind Jorn.

Drage got the hint. The air seemed to turn with him as he faced them. It carried the unique aroma of alcohol and whatever oil he used to sharpen his blades.

"You've brought practitioners," Drage said coolly.

"Khale and Pom," Jorn introduced.

Drage's eyes flitted to meet their own, before settling back on Jorn. "Shifters, huh? Replacements for the ones that ran?"

"Something like that. A little more loyal though... I hope."

"That's reassuring." Drage flashed him an easy grin, but the caution in his eyes was plain. "So, why do they want to join? Don't tell me they're trying to find someone, too. If they start screaming Cephas, they can turn around right now."

"We *are* looking for someone," Pom said, stepping in front of Jorn. Khale was by his side in an instant. "Not him though."

With trained eyes, they watched Drage sigh and discreetly hand a smiling Celina a silver coin, before asking, "Then who?"

"A friend."

"So, why don't you run along and search? Why come here?"

"It would be easier if we had others to help us."

"Really?" Drage leaned back, bored. He scrutinized them, before shrugging. "Sure, I'll let you join. We could always use more practitioners on our side. But first," he fell into a nearby chair and slouched contentedly against the wood, "convince me."

They stared at him.

"Come on now," Drage urged. "Bow, sob, throw me some coins. Do something! I don't have all day. I've got a meeting after this. Incredibly urgent. Can't miss it."

"Yes, I'm sure she's very beautiful," Celina said.

"Why, I would never," he repeated her words, all false indignity. "How could you even suggest such a thing? When—"

"Yer face makes me wanna punch kittens," Khale cut in. He

ignored the sudden, shocked guffaws around the room in favor of crossing his arms and staring at Drage with dead eyes.

"What did you just say?"

Purposely thickening his accent, Khale repeated the words, then tacked on a hearty, "I ain't droppin' ta my haunches before someone like you."

"Like me?" Drage said. Slow and dangerous.

"Haughty maroons with more air inside a' their heads than brains," Khale clarified, tapping two fingers against his temple. "I'd sooner have my head speared on a pike for the birds, yea?"

His words elicited a shudder throughout the room. All traces of hilarity died in an instant and numb silence stood in its place. They stared with bated breath at Drage's arched brow, waiting for the anger that would surely follow. But to their surprise, a half-smile tilted Drage's lips instead. It charmed a number of women around them. Then, he laughed. Solid. Rough. As if he wasn't used to doing so. His mirth was more than enough to ease the tension, and soon enough, others joined in as well.

Beside them, Jorn exhaled a breath of relief.

"Oh, I *already* like you." Drage snorted. He clasped Khale's shoulder. His smirk was wider now. Truer.

"You ain't playin' with a full deck a' cards then, yea?"

He laughed again, sizing them both up and judging them once more. Seriously this time. Pom's short stature and the snarl on his face. Khale's bright red hair and gaudy Astonian tongue. Two pairs of callused hands. They were dangerous; they had experience; and they were livid at—*something*. It was obvious. To him at least.

Yes, Drage fully decided then, *they'd make good additions.*

"Welcome," Drage said, opening his arms wide. His eyes crinkled, as he showed them the world. It was the best they could offer to cooped-up practitioners. "All tykes, terrors, and scamps have a place in the Hellion."

The cheers that erupted then, although still somewhat hesitant, were the loudest they'd ever heard. Neither of them, however, could be so easily stunned into silence.

"Rowdy bunch, yea?"

Khale looked out at them all. There was a second floor, he realized, seeing more than a few scruffy Nebbin leaning against the wooden rails. Khale nudged Pom, before using his head as an armrest. He whistled when he had his partner's attention. A wordless expression of just how impressed he was by their numbers.

"Guess we won't have ta worry about yer loud mouth, yea?"

Pom shoved him right back into Jorn. Khale wasn't discouraged. He'd been expecting it in fact. But that didn't stop him from clicking his tongue in distaste. He smothered the urge to grab his partner by the scruff of his collar, as his attention drifted to the troop that now surrounded him. They asked rapid-fire questions like he'd just come home from an epic war.

From the corner of his eye, Khale watched Floren seethe, before silently leaving the room. He knew that Drage noticed as well because he found the roguish man watching his subordinate leave with a complex look on his face. How would Drage react to knowing they killed one of his men? Would he have them killed, too? Would he do it himself? He seemed like the type that would. But the thought was quickly dismissed when Drage rolled his eyes at Floren's retreating figure, as if his sulking was common.

"You call your grunts, Imps, right?" Pom suddenly asked, forcing Drage back to attention. He jutted his chin at the daggers flanking Celina's hips before Drage could get a word in.

"You like them?" Celina drawled.

Pom didn't even bother trying to hide the longing in his gaze.

"Look elsewhere," Celina went on. "You wouldn't be able to handle these edges, sweet thing."

"Does the Hellion supply their men?" Pom asked, ignoring her jibe. He swiveled back around only to find Drage flashing him a perfect set of white teeth.

"You know it," was all he said.

Those three words were all it took for Pom to return his grin. Except two times as wild. "I'll hold you to that."

Olive,

Me an' Pom have a few errands ta run. You know how it is. Us Amorphs need ta feel the wind under our wings an' somethin' other than soggy dirt under our claws, yea? We'll see you soon. I give you my special eastern Amorph's word an' all that nonsense. (That's a thing right? I hope it is 'cause I've been sayin' it too long.)

If yer feelin' scarce, have Edanna cook. She's five years too young ta be handlin' kitchen knives, but frankly, yer stew is terrible. Don't even think 'bout puttin' the kids through that.

Go back ta Eriam.

Khale

***

Olivia,

Sorry for not telling you about leaving. It was sudden. I've left you my supply of spare daggers though. They're inside a leather satchel hidden in a gap between a few outgrown roots near the south side of the Mire. (Look at the map below). It's where all of those green wild berries are. If you're still not sure where it is, I carved my initials on the foot of the tree.

If you don't want them, then give them to one of the older kids. Don't just let them rust there. Those were expensive! I suggest handing it off to Nox. The black-haired boy that has the sides of his head shaved. He's dexterous for a kid. He even asked me to teach him how to use them a few nights ago. While I can't now (obviously), those blades will let him get a head start until I return.

I'll see you when I see you, Olivia. Take care of yourself out there.

Best,
Pom
[Followed by a doodle of trees, a dagger, and a flower pot.]

5

Tiv remembered enough to know they took him in broad daylight, but when he awoke, it was to total darkness.

I'm blind, he thought for a disoriented moment, panic rising in his throat, as he tried and failed to calm his breathing. The air certainly didn't help with his endeavors. It was hot and moist. Each breath seemed to stick unbearably close to him, as if trying to choke the oxygen from his lungs. It almost did, too. But when his eyes drifted downward and he found flecks of his pale skin peeking from the shadows, his terror stomped down on itself. It was quickly replaced with another, more infuriating thing— buzzing. Both inside and outside of his head. Tiv could physically feel the heaviness of his limbs, and distantly, he registered the sound of metal. Clinking metal.

At least he wasn't deaf.

He wasn't blind either, but he was... somewhere. His robes were exchanged for a thin cotton shirt, and he noticed a little too late that his ankles and wrists were bound by iron manacles. Tiv could smell them. He traced them blindly, feeling the fat chains that held them together. Another stemmed away from him and toward a nearby wall, where it was embedded inside layers of concrete. Tiv was taken aback by how close it was, providing little leeway inside of a room he couldn't quite see. But it must've been large. Because he could hear the steady pitter-patter of dripping water somewhere far from him. Ragged breathing, too, if he listened hard enough.

It was then he realized that he wasn't alone.

Eyes slowly adjusting, he could just make out a line of cells to the left and right of him. Most were empty. The vague shapes he did see were too small to be people, and he wondered for a moment if they'd locked him up in a kennel.

The strained whimper he heard in the cell across from him swiftly proved otherwise. His neck cracked as he tried to peer through the haze clouding his vision. There was no one there.

Had he just imagined it then?

Tiv opened his mouth to speak, then coughed uncontrollably when he found that he couldn't. His lips were dry, his throat even drier. He needed water. More than that, he needed to leave.

No more cages, Tiv thought with no small amount of determination. He called forth his magic and attempted to turn into a jail mouse out of reflex rather than any actual strategy. He preferred the form and had gotten quite good at it early on as a child when he and Jack would play in the older parts of the Tower. But when his hands failed to light and a shot of pain ran up his spine instead, he gasped in surprise. The hurt was unexpected enough to elicit a rough groan of pain that made his throat burn in protest.

But that didn't stop him from trying again.

Once, twice, six more times. All in rapid succession. It was as fruitless as sapping water from a stone. The pain of each attempt was muted by his snarls of frustration. Distantly, his magic thrummed beneath his skin. So far from the surface that it actually frightened him more than his current predicament. No sparks of blue, no transformation of limbs, there was nothing. Only the rising terror and his heart pounding in his ears. It pumped blood three times too quick. Tiv was sure he'd faint soon. He needed to calm down. But his awareness was stunted by one, single mind-numbing fact.

His magic was gone.

Tiv screamed.

Power didn't return to him and it didn't make him feel better, but he did hear someone shuffle from across the room.

Their noises were followed by the distinct ring of metal. They didn't speak, and he didn't raise his head to encourage them. As soon as his scream died, Tiv lowered his head to his hands, rubbing his temples and swallowing his fright. He couldn't even bring his fingers up completely because of his chains, instead he had to hunker in on himself. Tiv dipped down like a religious man. The manacles provided little freedom, but the way their coolness bore into his cheeks was a welcome distraction.

Don't tell me you need my help? Tiv's subconscious brusquely mocked in Jack's voice, and never before did he so desperately want to break something. *We split and this is what happens? Keep it together, you flaming turkey.*

Tiv viciously pulled at his chains, uncaring for the way they dug into his skin. It was a futile attempt. They were tight and seemingly unbreakable. For reasons beyond his own admittedly limited knowledge, he was exhausted. Even the simple act of pulling made him heave. As he eased his arms, smelling the scent of his own blood, his fingers brushed against the cuffs once more. Tiv tried to find a gap he could pry open with his fingernails, instead he found engraved markings that ran all around the metal. The lines were so thin and so fine, he would've missed them had he not been paying such close attention. But he was. Oh, he was. And as he traced their faux smoothness, he painted a picture in his mind.

He knew these marks.

Familiar as they were, he couldn't quite remember where they were from or what they were for. But he had time to figure it out, so he wasn't worried. Just as the thought entered his mind, his hands stilled, his eyes widened, and his breath caught in his throat. He looked down, unable to help the shudder that rocked his bones in realization.

Before laws were made against the brewing of lethal potions, the early embrocologists created many for the sole purpose of draining magic from a practitioner's veins, Tiv recalled Celaris say with an almost clinical detachment. *These are the same brews that Hunters use today to make deserters comply. They're dangerous, to be sure, but infinitely more humane than what they used back in the days before the First Zenith. The Mentalists preferred more… physical restraints.*

Tiv pulled again. The embers of urgency fueled him.

He'd rather die.

***

An immeasurable amount of time later, someone entered.

Each footstep was an explosion to his acute senses, and from the weight, he knew instantly that it was a man. An important one, too. Because the whispers across the room ceased, as did the clinking shackles. Everyone fell silent upon his entrance, except Tiv, who mindlessly kept slamming his wrists against the floor with no real force. He had little energy left to do so, but he'd been trying too long to stop now.

"What are you doing?" the newcomer asked when he saw his sorry state. No unkindness in his tone. No compassion either.

Tiv looked up then, seeing the man's blurred outline a short distance away. With eyes long accustomed to the dark, Tiv could tell that the man's cheeks were flushed from drink. Remarkably though, there was no unsteadiness in his movements as he took three deliberate steps toward his cage. The man fumbled with an unlit lamp, and Tiv shut his eyes when it suddenly roared to life. Though he knew that in reality it only provided a scant amount of light, it was still far more than he was used to.

He took his time opening his eyes, letting them adjust bit-by-bit until the flame became a little more bearable. His visitor didn't mind waiting for his senses to adapt. But when they finally did, Tiv couldn't help but flinch at the sight of the newcomer's face. He'd never been the sort to obsess over physical beauty, but the man before him had the kind of mug only a mother could love. Or maybe not, depending on the mother. Wrinkly, spotted, and grotesque. He had three nostrils and a long scar that creased his face from forehead to chin, sealing one of his eyes shut.

Tiv could honestly say that he preferred the unending dark.

He remained still, even when the bars of his prison creaked, trembling under the weight of the man that settled against them. They were shockingly unsteady and his insides twisted at the knowledge that he could probably break them had he not been bound by magical restraints, zapping him of what little strength he had left. It didn't help that they were starving him, or so he assumed, unaware of just how long he'd been trapped. Time passed strangely in the dark. But his growling stomach hinted to more than a few hours. Tiv could ignore his gut well enough. His parched throat, however, wasn't so easily dismissed, and when he saw the deformed man slide a canteen of water through the bars, his entire body trembled in anticipation. His cracked lips suddenly seemed so important.

"Drink," the man muttered.

Godsend, Tiv's mind cried.

He snatched the canteen with shaking fingers, carelessly dropping a few precious beads in his haste. The touch of water was divine. Tiv was too thirsty to think of how appalling he must seem, but he didn't think the man had any room to judge. He looked like the sort that scurried around in dungeons far worse than this one. So, when his tongue swirled around the outer rims for one or two extra droplets, he couldn't find it in himself to care.

When Tiv hurled the canteen gracelessly back—frowning at his too short chains—it was empty and sported a smidgeon of dirt at the edge where he'd held it. The man didn't even notice. He merely offered him a yellow smile that made Tiv's skin crawl. His good eye was kind and flanked by a whiskery eyebrow that reminded him of a few of his Masters from the Drowned Tower.

"Hello," the man greeted. Slow and unsure. "Good to know you're still alive."

Tiv almost scoffed. He pinched his thigh to stop himself.

"Good to know you care for your prisoners," Tiv retorted. His tone wasn't as derisive as he would've liked. It was nothing more than a low whisper, as drawn and hazy as a dream from another life. The water was still trying to work its wonders over his too thick tongue.

"You aren't my prisoner," he told him, pointing at a cracked door made visible by the lamplight. Tiv could just make out an armored guard standing beyond. He had dark skin and darker hair. More than that he didn't know.

"Then release me."

The man smiled tightly in response, his gaze apologetic. "I can't do that."

Tiv didn't bother asking why. "Then can you tell me where I am?" he asked instead. The question slipped from his lips, before he could stop it.

The newcomer's hands curled around the bars of his cell. His fingers tightened along with his expression, and for a hopeful instant, Tiv thought he'd answer. That he'd assure him in some way. That he'd tell him he was on his side. Perhaps luck had decided to throw him a bone. Pernelia knew he needed it. But then his fingers abruptly dropped, shredding the tiny flicker of hope in Tiv's eyes, before he picked up the canteen in a manner far too gentle for someone with such a monstrous face.

His gaze drifted to the cells beside him. Tiv distantly noted the people inside, but his attention snapped back as soon as the man took a step toward the door.

"Wait!" Tiv cried. "Where are you going?"

He didn't answer.

"No, wait, tell me where I am! Come back!" And because of his desperation, he didn't remember shouting, *'Please,'* over and over again.

The man expertly ignored him and when Tiv's world fell back into darkness, he was left with bubbling shame and sticky lips. They were drying up again. Tiv's fingers framed his shackles once more, searching for distraction. He found it by counting the iron links between them.

Four, five six, Tiv totaled, before beginning again, finding a newfound hate for the numbers.

Using one of the links, he tried his best to rub a tally in the wall, just deep enough for him to differentiate the mark from the rest that lined the stone. Tiv traced the line with a hesitancy that could've been mistaken for reverence.

One, he counted.

***

As the days pressed on, he met the eyes of the others around him. Two children, one woman, and two men. The children were curious things. They played strange games. Their recent favorite seemed to be who could find his pupils in the dark. The quieter one—Wynn, he thought, unsure—had won some time ago. From the way she'd avert her eyes whenever Tiv stared back, she knew she did, though she never mentioned it.

They were both proficient performers and took to practicing when they weren't lost in hopeful conversation. Tiv couldn't see them very well, but he heard their shuffling feet, their ragged breaths, and the annoying ring of their chains.

From the noisy exchanges of their guards, Tiv found that only one truly deserved to be down there. For manslaughter and pedophilia and a number of crimes that were lost to his ears as soon as he saw the fresh-faced man in the cell beside the alleged criminal. Despite the bars and the constant guards outside, the young man never slept. He was always huddled in a ball and didn't dare look up at anybody. Tiv didn't blame him. He'd have trouble sleeping, too, if he was next to a maniac. While the bars that separated them offered protection, they also just made the whole experience scarier.

Only the woman claimed practitioner—Elementalist, at that. With red eyes and redder hair, her appearance spoke of fire. But that was before she'd been clasped. What must've once been tan skin had become sickly gray. There were times she'd just collapse against the wall, only to wake hours later, screaming. She spoke too fast for him to catch the words and her pronunciation was always strangely garbled, but he understood enough to know that whatever nonsense she spoke wasn't anything pleasant.

It quickly became apparent that the Nebbin were treated fairly well for captives. They were fed every other day, allowed fresh water, and fastened in longer chains. It seemed they believed them less of a threat. They were right.

Thankfully, they were treated equally by the guards. None bothered them, only sneered when they were courageous enough to talk back. Not that many did. Not even Tiv. He couldn't waste precious saliva on people he knew wouldn't listen. To his disdain, it was mostly the criminal that had something to say. He had a rich voice that sounded sane for someone so shattered. It bounced like living dread off of the walls.

We're merchandise, Tiv realized, when one of the guards had to be physically restrained from breaking the criminal's face for a particularly nasty comment about his breath. He wondered how long they'd be kept here. Wares had to be moved sooner or later.

Would anyone actually want to buy a known criminal? He shook his head to rid himself of the doubt. On second thought, there were many.

It wasn't long before Tiv found himself counting time by their meals. He quickly noticed that he and the Elementalist were only given food and water after two of the Nebbin's had passed. It was another kind of torture to listen to someone eat and drink on an empty stomach, and sometimes he swore that a few of them ate louder on purpose. Even worse was the fact that the deformed man arrived like clockwork to offer his assistance. He emptied their buckets with a straight face and never once complained about his job.

Rat, the other prisoners called him.

He whispered things to them sometimes, but he never spoke to Tiv again. No matter how much he coaxed. Tiv didn't speak much either, despite the urging of some of his cellmates. Though there were times he'd eye the Elementalist across from him, encouraging her to talk with his gaze alone. She never did. But she at least had the audacity to glare back. Her eyes were bright in the gloom, if not a little weary. She lifted her eyebrows in judgment whenever Tiv attempted light exercise. It usually didn't turn out well. His body never cooperated with him and he ended up losing too much water. He gave up before long.

After some time, when the tallies on Tiv's wall accumulated and the voices in his head quieted enough for him to focus, he began to count the slavers. They periodically entered the chamber to check their chains. Tiv memorized what little details he could of them. One nursed a broken nose; a testament of their leader's disfavor. Another had a misshapen scar on his chin, and was always in the company of a man that donned a sleeveless tunic, showcasing muscled arms and an uneven tan. Field work? His skin tone certainly suggested it.

There were eight in total, and they all talked about each other. Some more than others. Tiv filed their words away, storing them for a time when they might become useful.

For now, he leaned against the wall, thinking of rescue and escape and the tales he'd tell upon his return. Pom would be enraptured and Khale would mock them both. In the back of his mind, Tiv quietly hoped that Jack survived the fall of their home and that he conjured a sea of icy water when he found him.

***

When he counted nine tallies on his wall, a new prisoner was brought in. A bloody little boy already halfway to the grave. He wore dirty white rags and the scent of submission. Though his eyes were shut, his chains were short enough for Tiv to know he was a practitioner and clearly not merchandise. The beady-eyed guard threw him in the empty cell beside his, uncaring for the way his limbs lopped lifelessly in every possible direction. Tiv's eyes widened in horror when the boy's head began to bleed, and when he saw his hands, his face morphed into a scowl he didn't think himself capable of producing.

"What did you do to him?" he roared, sickened. Disgust etched itself across his face as he snarled like a wild animal at the guard, who merely rolled his eyes at him. Like he didn't do a thing. Like this was *okay*. The guard left him to his shouting, as he picked at his expensive gauntlets that were stained with the boy's blood.

"Come back!" he yelled. The guard didn't listen.

Breathing heavily, Tiv assessed the boy's condition as best as he could in the blackness of their prison. He was even more grotesque now, than under the sparse light. With his hands and feet curled inward, resembling bird claws—too swollen to be of any real use—he looked like an Amorph forced to halt mid-shift. Red was everywhere. Made blacker without light. It reeked of steel and rust, and he heard the children in their cell's gag from the scent. By some miracle, the boy turned his head, and Tiv saw the demented smile on his lips. Tiv watched it grow longer and wider until he was laughing, delirious with pain.

"*Nonono*," the boy slurred. His broken fingers attempted to dig into the manacles around his wrists. "Magic hurts!"

Tiv struggled against his chains. He forced his powers out and disregarded the pain when nothing happened. But when the boy's eyes opened, flashing blue, Tiv's breath caught in his throat. Sheer shock halted him.

"Roval?" Tiv stammered.

He didn't answer, only stared unseeingly at him. But he didn't need to. Tiv shouted his name again, sure this time. He repeated it like a mantra, as he tried and failed to come closer. Without warning, Roval's arm jerked, curling at an impossible angle. Tiv knew what he was about to do.

"No, stop!" Tiv pleaded. "Don't use your magic!"

Too late.

Roval screamed like he was lit on fire.

The Elementalist, with her weary eyes looked at him with something akin to pity. On the other side of the room, that detestable criminal snickered. Even the scared young man lifted his head to see what all the commotion was about. He shrieked when he saw Roval's sorry state. For the first time since Tiv awoke, the young man opened his mouth to speak. To pray.

The criminal scoffed, shimmying his way to the very edge of his cell, so he could peer closer at him. "Bringing overpowered deities into this is meaningless. Do you really think someone here will listen to you mindless begging?"

His voice trembled, but he didn't stop. The names of the First Zenith spilled from his lips over and over again, until his tongue twisted, the words combined, and they became little more than the frantic ramblings of a man delirious from fear.

"Wishes aren't granted here," the criminal said, his deep voice a discomfort Tiv wanted to rid the world of. "This is Ferus Terria. God doesn't exist in a place like this."

"Shut up," Tiv seethed.

The criminal smiled in delight, finally getting a reaction out of him. Before he could retort, the door was flung open, blinding them until tears stung their eyes. By the time the light receded, a man Tiv had never seen before stood before his cell. He was old and leaned heavily on his staff. His hunched back was flanked by two lanky guards with sharp eyes.

"This one?" the old man asked the guard to his left, who nodded in response. Tiv glared at them both. "Look at those eyes. Definitely an Amorph's."

"What did you do to Roval?" Tiv bellowed. His throat protested every word.

"With bite, too," he went on, pleased. "He'll do."

Faster than Tiv could register, they opened his cell and hauled him up with strength their lithe bodies masked. He could hardly stand, but they had no qualms about dragging him out. Even if it was thrashing and screaming. The Elementalist caught his eye as he passed her cage.

With a shake of her head, she opened her mouth to warn him of—*of what?* Tiv wondered, only to still at what he saw.

She had no tongue.

As if he'd been doused in ice-cold water, what little energy he had left escaped him and he once more felt the heaviness of his limbs. The weight of his shackles were as familiar as his own two hands at this point. The men took advantage of his sudden compliance to pull him along.

Tiv could do little more than eye his surroundings at that point. They led him through a long hallway filled with ajar doors that led into rooms flooded with guards. It wasn't long before they forced him outside and up a flight of stairs that led into the biggest mansion he'd ever seen.

The inside was a different world entirely. All mustard floors and towering ceilings. Expensive oil lamps stood at regular intervals. He even saw several glass chandeliers with jewels encrusted along their steel tips. Several murals depicting nature spanned the walls. Stuffed animals stood in front of them in striking poses. Their dead eyes followed him as he passed. It was all so lavish. The air was no exception. Perfumed with enough lavender and vanilla to make his nose itch.

"Hurry now!" the old man urged, walking two steps ahead of them. "We're already late."

The men grunted, but didn't complain. Soon enough, they approached a solid, wooden door at the end of a sparsely lit hall. There were no other rooms in this area. Tiv wondered what kind of blue-blooded scum was behind this entrance, but he certainly wasn't curious enough to find out. With a particularly energetic flail, Tiv tried to elbow one of the guards in the throat, where he had no armor to protect him. He almost succeeded, too. But to his bewilderment, the old man socked him in the cheek with his staff, dislocating his jaw with practiced ease.

Tiv fell to the ground with a cry.

"Enough," he ordered, looking thoroughly unamused. His tone made Tiv's skin crawl. "It's time."

For what?

Sylvie,

Is it so hard to write one measly letter?
*I'm not asking for a flaming detailed account of your life. Just a note. A sentence. Creator, three words would do. One of them could've even been your name signed at the bottom. Just give me something, **anything** to know that you're alright. How much longer do you expect me to wait for what should be a common courtesy? It's been weeks, Syl. I'm tired of sitting on my laurels, hounding the messengers for a—*
When I see you, I swear I'm going to—
[Nine lines of heavily crossed out words mar the page.]
That was uncalled for. I understand that. Philip urged me to erase it. I swear that I've calmed down now.
This is what I really wanted to say:
Sylvie, if you died in some stupid, hilarious way, then you better believe that I'm going to tell everyone about it until Pernelia's falcon comes to take me, too. It's only right. As your brother, it's my duty even.
*But if you're still in Eriam, if you receive this, then please, **please** write back. For father's sake.*

Awaiting your response,
Dalis Sirx 16.27.CA

6

Ethil wouldn't stop fainting.

By the fourth time, Myrrh was already behind her, breaking her fall with her much smaller frame. Thankfully, she wasn't much bulkier than her, but Myrrh was starting to regret bringing her along. Not that she'd leave her be. She wasn't that heartless. Neither was she weak enough to abandon her responsibility because of a little unexpected hardship. Because that's exactly what Ethil was—her responsibility. Myrrh had taken it upon herself to save her life, to take her away from the dangers still surrounding the east. She wouldn't leave her now. Her pride wouldn't allow it.

Myrrh couldn't say for certain why she even bothered helping her. But Ethil had just lost her brother, and Myrrh didn't think she could stomach seeing the remnants of her home floating across the Zexin Sea. Perhaps she was underestimating Ethil's ability to adapt, but when she had first awoken and Myrrh recounted the brief details of what had transpired, where they were, and where they were going, her assumptions had held.

Ethil vomited all over her shoes, barely able to keep her eyes open in sick, startled panic. And here she was again, losing the battle with her subconscious. Myrrh had clearly underestimated the extent of her grief.

"Why are you doing this to me?" Myrrh muttered, as she gripped Ethil tighter. She struggled to wrap her legs around her waist. It didn't help that Ethil was a good foot taller than her. If Ethil woke up with an aching neck, then the fault was her own.

Once Myrrh finally moved her into a secure position, she began the task of trekking up the mountain slope once more. She wanted so badly to just transform and fly, but there were too many witnesses on the roads and the spread of sky above her was far too small for flight—at least for anything that could carry the weight of another on its back. But even as she looked up at the steep road ahead, the one that led straight to a slippery cliff she needed to take off from, she didn't envy Ethil. Her sleep was beset by nightmares. Ones Myrrh was tired of hearing every night. She knew what it was like to wake up panting, unable to fully process where she was and why she was there, and she didn't wish that on anyone.

Myrrh took a deep breath and trudged onward.

The dagger and waterskin on her side seemed like terrible burdens now. Even the slip of paper Master Dace had entrusted to her felt ten pounds heavier than it actually was. But Myrrh didn't dare leave anything behind. She couldn't afford to.

"You owe me for this," Myrrh complained with each step. "What in Snuff's name was I thinking bringing you along? I can hear Nickel and Ajax laughing at me from here."

Ethil didn't answer. Of course she didn't.

You better get over this soon, Myrrh thought without remorse. *The east is gone. Squandering your time mourning over the past makes no one happy. The dead don't care what you do, neither do inanimate objects. No matter how much you love them. Home isn't a place.*

Myrrh's grip tightened.

The faces of two partnered practitioners came to mind, as she thought of the Tower's destruction. Sylvie had survived. That, she knew for certain. But Reed... he was gone. She knew that, too.

Myrrh shook her head to vanquish her thoughts. She forcefully replaced them with far more pleasant ones. It wasn't hard. She thought of the raucous smiles of the other Hunters, her constant struggle to stay warm in the frigid temperatures of the Diamond Alps, and the immaculate sheets of ice that covered its buildings. They never failed to glint like jewels during the rare days of unhindered sun. She needed to get to her true home. There were people waiting for her there.

Fueled by her thoughts, Myrrh picked up the pace. The climb was a ceaseless struggle that happened in the blur of a moment and an age. When she finally reached the open cliff, she couldn't help but stare at the nostalgic sight before her.

The snow was breathtaking.

White blanketed everything within the ambit of her vision. Pointed trees sat below her, just shrill enough to guarantee a deep and painful impalement should she accidentally slip. It wouldn't be a swift death. Myrrh's eyes swept past them. She forced her mind away from her own morbid thoughts. Her demise wasn't something she wanted to think about. Especially not now. Thankfully, the thought of being speared by nature was overpowered by a herd of white Snuff that ran noiselessly across the land. She missed their squeaks.

And their taste, she thought, as her stomach rumbled in complaint. *They'd make a good stew.*

Triumph for besting the cliff forgotten, she continued to look longingly down. The cliff was higher than she remembered. She tightened her hold on Ethil's legs, shaking her violently to see just how far gone she was. Ethil didn't even stir. She grinned at that. It wasn't long before Myrrh was securing them both against the gale, as it tried in vain to call them to its side. As if she'd be so fo-olish. She knew this cliff's history, and it wasn't pleasant.

This area was once a hotspot for reckless Amorphs that sought a momentary rush of adrenaline. They'd jump off and transform mid-fall like the lunatics they were. It was even used as a place of initiation for some. That is until a spoilsport Elementalist decided to use this very edge to plummet to his death. The entire cliff face had been painted in red gore. It was quite the sight. The area was closed off by the Vanguard Circle after that. While the rumors of it being a hazardous area already kept most travelers away, their public announcement kept even the most raucous practitioners from the trail.

Their verdict was more effective than the plague.

In this case, however, the Hunters were the only ones that weren't required to comply. The cliff was turned into a path for those that needed quick entrance into the north without having to cross the Wymeran River. It was a highly guarded secret. The kind a number of her peers had died protecting. Not even the Elders knew about this path.

Conniving and terrifying, Myrrh thought, thinking of the three heads of the Vanguard Circle. *That's a lethal combination.*

But as she took off into the less than agreeable weather, she couldn't be more thankful for their cunning. Myrrh only hoped Ethil didn't wake up mid-flight. She was under no obligation to save her life a second time. Pride be damned.

As much as Myrrh didn't want a repeat of the sight of blood gushing down the mountainside, even she didn't fully believe herself capable of swooping down without nicking her wings. Certainly not with the frosty winds hindering her vision.

The cool air kept her alert and numb all at once, and she soon forgot all about Ethil sleeping on her back. Myrrh's senses funneled into the immediate. She sighed in pleasure when the rush of adrenaline finally hit. Nostalgia flooded her veins, warming her from head to toe. The rush of energy danced along each of her feathers until all she cared about was the endless expanse of pure white that told her where she was.

The Gelid Mountain ranges.

It sat atop the rest of the world, encasing the jewel of Ferus Terria within its icy depths. Natural streams of magic lingered in the air. It was enough to choke any Nebbin in a quick and timely fashion. But Myrrh merely breathed it in as deeply as she could. She basked in the sense of familiarity that came with it.

Because finally, after years of absence, she was almost home. It only took the destruction of another branch. But the pang of regret that lingered was lost to unbridled delight with every flap of her wings under the pale gray sky.

It wouldn't be long now.

***

Ethil heaved a sigh of relief when she dropped against the cave wall, unconcerned with the large spider that scurried away from her as she did so. The only thing that mattered now were the bleeding blisters on her feet and the grime coating every inch of her robes an unholy brown. She didn't even want to think about her hair or the kind of bugs that lived inside of it. Because surely, there must've been some sort of colony. It would explain the constant itch. Before she could actually lift her hand to comb through it, however, a hissing snake slithered inside of the cave.

She stilled, only to relax again when her eyes met deep black. Not a moment later, a bright light blinded her, warming the cave with a steady stream of familiar magic. Then, the snake was gone, and in its place was a body governed by a full head of brown hair.

"Myrrh," Ethil called, breathless, as she slumped against the raw stone.

Myrrh looked at her with one eyebrow raised, while both of her hands busily produced pieces of dry wood from her person. Ethil envied her alertness. Myrrh had been leading them to the Alps ever since she'd awoken. She flew them when the weather permitted and guided Ethil through the rough terrains of a few Hunter trails when the common routes along the Yovakine Plains held too many people. Yet the journey seemed to take little to no toll on her. Nothing did.

A Hunter, indeed.

Myrrh gave composure its definition. She observed the world from the sidelines, acting only when doing so struck her fancy. She was so different from the unruly Amorph from Ethil's memories. Though it was only during quiet times like this that Ethil really saw the full extent of who Myrrh was and who she had pretended to be.

There was no time for her to think about much of anything once her fainting spell passed because keeping up with Myrrh's breakneck speed required her full concentration. A part of her was thankful for that. The rest simply—*wasn't*.

Ethil was startled out of her thoughts when smoke rose from the pile of timber. The flames sparked sporadically at first, before they spread outward and consumed the logs. Once the heat of the fire reached her, Ethil suddenly realized how cold she was. She was shivering. Ethil blamed fatigue for her lack of attention because pinning it on Myrrh didn't seem like the greatest idea.

"Silas siphoned all of the air from the heavens, spread his hands without compassion, then rained fire upon friend and foe alike," Myrrh abruptly quoted. She cracked a small smile, while she settled into a seat before the flames. "Until the battlefield was no more and only the glimmers of triumph remained."

"The Dawn of Silas' Pyre." Ethil recalled the tale from the Battle of Yovakine, where the First Zenith destroyed the opposing faction that still held onto the reigns of slavery. It wasn't her favorite topic. But she'd read the story enough times to be familiar with every line of history those verses held.

"Some historians have a knack for making war and death sound beautiful."

"It keeps the younger generations interested." Ethil pointed at the fire. "Why are you quoting that now? Those aren't magical flames."

"Mystic inferno or no, all flames are associated with Silas, or so I've heard. The association is a curse for some Conjurers. More pressure apparently. Though that's assuming they give a damn."

Ethil paused, thinking first, before slowly nodding. "You're right," she said, avoiding Myrrh's eyes in favor of healing the blisters on her feet. "Where'd you hear it?"

"Sylvie said it once over a late night snack."

Ethil's head snapped up. She flinched when she met Myrrh's unwavering stare. But Myrrh hadn't mentioned anything about the Tower since they left, so Ethil hardened her resolve and met her gaze head on. She shoved every rumor of an Amorph's ability to swallow someone whole with their eyes to the far corners of her mind.

Myrrh smiled. Her face lit up in a way that reminded Ethil of home and kindness. But they were too observant for her liking.

"You're tired," Myrrh said. No question in her tone. No condescension either. Just pure fact. "You're scared. You miss home. You'd do anything to return."

Ethil frowned. "Why did you take me away?"

"Because I could. You were injured. Unconscious. It wasn't safe for you there."

"It wasn't safe for anyone," Ethil argued. "You took me away from my home."

"I never asked you to follow me," Myrrh said. Ethil opened her mouth in protest, but the words died in her throat. Myrrh was right. She hadn't. Ethil's frown only deepened at the realization. Myrrh jutted her chin toward the noisy forest outside, blanketed by a sheet of snow. Silence was non-existent here. The owls were oddly restless. "You're free to leave. I won't stop you."

Leave? Ethil thought in disdain. She didn't even know where they were. *Where would I go?*

As if she could sense her distress, Myrrh continued, "Master Dace should be reconstructing the Tower. You need only follow the slope down, then continue running east until you reach the Eirinne Mountains. It'll be a long run, but not an endless one."

Ethil's eyes widened in hope, but before she could ask more, very different words escaped her. "What about you?" she began. "Where are you going?"

"I'm going home," Myrrh said, puzzled, as if it should've been obvious. Ethil's cheeks heated at the fact that it was.

She knew where they were now. The incessant snow should have been a dead giveaway. Ethil blamed her worn mind. But how they got to the Gelid Mountains so quickly was a mystery. She could recall fainting along a few particularly steep paths, but nothing more. They couldn't have crossed the Wymeran River so swiftly. It was impossible. Not unless Myrrh had a truly splendid form with the ability to run miles in a second or jump across entire valleys. Maybe even fly at the speed of light. Perhaps she did.

She was a Hunter after all, so Ethil didn't discount the possibility, but neither did she know for certain.

"What will you do once you get there?" Ethil asked instead, knowing better than to ask the secrets of a practitioner's trade.

"I have a message to deliver," Myrrh paused, before slowly whispering, "to Leonas Dace."

"Jack's father?" she sputtered.

Ethil had only ever seen the man in pictures, but the stories that surrounded him were legendary—triumph against the Drakone family in council debates, victorious duels versus only the most lethal of practitioners, and a mind that single-handedly shook the politics of the north. The man seemed more god than human, and at times, had been hailed as such. 'The second coming of Thelarius,' the books said... and many believed it.

Then again, many also believed that newborn babies were already familiar with the faces of the First Zenith, and that their presence was the light that guided them into this world. Absurdity at its finest. The majority couldn't always be trusted.

"Are you a fan?" Myrrh asked, surprise in her tone, if not in her eyes. "I didn't peg you as the type. Mostly because I've never seen you stalk Jack before. Unless..." she trailed off uncertainly.

"What?"

"Have you?"

"No!" Ethil shouted, appalled. "I'm just curious. About him, about the stories, they're all so—"

"You want to know if they're true," Myrrh cut her off before she could start gushing.

Ethil nodded.

"Depending on what you've heard, then I'd say that most are." Myrrh shrugged in disinterest. As if her association with the man wasn't anything special. As if people didn't dream of meeting him, never mind actually having a conversation. "If I had to describe Elder Dace in a word it would be—ridiculous. Terrifying, but ridiculous."

"Ridiculous?" Ethil stammered. Of all the words to describe

the youngest Elder in history, ridiculous was nowhere near her list. August, certainly. Wondrous, she'd let it pass. Phenomenal, majestic, divine, a thousand others. Ethil would've even believed temperamental and reckless, based solely on Jack's personality—because he must've gotten it from somewhere—but ridiculous just seemed *wrong*.

"If you were expecting someone like Jack, then... don't." Myrrh's eyebrow's wrinkled in horror, as if she was recalling an especially traumatizing affair. "Elder Dace is floppy- haired and smiley. He's frightening, but very talkative when he wants to be. I'd say, almost skittish. That same catty grace is there though. You've seen Jack, so you know what I mean. It must be a high-born thing. Sometimes the temper is there, too. But Elder Dace is certainly more subtle about it. Now, don't get me wrong. He's not more forgiving, in fact, he's a tad too vicious at times. But I suppose that's what Master Dace likes about him."

"I—he..." Ethil trailed off, at a loss for words. Her image of him slowly shattered in her mind.

"Nevertheless, he's still an interesting man. Maybe even more so because of his quirks," Myrrh finished, as if she was describing a circus attraction. Her eyes flickered briefly outside. "Are you interested in meeting him?"

The lump in Ethil's throat grew as she looked down at her hands. She'd been healing the same spot for ten minutes now. How thoughtless. "You said Cheryll Dace was rebuilding?"

"I did."

Ethil's fingers twitched in contemplation. She busied herself by healing the rest of her blisters until they were nothing more than angry red marks. The thought of returning wasn't as great as she thought it'd be. Instead, all she could think about was an absent Duward and a devastated Institute.

She could always help rebuild. At least that way she'd be able to put her efforts into a worthy cause. But as Myrrh yawned, leaning back on her hands without a care, Ethil knew she couldn't leave. Not yet. She had to repay her somehow... or so she told herself, unwilling to admit that the thought of returning to that ruined place with no one beside her terrified her in ways she couldn't even begin to speak aloud.

Ethil clicked her tongue in instant regret of every action she'd taken since entering that cursed Iniquities Chamber. If they hadn't been chosen, then Duward wouldn't have died. If she hadn't argued with Tiv, then perhaps they could've been the ones to accompany them to Eriam instead of Reed and Sylvie.

She immediately clenched her jaw in disgust at her own thoughts. She didn't wish death upon any of her peers. If they'd chosen to go to Eriam, then they would have two dead practitioners to worry about instead of one. The only reason she'd survived was because of Duward's magic. It was exceptional, even amongst the other Healers in the east.

"Can I..." Ethil let the sentence hang.

"You want to come." It wasn't a question.

"I do," she said instantly.

Myrrh's response was silenced by a growl. Turning, they found a lean wolf baring pointy teeth at them. Flecks of red littered its muzzle. Signs of its latest meal. How it found them, neither could say, nor were they curious enough to find out. All that mattered now was the wolf's prickling fur and fierce snarl as it paced the entrance of the cave, deliberately blocking their exit.

Before they could react, Ethil felt sharp teeth break the skin of her arm, followed by the hot wash of blood. She screeched, kicking the wolf's face and throwing herself against the wall in a poor attempt to detach herself from it. Through the blur of her tears, she saw its nails dig into the snow. Its teeth sunk deeper as it let out a terrible howl. A flash of light in her periphery told her that Myrrh had transformed. But that didn't stop the rush of terror she felt when she looked down to find pure, black eyes staring up at her from the wolf's head.

An Amorph.

She screeched when a bear tackled the wolf away, tearing the skin from her bones and spearing pain throughout her body. Her good arm was already up, hand glowing, while she whispered a shaky incantation to mend the wound. She wasn't fast enough. Nothing was. Every second was agony.

Before she could register, the wolf was on its back, throat about to be mauled out. Then there was another flash of light, the desperate flap of wings, and it was gone.

"What was that?" Ethil managed to stutter.

Her hands shook in fear. She was exhausted and hungry and felt so utterly helpless at the moment. Her magic had a mind of its own, disappearing and reappearing in sporadic bursts of energy her body knew she couldn't spare. But she had no choice. There was so much blood.

"Stay here," Myrrh ordered.

And once again, Ethil was alone.

***

If Myrrh thought Ethil was going to sit around and wait for her to return, then she was insane. Ignoring her aching limbs, Ethil ran. The cold sun setting between the leaves only made her run faster. She barely even noticed the errant branches that scratched her skin or the hidden rocks that knifed her bare feet. She was close, and with the last vestiges of light fading into black, she couldn't possibly give up now.

A bright flash between two leafy bushes caught her attention and Ethil sprinted forward, straight into a clearing. It was empty, save for the pure white Snuff that soundlessly stretched its legs, as if preparing for an especially draining hop. It looked back at her. When her eyes met abysmal black, she realized why.

Ethil swallowed hard. Her numb heels scraped against frost. She prayed that she hadn't been chasing the wrong Amorph.

"Well, don't just stare at me," Myrrh's impatient voice came from its tiny muzzle, as if she'd been expecting her to pop up. "Get moving. We have a long night ahead of us."

"What about the Amorph?" Ethil asked. Her concerns were dismissed with an annoyed squeak. Myrrh sounded exactly like a Snuff, and Ethil couldn't help but gawk in wonder.

"He's a pro." Myrrh lifted her paw to point at a buckle in the corner emblazoned with six parallel lines. A small, barely noticeable streak ran horizontally across all of them. "See that mark? That Amorph was a Tipping. Not someone I, or anyone for that matter, would want to trifle with. Especially in this weather."

"A Tipping?" she whispered. "You mean that famous group of assassins? They're actually real?"

"What do you think?" Myrrh snapped. "He's long gone by now. I must've really gone and pissed someone off. Which isn't *that* surprising, but it would at least be nice to know who. Because for whatever reason, I'm that assassin's next target. One he missed. Spectacularly. He'll be back. They don't tolerate failure. The only question is when."

"Do you have a plan?" she asked.

Myrrh shrugged, and Ethil watched in fascination as she gestured with her paws. She'd seen many Amorphs continue their normal actions, despite transforming, but she'd never seen one do so in such a... cute form.

"Not really. But I'd rather be in the Alps next time he decides to strike. It's safer there. More witnesses."

"Oh," she said distractedly.

Myrrh rolled her eyes. Shuffling on her hind legs, she pinned Ethil with an exasperated stare, then hopped ahead. "Are you coming or not?" she asked without looking back.

"I am!" Ethil caught up to her, only to cringe at the smirk she wore. She never wanted to see such a cute animal smile so evilly.

"Then keep up," Myrrh said, just before she jumped. Her floppy ears stretched outward in prime Snuff fashion, sending her gliding a good distance away.

Ethil gaped, then called after her a moment later. Her voice was loud enough to shake the snow from the trees and send nearby animals scurrying away. She knew she should've been quieter, but it was hard to when she knew, without a shadow of doubt, that she'd just made a new friend.

Master Dace,

I've arrived safely in the Gelid Mountains. I'm currently two days of flight away from the Alps. A week if the blizzard continues.

Your letter is safe. I'll deliver it as soon as I pass the gates.

I encountered a few problems along the way, though it's nothing you need to worry yourself over. I'm more concerned if this courier will reach you in a timely fashion — if at all. I hope so.

Ethil is still with me. She isn't faring as well as I'd hoped. She might return soon. At this point, I'm not quite sure, but she has the option. I'll remind her just in case. If she does decide to leave, then I'll cast a Demar Spell on her.

I'll write again soon.

Your faithful apprentice,
Myrrh 19.27.CA

7

The sight of the Diamond Alps rejuvenated them both.

Myrrh, more than her companion. She ran from the trees like she hadn't just been complaining about the weather. Myrrh stopped at the base of the snowy mountainside. Her foggy breaths blended with the remnants of silver wind, as she stooped to pick up a white flower rimed with hoarfrost. Hundreds more stood sentinel across the clearing, and Ethil wondered if Myrrh might start frolicking. But her thoughts were soon forgotten when she looked upon the jewel of Ferus Terria.

The Institute poured from the mountainside. Almost as if a hundred Elementalists had one day decided to bend the terrain to their will, so that they might have a home. Prior knowledge, however, saved her from that ignorance. The Alps—just like every other Institute—was built on the backs of slaves. Thousands had died to perfect those marble towers, hundreds more from frostbite alone. Ice sheathed everything. It glinted under the natural light of the sky.

The sight was brilliant, almost offensive in its glory. The raw magic hidden deep within the land made Ethil's body tremble in pleasure. Her powers hummed along the surface of her skin, utterly delighted, like a separate entity. Ethil felt as if she could conquer the world here, best anyone that dared stand against her. It was a good feeling—confidence. It kept her thoughts away from her aching feet and half-frozen clothes, replacing them with ones of baseless assurance.

Birds looped between various buildings to fly in front of the infamous stronghold that housed the Zenith Council. It was easily the grandest structure in all of Ferus Terria. The building was carved right against the mountainside with the Council's symbol draped down its front. The cloth it was fashioned upon was the loudest, most garish yellow she'd ever seen. Flashy in every possible way. As if it needed any more attention. Everything else already seemed unsightly in comparison.

Ethil watched as billows of fire were released high into the air—*a class?* They were followed by howls of controlled wind that strengthened them. A few stronger gales blew the flames out completely and one errant fireball almost roasted an Amorph alive. She caught a glimpse of the tiny bird shifting back into a human out of shock. He was unreasonably large. Even for a man. When he fell, there was a loud crash, followed by laughter. Everything echoed down the mountains. The chatter, the tinkling metal, the occasional boom of mirth.

Her eyebrows scrunched in apprehension. "How haven't they caused an avalanche yet?"

"They have," Myrrh said, surprising her. "Twice. Though the Council erected barriers around the outer wall before any real damage was done."

"Smart *and* efficient." Ethil didn't expect anything less.

"Some," Myrrh refuted with a shrug.

As they made their way to the Institute's entrance, its walls looming eerily above them, Myrrh turned to shoot her a smile so bright, the light from the Alps seemed to dim in comparison. The fire behind her grin reassured Ethil in ways she didn't think possible. How Myrrh was able to slip from being a column of frigidity to just another lackadaisical practitioner was anybody's guess, but Ethil supposed it had something to do with her time in the east. With years of her life spent pretending, it was only natural that she perfected the art of switching into a different persona at a moment's notice. But Ethil liked to think that towards the end, Myrrh had stopped pretending. That the face she showed in the

Tower, with her fiery temper and desire for freedom, was her true self. The one she saw now.

"Let me be the first," Myrrh began. She spread her arms out in love and pride. "Ethil Mane, welcome to the Diamond Alps, the northern jewel of Ferus Terria. Where boldness is celebrated, wisdom is revered, and men rise into legends."

Ethil didn't look up at the buildings again. Not because it was too bright or because the wind kept attacking her already red nose, but because Myrrh's eyes told her everything she needed to about the warmth and splendor of the Institute before her.

Myrrh was home.

In time, maybe she'd be, too.

***

Passing through the gates was an uneventful affair. A pair of guards greeted Myrrh. They bowed their heads in a respectful acknowledgement that she didn't return. Ethil followed close behind. Her gaze lingered on the pointy architecture. She tried to ignore the eyes that followed them. Most were on Myrrh, who seemed exceptionally skilled in the art of ignoring people.

"Watch your step," Myrrh said, as she rounded a slippery corner. "No one will do it for you."

You just did, Ethil thought, but she didn't dare give it voice. She had a feeling that she wasn't talking about the ground.

"Wait." Myrrh held up a hand to stop her.

A pregnant pause ensued, as Myrrh looked around them. She drank in the sight of her hometown. It was just as she'd remembered. The Alps had never been a peaceful community. The people squabbled like ravenous wolves, always smiling derisively at each other and hurtling carefully masked insults like greetings. Surprisingly, a good number of them were religious. Myrrh almost scowled at the amount of sisters that flitted about, no longer used to their engaging eyes.

Thelarius' worshippers could be found on every street corner here. They chanted verses of praise that silenced those that passed. The local markets had altars sprinkled between tables of food and fabric. Even the armories sold statuettes of the four apotheoses. The larger ones went so far as to sell full bronze figures of renowned practitioners. Dead and alive. Myrrh had found one likened into Cheryll Dace once. It was a good replica, save for one small detail concerning her nose.

Myrrh saw a priest muscle his way atop a crate in the middle of a busy walkway. He had blue eyes and a thick tome in his hands, which he held up to the mob gathered around him. The priest encouraged the people to support an Elder she didn't quite catch the name of, then went on to spout nonsense about how the candidate he endorsed was particularly blessed.

What a waste of time, Myrrh thought. The public's favor was nothing more than a bonus trinket compared to the influential voices that directly dealt with those in a position to actually do something. In the end, it was the Zenith Council, the heads of the Vanguard Circle, and the Arch Potens that would have any say in who became the next leader of the Institute.

'*Let them believe what they wish,*' her mind uttered in Cheryll Dace's voice. '*If they aren't pushing their convictions onto you, then ignore them. Even fools have the right to express their opinions.*'

"Myrrh?" Ethil called, snapping her from her reverie.

"It's nothing," she replied with an ambiguous tilt of her head, before marching along again. "We need to go to the public archives. Elder Dace's office is there."

They walked on in silence. Ethil gaped at the marble columns they passed. The buildings grew larger the deeper they went, and by the time they stood in front of the silvery-white entrance of the archives, Myrrh had to tell her to close her mouth. An impossible feat because as soon as they entered, Ethil couldn't help the surge of excitement that ran through her bones.

Long lines of cherry red shelves stood in rows as far as the eye could see. There didn't seem to be any kind of general layout. But it was still amazing, despite the chaos.

Myrrh ambled along, turning down random corners with the

look of a woman that clearly knew where she was going. Ethil followed. Her fingers slipped along the spines of the novels lining the shelves. Some had become so overburdened that several books had to be settled on the ground, where they grew into piles, and those piles into heaps, and those heaps into miniature sections themselves that the keepers tacked little notes upon to remind others of what was buried within.

'*History 109B: King's Age, Pigmy Tonics A4, Crucial Herbs and Remedies Volume 12 (Stack 3), Crystals and Ore 67DCE,*' Ethil read, as they walked. *Just how many books do they have here?*

"This way," Myrrh said.

She led them to a dusty corner of the archives brimming with volumes of ancient history. Most of the tomes here were yellow and untouched, and—in Myrrh's opinion—better off forgotten. The tales they held were bloody. All of them were written by shaking hands and distraught minds. The ink from almost every page had bled over from where it had been initially laid, as if weeping at the stories they told.

Myrrh had read a few of them before, by her Master's recommendation. She didn't regret doing so, but she could've gone without knowing the tragic tale of a man whose entire life was stripped away from him by the cruelty of his peers. Or the hardships of a woman with a witty grin and—

She stopped herself. There was no use mulling over the past. Especially one that wasn't her own. Even if she wanted to, there wasn't anything she could do to change it. She looked around her instead. In the distance, Myrrh saw a few of the older keepers whispering behind their hands.

"Look at them," one said. "Wandering around and *touching* things! Those books are priceless. Priceless! What are they even doing here? They should just leave!"

"These are public archives," another argued.

"But they're going to break something. I'm sure of it! Who could be so ignorant as to let an Amorph into the building?"

Myrrh sneered at them. She'd spent years away, but was

unsurprised to find that they still hadn't learned that their voices carried. They were thick for such renowned scholars. Perhaps their age made them so. This was why she hated visiting. As far as she was concerned, the archives were nothing more than a giant hearth just waiting to be set aflame.

She cursed them under her breath, uncaring for the gray-bearded man down the hall that heard her. He turned to reprimand her... or so she thought. Because when his lips parted and no shout emerged, Myrrh squinted only to see the floor of his mouth and nothing else. It was wet and pink. No tongue or teeth to be found. Saliva trickled down his chin, and Myrrh flinched at the sight.

Behind her, Ethil squeaked in discomfort.

The man turned away, seemingly satisfied by their reactions. They moved quickly after that. The sight was certainly more effective than the mind-numbing prattle of the other keepers. But even with their swift pace, by the time they reached the main desk, they still somehow managed to upset half of the staff.

A dark-skinned woman was hunched over the tabletop, scribbling away on a long scroll that spread across the entirety of her desk. It was a pristine thing. The only other objects on it were an expensive ink set and a silver plaque that read: *Vivi Loakes*.

When the woman looked up, Myrrh stilled in surprise. She couldn't help but think that the Creator had really rolled up his sleeves during her conception. Bright orange eyes, perfect teeth, and a dash of whatever poison he used for gorgeous people. Wait, no, the Creator must've poured the whole damn bottle in. Her looks were that devastating. What in the world was she doing locked up with old coots that whispered too loudly and vented too much? Was it some new form of twisted punishment?

"Name?" Vivi asked with a frown. Her lips were pulled so far down her face, it looked almost deliberate.

That look told Myrrh everything she needed to know. Vivi was a keeper. A young one at that. She might've questioned it more had she not seen that expression. *'Refined reluctance,'* she called it, and all of the keepers were masters of the art. Personally, she thought it made them look like arrogant blowfishes. But if there was a telltale sign of the position, then that was it. Myrrh wouldn't be surprised if it was a prerequisite for working there.

"We're here to see Elder Dace," Myrrh said, not wanting to give her name and position.

Vivi's face brightened at that but not by much. She waved them in the direction of a shadowed hallway, tacitly giving them permission to pass, before diving back into her work. She hummed, pleased that they wouldn't be stealing her away.

"Pleasant, wasn't she?" Ethil whispered.

Myrrh didn't bother trying to hide her smile.

***

The walk to Leonas' office was blander than Ethil expected. She'd imagined impossibly detailed paintings mounted along the walls, chandeliers made of gold hanging gaudily above her, and whole suits of armor standing in uniform lines down every hall. But the stone walkway had none of those things. It was just a long stretch of emptiness, flanked by large windows that ended just before a pair of thick, wooden doors. It was appalling. She could only guess what the other denizens of the Alps had to say about this place with its lack of priceless lamps and droopy curtains. Certainly nothing pleasant.

Perhaps the appeal rested in its view. From where she stood, Ethil could see the main square on one side and an endless scape of snow on the other. Nothing impeded it, since the hall strangely led away from the rest of the building. As if it was added on when the builders realized that they'd forgotten to make space for another office. She could only wonder what it looked like from the outside. A pointed strip leading into a room hanging mid-air would give anyone pause.

How is it stable? Ethil wondered.

"Elder Dace requested his office to be built like this," Myrrh said, motioning to the entire hall as if she'd read her mind. Not for the first time, Ethil wondered if she had that ability.

"How's it even standing?"

"Enchantments. I'm not sure what kind. I didn't think there were any for something like this. These are an entirely different league of reinforcement. Maybe Elder Dace created them. It wouldn't surprise me. He wrote an entire series on the subject."

Ethil nodded, acutely aware of where they were and who they were about to meet. She'd read about Leonas Dace's exploits as a child and admired him greatly. He was the youngest man to ever receive the title of Elder, and the only one to simultaneously become one of the figureheads of the Vanguard Circle within the same year. He'd accomplished countless deeds during his time, and his name reverberated because of them. Ethil doubted she'd be able to speak to him without stuttering.

"Relax." Myrrh knocked, while Ethil wiped her clammy hands on her robes. "Oh, for Pernelia's sake, stop fidgeting!"

"Enter," a distinctly masculine voice cut in.

The door didn't creak like Ethil expected. Though she didn't know why she even thought it would. Of course someone oiled his door. Despite the scarcity of the hall, she wasn't visiting some no-name practitioner that never received visitors.

When they stepped past the threshold, her eyes drank in the startling contrast of her surroundings. She'd prepared herself for something stiff and sterile, but the office looked as lived-in as her old room back in the Tower. Papers littered the floor and books sat in mounds in a corner. A blanket was thrown haphazardly over a ratty sofa, both of which had too many holes. There was even a half-empty bottle of expensive liquor on a nearby table. No drinking glasses to be found. But perhaps the strangest thing of all was the ball of pink yarn that lay forgotten before her feet.

Does he have a pet? Because if he doesn't, then this is just—

"Cheryll's apprentice," Leonas said.

His voice inadvertently stopped Ethil from staring at his office. She fixated on him like a child that had just discovered how to control her magic. He was her long-time idol after all.

Leonas was a striking man with high cheekbones and skin so ashen, it looked gray under the light. He had slanted eyes that reminded Ethil of Jack, but the crow's feet that flanked them made the red orbs seem kinder in comparison. It was strange to see those eyes set neutral and not glaring at her... or anyone for that matter. But the way Leonas didn't even spare her a second glance, his eyes brushing along her face for a brief peek, before he dismissed her presence entirely, was so reminiscent of his son that she had to fight the urge to roll her eyes.

He was still a celebrated practitioner of the north after all. She didn't want to seem ill-mannered. But to her surprise, Leonas disregarded Myrrh as well. His attention was focused solely on the letter in her hands. Ethil watched in fascination as Myrrh handed over the wrinkled pages without so much as a greeting. Leonas didn't seem to mind, too busy breaking the wax seal to bother with either of them.

Even from where she stood, Ethil could see that the letter was blotched in some areas. Leonas didn't complain. He didn't even speak. He ate up every word written on the damp parchment, lingering occasionally to reread certain parts. Leonas looked like a man that had just been given the deed to the world. His face was full of veneration and joy, as if the words had been penned by Thelarius Merve, himself. A thank you letter for all he'd done during his time.

If Ferus Terria was destroyed in that moment, Ethil truly believed him incapable of caring. Whatever Leonas was reading must've been important, indeed. Something devastating enough to rock the very foundation of all four Institutes... or so she invented, unwilling to let her divine image of the man deteriorate any more than it already had. It couldn't be a simple love letter from his wife. It just couldn't. That would be ludicrous! She refused to believe that they travelled all this way for something so banal. But he didn't read it aloud, and they didn't ask what was inside.

So they waited, antsy, as Leonas forgot about the world.

Leonas,

Are you well?

Forgive the lateness of my correspondence. I've been terribly busy trying to fix the mess left by that detestable Serach. It is a slow process. Every day is filled with building, building... and even more building. I wasn't made for such tediousness. You should've ended that dreadful man's story long ago. How many times did you go back and forth on your decision to do so? Now look, I'm left to mend the consequences of that vile man's decisions. I expect this horrifying fit of sudden decency to be over upon my return, Leonas.

But I suppose there was some hidden boon in all of this. I was able to recover old records that might prove useful in the upcoming Summit. I'll try to find more, but I'm afraid the wrinkles on my forehead will soon become permanent if I'm forced to stay here any longer.

On a more serious note, I do hope my apprentice was able to reach you in one piece. Myrrh has a tendency of getting into... worrisome situations. She's an impulsive one, but she follows orders well. I'm afraid I must trouble you by leaving her in your care for the time being. She's brought a Healer along as well.

'A friend,' she says. Pernelia knows how much Hunters need more of those. Decide for yourself the girl's worth. I've never been fond of Healers and their mending powers, but perhaps she could be of some use. I've heard terrible things about the Weeping Grove, so perhaps having a Healer close at hand may prove useful in the future.

Be sure to stop and look around the world, love. Ferus Terria stirs. Even now. The north won't remain the center of the storm for long.

Oh, and do tell me if those old codgers finally go mad with their lust for power. I'd hate to be absent for such a long-awaited event, but such is life. Speaking of absence, I pray you've been caring for things properly in my absence — the leftovers of my legion in particular.

I've heard rumors, Leonas. Rather unsettling ones. Most have something to do with overwork. There have even been a few whispers of too much blood. I know that you're shorthanded because of those horrid Drakones and their incessant desire for more guards, but do take proper care of my practitioners. They're highly efficient workers, but all men have their limits. They won't last if you bully them so. I don't want to go through the trouble of finding replacements.

Your erraticism can be... problematic. As I keep telling you. But I trust you know what you're doing. Don't overwork yourself.

I've sent Jacques and his Arch Poten companion away. They're currently headed to the Alps. I know you're ecstatic to see him again, but I'm sorry to say that I sent them along the scenic route to visit a few rather... troublesome acquaintances in the Red Veld. For their sake, of course. But I'm sure they'll reach you soon enough. Be patient.

You should see him, love. Jacques is a mimic of you. Although I pray his companion figures out the secret to tempering him soon. She seems to know his moods better than most, so I don't believe we have too much to fret over in that regard. Jacques is still full of highs and lows with nothing in between. Another remnant of you. He's without a doubt your son. But I fear that my words are nowhere near as hard as his head.

I was shocked to learn that they had a certain stone in their keeping. Yes, **that** one. I left out a few explanations about it, though I'm sure they'll find them on their own soon enough. But never mind those terrible details. This companion of his—Sylvie Sirx—the primary apprentice of Columbus Cephas. A lofty position to be sure and more than impressive on its own. But that's not all. You'll be surprised, love, by the records I've found here. A family tree, detailing the offspring of certain men. Ancient, powerful men.

I fear to write more than I already have. So, I'll stop here for the time being. It's best to err on the side of caution, or so the saying goes. We'll speak more upon my return.

I know being an Elder is nothing but a pain for you, and it was my urging that made you vie to become head of the Zenith Council in the first place, but allow me to offer you one last piece of advice: it would be in your best interest to win the support of Victor Sirx. Advisers make for strong allies. Some more than others.

Stay safe.

Yours,
Cheryll

8

Folding Cheryll's letter with every ounce of gentleness he had inside of him, Leonas finally met the eyes of his dear wife's messengers. Myrrh kept a carefully composed mask on, though he could see the weary lines chasing the tired droop of her eyes, even when she tried to appear dignified and in control before him. She really didn't hide her exhaustion very well, but it was passable, he supposed. Myrrh seemed poise incarnate when compared to her companion. The nameless Healer was akin to a bird. Easily startled and very wary. She wore her emotions on her sleeve. It was easy to tell that his guard bothered her more than she'd ever admit and that her skin was likely tingling in disquiet because of it. But it was more than that. The way her eyes drifted up to meet his, inspecting his features, before falling down again. It was as if she was trying to pinpoint certain characteristics.

Jack's acquaintance, he concluded. There could be no other reason for such intense scrutiny. When Leonas gave her his signature dopey smile and her eyes widened in trepidation, he knew immediately that she and his son didn't get along. *Why am I not surprised?*

"Cheryll mentioned you were from the east," Leonas said, watching her squirm. "What's your name?"

"Ethil Mane," she introduced with an uncertain nod. Ethil opened her mouth to say more, but snapped it shut when Leonas stood from his seat. He walked to the front of his walnut desk and leaned upon the wood, before dismissing his guard with an elegant flick of his wrist. Leonas moved so fluidly that all she could do was compare it to her own more awkward movements. "Don't worry about Emery," he assured, flashing her a smile of sheepish delight. "He may look menacing, but that's about it. He's all milk teeth and broody faces deep down."

She visibly eased at his words, though he didn't make his guard leave for her sake. Cheryll was never one to send people on needless treks across Ferus Terria, and Leonas couldn't have another being privy to any information she could only entrust to her primary apprentice. But Ethil certainly didn't need to know that. Better she think him considerate, rather than scheming. Her partiality might prove useful in the future.

"So," Leonas began, "what other goodies have you brought for me today? Other than your first-hand insight into the Tower's demise of course. That would be better written in a report. I'm afraid I don't have the time to listen to any epic recounts today."

"Not much then," Myrrh said, not skipping a beat. Ethil seemed shocked by his blatant disregard of the subject. "I do have a request from Master Dace for you. About looking into certain colleges of the Weeping Grove."

"Did she mention which?"

"The Sanct Union, the Primordians, the Closions, the Lafertti Clan, and the Red Scripts."

"That's... I'll try," Leonas tentatively agreed. "Perhaps I'll send you there. What do you think?"

"Me?" Myrrh pointed to herself in surprise. It was flattering to be acknowledged by her Master's husband, but she'd just returned. Surely, he wouldn't send her off again.

"Ah, but you are in a bit of a bind, aren't you? What with the Tippings after your head," Leonas said, delighted when they jolted back. He smiled thickly at them. "Don't look so stunned! The Alps is the only place for someone to go once they've been injured in the Gelid Mountains. I'm sure he thought he could blend in with the practitioners here. Delirious thing."

"Where is he now?"

"Recuperating under my care. Would you like to see him?"

"No," Myrrh said instantly, stiffening at the meaning behind his words. Ethil's eyebrows furrowed in puzzlement at Myrrh's unexpected timidity.

"Don't look so tense!" Leonas laughed good-naturedly. His smile was so wide, Ethil wouldn't be surprised if he actually gave them a double thumbs-up in assurance. "You'll be under my care, too. Just like the rest of my lovely wife's legion. Cheryll requested it. Creator only knows why, but who could refuse so much extra help? Her scouts are delightful. I'm sure you are as well. And don't worry, I wouldn't dream of sending you out again. Not so soon, and certainly not with those Tippings lingering about."

"… I've been hearing things," Myrrh said, cautious.

"Oh?"

"About my juniors."

"All good, I hope."

"A few."

"How strange," Leonas remarked. He tilted his head in the most innocent gesture they'd ever seen. "Cheryll mentioned the same. I wonder who's been spreading all of these baseless rumors about me. To have her worried while she's so far away, why, that's unacceptable. Simply unacceptable."

"I just don't think Master Dace's legion can stomach your… usual methods."

Leonas blinked at her, stunned for the slightest of seconds.

"Well, you do speak your mind, don't you?" he drawled, unduly happy by the fact, and unafraid to show it. "I haven't had someone voice their concerns about my methods since I was studying under Master Savast Kerin twenty-seven years ago."

He eyed her carefully then, his gaze was steady and very even. Though the wry, almost playful smile that curled his lips betrayed his serious tone.

"He lost his tongue and all of his teeth not a few days after. Poor man. I hear he's working in the archives now."

Myrrh flinched, before swallowing her fear and forcing her mask back into place. Cheryll's disappointed gaze flitted past her mind. "I—I'm sorry. I meant no disrespect. What I meant to say is we're used to different approaches. Standard Hunter jobs. The sort of things that usually get brought to Master Dace's table."

"I'll keep that in mind. Was there anything else?"

"No."

"Allow me to ask my own question then. Do you know when Cheryll will return? She didn't mention it."

"I'm afraid not."

"That's a shame." Leonas deflated for a moment, then sprang right back up. "But I can at least look forward to Jack returning, so it's not a complete tragedy. He's even bringing a girl with him. They grow up so fast."

Leonas didn't bother asking if they knew his son's whereabouts, their body language said it all. Ears perked and backs straightened in sudden attention. He smiled, belatedly noticing the tiny mouse skirting around his table.

"Oh, shoo!" he howled. "Shoo, I say! No one wants you here! Ah, and would you look at all of these documents lying around? I can already feel Cheryll's correcting fingers on my neck. It feels like she's scolding me all the way from here. I really should clean up. If you'll excuse me, I... oh," he stopped abruptly, then looked at them as if he'd just realized that the sky was blue.

"What?" Ethil asked reflexively, her eyes wide and doe-like.

"I don't need to make excuses to you, do I? I'm not *really* going to clean. I want to respond to Cheryll's letter, so if you two would please..." he trailed off, before blatantly pointing at the door. As if he needed to make their dismissal any more obvious.

Silence descended around them. For a moment, they all stood there, blinking blankly at each other. Myrrh was the first to gather her wits. She coughed to get Ethil's attention. The effect was immediate. Ethil squeaked in embarrassment and threw Myrrh a desperate glance that Leonas only smiled at.

They were certainly amusing to watch. Or was that just him? He'd have to ask Cheryll's opinion on the matter. Everyone else always looked at him funny whenever he mentioned someone's behavior, as if they wanted to know why he bothered with people so far beneath his station. The answer was simple: Leonas loved people watching. They really should've known that by now.

Leonas waved cheerily, as he watched them bow and make for the exit as quickly as decorum allowed.

"Steady your thoughts, silence your emotions," he called out to them, before they could leave, "or you'll be eaten alive."

They didn't stay to question him. The door slammed shut, leaving him with that lingering mouse and twitching fingers.

"Didn't you hear me?" Leonas abruptly said. His smile dropped faster than the temperature. Remnants of his power seeped from his skin in the form of frosty smoke. It was followed by a violent squall that scattered the papers on his desk all around the room. "Leave, rat. You aren't welcome here."

"My name is Violet Llorens, sir. I have a message for you from the Council," the rat stressed, ceasing its scurrying and balancing precariously on its hind legs. Its head was bowed in respect, utterly terrified of the man, and rightfully so. "It's about the Lafertti Clan. They want to know what the Circle thinks of the Clan's appeal to—"

"I said, *shoo*," he repeated, uncompromising.

With a flash of light and a shift of limbs, the rodent before him transformed into a long-haired practitioner with nice shoes and a perky, carrot scarf. Too loud for the drab colors of his office.

Eyesore, Leonas thought scathingly, face dull and unamused.

"I apologize, Elder Dace," Violet said in an imploring tone that Leonas only associated with the fearful and near-death. She obviously didn't want to deliver this message. Just as much as he didn't want to hear it. "But your opinion on the matter is urgent and there's also the issue concerning Arch Poten Verne's refusal to attend the Summit. Even her husband has dismissed all forms of correspondence. The Council needs your permission to send a member of Captain Dace's legion to escort her."

"Don't you mean force?" Leonas muttered, his attention finally peeked. Barely.

"The Council said escort."

"Of course they did," he scoffed, scorning them in his mind. Little did he know that more than a few invective words escaped. "*Lavyana kahs.* The lot of them. They want answers? They want results? They're free to get them! *Vaklas in an den.* They shouldn't be sending my wife's men to do their dirty work. The factions are separate for a reason."

"Elder Dace," Violet called. But when his blood-red gaze snapped to her, she immediately lowered her head in contrition.

"Why are you still here?" he asked, no, commanded. Leonas wasn't looking for an answer. Before Violet could think twice, she was already transforming back into a mouse and dashing away from the Vanguard Circle's Head of Corrections.

Leonas hardly registered her squeeze through the rat hole in his wall—he really needed to seal that—as he rubbed his temples in unexpected irritation. Didn't she realize that he had more important things to do than fuss over the Council's petty concerns? He had a department to run, an absurdly bull-headed assassin to question, a number of colleges to look into, and a letter to write.

Leonas stilled.

… The letter came first. The Elders were fools if they thought anything else mattered where Cheryll was concerned.

His guard reentered the room then. He observed the crazed look in his eyes, the rodent darting away, and finally the explosion of paper around the room. Leonas' smile returned when his guard shook his head in a brief, but firm decision. He didn't want any part of whatever Leonas had just done. Smart man.

It was one of the many reasons Leonas had requested him to be his guard. There was something to be said about the menacing type that couldn't be bothered with asking questions.

Hand pawing blindly for a quill, Leonas fell gracelessly into his chair. He barely registered one of his ink bottles spilling all over the floor, as he began scrawling away like a mad man with a bright, new idea.

He had so much to do.

Cheryll,

I'm so glad to hear from you, love!

I admit, I was worried when it took weeks for you to write. I searched the skies for your birds, only to be disappointed every morning. And night. And morning again! I even left a bit of feed out. I had to stop unfortunately, because it attracted rodents. Not Amorphs, mind you. At least I don't think they were. I would've noticed. I doubt any of the Amorphs here are so starved anyway.

One of them shattered a glass statuette that Vidal gifted me ages ago. Once I figure out which one, there will be blood to pay. That was a collector's item! The carver died twenty years ago. I swear that the next animal—or person—to damage something of mine will share its fate.

But I'm losing the point of this...

In hindsight, I should've known you'd take different measures to send your letter, what with all of these blasted blizzards buffeting us. I'm starting to get tired of the constant snow. I envy you. I'm sure the Drowned Tower is far warmer, despite being underwater. Well, what's left of it anyway. Wait... is it warm? I can't quite recall. It's been so long since I've left the north. A shame, really. I would like to go, but— let me stop here. I'm rambling again, aren't I? I'm trying to fix that, but as you can see my success is next to nonexistent.

Still, identifying the problem is a good start... or so everyone tells me. Though sometimes I feel as if I'm the sole reason the ink merchants are still in business. I deserve a discount, wouldn't you agree?

Now, to put your mind at ease—yes, I'm quite well. Please worry over your own health. Your apprentice arrived safely. Somewhat. She was battered and terribly late. Had a bruise the size of my head and bluer than her own magic, but she's here. Her Healer companion as well. The Mane girl is a mousy little thing. She's clearly deterred by me in some way. Perhaps my title frightened her. If not that, then it must be the Dace name. She is from the Tower after all. I hope Jack didn't scare her like how he used to do with the other children here. Though I don't think horror stories have the same effect on adults. At least I hope they don't. I'd have to apologize to so many people, which I'd rather not do.

Ah, I can hear your scolding tone in my mind, love: "If you're not repentant, then don't apologize. It's insulting."

I miss you terribly.

*And I assure you, I'm not overworking anyone. Let alone myself. I'm merely making a few minor adjustments to the job description of your more talented Hunters. Nothing too problematic. Unless you count taking a few extra trips to the clinic—for very **minor** wounds— a problem. Oh, and that brings me back to the Mane girl. I'm sure the clinics would be grateful for another talented Healer.*

Now, if only Jack would drop by. That would be wonderful. But I have no doubt that you have your reasons for sending him off to the Red Veld. I await his return with bated breath. For now, however, I'll keep your words in mind. They've certainly... confirmed a few theories I had in my head, as well as excited me all the more. I'm sure the Alps will be buzzing once he and his companion finally arrive.

I'll prepare for them.

In truth, I believe others could do a better job. You know I'm no good at these things. But everyone else is busy making arrangements for the upcoming Summit. Every day, they scurry around like ants. It's an interesting sight. I'm sure you'd enjoy it. But why they even need so many decorations for a political affair is beyond me. What's the point? It's not like the Arch Potens are coming here with fifty of their best men. I'll be surprised if they even bring a dozen.

I'm afraid I must go now, love. Work calls. As it always does. I'm beginning to envy Peaches—that little orange cat with green eyes that comes by sometimes to take afternoon naps when it's cold out. She's terribly proud and has this awful snarl when disturbed. It reminds me of you, my love. It's honestly rather endearing... so please stop sneering at this. I'm thinking of training her to go after the rodents, so I can start feeding the birds again. But I'm afraid she might eat those, too. What do you think? I eagerly await your response.

For now, I'll content myself with praying for your quick return. And I'll see what I can do about Victor. Leave everything to me, love.

Yours,
Leonas

9

Rus observed them, feeling very much like a stalker as he did so. He was caught by their sharp eyes. They carried themselves with the confidence of twenty men. Both of them walked with their shoulders squared, each glide as deliberate as their tongues.

Are all practitioners so damn sure of themselves? Rus speculated.

The one's he'd met all seemed to be. But Jack and Sylvie were especially so. Together, they were quite the sight. The kind that stood out no matter the place and no matter the company. Rus envied them. He'd always been average. Mediocre looks, typical tastes, and a style that one neither liked, nor disliked. His handwriting wasn't neat, but it wasn't scribble either. He could hold his liquor, but by no means did he have a steel liver. He was just another face in the crowd. The kind one saw and forgot a moment later. Average of the average. King, if a man like him could be given such a title. A-grade support character material, or so his employer had told him when he'd applied for his current job.

Best decision of my life, he thought, taking his eyes away from the pair, before they caught him staring. Again.

Rus hadn't spoken a word since they set off a good four hours ago, but their constant squabbles about life under the Zexin Sea and every other trivial thing they happened to come across filled the silence nicely. They both had a lot of buttons, and just as many fingers. Though there were instances when they'd fall quiet, as if they'd just heard something disturbing. It was always promptly broken by Jack's cursing in a language he didn't know, but had long associated with practitioners of high degree. Vidal spoke the same language fluently. The forceful enunciation of their '*v*'s and the solid curve of their '*o*'s sent satisfying vibrations through his ears. For that reason alone, Rus wondered who they were and what business they had with Vidal. But he knew better than to ask. Curiosity got men like him either killed or maimed. He found neither option appealing.

"No," Sylvie suddenly stressed, sharp enough to snap Rus from his thoughts.

"Come on, Syl!" Jack pleaded. "Just one more time."

"I said, no."

"Everyone wants to see it." Jack huffed. He tilted his head toward Rus, who tried to hide the persistent quirk of his lips from Sylvie's narrowed gaze. An impossible task. She saw much, and her eyes weren't exactly sweet and forgiving.

"He doesn't even know what you're talking about."

Jack whirled to face Rus then. His lips curled upward into a dark, delighted half-grin that was just begging for entertainment.

"She has this wicked Khale impersonation," Jack told him, like he was supposed to know who that was. The way Jack looked at him made Rus feel like he was tacitly ordering him to jump in barely restrained excitement. He almost did, too. Whether it was out of fear of his eyes or instinct because of his unknown rank, Rus wasn't sure. But when Jack gave no further elaboration, he settled for a terse nod instead.

As soon as he did, however, Sylvie's face fell, while Jack's turned up in triumph. The man was positively beaming. The contrast between their expressions was so stark that Rus stopped to stare in wonder. Had he done something wrong?

"We're going to get along just fine," Jack said.

The comment was unexpected enough to make him stumble. Vidal would certainly laugh if he saw him now, tripping over his own two feet as he was wont to.

"Who would've thought?" Jack went on.

"Certainly not him," Sylvie chimed.

"Did you see that?" Jack turned back to her. His unexpected

like for the Nebbin already forgotten. "He wants to see it."

"He does *not*."

"He nodded, Syl! Nodded!"

"Because you forced him to."

"I did *not*," Jack said, using his best scandalized voice. It was nauseatingly posh, and Sylvie laughed in unbridled delight. The Elementalist shrugged in return, letting her laughter wash over him without even a snarl. Something he was prone to doing, Rus quickly realized the longer they travelled.

The pair shared a look, wordlessly speaking to each other in that way again. As if they were contemplating an extremely troubling matter. But then they both turned away, and the silence was broken by another one of Jack's sharp curses.

For the first time since leaving Yorn, Rus allowed himself to relax. They didn't seem like the type that would belittle him for being a Nebbin or command him to make miracles happen—not now anyway—and whenever Jack ventured into the subject of his work for Vidal, Sylvie would silence him with a scowl. Not that Jack ever listened to her tacit reprimands, but it was usually enough to distract him from the topic.

Rus didn't know if it was some sort of new social politeness he wasn't aware of or if Sylvie truly wasn't bothered by Vidal hiring him, but it didn't matter. It was enough.

So, he let their voices drown the silence as he thought of Yorn and the House of Silver Strings. They'd get their soon. At their pace, it wouldn't be long now.

He smiled.

Miran would never believe this.

***

Misfortune awaits tomorrow's dawn.

When that voice caressed the walls of Sylvie's mind, the frown on her face deepened to a noticeable degree. It sent unholy shivers down her spine that she blamed on the cold when Rus turned to her with a face of innocent confusion. He was far more observant than she'd initially given him credit for. But he was still deaf to that awful voice. Unlike Jack, who tilted his head to shoot her a warning look.

Stop reacting, his eyes said, still utterly terrifying with those black wisps parading around inside of them.

She made a face in response.

They didn't speak as they settled upon the ground to rest their weary legs. Conversation had dried an hour ago, and what needed to be said couldn't be done so in front of company. They lost themselves to their thoughts instead. Sylvie looked at, but didn't truly see, the yellow leaves blanketed over the dry grass. There must've been a decade's worth of piles beneath their feet.

Then, like they'd agreed upon it beforehand, they waited patiently until Rus fell asleep before speaking. It wasn't long. He was out five minutes after his head hit his sack.

"What do you think *she* meant?" Sylvie asked.

"There's going to be a storm." Jack looked up and sniffed the air with a very solemn look on his face. "Tomorrow... maybe."

"Be serious."

"Do I look like a prognosticator to you?" he asked. Sylvie scowled and threw a pebble at him. He dodged it with practiced ease, before lifting an unimpressed brow at her. "If you're curious, then ask."

"I don't want to."

"Then don't."

He was baiting her, she knew. Why? Sylvie couldn't even begin to fathom. But she grasped the stone, feeling its coldness against her clammy skin. Sylvie closed her eyes and tried to picture the type of woman that could own such a voice. Nothing came to mind. Just smoky wisps in place of hair and a faceless head, but that was good enough. At least she felt like she was talking to something a little more concrete.

"Hello?" she tried. Her head snapped up when Jack breathed in sharply. Sylvie glared as he made a poor attempt at covering his laughter. "Oh, stop it. How do you expect me to begin a this?"

"Ask a question," he said. "*She's* always answered before."

"Is it really that simple?"

"Why wouldn't it be?" Jack's eyes zeroed in on the stone. "Have you eaten yet?"

"Don't ask that!"

"It's common decency to—"

"Since when did you have common decency?"

"Yesterday," came Jack's instant reply. His smile was dishonest, though she knew his words weren't. The contradiction was bizarre. "I had this grand epiphany right after knocking you unconscious, and now you're telling me to get rid of it? There's no satisfying you."

"*Jack.*"

"Let me try."

He fanned out his fingers, signaling her to remove her hand. Sylvie shot him a hesitant glance, before her eyes ventured to Rus to see if he was still asleep. But she had no reason to worry; the boy slept like the dead.

Jack cleared his throat, then raised an impatient eyebrow at her. Sylvie let go of the Heartstone and allowed it to hang limply between them. For a brief instant, Jack's face morphed into something too terrifying to name, but then his eyes closed, and the moment was gone. He summoned his own image of *her* in his mind. Jack seemed to have an easier time, judging by the way his face eased almost immediately, before he opened his mouth.

"Another warning?" he asked, thinking of her initial words. "What is it this time?"

Untold dangers await in the city of slaves. Men with strange eyes are only welcome when clasped.

They shared an uneasy glance.

Jack produced his tattered map, opening it to reveal Ferus Terria's seemingly tiny geography and his blockish scrawls dominating every available surface. Had Sylvie not been familiar with the land, then she wouldn't have known where to begin. Jack didn't seem to realize that there was a problem with his note-keeping as he poured over the parchment.

"Here." He pointed at a spot half-covered with ink. "Yorn wasn't always the city of slaves. It was originally—"

"—Tor, I know," Sylvie finished, squinting to try and better understand his writing. To no avail. "Thelarius was born there."

"So... what? Does *she* think we're headed to Tor? The Pit? No way. The fumes alone would kill us. Or at least cut away one or two decades. I've read books about the bodies they drag out of there. Everyone writes about their green skin and black lungs."

"We don't exactly know what *she's* talking about. Maybe practitioners just aren't welcome in Yorn."

"Right." Jack frowned. He looked up at the purple sky, then at the unending expanse of nothingness around them. The lack of people was disturbing. "Get some sleep. I'll take first watch."

***

As the night lightened to signal dawn, Jack found himself staring at his hands. He had to consciously keep himself from allowing his magic to seep out and drop the temperature even lower than it already was. During that first week, when he tried to make the frigid night warmer, he cursed himself for forgetting that he couldn't. He was more careful now though. Careful to keep his secret tucked away, even from himself; careful to not show Sylvie how much he missed having the ability to command the elements; careful with... everything.

Jack wasn't angry about his magic being taken away. Not exactly. It was more accurate to say that he thought it was unfair. The *Orivellea* strengthened his magic circuit. It was a sign of favor from the Council and good fortune throughout life. It didn't give him any gifts that weren't his already. So, why, *why*, was so much taken away? He'd asked that lingering voice once, when Sylvie was asleep and the Heartstone had fallen over the grass, glowing blindingly for him to see.

But *she* didn't answer, and he was left to ponder.

The only thought that came to mind was that it did give him

power. More than he could imagine. More than any could ever know. It was a terrible secret that would rock the iron chain of command most practitioners lived by. Because if *she* was able to take so much away from him with a simple draining of the crystal in his head, would draining it completely make him Nebbin?

He'd immediately dismissed the idea with a wry shake of his head, but now that he had the chance to mull it over, the thought wasn't as far-fetched as he'd initially believed. Peose were granted magic from *Orivellea*, so why couldn't Elementalists be the same? The crystal acted as an extra circuit after all. But where did those circuits initially come from? Surely, not *her*. Or else that would mean that *she* was the source of all magic, which couldn't be true. No other practitioner had crystals imbued inside of their heads. So, there was definitely another source.

But did that mean that the Elementalists were nothing more than a horde of Nebbin given crystals at birth? Could all of the mundane be turned into Elementalists? Did the Council know? They must have. And why did that enigmatic voice decide to ignore all of his important questions, *she* could at least—

Jack paused at the feeling of someone staring at him.

Instinct told him to turn to Sylvie's huddled figure. He stared at the way her arms were drawn to her chest, how two slender fingers tapped against the ground in patience, counting the scant minutes until first light. She wasn't sleeping.

"How long have you been awake?" he asked.

"I haven't slept," she said, sitting up and combing her fingers through her hair. Slow enough for his thoughts to settle. He could still see that stupidly bright glow of the stone under her clothes.

"That's something the man on watch likes to hear."

"You seemed more focused on your hands than our surroundings. Care to share?"

"I'd rather die."

She frowned, though she didn't try to coax the words out of him. He was thankful for that, but still sore enough about her fake sleeping act to say so. Jack stood as soon as he saw a trace of the sun. Grabbing his pack, he called out to a groggy Rus. The man roused like a scared orphan that feared someone would pluck the shoes right off of his feet if he didn't wake fast enough.

Rus' eyes snapped open and he opened his mouth, lips forming what looked to be an apology, before he realized where he was and who he was with. The words died in his throat.

Neither of them needed to ask if he needed a moment, they just stopped and gave him one. But by the next second, Rus had already strapped on his pack and stretched out his legs in one fluid motion. His eyes were alert, and he looked fully prepared to sprint the rest of the way to Yorn. Rus was clearly a morning person. They were akin to grumpy, wet cats in comparison.

From the corner of his eye, Jack saw Sylvie's face morph into the strangest frown he'd ever seen, as if she couldn't decide whether she envied him or wanted to talk sense into him.

"Well, look at you," Jack said. A wry smile tilted his lips. "All excited and ready to return to your keeper." He expertly ignored the warning glance Sylvie threw at him.

"I won't slow you down, Sir," came Rus' unperturbed reply. His radiant smile outmatched Jack's mockery.

"Turn it down," Jack grumbled, shielding his eyes from his smile. "You're blinding me with that thing."

"What?"

"He's talking to the sun," Sylvie interrupted.

Jack frowned in disapproval. "Why would I ever talk to—" he coughed when Sylvie elbowed his side.

"He tends to do that," she went on. "Don't mind him."

"I completely understand, Miss!" Rus said, complete with an overly-enthusiastic nod. All traces of his nervous disposition disappeared to make way for whatever spirit of light that claimed him during the night. "The sun does shine brighter in these parts. It can get quite annoying, especially for those from the east. I've heard eastern practitioners usually stay under the Zexin Sea."

"We do..." Sylvie trailed off, shaking her head to rid herself of a few unwelcome thoughts. "Do you like the sun, Rus?"

"It makes for good farming," was his reserved response. Though his smile was brighter than magic. "I take it you're not a fan, Miss?"

"It's nice. Sometimes. When it isn't trying to bake me."

"I'm sure you'll get used to it soon enough," Rus assured with another wide grin.

Good god, Jack thought. He'd never seen such alacrity. It was nauseating. How did someone even achieve that level of pep after a nap? He wanted to know, so he could do everything he possibly could to avoid it.

Jack caught Sylvie's gaze.

She eyed him cautiously, just daring him to say something bitter. Oh, like he'd waste his breath. He flicked his wrist instead, urging the Nebbin forward.

"Come on," Jack said. "We don't have all day."

***

Yorn was a city of corridors.

Mazes within mazes that were laid upon what must've been the flattest land in Ferus Terria. There were no roads along the outer edge of the city, only worn, dirt paths that led into open markets or into lines of modest houses. Each household had only enough room to fit a family of four, but judging by the number of people they saw coming and going, comfort and privacy had given way to poverty. They held their packs a little closer once they stepped into the crowd.

They'd arrived in the middle of the day, when the entirety of Yorn was out working. Shopkeepers took one look at their clothes and beckoned them over, uncaring for their hooded eyes. Perhaps they already knew what they were? With so many people here, they must've been used to singling out the stray practitioner trying to avoid all human contact, and then milking them dry. Thankfully, they were quick enough to slip away.

As Rus guided them deeper, the dirt soon gave way to cobble paths. The hanging clotheslines disappeared to show clear skies.

They found themselves at the tip of the city proper. Where the buildings were taller and made of painted bricks, each grander than the last. Roofs were built on top of roofs. Made more for aesthetics than practicality. There were marble columns in places there ought not to be and peculiarly pointed archways lined with shining granite that was surely too expensive to be there. Well-trimmed bushes were on every corner and vines hung from balconies all around them, adding a touch of natural color to an otherwise synthetic world. Even the air was different. Perfumed and lighter. Perhaps due to the lack of people. There were still a good number of them, but not enough to fill the streets. Strangely enough, the guards outnumbered the citizens.

A bakery stood awkwardly between the two paths, caught amidst the classes. It was made from a combination of wood and white stone, as if it couldn't decide which ring it was a part of. Even the baker, with his large belly and balding head, couldn't choose. His apron was filled with holes, but the clothes beneath were made from fine cotton and lined with silver. The smell of fresh bread attracted all kinds of folk, it seemed.

Jack and Sylvie lingered there, startled by the contrast before them. On one side, a world where friends sold friends for pocket change. On the other, a world that bought those friends and made them theirs.

"Makes you sick, doesn't it?" Jack tilted his head to gesture around them. Even the expressions of the people were different. The poorer folk were noticeably more scared for night to fall. They kept looking up to track the position of the sun. "Maybe money makes people blind."

"And deaf," she added, then nudged him forward when Rus turned to see why they stopped. "Think you're up for changing their worlds, too?"

Jack's lips twisted in answer.

Reed,

Yorn's nights are cold. Not like Jack's magic, but like the Tower in the morning when the lamps are out and everyone is fumbling toward the lavatory doors. ~~I can't believe it's been thirty-six days.~~ I'm sure the outer ring is warmer. More compact as it is.

We visited a bakery with these fabulous flatbreads and golden custard pies. Rus helped us sell those silk linens we looted a while back, too. The saleswoman that manned the shop kept pursing her lips at our muddy boots, but she did give us a decent price. It was a little unfair, but we needed the money, so I don't mind being cheated out of a few coins. Rus brought us to an expensive inn after. For dinner, they served tiny sandwiches and colored water in quaint, ornate cups — 'micas,' they called it, or so Jack keeps reminding me. I don't know why he bothers remembering these things when he was the first to scrunch his nose at the mere sight of them. I think we've gotten too used to badly fried rabbit and unseasoned jerky to actually taste anything else. I wish they served Roco sauce here. Rus says he's never heard of it, and Jack told me that I'm the only one that actually enjoys the stuff.

Well, even if he is very, very, **very** wrong… I do miss it. Dearly. ~~I miss a lot of things.~~ Maybe its practitioner's food? Is there even such a thing? I probably could've gotten a jarful in the Veld if Jack hadn't —

I don't want to think about it. He'll apologize soon, I'm sure. When I least expect it. Emotionally useless bastard.

For now, I have to focus on meeting Vidal. Rus has arranged for us to see him tomorrow evening. He was sketchy on the details, but that's fine with me. As long as we have a chance to talk to him, then I'm satisfied. If Vidal is willing to humor questions other than business, then there's a lot about the Plains that I'd like to know more about.

Oh, flames. Now that I think about it, what am I going to say about the Summit? I wish Rus had told us more about the man. He's smart though. Made sure to run off before Jack could grill him. Good to know he has a good head on his shoulders. Still…

Jack's looking at his hands again. He's been doing that a lot lately. He won't give me a hint about what he's thinking though. He should really get some sleep. We both should. I'm going to tell him.

Sylvie Sirx 25.27.CA

10

Rus returned the following evening.

He had a spent smile on his face and a large pack behind him. It was so heavy that his shoulders drooped lower than Sylvie's, who stood a good six inches shorter. He'd develop a hunch soon, Jack was sure of it, and made sure to tell him so. But the way Rus shrugged in reluctant acceptance told him that he wasn't carrying it because he wanted to but because his job demanded it. Jack couldn't fault him for that.

Rus led them down the streets, offering small anecdotes whenever they passed an unapparent novelty. Sylvie entertained him for the most part, asking her own questions whenever there was a lull in conversation. Jack didn't bother. Instead, his eyes roamed the city streets. There were numerous statues scattered about. All used as altars, judging from the number of candles at the base of each.

Are they religious? Jack wondered. *Or did we miss a holiday?*

Jack didn't linger on the décor for long. His gaze drifted to the people. They were far more entertaining. He observed a woman and her daughter compare fabrics. Beside them, were two children that chased each other straight into a weapons stall with a grumpy looking salesman that had the bushiest brows he'd ever seen. And at the very end of the street, was a minstrel with worn boots and a sly grin. He spun a tale about secret trysts, catching the attention of young women with wealthy fathers. Clever.

The people were interesting, for lack of a better word. They were carefree, despite the happenings across the Yovakine Plains.

It might not have always been peaceful, but at least they were able to live their lives the way they wanted. He wasn't jealous... not really. Well, maybe a little.

"Jack," Sylvie called. His shoulders straightened out of reflex and he turned to blink owlishly at her. Sylvie's brow furrowed in confusion. "Your lips are twisting again."

"What?" he asked, puzzled.

"Are you alright?"

Their mouths are so expressive, he recalled in his mother's voice. Jack's hand immediately shot up to shield it from her curious view. His eyes thinned into a glare so severe, it made Rus squeak. But to his dismay, Sylvie wasn't even the slightest bit deterred. Jack didn't know if he should be happy or upset by her immunity, but he was in no mood to figure it out.

"Just thinking," Jack said after a moment.

"About a plan better than knocking me unconscious, I hope." She glanced at him sidelong, only to find him staring out into the distance, completely tuning her out. "Jack, are you listening?"

"No, but I'm sure it was a great story."

Her eyes narrowed, the light in them sharpening. "One more insolent word out of you and I swear I'm going to shower you in fire. I'll burn your hair, your clothes, and your eyebrows right off. Maybe even melt your teeth." Sylvie lifted her hand, fingers splayed in his direction. "Do you want that?"

"You and I both know that you're all bark." Jack smirked at her empty threats. Feral and wry. "It's not good to lie, Syl."

"Jack."

"I live for that weary tone." He laughed, then turned to Rus with a flippant smile crooking his lips. "You don't believe her either, right?"

Rus startled at the inclusion. His mouth opened and shut twice, before he settled on a placating grin. Jack was irked by his silence. Rus could tell from the way his smirk faltered. But never one to be deterred for long, Jack opened his mouth to speak in his place, only to be interrupted by a scream from across the square.

"Let me go!" a woman cried.

She was surrounded by three armed men with sneers on all of their faces, yet she still somehow managed to squirm her way out of their grasps and bump right into Sylvie. The two stared at each other, both unable to comprehend what had just happened.

Jack witnessed the exact moment the woman realized what Sylvie was under her hood. Her eyes widened to an almost painful degree, her jaw slackened, and just as Jack made to grab her by the cheekbones to silence whatever it was she was going to say, she was already gripping Sylvie's forearm with an excited gleam in her eyes.

"Help me," she squeaked. More thrilled than scared.

"What?" Sylvie asked out of reflex.

"Miran!" Rus called.

"You know her?" Jack asked.

Rus nodded. But before he could say more, Miran pulled Sylvie forward and hid behind her taller frame just as the guards stepped up to them. Sylvie's gaze flew from the shaken girl behind her to the disgruntled group of men before.

Well, this clearly wasn't fair.

Jack held back a laugh when, like the oh, so helpful person she was, she simply cocked her head at the ludicrousness of her position. Either unaware or uncaring for what was going on. Perhaps both. If Sylvie could help it, she never got involved. At least that part of her hadn't changed. It was a wonder that they were even in Yorn in the first place. Jack shook his head at the entire ordeal. They only wanted to meet Vidal. So, why did all of these people constantly insist on getting in their faces? It wasn't as if they were going around asking for trouble.

The middle guard—their captain, Jack assumed—stretched his hand out and wiggled his fingers in a soundless command. Sylvie blinked twice at it. While Rus looked like he wanted to say something to her. Jack guessed that it was something along the lines of asking Sylvie not to hand Miran over, but to his surprise, Rus only fisted his hands and kept his mouth shut.

Well, the girl was clearly important to him. Just not enough for him to risk his own skin… or did he just believe in them that much? He'd be sorely disappointed then. Because Jack didn't mind handing the girl over as long as the guards could justify themselves. Jack wasn't about to get into a scuffle with the town guard over a stranger, especially if that stranger was a criminal. But would Sylvie think the same?

He wasn't let down when she answered.

"Nice to meet you," Sylvie muttered, staring at the captain's hand as an excuse to hide her eyes. If it were him, he would've slapped it away. "Can I help you?"

"The girl," the captain said gruffly. "Hand her over. She doesn't belong here."

"Doesn't belong?"

"That doesn't concern you. Hand her over."

"Did she do something wrong?"

"No!" Miran yelled from behind her, startling them all. Rus threw her a sharp glare, but she didn't seem to notice. Miran balled up Sylvie's clothes to make sure she stayed in place, while she ranted. "It's them that's wrong! I was just on my way back to work when they stopped me. '*Go back to the slums,*' they said. Ha! As if! You guys sure know how to talk big for lazy tubs of lard!"

The captain was red in the face by the time she finished. He opened his mouth—once, twice—and each time Miran egged him on, chanting '*oaf, oaf, oaf,*' like he didn't hear her the first time.

Miran's face was flush with the promise of a fight, and Jack's eyebrows pinched at her moxie. At least she had spunk. But when their hands collectively settled on their blades, there Miran went cowering behind Sylvie. It was enough to make Jack double over in laughter and Rus have a heart attack.

Rus seized Miran by the shoulders, trying to tear her away from Sylvie's back. To no avail. The girl was clingier than vines. Just her luck, too. She latched onto the wrong practitioner. Sylvie wouldn't use her magic in the way Miran wanted, and from the way Sylvie's eyes drifted to his, screaming at him to not make a scene, they both knew it.

Finally done trying to take Miran away from them, the captain made to grab Sylvie's shoulder. Only to still in shock when she reached out and clasped his wrist before he could. Her hold was hotter than it should've been because the captain hissed as it tightened. Jack saw the familiar release of smoke, and when the captain's lips curled in realization, he wondered if Sylvie even wanted to get away from here. Because making enemies of the town guard certainly wasn't the way to do it.

"What are you two standing around for?" the captain yelled at his stunted underlings. He tore his scorched wrist away from Sylvie's grasp. "Capture them!"

They seemed shaken, but neither needed to be told twice.

Both guards drew their blades and charged.

Sylvie stepped back in apprehension. The indecision was naked on her face, as she twisted to face the gaggle of curious on-lookers behind them. There were so many children. Even that lying minstrel had stopped to stare in wonder. But when the captain lifted his sword with a furious roar, her expression hardened into one of decision. Sylvie lifted her hand. Her palm sparked, the burning light of fire prepared to burst forth, then—

—Jack squeezed her fingers shut.

"Easy, Syl," he murmured. Bitter frost lightly coated her hand, snuffing the flames and keeping her from doing something she'd surely regret.

Sylvie's body went rigid at his sudden intervention. Behind them, Rus somehow managed to pry the flabbergasted Miran off.

"Really..." Jack went on. "Why stop me when you planned to use your magic anyway?"

"Because I knew you'd make a spectacle of yourself."

"Oh? And you weren't about to?"

"*Without* first trying to scare them off."

"Little good that did you."

Sylvie opened her mouth to defend herself, but seemed to think better of it. Instead, she pulled her hand away... or tried to.

Jack held on tightly. His red eyes scrutinized her fingers, making sure all traces of her magic were gone and that he hadn't done any lasting damage before allowing it to fall back to her side.

He was unexpectedly fussy. Sylvie made a face at the realization. One that he returned with equal fervor.

Sylvie peered over his shoulder to inspect his handy-work. She was met with three shivering guards. They were covered in a thick layer of frost that made their teeth chatter. Key joints were frozen in place, leaving them unable to move. They looked like those marble statues she'd read about in books, sculpted sentinels forever forced to assume uncomfortable stances. When Sylvie looked down at their feet, she found their boots under a similar fate. It was enough to make her feel almost... bad for them.

Sylvie raised her hand, deliberating using her magic to thaw the ice from their toes a bit. They'd be there for hours if no one did anything, and the way they were glaring at them made her feel like they were trying to commit their faces to memory. Perhaps they were. It wouldn't surprise her.

"Isn't ice useful?" Jack said with a wide, triumphant grin. He flashed it gloatingly at the captain, before urging Sylvie forward. "Let's not wait for the townsfolk to start throwing things. Like rocks or knives or... apples." Jack shuddered. "I hate apples."

That did the trick. Sylvie turned to him with creased brows.

"You don't like apples?"

"Not the time, Syl."

She took one look at the mob behind them, drinking in their horrified expressions, before letting Jack tug her forward without further complaint.

They broke out into a run once they turned a nearby corner. Rus and Miran were at their heels, worriedly checking behind them every few seconds to see if anyone gave chase. No one did. But it was only when they slipped into a shady, puke-scented alleyway that they stopped. It was filthy, as alleys tended to be. There were three dumpsters lined side-by-side, but everyone took to leaving their garbage just outside of it, making it more disgusting than it already was. A homeless man was asleep beside the last one; a bottle of amber liquid the only thing to his name. By dawn, even that would be gone.

"*Filan vahs,*" Jack cursed, pinching his nose. The smell was so strong, he could taste it. Behind him, Sylvie gagged. Her entire face scrunched in displeasure. She looked like she was trying to hold her breath. But it was already too late for that.

"What *is* that?"

"Don't ask," Jack said fiercely. His eyes fell to the stone, actually terrified it might answer. "I don't want to know," he tacked on. Just in case.

"I didn't see anyone chasing us." Rus panted. He peeked outside of the alley for good measure, then nodded to himself when his statement held true. "We should head to the House of Silver Strings before anyone actually tries to."

He wasn't about to get any complaints from them. But Jack had something to say to the girl wheezing behind him.

"*Vaklas dalen.*" The wisps in his eyes stirred menacingly. "You've got some nerve using us as a shield. Now they know our faces. What were you thinking, you little *revonarahs karis?*"

"Jack!" Sylvie said, appalled.

"You're practitioners!" Miran cried, like it wasn't obvious already. She ignored Jack's bubbling anger as excitement from their mere presence took over.

Miran stepped forward with one hand extended in greeting, finally allowing them a proper look at her. She was boxy, short in stature, and the proud owner of incredibly callused hands. The delight in her voice made both of their eyes widen.

"Oh, please, please, *please* tell me about yourselves."

Two sets of eyebrows lifted. Jack and Sylvie stared at her like she was daft. Behind her, Rus groaned in exasperation.

"Please," Miran continued, her eyes falling when she caught their staggered expressions. "I promise to speak slowly and to never talk about things you don't want to and —"

"Excuse Miran," Rus interrupted her tirade. "She's, as you

can tell, unduly interested in practitioners. Everything about them. From individual backgrounds to magic."

"How do you two know each other?" Sylvie asked.

"We work for Master Verne!" Miran answered with stars in her eyes. She shoved Rus away, before slithering right up to Sylvie's side. "You're a Conjurer! What's your affinity? Last name? Any siblings? Are you from the Veld?"

Sylvie looked uncomfortable under her scrutiny, but then again, who wouldn't be? Miran was gazing so intently at her that even Jack felt his skin crawl. She had big eyes. Round and nosy. Sylvie looked around, desperately searching for an escape.

"Are you serious right now?" Jack cut in, catching their attention. He regarded them all individually. His eyes were like gory daggers in the darkness of the alley. "Is this actually happening? You've got to be—no, you know what? Forget it."

Jack walked off, his jaw set and his hands glowing blue. He left a trail of cold in his wake. It might take him a while, but he'd find Vidal sooner or later. He didn't need them. Yorn wasn't that big. And he could definitely do without the headache.

"Touchy." Miran frowned.

"He has his moments," Sylvie told her, before cupping her lips and calling out to him. "Don't just storm off! Wait for me."

Jack didn't stop.

"Do you even know where you're going?" Sylvie continued, struggling to catch up. She doubted he did, but the determined look he casted told her that she could question anything she wanted and he'd still find a way to make it happen. Suddenly, her doubts no longer mattered. "So, you'll find Vidal on your own? Fine. I believe you. But at least let them lead us there. It's better than wandering aimlessly for a few more hours, right?"

If he denied it, would she leave him be? Not likely. Jack sighed. His footsteps stopped completely, as he waited for the Nebbin to gather their bearings. Beside him, Sylvie's lips tilted into a happy, little half-smile that he ignored in favor of glaring at those plucky enough to complain at the fact that he'd stopped in the middle of a fairly busy street. They cringed back in fear from his blood-red gaze.

"Hurry," Sylvie called to the two Nebbin. "We don't want to keep Verne waiting."

Rus blinked, before he nodded and dragged Miran along.

"But I still have questions!" Miran whined.

"Save them for later!" he chided.

***

The House of Silver Strings wasn't anything like they'd anticipated. Perhaps because they'd expected an underground den and damp, humid tunnels that they'd be forced to trudge through—something that fit the persona of one of the players of the underworld. So, the long stretch of cobble road and pristine limestone walls were a pleasant surprise. The auction house was deep within Yorn, nestled at the very top of a set of shabby stairs that had definitely seen better years. There were carved faces along the walls leading up to the entrance that neither Jack, nor Sylvie recognized. But they were silent and stern and compelled them to go faster. A decision neither of them regretted because the view at the very top was breathtaking.

They could see the edge of the slums and the heath beyond. While the House sat high above many of the other buildings, it wasn't anywhere near Yorn's peak. That was reserved for larger households that were owned by older families with even older money. They saw a woman walk from that very district, then make a sharp turn towards the House. She was flanked by three weary boys with black iron cuffs around their wrists.

Jack stepped back in shock at the sight. His fingers twitched, as the beginnings of fury stirred deep within his core. He struggled to control the curve of his lips. Wordless, for once, in his anger. Jack's magic hissed in unmasked contempt. The smoke of his ice rose into the air only to fizzle out and die when Sylvie brushed his shoulder.

She caught his gaze with her own, much sharper one. There

was enough warning in her eyes to temper him. They weren't here to cause trouble. Not yet.

Six guards patrolled the doors. They were all fashioned in lightweight armor that had the blooming crest of the Verne family stitched proudly on its side. One of the guards opened the heavy wooden doors for the woman without so much as a second glance, apparently seeing no problem with her company.

A round of cheers echoed from inside, before quieting with the decisive slam of the entrance.

"Oh!" Miran gasped. "The Silver String auction is starting."

Jack whirled around to face them. "So, those *were* slaves," he said, his eyes narrowed in displeasure. The black wisps in his orbs moved erratically with his fury. "Why did they let a slaver inside? Wasn't Arch Poten Verne against this?"

"I thought so, too," Sylvie chimed. "I'm not going to work with someone that condones slavery. How can we help the Veld's Arch Poten with her problems if her husband is one of them?"

"No, no, you have it all wrong!" Rus defended.

"Then explain it to us."

"I—It's a front," he breathed, dropping his voice to a whisper. "Please just go inside and... look. Meet with Sir Verne after the auction. He can explain it better than I can."

They shared a skeptical glance. But eventually, they nodded in *very* reluctant agreement. They were already here, so they might as well go inside.

Rus let out a relieved sigh and signaled for the guards to open the doors. It was then they noticed that behind the uncomfortable helmet and matted hair, the guards all had practitioner's eyes. If they were with Verne, then they doubted that they were deserters. But what were they doing catering to Nebbin?

The guard, realizing his mistake, lowered his head. It was quick, tactless avoidance. He was young under all of that armor. But as they were led inside, where a grand hall fashioned in deep velvets and dark wood awaited, they thought that perhaps he wasn't the only one.

***

The auction hall was a grand place.

Of course it was. An auction hall had to be. Especially one that sported a name as extravagant as, '*The House of Silver Strings*.' Vidal had personally designed every inch of it, and contrary to popular belief, he had impeccable taste. Second to none. Nothing too plain or too gaudy about it.

Rows of seats were spread out before the stage and dozens more towered all around. Along the outer edges, were booths for the more esteemed guests. The Silver String Auction differed from the other, mundane auctions held here. During this time, only the booths above were occupied. Guests were seated high up where they could observe him like an insect, thinking thems-elves superior. But who was he to question the taste of nobility and self-important slavers? As long as they spent their money, then he'd keep his mouth shut. Besides, he secretly liked not be-ing able to properly look at their faces. They were round with fat and laziness. Only greed lingered behind their depths.

The stage was clear of everything save for him. A single spot-light flicked on, trained on his smiling face and the crescent tatt-oos under his eyes. Vidal was ready to excite the audience even if it was in no way a full house. They came for him after all.

He tapped the dark mahogany cane in his hand twice on the ground. An echo resounded all across the hall, signaling the start of the auction.

"Ladies and gentlemen." Vidal spread his arms wide. He closed his eyes and beamed an ivory smile. He didn't bow. Why would he? He wasn't here to serve. They were here to see him, and he wouldn't lower his head for their fancies. His voice was filled with affection as he exclaimed, "Welcome to my world!"

He smiled again. A feral smile that chilled to the bone.

"The House of Silver Strings is honored to have you here for tonight's auction! I am once again your host. Here to showcase the finest of wares from every hell in Ferus Terria."

Vidal didn't have one of those enchanted mouthpieces the ancient fossils in the north liked so much. His voice was loud enough for the entire hall. Practiced and fluid. How much time and effort had he put into his stage persona? Not even he knew. But the round of applause that followed his voice had his grin flaring. That was a special praise just for him. It was nice to be acknowledged. Even if the one he wanted to be accredited by wasn't among them.

"Tonight's leading commodity was imported from Sicin by a dear associate and generous supporter of the auction," Vidal went on with the self-confidence of a thousand men. "So, without further ado, sit back, admire the display, and do of course, raise those plaques."

He rubbed his thumb across the pads of his fingers in a universal gesture. Laughter echoed from the booths. A mixture of soft chuckles and high pitched echoes that collectively ceased as soon as the first item was brought on stage.

A boy no older than fifteen walked forward with a frantic, helpless stumble. He had enormous eyes that only widened at the sheer amount of people. Fear shook his bones. He was an honest thing. Vidal had seen many adults and children alike put on brave faces, but once they crept on stage to be dangled like fresh meat before a pack of starving hounds, all they could do was quiver, close their eyes, and pretend that they were somewhere else. The ones that couldn't usually wet themselves. This boy looked like he might.

Vidal watched on, feigning disinterest. He gripped his cane just a little tighter. He eyed the buyers above him and noted that the entrance now had a few new extras. Latecomers to his realm. They were practitioners like himself and were directed forward by one of his runners—Rus, he realized upon squinting.

Were they the ones Monet spoke about in her letter? Oh, he hoped so. He didn't want to deal with anyone from the Diamond Alps or even the Red Veld. He'd had enough of their constant prying. Vidal had no time for meddlers too caught up in their own ideals to understand his. But them... they were a breath of fresh, frigid air. New faces. Newer reactions. Even newer stories.

From his position, Vidal caught a glimpse of their faces. Angry, resentful, and wildly trying to tame their own disdain. The woman, dark haired and pale, buried her face in her hands when an overzealous bidder shouted his price. If it was from fright or revulsion, Vidal couldn't say. But she was quick to abandon her emotions in favor of securing her temperamental companion, who seemed to be trying his hardest to keep his hands from glowing any brighter than they already were.

Was he a Conjurer or an Elementalist? Vidal couldn't see his eyes well enough to tell, but the sudden drop in temperature was unmistakable. Foolish boy. He really should stop. He'd attract the attention of the Nebbin around them. While most were just rich loons, there were also a few representatives from slaver bands mixed in. The sort that were in charge of procuring exotic wares.

As the spectators calmed, waiting for him to get on with his performance, Vidal wondered if they'd be dazzled like the rest of these terrible people. Would they try to break him before it was over or would they linger in silence until he was finished?

Only one way to find out.

Vidal breathed deeply, lifted his hands, smiled—

Another copy.

—and stilled.

His eyes roamed the bewildered masses, searching for the owner of that abysmal voice. Had he imagined it? Instinct told him to look up, and he found those two newcomers still frowning, still looking down at him with disdain. But the girl's hands were wrapped around something by her neck. It should've been covered by skin and bone. Logic only demanded it. Yet, it gave off a glow even brighter than the spotlight he stood under.

How...? Vidal wondered, uncaring for the way the audience began whispering amongst themselves. Even the young boy beside him looked up in hopeful uncertainty.

The two suddenly realized that he was staring at them

because their eyes met, and then they turned to that foreboding object in her hands. The lullaby that came from it made Vidal shudder. Chills ran down his spine, as a cacophony of voices invaded his ears and made the magic in his veins ache to be released. The surge of adrenaline that coursed through him then made his blood sing. But as he looked frantically around, no one else seemed to be affected by the song.

Don't they hear that? Vidal thought, rattled. It was so loud. *How can they just ignore it… is it even there? Or have I finally cracked? Ah, Monet always said I would. I should've liste—*

Shall I trap you in an eternal hell?

—no, I haven't. Of course I haven't. It's there and it's…

Vidal regarded the pair again. He squared his shoulders, reclaiming his confidence. His eyes were red and piqued. Though his arms trembled with unease, he spread them wide in open challenge. When Vidal spoke, it was only to that voice.

"You're welcome to make the attempt."

Partner,

Yes, I'm writing again.

Sylvie… encourages it. Not that I'll ever actually send this. And don't you dare think that I'm doing this for her or because she said I should. I'm only doing it because it keeps her off of my back. I'll take as much peace as I can get. She asks too much about what's on my mind, and while she does let me off the hook when I don't want to talk it's still troubling. Ridiculously so.

Anyway, we're in Yorn. At an inn. The name? I don't remember. I don't care. The city? It's big, divided, and completely beside the point.

I found the strangest book in Yorn's bazaar. It's a history book—I know, I know, don't you dare roll your eyes at this page. I didn't burn it!—it actually isn't that bad.

Astonishing? Very.

Maybe because it isn't written in typical textbook fashion. It's more of an autobiography of sorts. I don't know what to call it. But it's about life in the Weeping Grove. The masters there, the enchanted trees, the colleges, and all of that. You'll never believe this, but it was written by Sirx! Dalis Sirx!

(Sylvie's brother if the name still isn't ringing any bells.)

*I skimmed a few pages and it has stories about her as a child and— Silas' holy pyre! All of the blackmail in my hands. I'm giddy, **giddy** with excitement. I'm going to tuck it away for now. Maybe I'll show it to her when I'm feeling particularly bored. I still can't decide whether that's a spectacular idea or an incredibly stupid one, but I'll settle on the former for now.*

Oh, Syl's looking over here. Scowling at my grin, too. Heh. I wish you could see it. It's hideous. I'd better go before she suspects something.

Althanni rhadin vashen elis rin.

May the morning be kind.

(Somehow, I doubt it.)

Jack 25.27.CA

11

Stiff silence followed Vidal's proclamation.

The auctioneer glowered in their direction, shoulders rigid and face defiant, but that dark voice didn't speak again. Black tendrils rose forth from the shadows to encompass the pair, though neither of them seemed particularly concerned by it. They were far more preoccupied with his unwavering stare, which prompted the curious audience to turn as well.

The woman was quick to hide her eyes. She urged her companion to do the same, but he seemed less inclined to listen. Setting his jaw, he glared at the crowd of Nebbin that surrounded him. Some flinched, while others proudly raised their chins.

Vidal opened his mouth to address them, but stopped when armed guards arrived from a back room with their weapons drawn and their faces stern. The man wasn't deterred. Instead, his eyes grew fiercer, the promise of a fight shined madly in their depths. Miran stepped up to coax them all back into the lobby, not wanting a fight to break out and ruin the auction. He'd have to reward her accordingly later.

With one strong jerk from the woman, the hotheaded man broke his stare down with the guards in favor of quietly scowling at her. There was a lot of contempt in his face and in his eyes. There was defense, too, and contrition, no matter how slight in comparison. The woman saw it all; Vidal knew she did. Because the look in her eyes reminded him somewhat of Monet.

Before anyone could move, she stepped closer to him and whispered something in his ear that was far too faint for anyone to catch. It made the lines of his face deepen, but he eventually conceded, throwing his hood over his head as if the entire hall hadn't already memorized his face.

Rus called out to them in a pitch that Vidal would be sure to tease him relentlessly for later. But even as his runner led the two practitioners deeper into his abode, presumably to wait somewhere far away from tasteless things like slave auctions, Vidal could still hear faint traces of that lullaby. It rang in his ears. The banked magic he hid pulsed in anticipation for the unknown.

There was immeasurable power there. His gut told him so.

But greed for power was detrimental and would only lead to ruin. His predecessors had taught him that. Over the years, he'd quietly witnessed their individual rise to worship—and their subsequent fall from grace. Satisfying as it may have been for some, he'd never found it entertaining. Vidal would sooner die than suffer a similar fate.

Beside him, the young boy let out a nervous cough. His chains rattled with the movement. It was enough to bring him back to reality, back to his stage and spotlight. The audience was staring at him again, wondering what he'd do, how he'd salvage the situation—could he? The more impatient ones were already asking for their coats, while the bored began their rumors. The latter were mostly withered biddies with nothing better to do with their time.

Vidal sneered. They'd unintentionally stolen his show.

Now, that wouldn't do.

"How unpleasant," Vidal said, just loud enough to catch their attention. He loudly tapped his cane on the ground before his feet, regaining his composure with each booming knock. It echoed decisively along the walls. Vidal cleared his throat and with a grin contradictorily sheepish when compared to the savage look in his eyes, he said, "Shall we continue the show?"

He was met with a round of approving cheers.

Vidal looked down at the trembling boy. He gave him a smile meant to comfort, but the boy only flinched. Opening his arms once more, Vidal quickly decided that he needed to get this show back on the road. Only then could he talk things through with his new friends... assuming they didn't attempt to rip out his tongue first. Vidal smirked at the thought. He'd like to see them try. Still, it had been years since he'd been so curious about anyone. Perhaps annoying them would be his new pastime. That sounded splendid.

Taking a deep breath, he tried again. Vidal arced the cane in his hand, and when his voice spilled forth, it was more excited than his spectators.

"Pick your poison," he began, "preach your passion, and choose your human. Welcome once again to my show!"

They applauded, praises spilling from their lips.

There were no interruptions this time.

***

Rus left them in what appeared to be Vidal's personal study, if the ten-foot tall, gold-framed portrait of Monet Verne staring imposingly down at them from the wall was any indication. There were more like it littered about the room in various shapes and sizes. Some hung from nails, but most—the older ones they gathered, from the dates helpfully tacked along the bottom—were propped up and gathering dust. It was a strange sight to behold, made stranger when Rus only shrugged, sparing their concern one, perplexed glance as if they were the creepy ones.

Candles burned before an unused fireplace; their wax spilled over the floor. A bottle of something strong and bronze sat beside various contracts on Vidal's desk. Judging from the smell, it could only be classified as liquid death. Jack was sorely tempted to tip it over in spite, and then freeze everything the man held dear to him. He settled for rifling through the papers instead.

Rus was quick to protest, but was ultimately held back by Sylvie, while Jack snooped. He found bills, receipts, manifestoes, pleas for protection, and random notes for a manuscript Vidal looked to be writing, but nothing on what he'd just witnessed.

They'd either need to get answers from the man himself or go with violent option number two. Jack turned to Rus, who stopped struggling in Sylvie's grasp as soon as their eyes met. The latter seemed more appropriate, given that Vidal was still pontificating on stage.

"What do you know?" Jack demanded.

Rus screwed his eyes shut, so he could avoid the looming threat of Sylvie waving her hand dangerously close to his face. The growing heat, however, piqued him enough to open them. Rus yelped at the sight of her roaring flames. He stumbled backwards. His eyes rolled to the large shield mounted on the wall, as if that might protect him from their magic. Fat chance.

Jack stepped closer. His fingers lit up intimidatingly.

On cue, the door flew open. It smashed against the adjacent wall, rattling its many portraits. All eyes settled upon Vidal, who strode in with a disturbing smile. Upon closer inspection, they noticed that he wasn't as tall or as menacing as he was on stage. Vidal was all points and sharp angles. He moved in a way that was entirely too sylphlike to be considered masculine. There was a dangerous glint in his eyes, the sort that characterized the bored and the deadly. Vidal took one look at the scene before him and dismissed it with a wave of his hand.

"Take a walk! I've got the floor," Vidal told Rus, his voice was just as theatric as his appearance suggested. Rus didn't wait for his captors to gather their bearings, swiftly fleeing down the hall without even a bow. Vidal watched him go, impressed by his speed. "Look at him go. What did you two do, I wonder?"

"Us?" Jack exclaimed. The wisps in his eyes shifted with his wrath. "What about *you*? We came all this way. Crossed the Yova Plains, passed the Red Veld, went through half a dozen decrepit villages for *this*?" he snarled, his magic escaping him without his notice. The temperature in the room fell just enough to be noticeable. He was fully prepared to charge the man and force him into answering when—

"What's wrong with your eyes?" Vidal asked.

For a brief instant, Jack's anger left him and in its place was confusion, realization, and the barest hint of wonder. But then the moment passed, and Jack marched forward to grab the taller man by the scruff of his collar. Red clashed with red.

Vidal was an Elementalist? Well, not that it mattered. Jack was going to beat him bloody.

We don't need his support. But even as Jack thought it, he knew it wasn't true. His mother would glare him into oblivion for ruining her plans. Sylvie seemed to realize that as well because she already had one arm on his elbow, the other burning with flames Jack knew she'd turn on him if he continued his assault.

Amidst it all, Vidal watched on in amusement. Like he was nothing more than a spectator and not the cause of their anger in the first place. Jack abruptly let Vidal go. He didn't seem ruffled, as he adjusted his collar with a supremely placating smile.

"You're pointing that fire at me, Syl?" Jack faced her, holding his chin high in defiance. "Really?"

"Because you never listen," Sylvie said, exasperated. "Let's hear him out."

"He's a slaver!"

"He has the right to explain himself!"

"Slavers don't deserve rights or opinions or whatever else you can think of in that flaming kind head of yours. He auctions people, Syl. Like cattle!"

"There must be a reason your mother told us to come to him. But how are we supposed to know what it is if you won't even let him speak, you—"

"What?"

"Brat!"

"Rich. Coming from a—" Jack stopped when he realized that arguing wasn't going to prove her wrong. Face red and temples throbbing, he whirled around, shouting an enraged—*Vaklas!*—that reverberated against the walls. Jack was beyond furious at the fact that he couldn't just walk away from this ridiculous fight. He needed to cool off. This wasn't the time to fall to anger. He knew that. Yet... Jack clenched his fists.

A bit crestfallen now that they weren't paying attention to him, Vidal cleared his throat and put on his best sage voice. "An opinion," he began, disregarding the full, combined force of their glares that they instantly shot his way, "is always worth a listen due to its uniqueness, but is overall worthless due to its nature."

They turned away again, finding each other's scowls more preferable. If his ego was less resilient, he might've been insulted.

"What? Never heard it? Well, not that I'd expect you to. I just made it up." Vidal laughed, as he watched them seethe. "Wow. Tough crowd. Alright, how about we begin with introductions? My name is Vidal Verne. I'm many things: a proprietor, an Elementalist, a Master, an auctioneer, a friend, even a husband. Pick what you like and feel free to classify me accordingly."

Vidal looked at them expectantly.

After a tense moment, Sylvie somehow managed to unclench her jaw enough to answer. "Sylvie Sirx." She met his gaze, trying to ignore the way his eyes promptly fell to the Heartstone hidden under her clothes. They hadn't seen another practitioner that could hear *her* since the Drowned Tower, so his scrutiny was beyond unnerving.

"And your companion?" Vidal asked.

"Jacques Dace," Sylvie answered, while Jack scowled and fixed his gaze on the wall.

"Big names." Vidal whistled, genuinely stirred. Those were monikers that rivalled his own. It had been a long time since he'd met practitioners of such import. "Let me guess, your fathers work in the Diamond Alps?"

"You know them?"

"Who doesn't? Don't you know that all high ranking men know each other? At one point, the three of us studied together under Master Kylle. Large class, though it was only Leonas I befriended." That caught Jack's attention because he finally turned to look at him again. Vidal pretended not to notice. "Kylle was an entertaining man. Excellent with ice and wind, but an absolute menace with fire. Singed my hair more times than I could count. But you aren't here for my stories, are you?"

Sylvie shook her head.

"You mentioned his mother." Vidal angled his head toward Jack. "What does Cheryll want from me? As you can see, I'm tangled up in my own affairs."

That provoked Jack. "Like selling children?"

"No. Well, yes. We buy them mostly. But it's not as bad as you're making it out to be."

"You... what?"

Vidal didn't answer immediately.

He opted instead to shut the door with his foot and click the lock into place, before grabbing himself a cupful of courage from the bottle on his desk. He was delighted to see that his papers remained undamaged. Vidal made a move to tidy them, but when Jack stomped over and Sylvie's forehead creased, he knew he'd kept them waiting long enough. They were impatient little things. He could see their parents in them.

"The Verne family is a wealthy one," Vidal said, never one to practice modesty. "That's no secret. Especially here in the Yovakine Plains. This is the middle of the world and boasts ground so fertile that anyone would be lucky to own land here. But lately, people only seem to come for the slave market. This auction house you're in now is the center of Yorn's. It isn't very big... yet. All of my contributors are small noble houses, but I'm working on attracting larger attention. I've been attempting to hammer a deal with one of the bigger dealers in Ferus Terria—the Fetters. But they're cautious, and rightfully so, I suppose."

"Wait," Sylvie muttered, disbelieving. She connected the gaps between his words. Her eyes widened more and more as the trickles of realization slowly dawned upon her. "So, you host a faux auction to make them believe there's a larger market here?"

"And buy their slaves in the process," he said, extremely pleased with himself. "I do sell the occasional Veld practitioner to infiltrate the bolder noble houses. I think that's what tipped the

Fetters off. Sell them a practitioner, then their house crumbles within the next few weeks? I should've been more careful."

"You free them then," Jack said, trying to take it all in.

"I hire a few as servants or messengers." Vidal shrugged. "The one's with nothing left to return to mostly. The rest are sent to their homes and those that don't want jobs are sent with Veld escorts to Heathe and Brantine."

An intricate mixture of relief and annoyance flooded Jack's veins. Vidal was irritatingly dramatic and—from the décor of his study—definitely had an ongoing obsession with his wife. But he could support his cause. Vidal seemed to understand his tacit concession because he smiled impishly.

Sylvie, on the other hand, sent him the smuggest look he'd ever seen. Jack pointedly ignored her. His eyes settled on the shield in the far corner of the room. He noticed again how imposing it was. Pure iron. The crest of the Verne family was dyed in red across its body. Like a bloody, blooming flower. It was definitely an heirloom. Jack doubted any average man would be able to carry it though. Let alone use it in battle.

"Do you like it?" Vidal asked, mistaking Jack's avoidant gaze for interest. "Her name is Valiance. The shield of the Red Veld. She once belonged to Arch Poten Haglynn Thareen's champion—and alleged lover. She caused quite the stir. Mistresses always do. Not that Valiance's previous owners matter. She's been passed to three dozen hands over the ages, and now she's mine."

"You dyed your family's crest on her," Sylvie commented.

"If she's going to belong to me, then I may as well leave my mark."

"I'm surprised no one stopped you."

"They certainly tried. But there are no explicit rules that say I can't enhance her to better suit my tastes."

"Don't you mean deface?"

"If by deface you mean beautify, then yes."

"Does she have a pair? Shields usually do."

"Ah, yes, Valor. He's in Monet's keeping."

"The blade you mean?" Jack asked, recalling its expensive sheathe. From the corner of his eye, he examined one of the near-by portraits of Monet. She held the sword like a butcher's cleaver. Her lips were curved down into an incomprehensible frown. Jack couldn't help but think that her features were too harsh when compared to the wilful smile of the man before him.

"So you've met?" Vidal asked, delighted. "How was she?"

"She seemed... exasperated," Jack said cautiously. He wasn't sure if the reason for her dour mood was him or the flood of refugees, but if asked, he'd definitely blame it on the latter. Vidal had a lethal mien that warned him not to press him too much. If nothing else, Jack trusted his instincts.

"You certainly know how to make a man want to run off, don't you? A trait that runs in your family it seems." Vidal's eyes lingered on the portraits along his walls. "I get awfully bored when she's not around. But as long as she's happy there, then I don't really care what happens."

There was a short lull in conversation, as they jointly stared at the portraits. Vidal looked as if he was going to speak, but Sylvie interrupted. She needed to finish asking her questions before he got tired of humoring them.

"Why'd you agree to this?" she asked. "Why not let someone from the Veld's Potentate Union go instead? Or did you just draw the short end of the stick?"

"I drew the longest," he said, smiling a fool's grin. "I'm not here because I lost, I'm here because I won. As you can see, this is a delicate matter. Those pesky Potens deemed only a select few suitable to carry out this task. Monet was among them. It wasn't much of a choice at that point. I couldn't let her come here. Monet, my heart, unfortunately lacks the necessary patience for such drawn-out tasks. Besides, I enjoy Yorn."

"In what way?"

"Some men dwell within forests, others under the sea. But I've always preferred urban cages. There's something about unnatural habitats that brings out the worst in people."

Vidal flashed them a winning smile.

They opened their mouths to continue their line of questions, but when his smile turned feral, they clamped them shut. Their teeth snapped audibly in the silence. It was so frightening that Sylvie completely lost her train of thought.

Vidal shot her a knowing look, irked that she'd interrupted him before. It was clear to her then that Vidal was the sort to bare everything out in the open. There was no second guessing with him. Vidal either liked you or he didn't. It reminded her of Jack. Without the temper issue. Well, almost. That Jack had a temper was obvious. Vidal, however, seemed easygoing at first glance, but his reactions were far more unpredictable, which easily made him the bigger problem.

"But that's a conversation for another time," Vidal went on, satisfied by their silence. "Why have you two come?"

They shared an uneasy glance. Monet had rejected them, but hopefully Vidal would be more open.

"How much do you know about the upcoming Summit?" Jack asked, holding Vidal's gaze.

"Exactly as much as I wish to—absolutely nothing. It doesn't hold my interest..." Vidal trailed off, his eyes shining in sudden realization. "Oh, let me guess, Cheryll wants me to convince Monet to back Leonas in the Summit?"

They nodded, then frowned when Vidal openly laughed. That didn't bode well for them.

"Since you've come to me, I assume my lovely wife said no," he said, amused. "Monet isn't the sort to be swayed by the pleas of men. Fortunate then that I'm no mere man."

"You'll help us then?" Sylvie asked.

"Not quite. As much as I'd like to make a nuisance of myself in the Veld, as I've said before, my hands are tied. Locating the headquarters of the infamous Fetters is more challenging than it seems. They cause all of these riots, traffic hundreds of slaves at any given time, and yet, no one knows where they keep them or from where they're procured."

"Have you interrogated one of their lackeys?"

"Thoroughly." Vidal sighed. "They were informative... for a time. I learned that the Fetters are divided into three jurisdictions, though how they divide Ferus Terria still remains a mystery. Their borders have been one of their most infuriating secrets. But I do know that they have one leader in-charge of each sector. They hardly ever interact with one another, save to exchange the occasional guard, so it's hard to pin their precise locations down. The pest wreaking havoc in the Plains seems to be the most candid of the lot."

"What else do you know about them?" Sylvie asked.

"Not much. One is a woman. The other, a man. The last— *nothing*. Smart, quiet, little bird."

"Are they practitioners?" Jack asked. "It could complicate things if one of them still has ties to the Institute."

"I don't even know that. There are rumors of course, but it would be foolish to trust them. I could point you in the direction of where they might be if you'd like to scout the areas for yourselves. I tried and came up short. But even if I was able to pinpoint exactly where they were, they have men with battle experience, while I only have practitioners lazy from peace. Oh, I'm sure Monet could lend me a good few, but it would be nowhere near the amount I'd need to stage a full-scale assault. Frankly, I'd be better off contracting mercenaries."

"Why don't you then?"

"Hiring the amount I'd need would be impossible without the entire underworld, the Alps, and anyone with an ear to the ground catching wind of it."

"Maybe we might be of help?" Jack offered.

"You?"

"Us," Sylvie affirmed.

"I suppose you want me to speak to Monet in exchange?" He stopped just long enough for them to nod. "While it's a nice offer, I don't see how two extra practitioners could be of much use."

Vidal paused when Sylvie dangled the pendant he'd been so

enamored with before him. It was a small, pretty thing. Not as eye-catching as his portraits, but still magnificent in its own right.

His eyes narrowed when something stirred within. It was followed by a chorus of incomprehensible voices that whispered to him in the silence. Vidal cocked his head to the side to better hear their secrets. He tried to discern that darker voice from all of the rest; the one he'd heard in the auction hall. Vidal distinctly recalled it being ancient enough to make his skin crawl, and he was *dying* to feel that sensation a second time.

Once the voices grew loud enough for him to pick apart, however, Sylvie tucked it back beneath her robes. They ceased immediately. Like howling children comforted by their mother.

Vidal blinked, then composed himself. "A Heartstone?" he asked, recognizing it after a moment's contemplation.

"*The* Heartstone," Jack corrected.

A pause.

Realization lit Vidal's features, before it was covered by a mask of solemnity. He'd heard the treasure mentioned in passing during his time in the Alps, though he never knew what they kept it for. Neither was he interested in the particulars of its origin. Vidal figured the stone was just another artifact that the Council kept because of its age, rather than it being of any particular import. Knowing those greedy loons, it was probably worth more than his and Monet's fortunes combined. But why did they have it? How did they get it? More importantly, what did it do?

As Vidal looked at the stone again, and then at the unusual blackness within Jack's eyes, he thought that perhaps they could be of some use after all. At the very least, they'd be able to sate his mounting curiosity. If Vidal was lucky, maybe he'd even get to hear that voice again.

Oh, he hoped so.

Opening his arms in the inflated manner he usually reserved for his stage, Vidal smiled. All of the color drained from their faces at the mere sight of it.

"Welcome to my show then, extras."

Reed,

Today was exhausting. I've done nothing but talk. About the stone, the Tower, a dozen other things. Yet I feel even more tired than when Jack insisted we sprint for a good hour across the Plains in the rain. (The pouring rain.) I know we had no shelter, but it wasn't like there was a village in sight then. But that isn't the point! The point is that Vidal Verne is the single most terrifying man I have ever had the displeasure of meeting. Oh, he's very smart and deceptively charming, but he's also borderline psychotic and unbearable and—

He just dropped by my room.

"Have a good night," he says.

Silas' flames! How can anyone have a good night knowing he's in the next room worshipping those portraits? Wait. Did he know I was talking about him? Maybe. I'm not going to risk it.

Until next time.

Sylvie Sirx 26.27.CA

***

Partner,

*I just had the longest, most excruciating day of my life speaking to Vidal-bleeding-Verne, and it wasn't even a lecture! If you don't know him or have never heard of him, then **good**. He has this annoying tendency to go off into tangents about his wife. Honestly, the man's been in Yorn so long, his wife probably doesn't even love him anymore.*

He told me a lot about his days in the Zenith Council—before he started running off and doing Thelarius only knows what—apparently he almost died from an allergic reaction to some unknown dessert my father made for him when they were younger. He asked me what it was, and if I'd try to poison him, too. Oh, like I have the time to bake things. The thing was apparently topped with Roco sauce. I told Sylvie only she could stomach that slop. But curses and hexes on all of these pesky Healers and embrocologists. Why can't people just stay dead?

Well, I don't completely hate the man. He does value his freedom and... forget it. I'm going to read that book by Dalis. I could use a laugh.

Jack 26.27.CA

12

Vidal was a scholar at heart.

Sylvie came to that conclusion while perusing the vast collection of books in the auctioneer's private library. Tomes sat, quiet and patient, filled with tales just waiting to be read—and read, she did. Sylvie mulled over everything from historical texts about the Yovakine Plains to autobiographies of the men that governed it. Vidal's library wasn't as large as the archives within the Tower, but it was cozy enough to pass as one.

The overburdened shelves were made of dark cherry-tinted wood that hinted at great expense; the chairs and tables were no different. Each sported meticulous engravings that blessed the library with an aura of luxury. Statuettes of ravens and owls were littered on top of furniture. They were carved into frightening and majestic poses, as if to warn others away from the books they stood over. In the far corner, stood rows of oddly shaped vials with even odder labels: *Sliced Moth, Newtweed, Caterpillar Legs*. All used for poisons no doubt. Sylvie knew little about the making and keeping of toxins, so she skipped that row in favor of the one below it that contained common ingredients for healing salves like *Dryvis Bitters, Tanged Moxie, Eriveen Stems,* and *Alicen Leaves*.

It wouldn't surprise her to learn that Vidal was a skilled embrocologist on top of everything else. With a background as stunning as his, nothing was impossible.

The library wasn't open to just anybody. Only those with permission from Vidal could enter. And despite the extravagance of the furniture within, Sylvie preferred the unforgiving coldness of the floor. The dark stones reminded her of softer times.

A mess of books and scrolls sat around her, encasing her with her thoughts. They'd been in Vidal's estate for a wearisome few days. Vidal filled them in on how Yorn ran and which families ran it; there weren't many. Two, in fact, and they squabbled endlessly. Their hate for each other left the city to be taken apart by other men. Those like Vidal and wealthier families from other cities.

Sylvie suddenly sighed. She rubbed her temples to ease the headache forming there. She'd been reading for the better part of the day, searching for clues about Silas Drayr, so she could confirm her lineage. An impossible task, she found, seeing as how most of the records from then were either long gone or reportedly kept in the north. Tiny footnotes at the bottom of each page included the title, volume, and even date of publication of the texts that the authors had gotten their information from. Their thoroughness was infuriating. Because here she was, hoping she could have their endless list of sources instead.

It wasn't long before she realized that the only books kept here were for public consumption, and most of them accounted tales she already knew.

Still, she read:

Wrapped in his solitude, the Creator decided to make animals that could speak—men, as we know them now. He shaped them into his likeness and gifted them the lands of the world, so that they could experience life and vigor; so that they could gain knowledge outside of his arms. It was in this way that the Creator lived a multitude of lives. Through his children, he felt pride, happiness, pleasure, and love. He no longer sat alone in his palace of infinity, and in his euphoria, he gave them more. Slips of magic bled from the ocean and the soil, tendrils of his divinity crept into the children who were faithful and true, who were generous with their blessings, who loved the deepest and the freest...

And it corrupted them.

Those that once adored peace grew deaf with power. Blinded by

*their own influence, they casted those unlike them aside and established
their own empire where they were the gods.*

That was the day the Creator experienced hate.

*Fearful and sickened by the blackness of their souls, the Creator left
them behind, granting them time to right their wrongs and come to their
senses. It was for naught, however, and when his tortured children,
those unfortunates that hadn't been touched by the light of his hands,
could no longer see past all of the terror and the blood, he decided to
intervene a final time.*

The Creator sent a champion.

*First Elementalist Thelarius Merve, a man of uncertain birth. His
exploits in the years that followed his rise to power earned him the title
of, Breaker of Chains, Redeemer of—*

Sylvie skimmed the rest.

It was an old story that she knew well enough to recite word
for word, though Sylvie had no doubt that it must've been told
very differently during the time of the Mentalists. That was the
problem with history, the stories always changed. They were too
dependent on the mindset of the people that wrote them.

Her gaze drifted to the stone that sat around her collar. Quiet
and peaceful. She supposed she could've asked *her* about the past
or even about the Fetters, but she wasn't exactly partial to the idea
of rousing *her* from slumber. Sylvie didn't want to risk sudden
asphyxiation. At least not until she had someone that knew how
to keep *her* at bay. But Jack was off wandering Yorn, traversing
the streets and peeking his head inside Vidal's auctions every so
often to jeer at the twisted man's obvious enjoyment.

Though they were confident they'd be able to help Vidal in
his task, neither had found anything concrete. Making friends
with the townspeople wasn't their strong suit, and in Jack's case,
neither was keeping his eyes hidden. But Rus hadn't come running down the halls to convey to her his woes, so Sylvie assumed
that Jack was at least trying to keep out of trouble.

Then, as if the world wanted to prove her wrong, she heard

Miran scream—*please! Oh, please!*—followed by Jack's vehement refusal and a string of colorful *íarre*.

So much for peace.

"They sound like they're having fun," Sylvie muttered to herself. "I wonder what Miran's asking for now?"

The girl seeks conversation.

Sylvie muffled a yelp with her hand. She looked carefully down at the Heartstone. The darkness stirred within. Though the bundle of wisps inside wasn't the same chaotic mess she usually found in Jack's eyes, so she took that as a good sign. Sylvie prodded it in caution. Her finger recoiled immediately when it swung to the left and back again. There was no change. No unexpected choking to speak of. Whatever it was seemed quite content to stay inside. But for how long?

"Hello." Sylvie paused, feeling silly for greeting a rock. But Jack had done it, so she supposed a few pleasantries from her would be perfectly all right. "… Did I wake you?"

There was no answer.

"Do you even sleep?" she went on with a nervous chuckle. But when the silence in the room continued, she sighed.

What did Jack say? Sylvie recalled their conversation before entering Yorn. *Just ask a question? Well, I did and got ignored. So, what now? Maybe my question wasn't good enough? Okay… let's try something better then.*

Sylvie nodded to herself. Maybe *she* was picky. Still, Sylvie found *her* newfound finickiness preferable to the disturbing way *she* constantly spoke out in the Tower.

"Do you know anything about the Fetters?"

When an answer finally came, Sylvie felt an immense wash of pride for successfully holding back her surprise.

Slavers of old. Larger, bolder then. They were destroyed by Thelarius and Silas during their time, although remnants remained. Their wills carried on, and the leftovers have been reunited by those once chained.

"Those once chained," she muttered, her mind racing. "Their

leaders are Nebbin then?"

They are lost imitations that aim to mimic an era long gone. An era they sought to rule. They stand against you. More than that, you need never know.

"Do you know where I can find them?"

Scattered across the lands of Ferus Terria.

"Well, that doesn't help at all."

Ages ago, they gathered in the slaver's pit. A tunnel of fire and ash. A fitting resting place. A fitting origin as well.

Sylvie frowned. She vaguely recalled *her* mentioning the city of slaves on their way to Yorn. Did *she* know they'd end up in Tor? Had *she* always known? Sylvie barely registered the echoes outside getting louder. They were coming closer. Oh, Jack would have her head for recklessly speaking to *her* without him. But that still didn't stop her from asking.

"Did you know we'd end up in Tor? Is there something you want there?"

Remnants of the past linger within the mines, scattered in the darkness. Where Thelarius was birthed, where Silas was lost, where friends sought solace.

Their final pieces remain hidden, still.

Come. I will show you the way.

"To my… lineage?"

To truth. To what you seek.

A trail of black tendrils shot out from the Heartstone, leading outside and into lands she'd only ever read about. Sylvie looked at the beckoning wisps, hesitant. They curled around her face, shifting too close for comfort, but they didn't try to hurt her. On the contrary, they were warm and inviting.

Sylvie gasped when the echoes of a hundred garbled voices entered her mind. She remembered Jack saying something about this—about the voices, the pain, the burning rush of power in his veins—she'd never forget the haunted look in his eyes then.

No! Sylvie mentally screamed, fingers pulling her hair and waiting for the pain to come. In her panic, she failed to notice that it never did. *I don't want—no, leave me alone!*

The voices ceased.

I shall not harm you, daughter of Silas. Nor do I seek to. Although previous instances might convince you otherwise, know that those were beyond my control. So long as you keep your magic turned my way, it will never happen again. We have no quarrel. Your gifts have always been yours to keep.

"What are you talking ab—"

Nothing your protector doesn't already have the answer to.

Her eyes widened, just as a pair of padded feet stilled outside of the door. The black trail disappeared, but she knew that if she called for it, it would return. She had plenty of time for that later though. For now, Sylvie cocked her head to the side, looking under the door at the frantic shadow and wondering who it could be. The stranger kept shuffling their feet, as if debating whether or not to enter. But when she heard another pair of footsteps, louder and faster, the door clicked open. The stranger's deliberation was clearly over.

Sylvie got on her knees, prepared to crawl behind one of the larger shelves in case Miran walked in. She stopped when only Jack slipped inside. He closed the door with as much softness as urgency allowed and pressed his back against it. His eyes flicked back and forth, fretful in a way entirely unlike him. As booming footfalls—Miran's, she assumed—grew closer, Jack's orbs finally settled on her. Alarm crossed his eyes, before it was replaced with suspicion.

Jack swiftly put one finger against his lips, afraid she'd give him away. Sylvie mimicked the motion, not wanting to be caught either. She failed to hide her smile when he sighed in relief. With a satisfied nod, he then pressed his ear to the door. Miran stopped before it, then shifted on the balls of her feet in consideration just like he had. Sylvie was sure Miran saw Jack's shadow from under the door, but luckily for him, Vidal's library wasn't a place for the uninvited.

"I know you're in there!" Miran said, infuriated. "I'll be back.

Just you wait!" She huffed and stalked down the hall, loudly saying something about permission and no escape.

Once her footsteps began to fade, Jack stuck his head outside to check how far she'd gotten. He smiled wickedly when Miran's back straightened with every creak of the door.

Oh, he couldn't resist.

"Vidal's hosting one of his auctions now," Jack called out to her. "You'll be waiting a *long* time, you little pest."

When Miran turned and charged at him, he slammed the door in her face with a smug grin. An agitated groan and a strong kick followed, before she stomped down the hall, still mumbling plans to herself. She was bold, but clearly not enough to chance angering her employer. Smart girl. Yet, by the time her voice faded, they already had a good idea of what she'd do—and what they could to avoid being caught.

"Good riddance," Jack said. "Flaming mule."

"Jack."

"What?" He raised his eyebrows at the disapproving frown on her face. "Oh, don't tell me you would've actually entertained her probing. I saw you trying to hide."

Well, he had her there.

"I didn't say anything," she defended, holding her hands up.

He gave her a deadpan stare that told her he knew what she was thinking. She avoided his gaze and eventually, he looked away. Jack ran frustrated hands through his hair. His fingers ghosted over the Orive crystal embedded there.

"I was minding my own business and here she comes like a bloody wraith, asking ten thousand questions about *everything*. And just when I thought that this day couldn't possibly get any worse, I saw a black trail. It led me here, but vanished as soon as I stepped inside. Know anything about that?"

She'd take Miran over this any day.

"I might," she said very slowly.

"Care to share or do I have to wait for common sense to catch up with you?"

Her eyes thinned into slits. She hated that tone, and he knew it. "Only if you share your secrets first."

Jack stopped to look at her contemplatively. As expected, she didn't back down from his gaze. It was foolish of him to think that after all of this time she would. His eyes drifted briefly to the Heartstone, silent and unhelpful. Sylvie seemed content to wait for him to speak, so Jack took his time. He walked closer and arrested her with his gaze. Neither of them moved.

When he finally did speak, his tone was harsh and critical. "I wonder which ones *she* told you about."

"So, you admit to having them."

"So, you admit to talking to *her*," he countered. They glared at each other for another age, before he sighed and fell to his haunches just outside of her wall of books. "Who doesn't have secrets? But speaking to her alone is dangerous. You know that."

Sylvie didn't respond. Excuses were for those that sought to lessen blame or avoid responsibility for their actions, she was neither. Sylvie could already imagine the line that would crease his brow if she answered with one.

"It was sudden," she said instead, struggling to explain. Her eyes locked with his. "*She* spoke so suddenly. I answered, though I know I shouldn't have. Speaking to her was… interesting."

Jack clicked his tongue, but didn't fault her for her curiosity. "Anything about the Fetters?" he asked.

She nodded, and he knew there was more, but he didn't push her. Sylvie respected his privacy when he didn't want to speak, it was only right that he did the same.

"They're in Tor. Well, actually the Pit… I think." She waved her hands when he didn't even try to keep the disgruntlement from his face. "She was vague about it!"

"The mines though?" he thought aloud. "There are a lot of slaves there, so it would make sense for their leaders to hole themselves close to where the market is. They'd just be another tree in the forest. But Vidal's been to Tor. He's been to the Pit, too, and he found nothing."

"You asked?"

"Obviously."

She frowned. "Well, from what *she* said, they might be inside the mines and not around it."

"Inside?" he repeated, taken aback. "With those fumes? You know they have to change out the miners every few hours, right? I'm surprised they haven't died down there."

"*She* seemed sure, and…" she trailed off, dropping her gaze in favor of drilling holes into the open books between them. Her fingers gripped her knees as she contemplated her next words.

"And?" he prompted.

"*She* wants us to go there."

"Go down the Pit?" Jack watched her nod. "Is *she* insane?"

Before she could continue her explanation, the voice spoke.

Where pieces of Thelarius lie, where Silas carries his secrets, where twisted men hide, she said. They stared at the stone in wonder, while the blackness within made itself apparent. *The slaver's pit is a place of answers written in ink already yellow from age. Answers that will lead this world into ruin. Answers that will fix your dilemma, yet thrust you into another with higher stakes.*

Still, you must go.

Silas' words belong only to those that carry his flame.

Sylvie and Jack shared a look.

It wasn't as if they could avoid going. Now that they knew the Fetters' base was situated there, they had little choice in the matter. They promised to help Vidal, and neither were willing to go back on it. Besides, the whole point of this journey was to shed light on the truth behind the stone and the First Zenith's past. They couldn't avoid the very place that could. No matter how much they wanted to.

But Sylvie still had to ask. "Why do you want us to go?"

I only wish to return.

"To where?" they asked in unison.

But the darkness vanished, taking the voice with it.

***

"You expect me to trust something so vague?"

"I know it's hard to believe, but—"

"No, I believe you," Vidal said with an amused smile. It was faint. Nothing more than an abrupt quirk of his mouth that steadily widened with Jack's growing aggravation. "Barely."

Jack's upper lip curled in distaste. He turned his head away to stare pensively at the wall before Vidal could see. Jack had a feeling that Vidal would only laugh at him for his blatant disdain. But when Vidal still did, despite his hidden face, he had no qualms about letting the sneer fully break free.

Jack had reiterated a few things to the older Elementalist, making sure to twist *her* words into something vaguer and never once telling him about what *she'd* done to help him and Sylvie in the Tower. Though Vidal probably saw through him anyway. He had an annoying look in his eyes throughout the conversation that said he did. Jack didn't trust his gaze. It was sly and shrewd and reminded him too much of the Elders from the north. Anything that even remotely reminded him of those manipulative codgers was never good. Jack kept those thoughts to himself, however. Far away from his mouth and his eyes.

"We'll head there first," Jack said. "You must need to gather a few men first, right?"

"You actually want to go?" Vidal asked. "I thought you were only here to rely the information. I suppose you have other business to attend to there?"

"Something like that." Jack shrugged. "I won't find freedom here in Yorn. I have to change my world a bit more before that."

"You have to change yourself first," Vidal advised. "Few are in a position high enough to free themselves from the binds of the Zenith Council. Fewer still, those able to roam the world without Hunters at their backs."

"Are you among them?"

Vidal pulled up the cloth of his pants in answer. It was just high enough that Jack could see the smooth skin of his ankles. Cocking his head to the side, Jack finally looked at Vidal like someone from his audience. He couldn't stop the smile that stretched his lips at the sight.

"That's a good look on you," Vidal said.

"No Demar spell," Jack muttered. His eyebrows pinched in thought. "Are you one of Arch Poten Verne's Potens?"

"Flames, no!" Vidal said, aghast. "Monet is wound tighter than a coil. She would've never even considered me if I worked unde—no. Just no. I... how to put it? I denied the spell."

"You *denied* the spell?" Jack repeated, shocked. "What? Just like that? A simple *'no'* was enough?"

"They were angry, but they were fools to think I'd agree to it in the first place. I'm a formally recognized Master of the Alps, not the Veld. The only reason I chose to remain in the south was for Monet. They can't order me around, and I won't submit to having such unreasonable chains placed upon me. Oh, they could try to punish me for that, but it would be a ceaseless struggle, I assure you. The Institute's rules have never once interested me, and I doubt they ever will."

Vidal turned to Sylvie then, bored of Jack's impressed gape. She sat on the floor off to the side with books from his private collection piled high around her like sentinels of paper and ink.

"That little thing around your neck does have its perks, doesn't it?" Vidal said, trying to catch her attention with his voice alone. "A shame *she* refuses to speak in my presence. Does *she* not like me?"

"A fair assumption," Sylvie said without thinking.

As soon as the words left her mouth, her back straightened and her jaw dropped. Disbelief kept her voice firmly locked in her throat, as the pair laughed at her expense. She cleared her throat, trying to grab their attention. To no avail. They weren't planning on stopping anytime soon.

"I didn't mean that," Sylvie said urgently, failing to keep her voice level. "What I meant was, 'I don't know *her* preferences.'"

Jack waved her off. "We all know what you meant."

"And I'm thrilled by it." Vidal smiled. "Thrilled!"

Sylvie grumbled something under her breath, but didn't attempt to dissuade them. She returned to her book with forced focus, barely registering Jack walking over and peering down at it. It was old and falling apart. Jack blanched when he realized it covered the Battle of Yovakine, a bloody fight that ended with a sea of fire engulfing friend and foe alike. It was what sealed Silas' name as the strongest Conjurer of his time.

He'd never been particularly interested in the topic... or history in general. But he could see why she'd want to go over it again. Hopefully she found something.

Jack turned back to Vidal. "We'll be heading out soon."

"I'll leave scouting the area to the two of you then," Vidal said easily, his posture confident.

"Are you sure about that?" Jack asked, smirking. "By the time you get there, there won't be any work left for you to do."

Vidal only laughed in response.

Monet,

Forgive the lateness! A thousand and seven apologies, my heart. I assure you that the outrageous runner you sent this missive with has been dealt with accordingly—fired, just so we're clear. I'd never do anything to harm the poor boy. And by fired, of course I don't mean with my flames. Not exactly.

But let's not dwell on such banal matters. Really, it's been so long since you've written. I thought you might've forgotten about me. Though I do believe you accidentally left out the part where you beg me to come home because you miss me oh, so much. Rest assured, I'll still arrive with gifts and fifty dozen daisies, and oh, a carriage! In typical noble fashion. It's okay though. I forgive you for your embarrassment. I'd be embarrassed (and extremely pleased) to read something like that as well. Strange, how some families raise their children to be so coy, wouldn't you agree? I'll try my best to find a decent horse rider.

In other news, I've met the unlikely pair. They're... interesting. Truly. They're after answers to questions that they don't even know how to word. I've agreed to help them after this slaver business has been seen to. I've been bored recently, so it's just as well.

And of course I won't bring the Veld into my affairs! Honestly, I was planning to. But you know I've never been skilled at refusing you anything, so consider the idea scrapped and in cinders. Happy you wrote to me now, aren't you? I do wish you did so more often. Demanding you give me more attention than those Union dogs is my favorite part of the day. If you neglect me too much, I may just have to come see you for myself. Oh, what a delightful idea! I think I'll do that. Soon. Once things calm a bit more here. It seems like things are finally moving along actually. Those two are quite helpful. Wild. Very talented. But just as young and prickly to offset it. I admire their tenacity.

I've been waiting for something interesting to come along and the suddenness of their actions is causing quite the stir in me. I'm going to move soon. You'll feel the ripples, I'm sure. So, prepare accordingly. They have a, how to say, well-informed companion with them. If what they've told me about their companion is true, then things are going to change. Soon. I'll return before they do.

Vidal 36.27.CA

13

Pain had the power to bend time, fueling eternity to make the mere act of breathing seem utterly unbearable. The taste of copper on Tiv's tongue had become as familiar as the scent of iron that surrounded him. But at least it wasn't dark. There was a little window high above his head, allowing light and rain to filter through his new cell every morning. It wasn't strong, but it was relentless. Come midday, the part of his cell nearest the window would be besieged by puddles. The water wasn't cool or soothing unfortunately. It was filled with heat. It dampened the air and made the world around him heavier than he thought possible.

The rain always started after a set of bells in the distance pealed, signaling the arrival of another day. Tiv had learned how to tell time by those bells and by how long it took for his blood on the floor to dry. Though it was getting hard to tell which stains were fresh and which were just damp because of the flood.

He hadn't been returned to his previous prison, but he didn't doubt that he would be. Soon. After they broke him, perhaps? Fat chance. But then he recalled the memory of himself sobbing two nights ago, and he bit his bottom lip in doubt.

Tiv counted the links between his cuffs again. The soggy squish of his rags kept him alert, as he waited for those bells to ring and grace him with the promise of water, assuring him that time was, indeed, passing.

He was alive.

Tiv looked up, seeing the outside world through his little window. It was right there. Just out of his reach. His one good eye twitched in anticipation, the other was swelled shut beneath an angry bruise. A memento from yesterday's beating. If he ever escaped, he'd be sure to appreciate the little things more. Like fresh air, clean clothes, hot meals, and… and…

When, Tiv thought, harshly correcting himself. *When I escape.*

The door to his cell creaked open. He didn't struggle against his chains or snarl at the pitiless woman just beyond the bars, as she assessed his state. She was flanked by two guards. Both as tall and proud as he'd once been. Behind her, Rat stood with his head bowed, nursing a tray full of bread in his hands. There were three small loaves arranged neatly on top of each other. Even from his position, Tiv could tell that they were stale. But it was still three more loaves than he'd expected.

If he ever received a blessing down here. That was it.

"You're awake," she said, pleased. "You're a tough one." She turned to the man on her left. He was scruffy and heavy from age, but he looked solid enough. The kind able to put up an ample fight, especially against starved prisoners and children. "Where did you say this one was from again?"

"We caught him in the Surbug Mire, Mistress."

"Wonderful. Just wonderful. Go back and see if you can find more. I've never met an Amorph so resilient. Do you think he came from the east? I hear the Tower trains the best Amorphs."

"I'm not sure." The man swallowed thickly when her eyes thinned in impatience. "It's possible, Mistress."

"What are you still doing here then? Go and find me some more homeless little birds. Go! Go!"

The guard flinched. He shared an apprehensive glance with his companion, who jutted his chin urgently, before scurrying away. His armor rattled as he made his way down the hall, and only when the noises ceased, did the woman turn back to him. Delight burned in her soulless eyes. Tiv glowered in contempt at the sight. But his scornful expression was lost in his beaten state. He was reminded again that, for the moment, he was all bark. No better than the spineless guards she kept around. All scared of her for reasons beyond his own admittedly limited knowledge.

"As if we'd bow that easily," Tiv said vehemently. It was no-thing more than a strained whisper, but the room was quiet enough for his words to carry.

"He talks!" she exclaimed, gaping at him. She stood like that for a good minute, pure disbelief on her face, before it was repl-aced by a furious snarl.

She whirled on her remaining guard and grabbed the start-led man by the back of his neck to shove his face into the bars, forcing him to look at Tiv. The man flailed. He scrunched his eyes against the cool iron, and even in his sorry state, Tiv pitied him.

"He's talking, yet you tell me you haven't gotten anything from him? Douse him in boiling water. Take out his teeth. Guillotine his tongue. You know I *hate* it when they talk."

There was panic in the man's eyes. Anger, too. But even that was stunted by fear. "Yes, Mistress!" the guard blurted out.

The Mistress seemed to be in a forgiving mood because she released him in an instant. She shook her hand out in open disg-ust, as the guard crumpled to the ground. He rubbed his abused neck, trying not to let his armor weigh him down. Then, she rose with her chin high and her nostrils flaring. There was nothing but calculation in her gaze.

Tiv squared his jaw and did his best to mimic her expression, still as obstinate as he'd always been. The pain he felt was lost to the throbbing in his veins. Mutual threats hung in the air between them, but they remained unsaid. Even as the woman turned to leave, shutting him away with his ignorance. With his sorry sem-blance of peace. Just what did they want from him?

Her guard was quick to follow her out, no doubt already planning on dumping Tiv's next torture session on someone else; someone with a more pronounced sadistic streak. Thelarius knew Ferus Terria had no short supply of them. Just the thought of another beating had him shrinking around the neck and shou-lders. He could only thank what was left of his meager luck that hardly anyone was there to see his moment of weakness. He didn't think he could stand seeing his captors' chests swell with pride when they realized just how terrified he really was.

Tiv didn't even know what they were after in the first place. But contrary to the Mistress' words about removing his tongue, they were doubtlessly waiting for him to spill whatever secret they thought he had because if they intended to just sell him off, then he was sure he'd fetch a far better price if he was able to stand on his own two feet. Or maybe they just liked prodding people with hotrods and beating them until they choked on their own blood? It certainly seemed like it. His captors always had these disturbingly large grins on their faces. The kind meant to break. He wouldn't though.

He wouldn't.

... But even he didn't fully believe that.

The clang of a tray brought him back to his senses. His head snapped up to find Rat behind bars—no... no, that was him.

Rat lingered outside.

He opened the tiny gate and slid the tray inside. It splashed along a particularly deep puddle, wetting Tiv's knee. Not that it mattered. It was still damp from before. Though the water was colder than he expected, and he jolted away out of reflex, only to fall still again a moment after. It hurt to move.

"Sorry," Rat whispered, as if that helped. But he did look genuinely remorseful about it. Tiv couldn't get angry at the only kindness he'd ever received in this place.

"Why are you here?" he asked, bowing his head because he couldn't look at his kind face anymore. The crow's feet along his one good eye spoke too much of laughter. There was nothing humorous about this place.

"To bring you food," Rat said, looking at him as if he'd gone mad. "Some of the others have been whisked away already. I thought you'd like their share. A man can't live on water."

"And that woman just let you?" Tiv's eyes narrowed in distrust, but he didn't bother looking up at Rat again.

Rat didn't answer.

Tiv knew better than to think he would. Rat was stalwart in his silence. His time in his previous cell was proof of that. But he wasn't going to ask why he was suddenly talking to him again. There were more important things on his mind. Like food. Tiv stared unabashedly at the tray, stifling a wet cough and failing to keep his hands from twitching in want. He hadn't eaten anything substantial in days. When they did feed him, it was usually some uncooked blend of dry oats and... the unknown. He was sure they mixed in chicken feed once though. Tiv knew because one of the farmers in Thyme had once given him a handful of pellets to toss at his brood. If he was nothing more than a farm animal, then they weren't doing a very good job of fattening him up.

"Who was sold?" Tiv asked.

"The twins."

"And?"

"No one else."

"There are three loaves here."

"Ah," Rat paused, his lower lip jutted out in thought. He opened his mouth to speak but no words escaped him.

Was breaking him with curiosity another kind of torture? Now, that was a first. But if the last person wasn't sold, then the logical conclusion was death. Roval instantly came to mind. He was already half-gone when Tiv was taken away. But Tiv didn't want to believe that just yet. Later, maybe. When Rat left and night fell, so his shadow was gone, too. No witnesses to see him sulk. For now, he entertained the death of others. Tiv cracked a smile at how twisted that seemed, though it was better than just mindlessly staring at Rat. Because the deformed man always, *always* stared back.

The red-headed Elementalist was also shoulder-deep in her grave the last time he'd seen her. Delirious for half of the day and asleep for the rest. Maybe she'd given up on trying. Or maybe that young man found the courage to use his chains to strangle that criminal with the nasty smile. Doubtful, but not impossible. Never impossible. It would be so easy, too. That maniac always slept against their cell's shared bars, his arms outstretched as if he wanted to embrace the boy. Disgusting swine.

"Aren't you going to eat?" Rat asked, snapping him from his thoughts. "Or would you like me to leave first?"

He caught on quick. But clearly not enough to just leave without speaking. Though Tiv liked that part of him. It gave him more time for questions. His stomach could wait. It had for a while now. Surely, just a moment or two longer.

"Do you treat all your merchandise so harshly?" Tiv asked. "Or only the practitioners?"

"Merchandise?" Rat cocked his head in confusion. "Oh, you thought, well, I see why you would, but no. *Nonono.*" He lowered his voice to a whisper. "The Mistress doesn't sell in the preferred trade of the rest of the organization. She stores. Though she does partake in the wares when something interesting comes along."

Partake? Tiv thought, the curiosity in his eyes vanished for a more dangerous opaqueness. That would certainly explain a lot of things: why they were treated so poorly in comparison; why only they were beaten. There was so much to be learned from practitioners. Tiv didn't doubt that. Maybe she wanted to know the secret behind their magic, though as far as he knew, it was already common knowledge that magic had none. You were either born with a magic circuit or you weren't. So, despite the glint in her eyes that made them shine like copper coins, she was still and would always be a Nebbin.

So, what does she want to know? Tiv wondered. *And why?*

"Does shifting hurt?" Rat suddenly asked.

Tiv blinked dumbly, before the question registered and he looked at Rat in apprehension. "...Why?"

"I was just curious."

"No, it doesn't."

"Ah." Rat nodded, nonchalant. "How do you do it?"

Tiv reeled back. He rolled the words around his tongue, deliberating. "I've always done it. It comes naturally."

"No, I mea—"

"Rat!" someone called from outside. Gruff and all sorts of impatient. "Time to feed the prisoners."

"I'll be back," Rat promised, already turning away. But before he left, he said, "That boy you were with. He's alive."

Tiv's head snapped up in disbelief. Both Roval's mind and body were patched together by little more than a prayer last he'd seen him. But when had Rat—good, kind Rat—who fed, clothed, and mended his wounds ever lied to him?

Tiv curved over himself, hunkering down with his head between his knees. He brought his six links of chain up and twined his hair around his fingers in a circular motion, thinking, trying to calm himself enough to do so.

"What's wrong?" Rat went on, his voice was sooty. Unhappy beyond words. "Don't you trust me?"

Tiv looked up.

He did! Oh, he did.

His eyes must've mirrored what he felt because the corners of Rat's mouth curved up enough to show his teeth. Then the door creaked shut, leaving him to his pondering. Made much more interesting now that the obvious choice of whose bread he was about to eat was gone. Even though it hurt, he smiled. A bloody, passionate smile that showed too much teeth.

Roval was alive.

He wasn't going to die here; he wasn't going to break. Because if no one else, Roval was counting on him. He'd either break free or wait for help. Whichever came first. Preferably the one that gave him the best chance of slaying that woman playing god.

Sometime after Rat had gone and he finished his meal, a new man came through the door. The underside of his fingernails were black and his clothes were heavily torn from negligence. His face was wet, suggesting a recent wash, but to Tiv, it looked as if he'd scrubbed his face with oil. Maybe he did it for a religious ritual of some sort. From what he'd seen of the men that the mistress employed, the idea wasn't too far-fetched.

They were all loons.

The man's lips curved upward, feral and ominous, with a promise of unpleasantness to come. But Tiv only smiled back. A demented smile that gave the newcomer pause. The pail of boiling water that the man carried fell dreadfully still as he regarded Tiv with newfound curiosity.

Not yet.

Tiv closed his eyes in a mix of acceptance and preparation. He pictured Roval waiting for him in his lonely little cell, so they could leave this place together.

I can't rest yet.

No matter how much he wanted to.

Father,

It's been weeks, and I've yet to hear anything from Sylvie. Nothing. Not a note or even a single word from her or from the few friends that I have there. I'm getting worried.

I have friends with relatives stationed in the Drowned Tower. Some have responded to the messages they've sent, although most haven't. But at least I know there are survivors. If she was okay, then she would've sent a message by now.

*Rumors about slavers acquiring new practitioners have spread to Wyvin. It's making the others antsy. It's making **me** antsy.*

You may hear things in the coming weeks about the Grove (and about me in particular.) I assure you that I know what I'm doing and that I plan to take full responsibility for my actions when the time comes, so don't worry about me. There's no reason to fuss. Absolutely none.

I pray this reaches you safely.

Dalis Sirx 28.27.CA

14

They were watching him again.

Dalis felt their eyes slink across his skin, over his worn leathers and sweaty face, as if he was the strange one. He ignored their stares, long used to them by now. The torpid passage of days had guaranteed that. Still, it was unnerving. His body reminded him of that when he couldn't quite find it in himself to lean comfortably against his seat.

They did the same thing when he'd first arrived in their small backwater village, at the end of his wits and out of coin. '*Hermit's Hovel*' they called it, with the sort of smile he only saw on children and the embalmed. They welcomed him with open arms; they were kind-hearted folk, despite their persistent glances. Though they did talk about him behind his back, sometimes even to his face. Not in a demeaning way. Because apparently that was possible. They said it the way a grandmother would when looking upon her misbehaving grandson. Full of understanding. It was terribly disturbing.

But even if he didn't exactly hate it, he couldn't stay.

Dalis had somewhere to be, as all men did these days. He couldn't afford to waste any more time here. He'd already spent too long and too much in the last two settlements. Gathering information, he told himself. But deep down, he knew that he'd simply grown tired of his search. There were no slavers here. The rumors were the over exaggerations of a coward, and the packed caravans were a lie. But he couldn't turn back. Not yet. Master Rhone would have his head if he came back with nothing to show for his absence. Thankfully, he was proven wrong, and by a smelly vagrant no less. The drunkard laid flat across a garbage heap outside of the Hovel's local tavern.

With the help of a little unfriendly persuasion, the bum warned him of a group of slavers that sometimes dealt in practitioners. Torture them, too, or so he murmured with that atrocious look of fear clotting his voice. Dalis didn't trust his words. Who would trust the stammers of a man with a knife against his throat? But cowards weren't known for their lying tongues, and that drifter was undoubtedly a coward.

The vagrant sputtered one name—the *She's Disciples*—before Dalis knocked him out cold. Now, the only problem was finding them. Dalis could go whenever he pleased, but with little money and not enough food, leaving without a specific destination wasn't the smartest move.

A waitress approached him with a bottle of his favored poison balanced atop her tray. She was the same one that came to him every night when he'd leave his leaky hostel room for an extra sip of wine. She knew his drinking habits well enough by now to leave the bottle and scurry away. Dalis wasn't one for idle chatter, neither did he touch the food, despite his grumbling stomach. His diet of wine would kill him one day, he mused, but he still found it preferable to what the local markets had to offer.

Despite growing up in a place as isolated as the Weeping Grove, he considered himself well-traveled. But he'd never seen food quite like theirs before. Sticks dipped in water and mush that they called oats. It didn't look like any oats he'd ever seen. The sticks that were haphazardly mixed in were brown, thin, and horribly unappetizing. There was no other food on this side of Ferus Terria, or so they claimed. Dalis didn't believe them. The ruined city of Purine had strived here for centuries, and they were known for their agriculture.

The townsfolk seemed to wholeheartedly believe their false lore, however, so he didn't dare say anything on the subject. But he couldn't help but think that his peers in the Grove would never believe this. Dalis didn't know why they secluded themselves in the so-called, *'wasteland of Ferus Terria.'* This place was a mess. He wanted nothing to do with anything here. That included the people.

As if to spite him, a man dropped gracelessly into the empty seat across from him. The man looked like a drowned rat. His hair was an oily mess with a stump for a nose and a livid scar sealing one of his eyes, rendering him half-blind. But that didn't stop his one good orb from shining audaciously in the gloom.

"Dalis Sirx," he rolled the name on his tongue. His voice was a harsh and guttural thing, as if he wasn't used to speaking. "You the outsider everyone keeps yakking on about?"

"That depends," Dalis replied, leaning back in his seat. The man eyed his blue eyes curiously. "What kind of things have you been hearing?"

"Only the good kind." The stranger shook his head and cast a sidelong glance at the group of young, lovely women lingering by the door. Something dark and envious crossed his face, before it was covered by a smile that didn't quite reach his eyes. "Around here, I go by Larce Adannes."

He offered his hand.

Dalis didn't take it. His mind ran instead, dwelling over the strange greeting. Dalis wondered what he happened to go by elsewhere. "What brings you here, Adannes?"

"Larce," he corrected, then dropped his voice to a whisper, "I hear you've been searching for slavers."

Dalis' fingers flexed under the table. "And where did you hear that?" The animosity in his voice was clear.

"Here and there." Larce showed him his teeth, yellow and rotting. All false helpfulness. He wiggled his fingers and urged him to shake. "You know what they say, everyone always has at least one rumor following them... or was it that everyone is following a rumor? It's been so long since I've heard it. In any case, it just so happens that I'm following yours."

Larce's grin was beginning to scare him. Dalis grasped his

hand all the same. It was small and bony. Just like the rest of him. He was clearly malnourished. Perhaps the dread he felt just came from the fact that he wasn't used to being smiled at by someone like him. Dalis didn't discount the possibility.

"So," Dalis began, "what can you tell me about the rumors *I'm* following?"

"Not much. There aren't any slavers here. But your eyes look like they'd be worth a coin or two. So, you should go, befo—"

"Stop crowding!" the innkeeper yelled, drowning out the rest of Larce's whisper. The fat man shooed away the women by the door with a bottle. An awful sneer marred his lips. "Kids," he grumbled, "they see one handsome man and they come in droves. Squealing little slops."

Dalis didn't bother listening to the rest of his tirade. He turned back, only to find Larce already standing.

"Wait," Dalis called, but he ignored him. Larce ran outside. His good eye was wide in its socket, seemingly troubled.

One of the girls that had been eyeing him suddenly yelled at the top of her lungs. "Mistress!"

The girlish shriek attracted the attention of the rest in the inn, and soon enough, they were all shoving their way outside. Even the small bartender that Dalis had never seen leave his domain jumped over the counter to squeeze between the larger men.

When all had gone, screaming and kicking their way out, he was left with silence. Wordlessly, Dalis raised his glass. His reflection on the empty bottle toasted him in his isolation.

Dalis smiled, as he downed his drink. He had a feeling that he was about to find what he'd been seeking. The timing of Larce's sudden appearance was no coincidence, and by the time his feet met the inn's porch, he wasn't disappointed.

No slavers? he guffawed at the lie.

The prison carts that followed the woman said otherwise.

They were practically paraded down the streets. The people inside were chained, wide-eyed, and dirty. They were too far for him to see their eyes, but he assumed they were Nebbin. Not that anyone noticed. They kept their attention on the woman, and really, he didn't blame them. She was stunning. Her gaze swept over the crowd, and he made sure to hide in the shadows of the inn's porch.

She's Disciples, he thought, as they continued on their way. *Probably off to sort their wares.*

He eyed each captive, but even if the one he was searching for wasn't there, he'd still free them. His principles demanded it. But… not now. First, he needed to return to his group. They were camped deep inside the marsh, and vocal enough to let him know just how unhappy they were with the arrangement.

Dalis saw Larce follow the woman. Briefly, he watched the ratty man turn and wave in his direction. His smile was a little more thrilled than before, his good eye alight with mirth, as he gestured absurdly at the enchanting figure disappearing down the road, before frolicking behind her.

Frolicking. Like some sort of woodland fairy.

Dalis rolled his eyes.

The crowd trailed behind the carts, uncaring for the startled people within and seemingly unaffected by the blistering heat. Being this close to the Narrow Marsh made for hellish mornings. Dalis envied their tolerance. The useless clouds drifted along the edge of the horizon, uncaring for those baking beneath the sun. It was a beautiful day, although overly so. The kind of beautiful that he just had to grumble about, since responsibility loomed over him like the tall shadow of a disappointed parent.

Dalis came here for a reason, and he'd be damned if he returned empty-handed. After the stormy exit he'd made when he left the Grove, he had no doubt that his peers would ridicule him should he return with nothing to show for it. But really, could they blame him for being upset? After news of the Tower's destruction crossed the Wymeran River, he'd been shocked, worried, and—finally—angry. His anger only heightened when he heard his peers gossiping about the sudden spike of practitioners in the slave markets.

Dalis waited for weeks. He pestered their couriers for letters every chance he got. After receiving a grand total of seventeen missives, all varying in length, with none of them from his sister, he couldn't wait any longer. Apprehension clawed at him. So, he set out with those that shared his desire to search for their lost relatives from the Tower. Their exit had been anything but quiet. He distinctly recalled a Master knocking one of his unsuspecting friends in the head with a tome thicker than his torso.

The Potentate Union acted as if they'd never return. They weren't fools; they knew better than anyone the consequences of deserting.

Soon, Dalis thought, unclenching his fists. He'd definitely return soon. He just needed a little more time.

Turning, he found a group of people seated on the edge of a stone fountain. It was a simple thing, placed right in the middle of the town square. Much too artless for a centerpiece, but the town was poor enough that it looked halfway decent. Tin cups were attached to chains embedded near the fountains spout.

It doubles as a waterhole, he realized.

A little boy scooped a cupful. He brought it to his chapped lips like a starving man unearthing moldy bread. Dalis stared at the stray droplet that trickled down the boy's throat. By the time the boy drained the cup dry, he was panting from exertion. As if the act of drinking was a chore in itself. It certainly looked it. His face was more contorted than before.

Then, like he knew he was being watched, the boy faced him. He cocked his head to the side, curious and fearful of his much larger presence. Dalis doubted he'd grow up to be as big as him — and he pitied him for it. Pitied all of them.

***

Dalis followed their convoy to a large estate just outside of the Hovel. It was an old building with high arches and deadly points on top of its gates. The kind used to pike heads on. Square pillars of rock and dirt rose unnaturally from the ground. As if a practitioner had come through and decided to raise the floor for no other reason than to display his power. Because the longer Dalis looked, the more he realized that there was no particular order or reason for them. Were they remnants from a fight or just another strange decoration? It was likely the former, but he couldn't be certain.

He found no symbols that could tell him of their allegiance. But he did see Larce. The man shrugged on a hood and led the cart pullers to another entrance off to the side, while the Mistress disappeared through the main gate without a word.

There was something about the way they handled the prisoners. An arrogance that Dalis didn't fail to notice. Their caravans had no locks, as if they fully expected them to comply. Desperation was good, but fear was better. He wondered how many had tried to escape with their hands and feet bound only to end up pierced in the collar or impaled with a sword and left to bleed out on the side of the road as the others watched. From the terror in the prisoners' eyes, probably one too many.

Dalis blended with the shadows just outside of the gates for a good half hour. Foliage obstructed his view of key areas. He groaned in annoyance at that. Shifting on the balls of his feet, he squinted at a shadowy corner where a rock path was hidden. Dalis could just make out a row of warehouses at its end.

Is that where they keep the slaves?

The sudden, almost joyful ring of manacles was as distinct as the cry of cicadas in the bushes. He scowled when he heard someone yell: *'Gentle with the merchandise, you cob-headed idiot!'* Dalis couldn't decide if it was a good thing that the slaves weren't kept here for personal use or awful for that very same reason.

So, they're being stored here? Dalis thought, leaning closer and trying to hear more. *For who?*

He reeled back when two men rounded the corner. Their voices were louder than drunkards arguing about politics.

"Have you seen the Amorph yet?" one asked. He had a distant look in his eyes.

"The one the Mistress brought to the inner chambers?"

"That's the one!" he exclaimed. "Tough little shit. He's worse than the Elementalist. Are all practitioners so bloody resilient?

"Well, the kid seemed normal."

"Good point. But he was a kid, so that's moot. I bet they go through some kind of torture training."

"Think the Mistress'll stuff him?"

"The Amorph? Who knows? I'm going to make that bloody cyst scream today," he said, determined. "I don't care what the others say, it's possible. You'll see."

"What I can't believe is how many of them she goes through. It's ridiculous. I mean, is there even a secret to their shifting? I'm sure we would've found out by now if there was."

"Well, it isn't natural, I can tell you that."

Dalis listened to their boasting until their voices were muted behind a door. His curiosity was more than a little piqued. So, their Mistress was interested in Amorphs? For what purpose? He sighed, wishing he could've followed them. But the sun was still out and there weren't enough shadows for him to blend into. Not for the first time, he wished he could transform into a bird or a fly. It was just so convenient.

Now that he thought about it, that was probably why the woman was so interested in their abilities in the first place. But a Nebbin developing magic? It was unheard of.

He looked back at the warehouses. The doors weren't sealed, but guards did patrol the area. They came and went at seemingly random intervals. No noises came from within, so their captives were obviously well-behaved. It shouldn't have surprised him that they kept practitioners here, but he didn't want to believe it.

Dalis clenched his fists. They needed to clean this place out. Soon. He didn't know if he should hope that they had a few eastern practitioners or not, but he didn't dwell on it. His gaze drifted to the entrance of the estate. No guards. It was almost too easy. But he couldn't storm this place on his own. He needed to return.

Just as he thought it, someone gripped his shoulder.

Dalis instinctively reached for his dagger. Only for the newcomer to raise his palm in the area over its hilt to silently prevent him from drawing. Dalis was deathly still, unable to look at the newcomer's face. Not even when the stranger stepped back with both arms raised in apologetic surrender.

"No harm," the stranger said. "I didn't mean to startle you."

Dalis didn't believe that. But he swallowed his uncertainties, along with the string of colorful invective that sat fresh on his tongue. His fingers never left the dagger's hilt. Still wary, still ready to draw. What a violent Healer he made.

He lifted his head to find Larce standing there with a worried expression crooking his face. "You shouldn't be here," Larce said, pacing frantically. "Oh, *nonononono*... the Mistress will be angry. Very, very angry."

"Calm down." Dalis warily eyed their surroundings. "What are you doing here?"

"Me? Why, I'm in charge of," he stopped, looked at him, and then shook his head. "You shouldn't be here. You must go! She'll find you, and we—she has no use for Healers."

"What?"

"Go!" Larce pushed him away with more strength than his decrepit body suggested. But it still wasn't enough to move him.

"There are slaves in there," Dalis hissed, then seized Larce's wrist. He coiled in on himself immediately, as if afraid he'd be beaten. Dalis had to hand it to him, he knew how to make him feel terrible for a thoughtless action. "I want to set them free."

"Free," Larce repeated, dumbfounded for all of a second, before he shook his head again. "*Nonono,* you must go. Leave this place. Return to your companions in the marsh."

How did he... Dalis' eyes narrowed into slits, though Larce didn't seem to notice. He didn't need to think twice.

Before Larce could react, Dalis drew his dagger and knocked him twice on the back of the head. Larce's voice died in his throat, as he crumpled to the ground. Dalis grimaced at the thought of having to drag him all the way back to the Narrow Marsh, but it was better than letting him roam here with the knowledge that he and his group were near. He only hoped that no one noticed Larce's absence, before they could figure out a way to break into the estate.

***

Tiv could hear himself breathe. That scared him.

It wasn't the steady breaths of the healthy or the heavy whee-zes of the fatigued. No, this was different. This was thick, sloppy noise. Every time he inhaled, he heard the wet gurgle of his throat groaning in protest. Each swallow was pain. Tiv was afraid of coughing because he just knew he'd hack up a lung if he did. Judging by all of the blood and saliva that he spattered over his clothes whenever he opened his mouth more than a fraction, he didn't think that idea was too far-fetched.

His feet were crusted with blood; a consequence of the beat-ing he received today. They'd been getting progressively worse. But the worst by far would have to be when that vile woman sat in for a ringside seat. She didn't look entertained—he could only thank whatever god was still on his side for that—but calculating. The Mistress stared at him like she was trying to figure something out. It didn't help that they seemed to be beating him for no reason. Couldn't they at least tell him what they wanted? Or was breaking him first really so high on their list of priorities? When did beatings come before demands anyway? Stupid Nebbin.

He bit his tongue throughout each session only because he was afraid that if he opened his mouth, then the agony would overcome his senses and he'd scream. Tiv wouldn't give them the satisfaction. He hadn't so far. That was the only thing he could be proud of now.

Tiv wiggled his left hand and flinched at the three fingers that remained. He didn't even attempt to move the right, as he turned to look up at the darkening sky. It would rain soon. He'd stopped counting the days some time ago. Not out of his own volition, but because the state his captors left him in always made him blissfully unaware of everything. Like the pealing bells in the distance or the glass droplets he once adored. Recently, he was always tethering on the edge of blacking out. Once they walked out of his cell, the darkness that crept along his periphery would consume him completely.

Tonight, however, was different.

There were usually random lulls throughout the day where Rat would come in to pat the blood off of his wounds or to help him eat. That happened at least twice. More, if his interrogators left early—like they had today. But strangely enough, Rat wasn't here. Tiv wasn't about to call and ask where he was, afraid to get his only companion in that woman's bad graces.

So, he waited, and for a long time he kept his eyes on the door. The grooves on it were familiar. As was the silence. Yet his cell felt almost... wrong. It was as still as it always was when he was alone, though there was something deeper, an implacable emptiness that settled without his permission. One moment, his small world was crimson and complete, then the next, there was *that*. A profound bareness that he couldn't explain.

Tiv just suddenly felt so... *lonely.*

He was startled out of his thoughts when the soft pitter-patter of rain reached his ears. It sprayed overhead. Droplets trickled down the wall to wet his back, and he hissed at the sensation. Tiv faced the downpour, wanting it to heal his puffy face and assuage his hurt. The rain was sharp, but it felt real.

His cuts and bruises stung as the rain fell fiercer, almost as if it were attacking him. Tiv groaned when the cool droplets fell upon his face and down his neck to wash away the blood. The sound was foreign enough for the sentry stationed outside of his door to peek inside and shoot him a quizzical stare, as if bewildered by the realization that he, too, felt pain.

Of course he did.

Tiv mumbled something under his breath, but otherwise ignored him. How many weeks had passed since he'd last used his magic? He didn't know. He didn't want to. But he felt it banked under his skin, just begging to be released. And oh, did he want nothing more than to do just that. But he couldn't, and right now, he needed rest. He needed to be in his dreams, where he wasn't bound by chains that sapped his magic circuit dry. Tiv wanted to go back to a time when his binds were only spells, not physical bands made of cold iron that chafed his skin raw. The infected sores under them were so pungent that he actually preferred the smell of his own blood.

As he closed his eyes, he realized that the stones of his cell were humming. It didn't have the same skin crawling effect as a wall infused with raw magic and he didn't think this was what Jack heard whenever he yelled at the invisible spectator that he claimed whispered things in his ear, but it might've been close. Because it was quiet and it was there, at the very edge of his hearing. Just loud enough for Tiv to fall asleep to.

It coaxed what was left of him into a safe place that felt a lot like the humid days he'd spend camped out with Jack in the mountains or holed up in the Iniquities Chamber for something they were never — *never* — responsible for. It was like that perpetually noisy archive where Master Celaris would outsmart him and then smile smugly or those moments when Rat would talk to him about Roval, and how nicely the boy's wounds were healing.

It felt like peace.

The back of his eyes stung, so he closed them. Tiv could hardly keep them open now anyway. He'd been blinking away the heavy dregs of sleep like an afterthought, and he didn't want to anymore. Tiv drew in a breath. He tried not to shudder when a terrible noise erupted from his chest. Although he could still hear himself breathe, the pain of his wounds were numbing now. If that didn't count as a blessing, then Tiv didn't know what did.

Living hurt.

Creator, it *hurt*.

But if he was finally slipping, then he didn't want to remember the way his captors kicked him on the soft spot behind his knees and held him up by the oily strands of his hair. He didn't want the last thing on his mind to be visions of their morbid grins that filled with delight as he lost fingers and nails and toes—*no.*

Instead, Tiv recalled the thrill of flying, of rising above the rest of his grade with his partner by his side, of marveling at the lucid shine of Pernelia's statue in the early hours of dawn.

Don't worry, Tiv, he heard in Celaris' oaky voice. *The days may seem long, but as time presses on, even the sun must yield to the moon. So, be patient. I promise you that the world won't always feel so restless.*

If he died now, he wanted to be surrounded by the familiar waters of the Zexin Sea.

The skies continued to weep long after he fell into the dark.

Arch Poten Cole,

News of my son's most recent venture has reached the Zenith Council, and I would like to apologize on his behalf. He's worried for his sister, Sylvie, a practitioner of the Drowned Tower.

We've heard no news concerning my daughter's whereabouts from the primary Hunter Captain in charge or from any of the practitioners currently stationed in Eriam. Neither has Sylvie reached out to ease our worries. Dalis feared the worst and has thus acted out for the first time since he was a juvenile apprentice. I can assure you that he has not deserted, nor has he ever considered the thought.

Dalis sent me a letter not too long ago with a promise to return and suffer the ramifications once he finds his sister—dead or alive. When that is, I cannot be certain. But knowing this, and seeing with your own eyes Dalis' unwavering loyalty as a proud practitioner of the Institute, and of the Weeping Grove in particular, I implore you to not force him to take part in the crystal creation process upon his return.

However, should he decide not to take responsibility for his actions when the time comes, then I vow to hunt him down myself.

Victor Sirx
Zenith Council, First Adviser

Signed this day on the 34th of Crown Age

15

Ethil bunched up her sleeves as she ambled down the Alps' Healer's Corridor. Though the word 'corridor' was a ridiculous misuse of the word because it didn't take her long to realize that the area actually spanned an entire wing of the Institute's main building. It even had another section beside it with tiny, blockish structures and open-learning clinics where practitioners came and went at all hours of the day.

The public archives were near enough that the Healers could pick up a manual, then return in under five minutes, assuming they found what they were looking for. There was even a row of heated greenhouses in the far back for embrocologists. Ethil made a mental note to stop by and see what they grew. But for now, she simply assumed that most of them housed only the necessities, since the plants that were regularly used for basic poultices and tonics didn't naturally grow in the Alps. While they were common enough to not be appealing to her, she was interested in their heating system.

Are all of the other Institutes like this? she mused, but promptly dismissed the thought. The Alps was more like a city, rather than an Institute. There were so many buildings and back alleys that she doubted anyone got their work done on time. How could they when just walking was equal parts daunting and arduous?

The perpetual cold certainly didn't do them any favors. Ethil paused to stare at the white puffs of smoke that emerged from her mouth. They disappeared with the wind.

Even the wind is icy, she thought, shivering.

After their talk with Leonas all of those days ago, Myrrh had shown her to her room. It was a small place with only a bed and a dresser, but it was still warmer than sleeping in a tent outside. She was surprised at the amount of privacy she had. It was much more than what she had when she shared a room with that mousy Amorph from the Tower. Ethil caught herself wondering what happened to that roommate of hers from time to time, but she always shook her head of the thought quickly after. It wouldn't do her any good to dwell on it.

Instead, Ethil found solace in exploring the Alps. To her surprise, only a scant few areas were restricted, and whenever she asked someone about her little adventures away from her room, they only encouraged her to wander and learn more about whatever she pleased.

Today, Ethil decided that it was finally time to stop dawdling and head off to see what the other Healers did. What did they learn? Were they required to take up Embrocology? Were they taught in groups or individually? They were all brought here after being selected in Choosings after all, so she didn't doubt that they were all good enough to warrant their own mentor. Ethil was afraid she'd seem incompetent in comparison, but Duward had never taught her to back down from challenges she had yet to face. So, she steeled herself as she continued the long walk to the nearest clinic. Even the thought of her brother couldn't stop the nervous butterflies from pooling in her belly, however, so she found herself waddling awkwardly the entire way.

Ethil stopped when she saw an unnaturally bright light ahead of her. Curious, she peeked around the corner to see a pair of laughing Elementalists. There were so many of them here. They easily outnumbered all of the other practitioners three to one. But, then again, there weren't that many other subgroups to begin with. The Healers and Amorphs combined numbered in the low hundreds, and the Conjurers even less. There were hardly any children either. The few she did see were about to enter their teens, most having just arrived. Seemed the Diamond Alps didn't favor kids, no matter how talented.

She lingered around the corner, as the two Elementalists spoke rapid-fire *Íarre*. Each word was foreign to her ears. If she was going to stay here, then she really needed to learn. Maybe Myrrh would be willing to teach her if she wasn't too busy.

Blue light suddenly caught her attention. Her gaze fell to their luminous hands. Sparks of fire fizzled from their fingertips, as they ran them over their exposed arms. Upon closer inspection, Ethil noticed that the edges of their sleeves were singed black. Whatever happened to their robes must've had one amazing story behind it because the smiles on their faces were dazzling enough to make her want to do the same.

As if he knew he was being watched, one of the Elementalists turned to face her. He was short with messy brown hair and a pair of thick glasses balanced on the bridge of his nose. His eyes were guarded, but not unkind.

"*Ravas a sûn?*" he asked, caught her flustered gaze, then corrected himself. "Are you lost?"

There was an uneven drawl in his voice that showed he was unaccustomed to speaking in the trade tongue. But at least he was trying. Ethil couldn't fault him for that. Especially since she didn't know a word of *Íarre*, barring the curses she'd heard Myrrh mutter of course. Ethil doubted they'd take kindly to those.

"No." She pointed to the clinics. "I was on my way there."

"Ah, for," he paused to hum, as if searching for the proper word, before finally settling on, "classes?"

"*Vahan arí vësa?*" his tall companion cut in before Ethil could answer. The brunette shrugged absentmindedly, before replying in a low voice that she could barely hear.

Ethil wanted to know what they were talking about, but she knew better than to ask.

"My friend was wondering if you were new to the Alps," the brunette said, louder, once he saw the look on her face. He was clearly adept at reading expressions. Everyone here seemed to be. Ethil would have to keep her guard up like Myrrh warned if she didn't want to be read like an open book by every stranger she happened across.

"I am," Ethil said. "How did you know?"

"You have a, what's the word, *adûrkarïas vïla na sarahsë*," he muttered under his breath. His tone sounded more bothered than she expected. If it was because of her or because he needed to practice speaking in the trade tongue, Ethil couldn't say, but she hoped it wasn't the former.

"Umm..." she hesitated when he didn't continue.

"Distinct!" he exclaimed. "That's it! There we go. *Vïa ne rûna sï lenûrivahs*, that was driving me crazy. You have a very *distinct* accent. Better than the others here. Even those chosen as adults lose that kind of fluidity after a few years. The tongue forgets."

"I arrived a few days ago," Ethil confirmed, careful not to give too much away. She didn't want them to suddenly start asking her questions about the east.

There was a short, awkward pause.

Ethil looked around, about to excuse herself when he spoke again. "Do you need help or...?" he let the question hang, opting instead to give her a meaningful stare.

He was giving her a way to escape from the conversation, Ethil realized. She smiled in appreciation.

"No, thank you. My friend, Myrrh, was kind enough to show me around the main parts of the Corridor when I first arrived."

They shared an uneasy glance at her words.

"Myrrh," he said slowly, "Amaurisse?"

Ethil blinked. Well, she didn't know honestly.

"So, has Master Dace returned?" he continued, disregarding her confusion.

She stared, wondering how much she should say. Ethil settled for uncertainty. "I'm not sure. I didn't ask. When I arrived, Myrrh only brought me to see Elder Dace."

So many Dace's, Ethil suddenly thought. She was tempted to just call them by their names. It would definitely be easier to understand, but she'd probably die of discomfort. It was one thing to call Jack by his name, it was another thing entirely to call one of the leaders of the Vanguard Circle by his.

Ethil shook her head to rid herself of such pervasive thoughts. She peered at the two practitioners before her, hoping that she hadn't missed anything important, only to find that they'd gone completely still.

"Is everything alright?" she asked.

"Fine!" the brunette blurted. His companion nodded along. "We need to go—*arïvós da shalen a, Heldes*—good to meet you, Healer. May Maurice light your path!" he shouted, before racing off with his friend at his heels.

Their eyes shifted along the walls, as if someone other than Ethil was watching them. Their voices echoed from down the hall, and she heard them say something in *Íarre* again, but in far more dire tones.

"What was that about?" she thought aloud. But of course no one answered.

Ethil dwelled on it all the way until she reached the clinics. They were small, but pristine and neatly lined up in rows. Each had large windows beside the door, where she saw Healers patching up wounded practitioners or handing them foul-smelling balms that they scrunched their noses at. Some had even crowded together to watch an Elder cast a tedious healing spell in record time. There was a young girl beside him with sharp, blue eyes. She carried a tome thicker than her own body. His apprentice? It was likely.

Not wanting to shove her way through the pack, she entered the quieter clinic across from it. There weren't many people here. Only a sleeping practitioner in a cot at the far end and an older Healer with wrinkles around her mouth. Whatever she'd done in her younger days left her with leathery hands and shrewd eyes that seemed to swallow Ethil whole. It reminded her of an Amorph's gaze, except less fearsome and more empathetic. She couldn't decide if she liked it or not, but as soon as the woman smiled at her, she found that she couldn't hate such expressive eyes. Not when so many around her kept their emotions secured behind walls taller than the mountains they lived in. She'd bet they were harder to scale, too.

"Oh, what brings you here?" the woman asked, taking note of her eyes first. "Don't you want to see Elder Ildred cast his special rejuvenation magic? It's what got him a seat on the Zenith Council. All Healers should see it at least once in their lifetime."

"No," Ethil said as politely as possible. She didn't even spare a glance back at the other clinic. "I'm afraid there's too many people for my taste."

"Oh, he's never been good at shooing them away. Talented man. Terrible orator. I wonder how he survives the Council's meetings." She ushered Ethil inside. "Come in then, and close the door. We don't want the chill coming in with you. Did you need something? I don't think I've ever seen you before."

"I've only just arrived. I was hoping I could take some work off your hands."

"A greenhorn, are you?" She smiled brightly. "I'm afraid you've come at the wrong time. It's rather slow at the moment. My only patient is asleep, rather deeply at that. The poor boy exhausted his magic circuit. He'll be thoroughly scolded by Elder Seraphin later. But oh! Sit, sit. What's your name, dear?"

"Ethil Mane," she said, failing to hide her grin.

"It's a pleasure, Ethil. I'm Master Floris." She spread her arms out in welcome. "I'm the Matron of Channel Two's clinics. You're lucky to have found me and not Master Macee. He talks ceaselessly about the heart and all of its intricacies."

Ethil was beginning to think that they all had their own little quirks because not two minutes in and she could already see that Master Floris was the fidgety type.

"Oh, but he's still a good man," Master Floris went on, her eyes wide with embarrassment. "And we're both fully qualified to teach you everything from mending wounds to brewing tonics. Since you've come all this way, is there anything specific you'd like to learn?"

Ethil hesitated a moment, before taking out her tome. The familiar weight of it calmed her nerves. It had been so long since she'd healed anyone, let alone written any recipes. But this was as good a time as any to brush up on her skills—and hopefully acquire a few more. She leafed to a crumpled page with the formula for a blood clotting tonic she'd never gotten the chance to try. It was one Duward had shown her, before they were called to the Iniquities Chamber. It felt like a lifetime ago.

"This." Ethil showed her the page.

Her eyes lit up in recognition.

Master Floris scurried behind a counter, grabbing a tray of flasks, two mortars, and more measuring spoons than she could count. Ethil couldn't help but smile in delight.

She didn't doubt that if given enough time, she'd be able to one day call this place home.

***

Why is the head office always so packed? Myrrh thought, as she walked down the halls of the Vanguard Circle's Hunter Division.

Used to slipping by unnoticed, her steps were lithe, yet firm. They didn't echo against the stone floors. Those whose did were easily discerned as either newly promoted Hunters or potential recruits.

Speaking of recruits…

Myrrh caught two restless ones standing in a teeming corner near Cheryll's office, and for reasons beyond her comprehension, they were missing their sleeves. They recoiled as she passed, and Myrrh had to question the sanity of the idiot that chose them for the Hunter Division. They'd more than likely be passed off to the Council or be given some mundane job like studying geology or cultivating plants. It was what all of the other rejects did.

Myrrh stopped when she saw a familiar face.

"Charlotte," she called.

The woman turned, giving her a full view of the freckles scattered chaotically across her cheeks.

"Myrrh," Charlotte said, relieved. "Do you know what's going on? People have been saying that Master Dace has returned. I've been trying to keep them away from her office, but they just won't listen to me. It's all, *'My father wants her to look over my Hunter application,'* this, and, *'I've been waiting for months,'* that." Charlotte scowled darkly at them. "Idiots."

Myrrh raised an eyebrow. "So, they all decided to stake out here? Master Dace would burn their applications in front of their faces if she saw them now."

Charlotte laughed and Myrrh's face softened at the sound. It wasn't the dainty laugher her highborn parents had ingrained into her, but hearty, throw-your-head-back laughter. Noisy and filled with gasping breaths in between. As Charlotte struggled to get ahold of herself, Myrrh whirled around to address the mob.

"Master Dace isn't here," she announced.

A series of groans followed.

Who even let these people in? she thought.

"And she isn't returning anytime soon," Charlotte declared. "So, scram, you whiny Snuff eaters!"

They turned away at her words, their mouths twisted into gnarled frowns. Most left, but they could still hear the uncertain scuffles of boots as a few of the more persistent ones lingered just past the bend.

"Maurice, help these blunted fools," Charlotte grumbled, stomping down the hall. Terrified shouts exploded into the air as soon as she rounded the corner.

Myrrh grinned. Same old Charlotte.

"I heard you were back," a voice abruptly said from behind her. It was deep and distinctly masculine.

Myrrh turned to find a mop of brown hair and black eyes obscured by a proud nose. Too proud. A crab sat on the newcomer's shoulder, rapidly clicking its pincers at her. Frankly, Myrrh was surprised that he hadn't exchanged the thing for a snake yet. It didn't suit him at all.

"Where's your Peose?" he asked.

"With Master Dace." Myrrh shrugged. She'd never been attached to the thing. Unlike his tiny pet, her toad was larger than a
wagon. It was the very opposite of stealth. "What do you want,
Dwyn?"

He smiled patronizingly. "Just passing through."

Myrrh sneered. Even a child wouldn't have believed him.
"You're so transparent."

"I don't know what you're talking about," he said, gliding
past her. The smile never left his face. "If you're looking to report
to Elder Drakone, then he's in his office."

Myrrh tilted her head, warily watching him leave. How did
he know she was going to see Elder Drakone? Hadn't he just doubted her return? She shelved the thought immediately. It didn't
matter. She'd worry about Dwyn's creepy grins later.

She had already finished her meticulously written account of
everything she'd been through and handed it off to Leonas. Now,
she needed to speak to the man in charge of the Vanguard Circle's
renowned Hunter Division, Roderek Drakone. He wasn't much
to look at—broad, bald, and riddled with scars were the top three
descriptors that came to mind when she thought about him—but
Roderek did possess the impressive ability to strike fear into the
hearts of anyone foolish enough to stand against him. Perhaps
that was to be expected from someone with his name, or better
yet, his position. Because as far as she could tell, the other two
Circle heads were just as frightening. She wouldn't be surprised
if it was an unspoken prerequisite for the job.

I wonder who's worse? Myrrh mused.

She couldn't decide.

The thought of standing in front of Roderek unnerved her,
but she crushed the feeling just as quickly as it appeared. There
was no use fretting over their meeting. She needed to see him, regardless of her feelings on the matter. Thinking about it would
only make it worse.

Holding her head up high, Myrrh made her way down the
familiar path to his office. Unlike Leonas', which was a sight on

its own, Roderek's was inconspicuous. It was remarkable for being incredibly... *not*. The door was of normal size and made of plain wood. It stood amidst a number of similar doors that stretched out in a long line down the hall. The deer head carved on its jamb was the only indication that it belonged to Roderek and not one of the Hunter Captains. Myrrh didn't know if denying luxuries was just a hobby of his or if he was actually comfortable situated here with the rest of his lackeys, but she doubted his Captains were happy about it. More than once, she'd heard her master snippily speak against Roderek. It was always for one thing or another.

'You really should go, your face makes Bellin's stomach ache,' or, *'We aren't so incompetent that we need you watching over us. It's insulting. Get a bigger office. Now.'*

Cheryll Dace had guts. No one in the Alps could deny that. Forget that he was a Drakone or that they once studied under the same Master together, her scathing tongue spared no one. Equal in every sense of the word. But Myrrh wasn't Cheryll, and as she stood outside of his door with her hand poised to knock, her insides churned in unease.

"Enter," came a stifled voice from within.

He didn't even give her a chance to announce her presence. Myrrh opened the door to find Roderek seated behind his desk with a very grumpy look on his face. The scars littered across his head made his demeanor all the more menacing. He was clearly in a bad mood. She should've stayed away.

Is this why Dwyn was laughing? Myrrh wondered. Realization settled in the pit of her stomach like poison. *That snake.* She did a quick sweep of his office. It was neat. Almost sterile.

"Elder Drakone," Myrrh greeted with a bow.

"You returned a few days ago, didn't you?" he said, terse enough to make her wince.

"Please forgive my lateness. I was helping someone settle."

"The Healer from the east." He nodded. "Did Cheryll order you to bring her?"

"No," Myrrh denied, forcing her mouth into a thin line when Roderek raised an inquisitive brow. "I brought her with me because she lost what was left of her family just before the Tower collapsed and she didn't have—"

"Enough," Roderek cut in. He didn't want to hear another sob story and the impulsive decisions it forced. "Has Cheryll located the stone?"

"No," Myrrh lied, hoping against everything that her voice didn't crack. It sounded steady to her. But the way his eyes thinned told her there might've been a lilt even she wasn't aware of. "Master Dace waited for Elder Serach to expose himself by harnessing the stone's power only to realize that she was too late. It destroyed the Institute. By the time she fished his body from the Zexin Sea, the stone was gone. She's been searching tirelessly for it. But it's transparent and small, while the sea... *isn't*."

"So, she's decided to remain there?"

"Yes, to rebuild. For now."

Roderek folded his hands together, thoughtful. "What of the Tower's Arch Poten?"

"Columbus Cephas is still missing. Master Dace presumes him dead. But she did send his primary apprentice in his place, along with her son."

"His primary apprentice?" he repeated. "Name?"

"Sylvie Sirx."

His eyebrows rose and the lines on his forehead deepened with the motion. The flicker of the lone oil lamp atop his desk casted a terrifying shadow over the weapons mounted on the walls. It forced their metal to shine, and Myrrh didn't like how the steel edges seemed to reflect his eyes.

Myrrh gulped when those same hard irises zeroed in on her, boring holes into her, as if trying to split her apart with his gaze alone. His eyes were too horrifying to be human. Were the offspring of Maurice part-god? Because she'd believe it if they were.

"You're dismissed," he said after a moment's deliberation. "I expect you to report back to me if Cheryll finds out more."

Myrrh didn't need to be told twice.

With a nod, she all but ran out of his office. It was only when the door closed behind her that she finally allowed herself to breathe. Deep, long breaths that filled her lungs and gave her peace. It was a standard report, but relaxing in front of someone like Roderek Drakone was out of the question.

She dreaded having to do it again.

It's him, Myrrh thought, forcing her stiff legs forward. *Out of the three of them, Roderek is definitely the worst.*

For once, she wasn't happy to have found an answer.

Master Dace,

I've done as you've asked.

Your letter has been safely hand-delivered to Elder Dace. He opened it before my eyes, and while he did have some concerns regarding your request to look into certain colleges within the Grove, he wasn't opposed to the idea. I'm sure he'll conjure up a proper plan soon.

He hasn't mentioned who he'd send to the Grove yet, but hopefully it isn't me. I'd like to stay in the Alps for a while longer to see how the men are faring under Elder Dace's leadership. From what I've gathered from the other divisions, they aren't doing well. I brought this issue up to Elder Dace when we met, but I'm not entirely certain my words got through to him. Even if they did, I doubt he'll listen to me. It would help if you could write to him again, Master. (Perhaps you can mention my desire to remain in the north as well?)

While I'm on the subject of Elders, I've also given my report to Elder Drakone regarding the stone. He seemed… skeptical.

I tried my best.

Your faithful apprentice,
Myrrh 20.27.CA

16

A loud bang shook the dust from the walls.

As soon as the door closed behind him, all talk ceased. Even from where he stood, he could smell their fear. Their anxiety. It was a wonder they were able to remain so composed when out in society, mingling with the very people they plotted to overthrow. But that wasn't his concern. So long as they showed respect where it was due and kept their mouths shut, then he had no problem with them. Even if their fretful eyes did make him sick to his stomach.

"You're here," one said, boldly drawing nearer. "We've been waiting for you, Elder."

"I was held up."

"If I may ask, what have you learned?"

"What happened in the Grove?" he asked, ignoring the question. If the man was annoyed at his blatant disregard, he didn't show it. "Has the Lafertti Clan backed out?"

"No, err... they've run into a few unexpected hitches, Elde—sir. Half of them are still in disagreement."

"Have you looked into the other colleges?"

"Y—Yes! Of course! But they're talking it through. It seems as though the vote is leaning towards stopping the production of *Orivellea*. A startling number of the Healers are tired of it. Very tired. Bloody, ghoulish work, they say. The Union, however, has disagreed. They're trying to keep their affairs quiet, so they've become even more isolated recently. Much good it did them though. I'm sure things will heat up soon. I believe our allies will make their move once it does."

"Good." He grinned madly. "I'll send men to the Grove as back up should they decide to foolishly act beforehand. Have Rix send a message to Lynol. He's efficient, but even the most capable men need time to prepare their forces."

"Of course, sir."

"What about Zacarias? Is he still overseeing production in the Anvil? I expected a report from him six days ago."

"I tried getting in touch with him, but the Grove is currently in a state of disarray. No messages in or out over the last few days. But I assure you that my contacts will inform me as soon as they start allowing messengers back inside the Grove."

"What happened?"

"According to my sources, a batch of their senior practitioners set out without permission. I have their files here."

He snatched the outstretched folder from his hands. It was thick and filled with detailed sketches and personal files of twenty odd practitioners. It had everything from their first master to their kill count. Even their specialties. Invaluable information. His eyes lingered on their supposed leader. Primary apprentice to the Red Scripts' representative and eternal pain in his side. He knew that his Master was loyal to the Institute, however, so he assumed that he was as well. Few Masters took on apprentices with different values. It made little sense to spend years mentoring someone they couldn't stand... but still, he had to ask.

"Did they desert?"

"No one believes they did."

"Why not?"

"If you look here, sir." He pointed at the *past and living relatives* section on each page. "They all had family from the east, and they made quite the ruckus about no one sending out search parties before they left. The Potentate Union, and even the college representatives, all believe that the only reason they left was so they could find them."

"And if there was another reason?"

"Highly unlikely, sir."

His eyes settled on the man for a moment, observing his sure gaze and amusing himself with how his hands trembled in contrast. Was his face really so upsetting? In all honesty, he always tried his best to school it into something less threatening. But it seemed he had yet to master that particular skill.

He rubbed his temples, waiting for his nonsensical thoughts to vanish. When they didn't, he decided to distract himself in a different way. He leaned forward until he was uncomfortably close to the quivering man before him.

"What have you learned from the Council?" he asked.

The terrified shriek that left his lips when he tried to answer made him grin.

***

Ethil stopped before a small kiosk hidden in a corner beside the public archives. It was a small thing, run by an even smaller boy. About fourteen from what she could see. He was gangly with big, black eyes that peered up at her as she looked at his wares—statuettes of several practitioners carved from bark, iron, and jet. She didn't recognize most, and the few she did all had dour expressions that contrasted sharply with her knowledge of them. Ethil didn't think Elder Dace ever stopped smiling dopily or that Master Floris could ever be anything but endlessly kind, but there they were... perpetually glaring at everyone that passed.

Littered between them were clay dolls in the shape of mythical beasts with large eyes. There was a lion with the head of a ram, a cat with frog legs, and a bird she couldn't name, but it had veiny, insect-like wings that crept her out enough to not want to learn it. They were fascinating. Certainly worth more than a second's glance. But Ethil wasn't so infatuated with statues to consider spending even a single piece of copper on them.

"They look constipated, right?" someone whispered by her ear, startling her into dropping the statue of a chicken she'd been holding. The boy was up in an instant. He caught it with reflexes that could put a Hunter to shame, before sending her a glare colder than death.

"Myrrh!" Ethil shouted.

"Sorry, sorry," she said, before giving the boy a look that he curled his upper lip at. "Who do you think you're sneering at?"

"What are you doing here?" Ethil asked.

"I'm here for the kid." Myrrh pointed at him, then thrust her thumb over her shoulder meaningfully. He stood a little straighter when Myrrh's eyes flashed in annoyance. "Charlotte has been looking everywhere for you. Stop running away when you know you hav—hey!"

The boy ran off, clutching his little knife and a piece of wood, leaving the stall without a care.

"*Vaklas dalen*," Myrrh cursed after him. "That brat."

Ethil's eyebrows furrowed. "What happened? Why did he run off?"

"Salace is a junior Hunter," Myrrh revealed, then shrugged when Ethil's jaw dropped. "I know his partner. She asked me to help her find him. They've been tasked with thinning out a few of the growing Truffalo herds further north. Those beasts will eat literally anything. Leave them alone long enough and they'll start killing all of the local wildlife. We can't have that."

"Is that safe? He's so small and Truffaloes... aren't."

"Salace is a gifted practitioner, but absolutely terrible when it comes to following orders. Which doesn't make him the best Hunter. He can be disciplined of course, but I doubt anyone would bother, since Elder Dace will likely be picking him to serve in the Corrections Division soon. He's already asked about him on several occasions. It won't be long now."

"Pick him? Is he really *that* talented?"

"Very."

"But to be taken as an apprentice at such a young age, and by someone like Elder Dace no less. That's incredible!"

"Not exactly an apprentice, but yes, it is impressive. Salace is barely into his teens. Grown men with years of experience get passed up by Elder Dace. Even I don't know what his requisites are. No one does."

"Wait, what do you mean not as an apprentice?"

"Elder Dace has never had a primary apprentice or even a regular one for that matter," Myrrh explained. "While he hasn't made any official statements, it's obvious that he's saving that privilege for Jack. Keeping prestigious positions within the family is common everywhere, and this is one mantle that's been with the Dace family for generations. Perhaps not continuously, but enough that the people see it as natural for a Dace to hold the title. Besides, I'm sure Elder Dace would like to retire soon. He'd be a fool not to groom Jack before he does."

"So, they just allow Elder Dace to take whoever he wants? Even when they know that he won't give them the same attention as a proper Master would?"

"The Council usually files complaints whenever Elder Dace wants to pull out a regular practitioner. It's rare, but it has happened once or twice. It's different for those in the Vanguard Circle. Even if Elder Dace is only taking them on as lackeys, he still gets first pick of the new arrivals in the Hunter Division. It goes like this," Myrrh began, complete with elaborate hand gestures to better explain it to her. "First, Elder Drakone approves their applications, then the new recruits spend a few weeks under the supervision of any available seniors. It's essentially a trial period to see where they'll end up. Corrections will pick who they want during this time. After Elder Dace chooses one or two—or more often, none—Research snags a few more, then finally, the Hunter Captains squabble over the leftovers. There's always a lot of them left, so it isn't all bad."

"But doesn't that mean the Hunter Division actually gets the short end of the stick? That doesn't sound fair."

"It isn't, but it's how it's always been. There have been appeals to change the system, but none of them have ever gained traction. It doesn't help that most consider it an honor to be among the few chosen by Elder Dace."

"But won't that cause a rift between the divisions? I'm sure they've argued over practitioners at one time or another."

"In the past, sure. I heard that before the current heads took office, there was a lot of in-fighting."

"What changed?"

"Just leadership. You'd be amazed what a difference that can make. Master Dace told me that it's because all three of them understand that talented practitioners come and go. It's a good philosophy. A right one. That, and no one actually wants to teach newcomers in Research and Corrections the ropes unless they're *really* worth the effort. They've passed up a lot of good men because of that."

Ethil paused for a moment to take it all in. "What's going to happen to Salace once Elder Dace chooses him?"

"Assuming Salace doesn't refuse his offer, then Elder Dace will likely hand him off to study under one of his more capable underlings. Thelarius only knows how talented his practitioners are. His training methods are brutal. Vicious or cruel doesn't even begin to describe it. While I've never heard his men talk about them, I've heard a lot of the Hunter Captains say that Elder Dace appealed to the Council to grant him a special clinic, where his practitioners could spend their mandatory recuperation periods away from prying eyes."

"What does he do?" Ethil asked.

"I don't know," Myrrh said honestly. "But I've seen a few of his new recruits return with third degree burns and infected boils covering their entire bodies. I even caught one running to the infirmary with flayed hands once. He threw up the entire way. Nothing normal either. His vomit was purple and green from poison. Elder Dace eliminates the weak like weeds."

Ethil could imagine it so vividly that she shuddered. She didn't doubt Myrrh's words. How could she when she'd felt his menacing aura for herself? Though, she amended, Elder Dace did go out of his way to make her feel more comfortable, so he couldn't be *that* harsh. Even the books in the archives painted him as someone approachable and mild-tempered. Then again, those were likely biased opinions.

"What about the cart?" Ethil asked, needing to change the subject before she gagged.

"What about it?" Myrrh shot back.

"Should Salace really just have left it here? What if someone steals his things?"

Myrrh blinked, as if questioning her intelligence. "That was just a ploy. He rounded the corner some time ago."

"Huh?"

"He's right there."

Myrrh pointed at a gray spider the size of Ethil's head. It sat on top of a block of wood, extremely still. It blended in with the other strange creatures on the stall's counter, but as soon as she spotted it, the spider's fang-like chelicerae clicked together. The long, hairy legs that surrounded the wood ambled forward, as if preparing to jump and hug her face.

Ethil screamed at the sight. She stumbled backwards, barely registering Myrrh's laughter. There was a flash of light, and then Salace was back. He jumped off of the counter that tipped dangerously to the side at his sudden weight, before sticking his tongue out at them.

"If Charlotte catches you, she'll tear each and every one of those legs right off," Myrrh said plainly, uncaring for the way the boy huffed in response. He was quiet for a child. "Scram, Salace. Elder Dace hasn't chosen you yet, so you need to do your job until then."

With that, Myrrh turned on her heel and stalked away.

Ethil looked between her and the defiant boy for a moment longer. She grinned sheepishly at him, before following after her friend. Myrrh was short, but she was fast. She expertly weaved her way through the throng of people, ducking under arms and dodging food carts with practiced ease. Ethil wasn't nearly as quick, and she found herself mumbling apologies every other second, until Myrrh stopped in front of the entrance of the Zenith

Council's meeting hall. She waited patiently for her to catch up.

With another grin, Ethil hurried her steps, trying to copy Myrrh's movements. She almost got the hang of it, too. But by the time she did, there weren't any people left for her to slip between. Ethil settled on the cold marble steps instead, made colder from their coat of snow.

"Where are you going?" Ethil asked, her nose red.

"You want to come?" came the response. Myrrh went on before Ethil could answer, but her gait was noticeably slower this time. "I heard Master Floris has been teaching you."

Ethil looked at her, surprise flashing in her orbs, before she remembered who she was talking to. "She's skilled with salves. I've learned a lot so far."

"Have her show you how to make those enchanted bandages she hands out to the juniors. They promote natural healing and smell absolutely amazing."

"I will!" Ethil said, delighted. "What have you been up to?"

"Reports, among other things."

Ethil lowered her voice. "Like dealing with the Tippings?"

"What Tippin—oh!" Myrrh blanched. "No, that isn't my problem anymore. That unfortunate soul was left in Elder Dace's care. He's usually quite private with his affairs, so I haven't heard much." Not that she wanted to. Myrrh swallowed discreetly, before opting to change the subject to something more appealing. "I have a feeling I'll be sent out again soon though."

"Now that you mention it, who are you sent out with? Do you have a partner?" Ethil asked, unsure. She could hardly imagine her even having one. Myrrh worked so well on her own.

"Only temporary ones." Myrrh answered. "Redmond was the latest. He's currently with Master Dace. Bet that suck-up is real happy about that."

Ethil didn't quite get it, but she didn't bother asking. If he was helping Cheryll rebuild, then surely he wasn't all bad.

As if she knew what she was thinking, Myrrh shook her head and said, "He doesn't deserve even one nice thought."

"I'll be the judge of that."

"It's your mind." Myrrh shrugged. "So, tell me more ab—"

She was interrupted by a loud crash.

They turned when the door beside them rumbled with the sound of furniture being thrown at it. A pitiful yelp followed. Ethil was about to throw the door open and end whatever was going on inside when Myrrh held out an arm to stop her.

"Don't," Myrrh commanded.

"Someone could be hurt," Ethil protested. But her voice died in her throat when Myrrh pinned her with a dark gaze.

"That's one of the Zenith Council's lounges. We can't just walk in. Besides, there should be guards inside."

"But it's quiet. What if they knocked them out?"

Myrrh hesitated, before shaking her head. "We should go."

"No! I'm a Healer. I can't just—"

The door opened.

Ethil barely registered the flash of light by her side, as someone she didn't know came striding out. Three others followed, giving her funny looks, before covering their faces and scattering in different directions. The first man, however, heavily scarred from head to toe, lingered by the door, appraising her.

"You," he called and Ethil straightened. She looked around, panicking when she found no trace of Myrrh. Ethil pointed a hesitant finger at herself, leaving the question unvoiced. The man understood immediately. He nodded, not once uncrossing his arms. "Yes, you. Come here."

Ethil took one cautious step forward... and no more. The man seemed to find it adequate.

"What did you hear?"

"Nothing!" Ethil held her hands up, as if to further confirm her innocence. "I was just walking and then the door shook—"

"Where's the Amorph that was here with you?"

Her eyebrows raised for an instant, before she gathered herself. Ethil tried to look as confused as possible. "A—Amorph? I was alone."

He didn't believe her. She knew he didn't. With every fiber of her being, she did. But to her surprise, he only closed his eyes... and sighed.

Is he letting it slide? Ethil thought. *Oh, I hope so. Please let it slide. Please, please, please let it slide.*

"You're the new one, aren't you? The Healer from the east?"

"Yes," Ethil stuttered like a leaky faucet. Thankfully, he didn't question her nerves.

"So, I assume you've met Leonas. He personally welcomes everyone that's had the chance to see his wife. Watch out for him though. Don't let him send you or your tiny friend to the Grove."

"What?"

"He isn't what he appears to be," he warned ominously.

He placed a large hand over her shoulder. His grip was firm, and Ethil had the distinct feeling that even if she tried to escape, she wouldn't be able to. Sweat ran down her brow and her knees quivered in apprehension. But as quickly as it had come, the weight of his hand disappeared and in its place was the frigid wind of the Alps. Ethil had never loved the cold so much before. She looked up, only to find the man already walking away.

He didn't even glance back when he said, "That goes for you as well, Hunter."

Ethil shivered.

She stifled a scream when she saw a tiny lizard crawl down her shoulder and settle in the soft crook of her elbow. It blended with her robes. The dark eyes that fixed themselves on her face told her that there was no need to worry.

"Myrrh," Ethil called tentatively. "Who was that?"

The lizard opened its mouth, and for a moment, Ethil was distracted by the way its tongue slipped unnaturally out to mimic Myrrh wetting her lips.

"Roderek Drakone."

Master Dace,

Forgive the number of enchantments attached (especially that tiny detonating one). I asked Charlotte's new junior, Salace, for help. He's extremely skilled with them. Elder Dace has his eye on him.

To start, Elder Drakone has warned Ethil and myself away from Elder Dace. I've always been cautious around both of them, but never to such a degree. I don't think—

He told us not to follow Elder Dace's orders to the Grove.

Something must've happened that I'm not aware of. I'm sorry. I'll find out immediately. It would help if you could also send a few messages to the council members. Those you trust anyway.

I need your guidance, Master.

But even I know what a terrible idea asking for it is. Especially now. My previous message may have been intercepted. I'm not entirely sure how, since I made certain to personally deliver it to one of your Peose stationed along the border. But I'd rather not take any more chances. Thus, the enchantments.

Read, reseal, and resend... I never thought that old ploy would be used on me. Whatever the case, it's safe to assume that this one will be intercepted as well. But if it isn't, and I'm just being overly paranoid, then, again, I'm very sorry about that explosive enchantment.

Very sorry.

Your faithful apprentice,
Myrrh 22.27.CA

17

Vidal had always been a betting man.

It was one of the many traits Monet liked least about him. Vidal could name over a dozen other things she didn't care for — '*How are you so bad at being a functional person?*' he recalled fondly in her voice — but gambling was perhaps the one thing that truly got under her skin. Although she wasn't fond of it, Vidal had no intention of changing that particular aspect of his personality. By this point, it would be close to impossible anyway. He constantly started betting pools with Monet's Potens in the Veld. Back when he was in the north, he'd even get the Elder's to play along with him. Rocous was always the easiest to rope in.

Contrary to whatever they might've believed, Vidal didn't bet for the thrill of the game or for the pouches, sometimes *heaps,* of gold — though that was certainly a good guess — he bet simply because he always wore the biggest smile at the end of it. His craftier friends had noticed that immediately, while others took to blaming their horrid luck. Then there was the occasional group that would smile smugly whenever they thought they'd beaten him. While it might not have always been apparent, Vidal never lost. This time would be no different.

People always assumed that his mind worked in abstract ways. That his imagination painted things into being, which was true in a sense. When it came to his shows, he was a free thinker; when it came to his speeches, he was a wild spirit. Even his clothes differed from the norm. But when it came to strategic manipulation, to how to best utilize his men, Vidal's mind worked in bullet points. Organized and ordinary. As plain as can be. Once he crossed one out, he moved onto the next.

Today, it was finally time for the next step.

Vidal looked down at the playing cards he'd laid out before him. He flicked a card with a decrepit old man carrying a boulder on his back off of the table with a little more force than necessary. It flew under a sofa. Left to rot there until the maids came. Perhaps longer if they didn't do their jobs properly. By the dust that always lined his upper shelves, he knew they never did.

Trapping two more cards with his finger—one, a regal mage with his familiar; the other, a wanderer burdened by chains—he moved them right into the middle of a pile of common gold sack cards, before shrouding his hand in flames.

They lit up brilliantly.

The two center cards, having been made of a different material, blazed differently than the rest. But even with their special covering and smoother surface, their smoke was visible, too, after a minute. Vidal watched their edges burn, before he threw in another group. A seeker at the top with a herd of Snuff below. He encased the sizable deck in a thin layer of ice, then stared as the fire continued to hum, slowly melting it.

Vidal doused the growing flame with water from a nearby pitcher before it could. He stared at it long after the flames were gone. The fact that he'd just ruined a perfectly good table and an even better deck of cards was the furthest thing from his mind.

Powerful lures make for worthy distractions, Vidal thought. *Especially if they have something the Fetters' want.*

He doubted Jack and Sylvie would be able to do much in the face of a horde of enemies. But since they were so willing to make the sacrifice, then who was he to stop them? Now that they'd moved, he couldn't allow himself to dawdle any longer. He needed to gather his herd, before either of them were roughed up too badly. Leonas would strap him to one of his interrogation tables if Jack died under his watch.

What's going to happen after all of this? Once they've found their secrets and flipped Ferus Terria on its head, what then?

The need to know burned him, needling its way under his skin like disease through a brothel. Vidal knew that the events transpiring now were just the lead-ins to the real show. The turning points. Who would be at its center once the stage was finally set? The one peacefully watching over everything, surrounded by a sea of blood with only corpses for company?

Vidal didn't know, but he wanted to find out.

Bad things were currently happening in all of the Institutes. With the Tower gone, the whispers of betrayal in the Grove and the shouts of discord in the Alps rang louder than ever. Everyone was angry at something. The Veld's impact in Institute politics was minor at best. Monet didn't care for their ways. While he adored her for that, he also knew that she'd have to kindle a spark of interest within herself soon. Whether she wanted to or not.

The eye of the storm was no longer clear. It couldn't be the north anymore. Not with their squabbling over a new leader. Vidal scoffed at the thought. There were an infinite number of things for them to concern themselves with, yet they chose the most irritating. They needed to deal with the problems in the Grove first, as they should've done with the Tower and the Veld.

Egotistical half-wits, he thought scathingly.

If they handed control over to the Vanguard Circle for a day, they might actually get somewhere. Even if their leaders left a trail of blood and ashes in their wake, it would still be progress.

"The cards!" a girl whined, snapping Vidal from his stupor.

He looked down to see two little hands grasping the edge of his desk, fingers now wet and dirty from the mess, before a tiny head popped out. Vidal stared as brown eyes, smoother than warm liquor, blinked owlishly back at him. He smiled at the slight puff of her cheeks. She had a very grumpy look on her face.

"What did you do to the cards?" she accused.

He at least tried to look remorseful. "They needed to suffer."

"Why?" she asked, no longer flabbergasted by their sorry state. The way she tilted her head reminded him of her mother. It was the exact same motion. Half-frown, tight eyes, just daring him to say something she didn't want to hear.

"Because it was the only way I could lure them out."

"Lure them out?" she repeated. She had a habit of pursing her lips when she thought. "Were they hiding?"

"Yes."

"Where?"

"In a deep, dark place. Just on the edge of my reach. But my men aren't ready for the truth and your mother would've never let me do it on my own."

"Why not?"

"Because of the danger, my dear."

"Danger? Why was it dangerous?"

"They wanted something from me."

"You didn't want to share?"

"This wasn't something I could give."

"What was it?"

Vidal shushed her with a finger.

She was a curious thing. That lively tongue would get her into more trouble than she could ever know. She needed to learn how to hold it. There was no magic in her veins for her to call to her aid should she stumble upon someone that lacked his... tolerance for questions.

"Shhh!" she mimicked him by pressing her finger to her lips.

Vidal smiled at the sight.

"Run along now," he told her. "Go back to the library. Your mother will maim me if she finds out you skipped your history lesson. Again."

She made a face, but conceded nevertheless.

With an exaggerated flourish, she flicked her hands out and rubbed them together to get rid of the water and ash that clung to her fingers. She took a moment to scrape the remnants under her nails, then had the audacity to dry her hands on one of his horrendously expensive throw pillows. Little pest.

Vidal waited patiently for her to leave. He narrowed his eyes when she lingered by the door with another question dancing on the tip of her tongue.

"Was there something else?" he prompted.

"Did the crazy lady leave?" she asked. Vidal raised an eyebrow at that. "The dark-haired one that talks to herself. I saw her from my study room!"

Mistaking his sudden amusement for disbelief, heat colored her cheeks, and she hurriedly tried to explain herself.

"She was asking herself questions, I promise! She might've been asking the books questions, but that's weird. Well, I ask the books questions sometimes… but never seriously! But I saw her and she was real and she stopped talking to herself when that creepy man came in!"

"Creepy man?" he questioned, unable to hold back his smile. Not that he was trying very hard.

"He had red eyes like you, and bad skin like I do when I'm sick, and a loud mouth, and really big, visible veins right," she pointed at her temples for emphasis, "here."

"I think," Vidal began, "that you should take a break from studying and take a nap instead."

"I'm not lying!"

"Oh, I know you aren't."

His voice must've come off more patronizing than he'd intended because not a moment later, she raised her chin and slammed the door with an indignant huff. Vidal heard her stomp all the way down the hall. He smirked in amusement at that.

She was definitely like her mother.

Speaking of the woman, he'd have to contact her about sending a few men over soon.

***

Sylvie's fingers danced along her side. They lingered over the cauterization scars there; a reminder of how far they'd come. She sat with her legs crossed and one hand tensely rubbing the wound, as they waited in the back of a wagon that Vidal had been kind enough to supply them with. A midnight horse pulled it, while one of Vidal's lackeys—a burly man that grunted his way through conversations—kept it on track. They'd been travelling for three days now and had just passed Aston's border, where the man promised to take them past the marsh, but no further.

"The Pit's dangerous for someone alone and uninvited like myself," he'd said. His first and only complete sentence to them, before he revealed a slave's brand on his wrist. White and puffy. It was barely noticeable under the light of the sun.

Sylvie raised her eyebrows at it, unsure how to react. Jack was more open. He cursed a colorful string of words that she couldn't quite make out. But the way he ran his hands through his hair told her that it wasn't anything pleasant.

The man forced a smile and shrugged, before facing forward again. It was uncomfortably silent after that. And none of them made a move to break it.

Feeling as though she'd prodded her wound long enough, her fingers automatically went to the Heartstone, before settling back beside her. Then she did it four more times. Once to make sure it was still there, the other three for no real reason other than she was bored. Intolerably so. Sitting there, just waiting for the unknown made her antsy. Sylvie thought about *her* words. About magic and secrets and things that supposedly belonged to her. Would going to the Pit really lead to answers? Would Jack be willing to give her insight?

Sylvie's gaze involuntarily drifted to Jack, who threw her a look that questioned her sanity. He knew something. Jack always did. She ignored him in favor of peeking at his hands. They were fiddling absentmindedly with the hem of his robes. The Demar Spell on his ankles glanced out at her. His very own set of brands placed upon him by his mother. If overprotective had a physical form, then that was it. They must've been incredibly effective for her to resort to such permanence. Incredibly painful, too.

Was it worth it? Sylvie pondered. *Does anyone else have them?*

She squinted to get a better look, only for Jack to smooth his clothes down. Sylvie looked up, unsurprised to find him glaring at her. The veins along his temples were unnaturally bright today. Like they were audaciously trying to compete with the sun. It made his already pale skin glow unnaturally.

"Can I see it?" she asked, careful.

"Why?" he shot back, catching the way she gripped the Heartstone. "Are you that nervous?"

Sylvie schooled her expression into neutral, but didn't try to hide her anxiety. Holding her thumb and forefinger an inch apart, she muttered, "A little."

He had to lean in just to hear her. But as soon as he did, Jack's immediate reaction was to scoff, pause, then intensely scrutinize her until she met his gaze. She was more defensive than she ought to be, he thought. Her expression took a turn for the defiant, just daring him to mock her.

Distantly, Jack heard the wind rustle the long grass and the soothing trickle of water. They were close to the Narrow Marsh. Disturbingly close. In front of them, Vidal's lackey turned to shoot them a look, wondering at the sudden tension. But when the wagon stumbled over a rock, he hurriedly looked away.

Jack stared at Sylvie for a second longer. He blinked twice. Very slowly. The third time, he left his eyes closed and with a shrug, he inched his robes up for her to see.

Sylvie scurried forward on her hands and knees. She examined the white lines that made up the words and how they looped together. Sylvie traced the outline with her finger, then pressed experimentally on a puffy portion along the inner curve of his ankle. It looked like it hurt. But Jack didn't even flinch, so she took that as a good sign.

"That didn't hurt?" Sylvie asked just to make sure. She found herself pressing it again, before he could answer.

Jack raised an eyebrow at that.

"Did you want it to?" he countered, suspicious.

She laughed. Loud and amused. There were so many other adjectives he could use to describe it. None of them good for his pride. Jack swatted her hand away when the corner of her lips finally settled into a small quirk.

He was so touchy when he wanted to be left alone. But that was half of the fun. Sylvie preferred this over his attitude when he was bored and in the mood for company. Jack could be utterly maddening then. She wondered how Tiv dealt with his erratic mood swings—he'd probably called him a woman. Sylvie could imagine him saying that. Did Jack miss him? Because she did. She missed Reed, Myrrh, and Master Cephas, too. Sylvie was tempted to ask, but mercy won when he lightly pushed her on the shoulder, urging her back to her side of the wagon.

Sylvie scrambled back.

She rummaged around her pack and brought out a small box of bread and her journal. Sylvie leafed through the pages until she found where she'd left off. It was a wrinkled page with a spatter of ink on one corner. As she reread her words, she couldn't help but shiver at what she'd written about Vidal.

Sparing the sun a glance, Sylvie noted that it was still high above them. They had plenty of travel time left. Their guide was whistling a familiar tune now. If she tried, she'd be able to place the words that went along with it. Sylvie didn't try though.

They'd be arriving at the Pit soon. Tomorrow, at the earliest. She'd write until then.

***

Jack's hands quaked.

He looked down at them, distraught. There was an unknown black residue on his skin. It hardened over the veiny parts in a decidedly repulsive manner. Turning his palms upward, his eyes widened at the sight of his hands. Bone thin and gray. His palms were more callused than he remembered them ever being; his fingers were too short and too wrinkled to be his own. Yes, they couldn't be his. He breathed a sigh of instant relief, before the thoughts registered and he stiffened.

Then whose?

Jack's immediate reaction was to look around.

He was surrounded by darkness so deep that he doubted even sound could penetrate it. There were slight blurs along the edge of his vision, so there must've been something there. He just couldn't see it. As he looked down at himself, however, he realized that his form was as clear as day. Jack mapped out the contours of his face with his hands. Awkward nose, busted lip, no veins along his temples. He felt a minor bump under the skin of his left eye—a mole? Definitely not him.

As his senses sharpened, he began to feel things, too. Jack looked down to see a puddle of red under him. Blood.

Of course, he grimaced. *It's always blood.*

And there he was… kneeling in it.

Instead of moving, he looked into the puddle to catch a glimpse of his reflection. He squinted when red eyes stared back at him. An Elementalist then? Before he could make out anything else, the puddle rippled. He saw a shoe. Someone had stepped into it. Then, like a light had been turned on, the rest of the world came into focus.

A startled gasp left his lips at the sight of the butchery before him. Practitioners. He could tell from their robes. Fifty or so—all dead. There were people trapped in cages, crying and screaming. Their ankles and wrists were bound by chains attached to iron rings on the stone floor just past their reach. He doubted they'd be able to get anywhere near them. The cages they were trapped in were held in place by long, black cables from above. While the prisoners looked so malnourished that he questioned their ability to stand. Never mind breaking free.

Roots of raw magic lingered on the walls; Jack knew those walls. Before he could place them, the man in front of him seized his arm with enough force to snap it in two. Given how skinny his wrists were, Jack didn't doubt that the man had actually made an effort to restrain himself.

He was lost in the orange hue of the man's eyes. Distinct and familiar. They were easier to place. Jack had memorized the way they curved a long time ago after all. But the man that stared at him was one he didn't recognize. His face was youthful, but weary. The lines that creased his forehead were too numerous to count. His dark hair was a short, wild mess that looked as if he'd just rolled out of bed. They definitely weren't acquainted.

That hostile, yet pensive look was unmistakable however. He'd been on the receiving end of that stare enough times to be intimately familiar with it.

Sylvie, Jack wanted to call, but found his mouth drier than callused skin in the cold. This wasn't her. Of course it wasn't. *She's a girl,* he thought the obvious, wanting to smack his head for his own folly. *Her brother? He looks young, but… maybe.*

"Are you… Nebbin?" the Conjurer asked, unintentionally interrupting his inner, panicked monologue.

Do I look like Nebbin to you? Jack wanted to say, affronted by the mere inquiry, but something held him back.

He was insane. Jack was sure of it now. He had definitely lost his mind sometime between speaking to Sylvie and falling asleep because this was solid proof. Unless… *do crazies even know they're crazy?* he thought, genuinely curious. *They should, shouldn't they? Somewhere deep down or maybe they even outright accept it. Then again, that doesn't sound right—filan vahs.*

Not even a minute into being insane and he'd already made an argument against it. Not a great one, but how else was he supposed to explain this?

"What's wrong with your eyes?" the Conjurer went on, while his own narrowed in a familiar way. His question, too, was familiar. Then, like he'd been burned, Jack shoved the man as far away from him as possible.

Jack felt more than saw his fingers light. His entire arm blew up in flames. Behind him, his other hand conjured ice.

They both startled at it.

Why the man did, Jack couldn't say. But the feel of the two elements erupting from his skin was something he hadn't felt in a long, long time. Jack reveled in it. His magic reacted to his pleasure in the form of a soft gale breezing its way around him. He stared in awe as he splayed his fingers wide. Dirt sprang forth between the gaps, mixing with the blood on the ground to make mud. It ruined his clothes, but he didn't care. They were already torn for reasons he didn't know.

Absently, he noted the Conjurer's bewildered gasp. The stranger was perfectly still, his face uncomprehending, as if he'd just seen someone blessed by the Creator. But that couldn't be true. Because Jack didn't believe in one omniscient being responsible for all of the life on their wretched land. He only believed in the four apotheoses, and even then, he criticized their ways. Jack wasn't blessed. He just got his magic back.

His magnificent magic that rolled out of his veins in steady waves with no signs of stopping. As deep and as profound as the ocean. Oh, how he missed this.

Thelarius, she unexpectedly called. *What are you doing?*

***

Jack gasped for breath.

Unable to blink it away, he was forced to stare at the colorful blurs that all too suddenly filled his visage. They were meshed together in such a disorderly fashion that he flinched around the shoulders in physical pain. The blurs moved, closer and closer until something warm and soft settled on his face.

Jack finally found the sense to close his eyes. The relief was immediate. He gripped his unsettled stomach, as he tried to focus on his breathing. He waited for it to slow into deep, even breaths, before he chanced peeking his eyes open again.

Orange eyes greeted him as soon as he did. This time, from features he definitely knew. His gaze drifted to the stone that sat inconspicuously under her robes. Jack scowled at it. Somehow, he just knew that his recent dream was once again *her* doing. Why did he have to be the one subjected to those strange dreams? Wasn't it enough to take his powers once?

Jack shuddered when he recalled the encompassing sense of

release he felt when those elements spilled forth from his hands. The way they blended into each other and surrounded him. All he had to do was think of them, and they came. His expertise hadn't diminished at all. He wasn't masochistic enough to try conjuring them now. Jack breathed, trying to reign in his deep seated desire one step at a time. He hadn't longed for anything this much since he was stuck in the Tower...

... *The Drowned Tower!*

Jack choked on his own spit in realization. He hunched forward, coughing harshly. Sylvie said something—he knew she did—but his ears didn't care to register her words.

In his dream, he'd been in Thelarius skin. It had happened before, but the experience wasn't as... intimate. He could move; he could feel; and it explained the Conjurer's surprise to his red eyes. Thelarius was the world's first Elementalist after all. But, more importantly, they'd been in the Drowned Tower. Thelarius Merve, head of the First Zenith and man that had ascended into godhood, was chained up in the Drowned Tower and mistaken for Nebbin. In the same spot he and Tiv would play as children.

He wanted to laugh and vomit all at once.

The Conjurer was Silas then. It could be no one else. He bore a startling resemblance to Sylvie... or perhaps it was the other way around. Jack didn't know if he should've expected that or not. His genes were ridiculously dominant if his traits were still present after so many generations down the Drayr line. Speaking of features, all of the portraits and statues over the ages had gotten Silas' nose wrong.

"Jack!" Sylvie yelled.

Her voice broke through the haze around him. He blinked, trying to rid himself of it completely. When he saw the clear line of her jaw, his own dropped open, as if now only seeing her for the first time. She really *did* look like him.

Jack raised his hands to grasp her face, so he could turn it this way and that, but the look in her eyes told him that she'd strike him if he tried.

"We're here," she remarked, eyeing him warily. Jack turned, trying to make sense of their surroundings. The Pit was but a speck in the distance, though they'd be able to get there in under an hour. Less, if they sprinted. "Are you alright? You fell asleep and now you're..."

"What?" he asked out of reflex.

Sylvie pointed at his eyes, swirling her finger repeatedly. He got what she was trying to say. But he didn't exactly know how to get the wisps to stop. Placing a hand on his forehead, Jack breathed as deep and bolstering as he knew how.

He needed composure. Now.

"What did you see?" she asked knowingly.

Jack could already tell she regretted not having slept as well, so she could see what he had. Would she still feel that way if she saw the manic look in his eyes when his old magic spilled forth from his fingertips?

"Nothing you'd like."

Sylvie stopped to give him a look. Warmth settled in the pit of his stomach whenever she made that face. He liked her best like that. With her lips tugged downward in an infuriated scowl and fire burning in her eyes. Always biting back. Jack felt some semblance of normalcy from it. As if nothing had changed from the day he stumbled upon her in that dark archive on their shared floor. His heart hammered in his chest, and Jack dipped his body forward for no other reason than to be near. Like she was the only thing solid that he could grasp in the shifting sands around him. Her presence was constant and sturdy. A lifeline that kept him from drowning under the leagues of dirt thrown his way.

When Sylvie still didn't look away, Jack let out a long, heavy breath, thankful that she gave him time to regain his composure. With each steady exhale that left him, he realized more and more just how big this dream of his was. Combining it with the other he had all of those weeks ago, his mind worked to fill in the pieces. It wasn't that hard. The answers were right there. They'd always been. Like shattered glass, he just needed to line up the shards. Why had he ignored it for so long?

Denial? his mind supplied. *Because...*

Thelarius had been mistaken for Nebbin—*Nebbin*! His eyes were brown in that initial dream. He'd even been staggered by his own magic.

Thelarius was in chains... like the rest of the slaves.

His fingers trembled, as he brushed the *Orivellea* in his head.

Human Peose, he considered, disgusted. Jack recalled the brutal stories of how Elementalists were handled whenever they tried to escape the Institute. The Zenith Council must've known. It would be impossible not to. Jack's thoughts drifted to the stone. It always led back to that damn rock. *She* had helped Thelarius, given him power, and had just as easily taken Jack's away.

What is she? What does she want?

To return, *she* answered, **to take back what's mine.**

Sylvie's eyes were on him in an instant. Her entire body was straighter than Jack had ever seen. Behind her, the man that had accompanied them grew impatient. His face twisted as he waited for them to get off of his wagon, so he could return to Vidal. He made no physical move to rush them, but Jack did so anyway. He didn't want to look at a Nebbin right now.

Grabbing his pack and trotting off with only a terse nod of gratitude, he stiffened when Sylvie roughly grabbed his arm. The same way Silas had done in his dream. But his wrists weren't so breakable now, and she was nowhere near as strong.

"Jack," Sylvie said. Very unhappy.

The warning drawl of his name was something he needed a good defense for, but nothing came to mind at the moment, so he let it be. The matter wasn't all that pressing anyway. What was important was the upset gleam in her eyes. She wanted answers. Jack knew that look all too well.

Well, he'd already gotten his proof, and as intangible as it might've been, it was still proof. So, there was no reason to deny her what she wanted.

"I'll tell you on the way."

Partner,

We've left Yorn. We're headed to Tor now. Well, not exactly. We're going to the Pit. I **wish** we were going to Tor. Now, I have to deal with smog-filled mines and dirty miners. What's next? A horde of incensed Nebbin after my head? I doubt I'd be able to handle that. Not anymore. I miss my powers.

Jack 37.27.CA

***

Reed,

We've gotten invaluable information. While I don't doubt the truthfulness behind the words, they were vague enough that I'm afraid I might've interpreted them wrong. Well, they were clear in a sense, but... I don't know where I'm going with this, so I'll stop here. My mind's been fuzzy ever since entering Yorn.

Jack and I have finally arrived in Aston. Even though the wagon we're riding moves slower than an injured hound, it still beats walking. Speaking of Jack, he's halfway on the path to sleep now. All drowsy and curled up into himself. I wish I could capture this moment. Maybe then I'd have some proper blackmail to use against him when he's in one of his more aggravating moods. He's been laughing to himself a lot lately. Like he knows something he shouldn't. (I think he might be losing it.) This mood of his started back in Yorn when he bought a book from the bazaar. He won't breathe a word about it to me. I can't believe this dozy bastard is the same one that was arguing so heatedly with me over what I should and shouldn't bring on this trip. Like I don't know how to pack! I think he was just extra upset because I wanted to linger in Yorn.

Vidal gets this weekly plant shipment for his tonics, you see. Turns out he's a gifted embrocologist, on top of being a celebrated practitioner and rich landowner. I wonder if there's anything he isn't. I'd hoped to swallow my fear and learn a few things from him, but lack of time and Jack's insistence trumped that desire. So, it seems that it'll have to wait until we return. I was able to brew a few clotting tonics though. I even made this nice salve. I can only pray that we don't need it.

Fifty-one days. It's been fifty-one days.

Sylvie Sirx 40.27.CA

18

Sylvie's stare was unnerving.

Jack had always known it was. He'd been on the receiving end of it for a while now. There wasn't anything pleasant about the way her lips pulled together before straightening or how her eyes narrowed in warning. It was enough to send lesser men running. Most days, it did. Jack distinctly recalled a merchant's grin dropping when he saw her eyes, while off to the side, an urchin stepped back in caution. She liked to claim that it was unintentional, but he didn't believe her. It could've also been because they were shocked to see the eyes of a practitioner, though Jack doubted it. He'd seen the Conjurers in the Veld with their orange glares and their stern faces, and he'd met his fair share as a child during his short time in the Alps. Jack always met their gazes head on; the same way he met hers. But none of them, *not one*, made him want to rear back as much as he did then.

She just sat there in contemplation.

Her eyes bore into his own. They drifted away only briefly to the side of his head where his Orive crystal throbbed, giving him a sleepy kind of headache. Jack knew the veins there were pulsing erratically. Not because he could feel them, but because he'd self-consciously examined them in the mirror enough times to know how they looked during all of his moods.

Breaking the stare down, Jack turned to the mountainside the rest of Ferus Terria had so adequately labelled, 'the Pit.' It was called something better before. Something more creative. Worthy only for the most lucrative land in the Yovakine Plains—and the most toxic. Its ore brought centuries of prosperity to Tor. But like so many other things, its true name was lost over time. Jack hadn't cared enough during his time spent studying the different civilizations of the south under Master Cutward to read that far back. He still didn't now. It wasn't important anyway.

The only thing that mattered now were the rails he saw running all along the cliff side. If he squinted, he could just make out the ragged people pushing carts. Their skin had so much ash that Jack could barely make out their shackles. But if he tilted his head just so, he could hear them clink on the ground along with their picks. Great, unwieldy things. They swung them down like hammers to harvest stones he'd never seen before. They didn't look like they were worth much though. None of them were shiny or glinting. Were they for building, then?

There were towers and ladders scattered all around the Pit's face. Its entrance was a gaping hole that was so dark Jack couldn't see anything past it. He wanted to amble closer, but the armed watchmen that patrolled the area made him wary. Jack doubted they were hired to keep the workers in line. Even from his position, he could tell that those sorry men had been cowed into obedience long ago. The guards were there to protect whatever lay inside. Jack wished he could creep close enough to see the color of their eyes. How was he supposed to devise a plan if he didn't know what he was up against?

Jack's gaze travelled upward, where clouds of thick smoke blackened the sky, expelled from various openings along the Pit. If he was an Amorph, he could've used it as cover. But he wasn't, and he wasn't about to ask the stone if it could make him one. He was sore enough about the idea of being a human Peose created by the Zenith Council. Transforming into an animal now would only cripple what was left of his pride.

It was no wonder all Elementalists came from the north. They were all summoned back there, too. Even those that learned in other Institutes. He'd once thought that invitations to the Alps were a privilege only offered to his class. Now, he knew better.

He chanced another glance up at the sky, wondering what they could do to slip in unnoticed. Of all the places, why did they have to hole themselves up in a slab of rock filled to the brim with poisonous gas? Were they that eager to greet death?

For a moment, Jack questioned if they were really in there, but quickly erased the doubt from his mind. Of course they were. Jack trusted *her* words. *She* hadn't led them astray so far, so there was no reason not to. He just hoped that the ones they needed to apprehend weren't off gallivanting around the Yovakine Plains because if the rumors about the Pit were true, then he doubted they'd be able to stay down there for long. Not without sullying their lungs beyond reprieve at least.

Jack dug into his pack for his map. He needed to scribble in a few notes while he was here. They were mostly general things that weren't written in books. Like their precise location's terrain or landmarks that scholars didn't consider important.

He was taken aback when he realized that Sylvie was still staring at him. Well, not exactly. Her eyes were on his jaw, hazed over in thought. There was a frown on her face that he couldn't comprehend.

"For the love of—Syl!" Jack snapped his fingers in front of her face. "Get your head out of the clouds and into the game."

When she spoke, her voice was controlled and very even. As if telling him to piss off. Like he would.

"I'm thinking, Jack."

"You do realize that we're about to sneak into the Pit, don't you? Think heavily on your own time. Preferably when we're safe in an inn that's far from anything even remotely Astonian."

Jack balked at his own words. This place smelt like Khale. Not that he went around sniffing the red-headed Amorph, but Tiv had a keen sense of smell, and his partner would regale him with unwarranted tales of the things he unfortunately got a whiff of. Like wet fur, dirty spoons, foul breath, and… Khale. He smelt like metal, or so he'd been told. And this place reeked of it.

Squeezing his nose, Jack scowled when he saw the questioning glance on Sylvie's face.

"What's wrong?" she asked. Her previous train of thought seemingly forgotten.

He'd rather freeze himself blue than tell her. Besides, they couldn't dawdle any longer. They'd already wasted enough time.

"Are you ready to go now?"

"You're the one that's been staring for ages at the sky."

"I've been trying to think of a way inside."

The look she gave him then was filled with all kinds of things. None good for his self-esteem. Disbelief, confusion, and a disturbing lift of her brow that said what she thought without her having to voice any of it—'*did you hit your head on a rock?*'

When she pointed a finger over his shoulder, he wanted to.

There were black tendrils there. They led them to where they wanted to go. The tendrils tunneled off to the side, before disappearing behind an outcropping of rocks where a group of sentries were huddled around each other, playing cards and smiling about something he couldn't see.

On the very edge of his hearing, he heard *her* and the voices that always whispered whenever this path of misfortune appeared. Vidal would've had a field day if he saw it now. That lullaby called out to him again. A promise of power and answers unknown. How could he have missed something so alluring? But his bewilderment was snuffed by the realization that Sylvie could actually see the trail now. Jack knew something more happened when he found her in Vidal's library. But before he could ask her about it, Sylvie dashed forward, holding her robes so they wouldn't billow with the wind. She crouched behind a boulder just large enough to cover her and not much else, before signaling with her hand for him to hurry up.

Just where does she expect me to hide? he thought.

The rock he was behind now was further, but certainly better camouflage than thin air. By the exaggerated roll of her eyes, he knew that Sylvie understood his dilemma, though she held no sympathy for it. He swore that the emphatic shake of her head was wholly deliberate, and so was the way she made sure he saw every second of it.

And I'm the infuriating one? Jack scoffed.

With another flick of her wrist, she called him over and did her best to make enough space for him. It really wasn't much. Jack didn't fancy having to squeeze behind a too small rock, so he tried to find something else instead.

Nothing, he thought bitterly. *As expected.*

But that didn't mean he was about to give up. If there was no way forward and no way back, then he'd have to create an alternate route. Jack picked up a handful of pebbles, then threw the biggest at the nearest guard's head. The man dipped forward, his crouched knees gave at the sudden, harsh impact. The others leapt back with a surprised chorus of *'what's'* and *'who's there?'* before they eyed their surroundings critically.

Jack threw another pebble, but this time he let it roll a short distance from his feet. Sylvie shot him a withering look that he expertly ignored in favor of running to the other side of the large boulder just as the group of men neared it.

They were likely surrounding it by now. One on each side. Two more men waiting at the back. He knew because that was exactly the sort of tactic he'd employ... if he wasn't a practitioner.

They aren't practitioners, he surmised.

Jack watched their tall shadows creep closer. From the corner of his eye, he saw Sylvie tense. Her fingers twitched, as one of the two that lingered behind stepped uncomfortably close to where she was hiding. She spared him a glace, livid and bursting. Jack answered back with an expectant grin that told her to handle it. He knew she could. Quietly, however, was another matter. Her flames weren't made for silence.

The shadow to his left finally neared enough that Jack heard the man's anxious exhales. The squish of his boots over the pliant dirt made Jack's veins burn in excitement. Before he knew it, he jumped out and elbowed the man right in the jugular.

Jack paused... he'd been aiming for his nose.

For a moment, he stood there, simultaneously dumbfounded and embarrassed by his shorter frame. The man fell back, holding his throat and trying to recover from the blow.

Well, he supposed that worked, too.

Someone yelled behind him, and he turned just in time to gracelessly duck away from a blow that would've split his shoulder in two. He barely registered Sylvie leap from her hiding place with her hands up. She spewed fire at enemies he couldn't see. Her flames blurred the air. They made men scream. But the two he faced weren't at all surprised by her appearance. Perhaps they expected him to come with a partner? It was common knowledge that practitioners travelled in pairs. But did they really have that much experience dealing with practitioners? If they did, then this would be harder than he thought. Especially since he could hear the others already running towards them.

Hard, he thought. *But not impossible.*

Never one to be outdone, Jack rolled away from another strike. But he wasn't fast enough. It nicked his shoulder, tearing his robes just as he let loose his magic on the ground. It wasn't like his usual ice. This one surged desperately forward. It had spikes that pierced their boots and coated their legs, effectively halting them in place.

Their blood pooled inside of the ice. But Jack didn't feel bad enough to linger. He let them rage their lungs out. There was no time to shut them up when the others were already on their way.

Jack followed the black path until he reached the rock it sunk into. Glancing cagily at it, he used both of his hands to pry it aside. His fingers clutched deep into the stone's back. He didn't stop even when he felt the slick touch of warm liquid that told him he was bleeding. It opened slowly at first. The cries in the background almost seemed distant to his ears. But with one more forceful tug, it tumbled right out and nearly crushed his legs.

An outpour of stale, black air greeted him. The tiny hole functioned like a chimney, letting out just enough smoke to give away his position. Maybe it was a sealed vent? From the struggle he just had with a damned rock of all things, he didn't doubt it.

"Does that she-devil really expect me to crawl down here?" Jack complained, coughing. His eyes roamed the area for Sylvie. She stood beside one of the men she'd burnt beyond recognition. Fire still sparked in her hands, as she stared mutely in the direction of the horde of approaching Nebbin. From their shouts, he could tell that they were frantically trying to pinpoint the sobs of the men he'd left frozen. Did she want to stay and fight them all? Was she that furious by their disregard for the slaves here?

Who was he kidding? Of course she was. Because he was, too. The abolition of slavery was arguably Thelarius' greatest acc-omplishment, and while he may not have been his biggest fan, it went against all of his morals to stand idly before it; went against everything that had been ingrained into his head since he was a child. But even with all of his powers, Jack doubted he'd be able to fight so many men. So, what was Sylvie going to do? Glare at them to death? They needed to go after bigger fish. Not risk their lives offing an endless sea of grunts.

Before he knew it, Jack was tossing a large stone at her to get her to hurry up. It socked her right in the shoulder, and she crumpled sideways.

Jack paused.

He felt bad about that one. Kind of. The guilt dissipated as soon as she turned furiously in his direction. Jack called her over with a wild wave of his hand. He didn't have to wait long.

Sylvie stopped when she was by his side, her mouth ajar, as she pointed at the miniscule opening that's singular purpose at the moment was to look as unwelcoming as possible.

"You can't possibly expect me to climb down there." Sylvie took a step back to further prove her aversion. "Those fumes will kill me, Jack. *Kill me.*"

"You're talking as if we have a choice," he bit back. "Who's the one that led us all the way to the Pit in the first place?"

"Not me!"

"Well, we can't exactly blame a stone now, can we?"

"Why have you already decided that this is my fault?"

With swift fingers, Jack caught her wrist in a bruising grip. He didn't care that his hand was still dripping with blood or that she tried to kick him in the shin in an effort to get away.

One of the Nebbin shot an arrow in their direction. The bolt missed him only because of a sudden flurry of smoke. That was some incredible marksmanship. The kind he needed to get away from. He wasn't about to sit around and wait for them to fire off an entire volley. There was no way the smoke would protect him from that.

Jack didn't waste any more time.

It only took one, harsh tug for Sylvie to tumble forward onto her knees. Jack shoved her head first into the darkness. But when she hit her shoulder instead of falling face-first into never-ending abyss, he couldn't help but stare in surprise. There was solid ground after all; a tunnel just small enough to crawl through.

Sylvie coughed, the smoke having blown straight into her lungs. It stopped for a brief instant because of her obstruction, before moving just as strongly as it once had.

Jack leapt in after her, already hearing the cries of the Nebbin that ordered their hesitant men to give chase. They were fools if they thought he'd let them. With quick hands, ice leapt from his fingers and coated the entrance just as an arrow came soaring down to strike it.

When he opened his eyes, he found the arrow's tip frozen dangerously close to his forehead. Jack breathed in relief. Only to erupt into a coughing fit at the amount of smoke he inhaled. The Nebbin hacked away at the ice with their weapons. Jack didn't plan on sticking around and waiting for them to finish, but even breathing was a struggle now. He felt like he was about to cough up a lung.

Before he could conjure up a plan, a pair of hands grabbed his robes and dragged him further into the tunnel. Jack crawled along blindly, while burying his nose as best as he could into his shoulder. He let himself be pulled until they reached what he assumed was the end of the tiny hellhole because Sylvie stopped. Her hold on him tightened in apprehension and she backed right into his face. Her scapula hit the side of his head, harshly pushing his face into his own collar.

He couldn't breathe.

Jack tried to call her, found that he couldn't, so he pushed her forward instead. They both stifled a scream when they tumbled down into a larger space. It was noticeably less dark and a thousand time less stuffy. His joints ached and he swore he bruised something on the way down, but Jack couldn't find it in himself to care.

He could breathe.

Pernelia's blessed falcon, he could breathe!

Jack inhaled deeply, exhaling through his nose and trying to get the final vestiges of smoke out of his system. Sylvie was in a heap beside him. Her forearms settled on the rock hard ground as she panted, still trying to comprehend what had happened.

Distantly, Jack heard the aggravated echoes of a few men still struggling to shatter his ice. Fools.

He looked around them. They were in a boxed room with no door and no artificial walls. Just brick-colored rock. Jack didn't know if it was natural or if the oil lamp positioned just outside of the room was to blame for the stone's reddish shine. The little lamp sat atop a crate. For the miners no doubt. Thankfully, none were in the room at the moment. Their only companion was a groaning exhaust machine attached to three small pipes that's mouths were pointed into the tunnel they'd just exited. Each of the pipe's openings were no bigger than his fist. How such small things could expel that much smoke was a mystery for the ages. One Jack didn't have the time to ponder, as he noted the insane amount of crates around them.

He opened one of them to find glittering stones. Pricy things. Jack grabbed a handful, before opening another. This crate was full of tall, glass bottles with thin necks. He knew they were filled with wine by the smell. Possibly a rare vintage. Jack didn't know enough about wine to tell their age or their worth, but they were too large to lug around with him anyway. So, he grabbed another handful of expensive stones in preference.

Once he was finished, Jack dusted himself off and slapped his hand over his chest. Twice for good measure. He kept his eyes on the hall outside. The tendrils had already formed, leading them to where they wanted to go.

"You pushed me," Sylvie said in disbelief. She stood up and gave him a dirty look. He had to keep himself from laughing at her disheveled appearance. Her face was painted black. He doubted his was any better. "I can't believe you started this ruckus, threw a rock at me, and then *pushed* me down a tunnel you didn't even know had solid ground."

Jack fully turned to her then. Only because he was surprised that she referred to his first push and not the one that ended with them falling into this mess of a room. Although she was probably mad about that, too.

"You noticed that I didn't know?" he asked, more than a little impressed by her rushed observation. "That's kind of amazing."

Her response was a kick to his ankle. "Don't patronize me."

"I was serious!" he said, backing away.

"You liar!"

"How many times do I have to tell you that I don't lie, so—"

Sylvie clamped his mouth shut with her hands. "Shhh!"

Jack pulled away, prepared to protest, but stopped himself when he heard someone yawn. A drowsy, grumbling old man appeared not a moment later to stand beside the crate with the lonely oil lamp. He had an iron pick balanced on his shoulder and more muscle in his arms than Jack had in his entire body.

They pressed themselves to the wall, as the miner settled directly opposite of it, whistling his buff heart out.

"Wonderful," Jack griped. A string of invective danced along the tip of his tongue. "Now what?"

On cue, another miner appeared. They only got a glimpse of his long and imposing shadow, but that was enough for them to know he was big. Maybe even bigger than the first. He had a cheery disposition though and that helped ease their nerves.

"Wake up," Cheery Man said in a thick Astonian accent. "Those fishskins're out there gatherin' the rest a' the boys."

"What now?"

They watched with bated breath as Cheery Man's shadow quivered in the light. "Somethin' 'bout stayin' outta their way 'til they catch a dozen or so intruders."

"A dozen?" the old man laughed. "We woulda noticed if a dozen men suddenly barged in, weapons ready."

"They say they're practitioners, yea?"

"What do they want? A lump a' shiny gems? Those cretins should just let 'em take it! S'not like we don't 'ave enough rottin' away down 'ere."

"Right, right," Cheery Man said, assuaging the old fool and coaxing him away. It took a few minutes, but eventually, their shadows grew smaller as their steps faded in the distance.

"Bless him," Sylvie said. She practically merged into the wall behind them in her relief. Jack was no better. He drew in a deep breath to quell his nerves.

Not a step in and they were almost caught.

What kind of self-respecting Elementalist sneaks around anyway? Jack thought in disdain. Each of his powers were storms in their own right. Even if he only had one left; even if that one was never really his to begin with. Jack's hands trembled at the thought, so he balled them until they stopped. If he didn't control himself, he had the sinking feeling that he'd alert the entire mountain of their presence before they even had the chance to leave this room.

He almost didn't want to leave.

Unfortunately, that wasn't an option. His only solace was the realization that the guards actually lied about their numbers.

To save face? he wondered, scoffing. *Fluffs.*

"Ready?" Sylvie asked, as she peered around the corner.

Jack threw her a sharp glance that she failed to notice.

"Like you have to ask."

***

The tunnels were foul.

While they weren't as dark as Sylvie was used to, the torches mounted on the walls were scarce enough that entire paths were shrouded in shadow. Unwilling to use her flames in fear of someone catching them, they walked blindly through the darker paths the tendrils led into. Their steps were guided only by the group of hushed voices that led them deeper into the Pit's center. Twice, they happened upon large mechanisms that regulated fumes from an area below. The smoke was pumped through pipes that led into openings outside.

Sylvie couldn't count the number of times they had to press themselves into tight corners because a stray miner passed. It seemed a good number of them had either decided to ignore the repeated calls of the guards or were so deaf that they hadn't heard them. Permanent injury seemed a very real possibility here. The miners that remained all walked like the dead. They were still bigger than either of them, but they were also exhausted. They dragged their tools on the ground. Their iron heads trailed pathetically along with the links between their cuffs.

Whenever Sylvie's fingers twitched, hoping to unclasp them from their binds, Jack would shoot her a critical gaze. She knew they couldn't afford to alert anyone of their presence and that it was sheer luck that they hadn't been found yet. But…

… They were struggling so much.

Sylvie scowled when Jack pushed her forward. Again. She kept his promise that they'd free them later in mind, after they finished what they needed to do. Sylvie was sure that the leader of the Fetters already knew about them and that it wouldn't make much difference if they went around freeing people now, but she decided against bringing that up, knowing Jack would refuse because they might get in the way. His reasoning was sound, but that didn't mean she agreed with him.

She shook her head.

It didn't matter who was right. Slipping into an argument now was wrong and neither of them wanted that.

Come to me, she said. Her voice bounced around them.

They shivered at the sensation of magic coiling in their guts. Sylvie grasped the stone, as if that might quiet it. Its cool surface slipped in her hands. Lucid and brilliant, despite her death grip.

Eventually, the path led them to a set of narrow tunnels that winded round and round to form a maze. Wagons and rails were few and far between here and stragglers had all but disappeared. But they still heard the heavy huffs of men at work. The sounds that echoed along the walls were different from the loud, hacking noises of digging men though. This was softer. A slush of water, heavy puffs, and someone constantly yelling:

'Hurry up, you blighted half-wits! It's almost done!'

They followed the sound, not even glancing at the trail that lingered above their heads anymore. Sylvie wiped the sweat off of her brow. She grimaced at the ash that coated her fingertips when she did. It was hotter here. Sylvie was tempted to strip off a few layers of her clothes. Even Jack was fiddling with his collar in an attempt to air the heat out.

Sylvie glanced up when the endless walls finally opened into nothing. There was simply a stretch of stone one moment, and then an open cave the next. They lingered just on the edge of it, peering over the side so as not to expose themselves.

That's when they found it. The core of the Pit.

From the other winding paths, theirs seemed to be only one of several entrances that all led to the same thing—a wide, black pool of thick liquid, which enveloped the entire ground floor. It bubbled and exhaled fumes into the open air. In the ceiling above were large, elastic pipes that led into the machines they'd found along the way. So, this was where the gas came from? And they'd inhaled a good deal of it on their way here, too. Sylvie had no doubt that it had already done some kind of permanent damage to her lungs, despite the scant few hours they'd spent wandering. It was no wonder the miners had to be continuously swapped.

The ones here, however, were different. The men that stood in chains around the pool, stirring with tall, steel rods, all had a greenish tint. Some had been there so long that their cheeks were sunken in, the rims of their eyes purple with exhaustion. They were noticeably sick from the fumes. It was likely that they were worked to death, and then exchanged by some other unfortunate soul. They panted and wheezed, but the man that stood off to the side of the pool's dense waters only told them to stir faster. He was short, but imposing with a strong jaw and wide shoulders. An extravagant white robe dwarfed him, sullied only by the specks in the smoke that stuck stubbornly onto him. His eyes were mad and haunted and oh, so cold. They were colored with the lightest green hue they'd ever seen. The man screamed at the men to hurry. Clearly not one to be trifled with.

"Syl," Jack whispered. He angled his head ever so slightly to better stare at something that she couldn't see. "Look."

She craned her neck over his shoulder and gasped when she saw an enormous blue crystal in the pool. It was pointed and familiar, swaddled inside of the waters like a sleeping infant. Her gaze settled on Jack, whose fingertips ran along the *Orivellea* embedded in his head.

"I thought," Sylvie swallowed thickly, "Orive Crystals were only made in the Grove."

"They are," Jack said, his gaze ran over the entirety of the floor. His fists clenched in what looked to be impatience, but she knew enough about him by now to know that it was unease.

Sylvie stifled an angry scream when one of the worker's knees gave in to fatigue. He dropped his rod and fell right into the pool's murky depths. There was a hissing sound, and then the man yelled, fully conscious once again. But it was too late. Smoke rose from his body. They watched in abject horror as the skin melted from his bones and he sank deeper into the liquid, until not even a drop of him remained. The others around the pool stilled, but promptly discarded their fear in favor of closing their eyes and mixing faster. They were crying now.

"What's going on?" Sylvie's voice was barely audible amidst the noise. "What's all of this even for?"

"I don't know," Jack whispered back. His tone was harsh and uneven. "I've never seen an Orive made before. This is... wrong. It has to be! That can't be a legitimate crystal. Look at their chief. He's Nebbin! The Orive has magic infused into it by Healers."

Just then, the man stepped forward and retrieved a ruined journal from his robes. It was no bigger than his hand. He flipped reverently through the pages. The man read through three sheets, before pocketing it again. Then, like he knew he was being watched, his head tilted upward in their direction.

They recoiled behind the wall.

Silas' journal, she said, startling them. Sylvie bit her tongue to keep herself from shouting out. *His words hold the secret to Maurice's Orivellea, to your truth, and to my return. Thelarius' presence lingers here. I can feel it. Silas was close. Although not enough. Never enough.*

"Maurice's *Orivellea*..." Jack ignored everything else *she* spouted. *She* was always mouthing off about something *she* was never willing to properly explain. "I thought the recipe for the crystal was made by Thelarius. Why would Maur—is that why it's only made in the Grove?"

I cannot allow myself to be ripped apart any longer.

"What? Explain from the beginning before you drop vague lines from the middle, you flaming—"

"Quiet!" Sylvie hushed, pinching his shoulder.

Jack clamped his mouth shut. He flinched not in pain, but in realization. But it was too late. The man had already heard them.

"I can hear you," the man called. His voice was an angry, guttural thing that made them shudder. "Come out!"

Don't let him take me.

Monet,

How are you, my dear? Well, I hope.

I'm terribly sorry about this, but I'm afraid that I'll have to cut my usual pleasantries short. Do forgive me for being so crass. (Though I think you like this side of me better, no? Seems I will never truly be a Veld man. Concision isn't exactly my strong suit.) I know I made a promise to you about keeping your delightful Institute from my personal affairs, but this particular issue isn't exactly... personal. As an aside, I told you those two were interesting and frankly, I'm glad they came.

I've assured you on numerous occasions — no less than forty-nine, I believe — that I could've handled going after that feckless ~~revonarahs karis~~ rat myself. Given enough resources, I would've been successful, too. Now look, we rely on children to handle our affairs. I can hear the entire Alps laughing at me from here. It stings. Oh, how far I've fallen.

Yes, this could've all been avoided if I refused their help. But they would've left even if I had. They want something from the Pit. Neither told me what it was, but it's obviously something valuable. They don't hide things as well as they think they do. I'll have to help them with that.

I hope you can force those Potens of yours to move now. If they want to point fingers, then tell them to pin the blame on the children for their recklessness or say it's just one Arch Poten reaching out to help another. Maybe even lie and tell them that those two were sent by the Zenith Council or the Vanguard Circle to aid us in our... dilemma. I'm sure Leonas would be willing to cover for us. He's the keeper of so many secrets, what's one more?

Truthfully, I don't care what you decide, just send men.

And tell that dullard, Wilhelm, to keep his mouth shut. Don't let him sway the other Potens to skimp on forces. When I say I need men — I. Need. Men. Whoever you have to spare. If they're inexperienced, then now is their chance to remedy that. Though I do caution you on sending too many greenhorns. I don't want a throng of untested practitioners at my back, or worse, those that feel they have something to prove. They'll die, Monet. I can't save every fool.

I'll return to the Veld once this battle is won. Until then, be safe.

Vidal 38.27.CA

19

Jack stepped out with a brisk, echoing boom.

Heads turned from all around the room. The slaves stopped mixing just long enough to meet his eyes. Red and prickly. They flinched back at the sight. Jack's glare was acidic enough to scald, and it was pinned on the nameless man that stood on the ground below. The man held his ground well. His chin was raised high, and his lips were curved into a perplexed frown. There were no signs of trepidation on his face.

Jack continued to stare at him, entirely unrelenting, despite how his head throbbed in his sorry attempt to master himself. The ground froze beneath his feet, cracking and spreading cool air throughout the humid room.

He looked over his shoulder only once to see Sylvie cross her arms in displeasure. He didn't know if it was because of him or the morally questionable things going on around them—likely both—but he didn't care enough to ask; he couldn't even if he wanted to. Unclenching his jaw was a long and arduous process that he wasn't quite ready for. He physically felt his own frustration clawing up his throat, words as sharp as freshly brandished swords just waiting to be unleashed, but in the end, those were just words. Jack couldn't get any answers out of this man with criticism. No matter how biting.

As if responding to his resolve, his magic surfaced. Its light was bright enough to outshine the monstrous crystal in the center of the room. Jack flinched when the Heartstone's whispers grew louder in his ears. It fueled the angry flow of ice in his veins, powering him into a cold, gray sun.

Jack felt a foreign tickle centered just behind his eyes. Then all at once, it exploded. Jack knew the wisps moved. He could feel each individual strand as it stirred in the small span of his irises.

He stifled a shout when darkness crept from his feet, steadily rising over his ankles and latching onto his legs. There was a call—*come to me*—and then he felt the wash of a river, before the blackness receded. His head snapped to the side, where Sylvie gripped his shoulder. He observed her fingertips as they glowed, heating his body from head to toe. Her hands were alight with the same strength that fueled his own. Except Sylvie's burned in a different way. Hot and severe. It was almost too much to bear.

"Jack," she called. Soft, yet arresting. He was unintentionally letting another take control. Like Rior and Serach. He was neither. And as far as she was concerned, he was never going to be.

"I know," he bit out.

The realization, however, didn't stop him from struggling to control his flaring temper. Absently, he listed another man slip in fear from their sudden appearance. He fell straight into the pool, shouting and trying to claw his way free from its depths. The workers watched on in fright. A woman, bolder than the rest, reached out to pull him out, to become the lifeline he so desperately searched for. But as soon as she grabbed his hand, she tumbled right in with him, taken off guard by the strength of his grip and the viscosity of the liquid. Jack and Sylvie froze at the sight. They watched, dazed, until the two were enveloped completely. Their cries were muffled by the liquid.

The man—their leader—simply stared curiously at them. He didn't move. Not even when the workers stopped stirring and fell on their backs; scarred, sobbing, and useless. Jack couldn't hold himself back anymore. The ice that had lingered under his feet spread, encompassing the slim stone path they stood on and coming dangerously close to the edge of the pool.

"What," Jack began, wrath dripping from every word, "do you think you're doing?"

The man's eyes thinned and one delicate eyebrow rose in unspoken threat. His voice was nothing like the thunderous roar they'd heard when he shouted. It was careful. Piqued.

"Who wants to know?" he asked.

An enormous spray erupted when Jack's ice suddenly met the dark liquid. As if the waters themselves jetted in protest at the touch of magic. The water froze mid-air in long, curved lashes, unable to escape his frost. They glinted beautifully in the gloom, and for an age, everyone just stared. Then with a thousand cracks, the entire lake was frozen. Steam rose high into the air, and the slaves yelped when their rods were forced still. Those that were quick enough to step back were spared from his ice. Those that weren't screamed in agony.

The man looked on, mouth agape, yet, for reasons they couldn't fathom, his eyes still shined. As if all of this interested him in some sick way. He dived deep into the pocket where he kept Silas' journal. His fingers splayed reverently over its cover.

Touching it for reassurance? Jack scoffed, his mood darkening by the second. He'd freeze the blood in that vile man's veins until he couldn't feel anything anymore, and then shatter his hands for his *own* reassurance.

There was a loud snap and Jack's head whipped around to find a fissure in the ice that had encompassed the Orive crystal. His brows furrowed in confusion. Why would it react to his harmless frost, yet remain unperturbed by the water's acidity?

"You're an Elementalist," the man finally spoke. There was something pleased about the way he said it. He pointed at the side of his head, right where Jack's Orive sat. "My kin."

Jack knew exactly what he meant by that, and he hated it.

Human Peose, he thought again, shuddering. *Nothing better than another ancient experiment.*

"You aren't surprised," he went on, catching the flash of recognition in Jack's gaze. "Does that mean you already know?"

"Don't compare him to you," Sylvie cut in. Her lips were pulled into a tight line of displeasure. "I don't see him chaining anyone up and forcing them to work."

The man laughed. "Maybe because he's the one that gets chained wherever he goes?"

"The only slave I see here is you."

"What bold words!" he exclaimed, uncaring for the way their hands continued to flare. "Spoken like a true practitioner. But how quickly you forget that he isn't one. I admit, I'm shocked to see you both here... and aware at that. Who told you? Have your leaders finally exposed their lies to the rest of the world or did you strangle the information from Verne?"

"Verne?" Sylvie paused. "Vidal Verne?"

"Oh, so it was him!" He nodded his head. The mere mention of Vidal's name all the proof he needed. "I didn't think he'd tell anyone. I never thought he'd be so desperate to get rid of us. Did he get tired of the distance from his wife or has something interesting finally happened up there?"

The man suddenly shook his head and turned to the frozen *Orivellea*. The crystal was so much bigger up close. Without an ounce of fear, he stepped on the pool of ice and slid his hand over the crystal's surface. It squeaked awfully.

"No matter," he continued. "I'm almost done. Only one more ingredient left."

"Do you really expect us to just sit back and watch you finish this?" Jack asked, already making his way towards him.

"You'd deny your kin the right to the same powers you were fortunate enough to be given at birth?" the man asked, genuinely puzzled by the thought. But the moment passed, and then it was replaced by a luminous smile that brimmed with clarity. "Why don't you join us? We have the same goal. The Fetters, or rather, my grand division of it, was brought together to realize Thelarius Merve's wish! To unite Nebbin and practitioner under one rule. That's why the First Zenith created so many Elementalists."

Sylvie and Jack startled when *she* hissed at his words. A threatening sizzle that made their hearts hammer in their chests.

Liar, she roared and echoes of smaller voices followed. *There*

should have only been one! One! As agreed upon! That avaricious
Maurice… always covetous of what could never belong to him.
Green-eyed snake. He wanted it all for himself.

The man didn't hear, so *her* wisdom and *her* unspoken threat
were both left hanging uselessly in the air. With an exaggerated
flourish, the man held up Silas' journal for everyone to see. He
held it the same way Thelarius' priests held statues of him during
processions, as if it could absolve everyone present of their sins;
as if that singular block of lifeless stone held the secret to the creation of the world. In this case, however, it actually might. They
could only guess at the kind of secrets kept in Silas' journal. And
if *she* wanted them to take it from him, then the possibility of it
discussing more than just mere creation was a very real one.

The man's hands trembled in excitement.

"But those damnable extras in the First Zenith were jealous
and got in the way," he went on, speaking as if he knew it all.
"Always, always getting in the way of us Nebbin. Maurice, bless
his soul, realized their plan! He killed the great Conjurer Silas and
left his journal here for us to find. So that we could free Thelarius
from his binds to the ultimate being and enslave it in return!"

He was ridiculously insane. No other explanation for it. Jack
didn't even try to make up an excuse. In his mind, this nameless
man was off of his rockers—and that was that. The last time he'd
heard *her* get so upset was when Serach was spouting out his own
notions. For an absent second, Jack pondered the reason why all
of their enemies talked so much? Was it some kind of necessary
trait before crossing the line into lunacy? His words made him
want to bang his head against the nearest wall. Jack looked to his
left. It was close.

Jack noticed some of the workers futilely trying to pry their
manacles off, but they were weak and shivering now due to the
aftereffects of his ice. He only noticed the sudden drop in temperature when one of the workers wheezed, his teeth chattering so
much that the sound echoed all around the room. Jack watched,
as the slave's breaths left a visible trail of smoke that disappeared

into the open air. Some of them were still stuck to their stirring rods, desperately trying to crack his ice with their weak fists. To no avail.

He'd need to finish this quick then. Preferably before they got caught up in their problems and died in their attempt to run. It would be his fault, too. Jack couldn't have that.

He stepped forward, debating jumping down to the edge of the path and making a mad dash for the nitwit before him or taking the long way and freeing the prisoners first? The decision was made for him when Sylvie caught the end of his sleeve. Her face hardened into an expression that gave him pause.

"I'll take care of the people *and* the crystal," Sylvie told him, leaving no room for argument.

It wasn't as if he could shatter the crystal with his ice anyway. Neither of them were strong enough to hack a block of ice into snow. Sylvie, on the other hand, could melt it down.

"You're leaving me with the raving lunatic?"

"*You* shut him up, before he makes both of our ears bleed."

The corner of Jack's lips twitched. She knew just what to say.

"Have you decided already?" the man interrupted, strangely delighted by their whispers. He looked at Jack with a smile that was anything but real. "What do you say? We could always use another Nebbin on our side!"

Jack bristled at his words, barely registering Sylvie leave his side to run down the path and to the nearest quivering worker. The slave batted her away, but she caught his wrist in one hand and broke the frozen iron ring that kept his chains in place with the other. She moved onto the next with methodical precision. No moves were wasted, no step squandered. The man idly watched her from his position on the ice, as if he could care less about her releasing them. Then again, what were a few half-dead slaves compared to their current situation?

Jack jumped. She was doing her job, now it was his turn to do his. His hands glowed bright enough to capture the man's attention once more.

"No," Jack finally answered, slow and clear, so he could get it through his thick skull. "Why would I ever want to join a senile turtle that can't even tell the difference between Thelarius' goals and the petty ones he wants to achieve?"

The man froze, every bone in his body screamed livid. "You can't lie to me! I've read the history. The *true* history. Or do you doubt my words? Are they too hard to comprehend for someone raised to dance in the Council's palms? I can show you the truth! It's all here in this journal."

"Is that head of yours as empty as the words you speak?"

"What," the words caught in his throat when Sylvie rushed by them. Fire in her hands, aimed directly at the frost covered crystal. The man was quick to gather his bearings, drawing a knife from his robes. "Get away from my creation!"

Jack didn't think.

He sprung forward and blocked the blade in what was possibly the stupidest manner of blocking he'd done to date. He certainly felt the consequences. Both physically and mentally. Behind him, he heard Sylvie yell his name. He ignored it in favor of watching the man, whose eyes widened in surprise, but not enough for him to let go. Instead, the man's grip tightened over the hilt and he dug the knife deeper into Jack's forearm. Jack ground his teeth together to keep from crying out.

But then ice seeped from his veins, encasing the tip of the dagger all the way to the hilt. The man gasped and let go just in time, but Jack snatched his arm, before he could fully pull away. His ice rose with a vengeance. It crept up the man's arm, freezing everything up to his elbow a sickly purple. Just as he was about to envelope the rest of his body in ice, so he could milk the demented fool for answers, his fingers stilled.

Jack didn't know what happened. But one minute his vision was sharp with rage and the next, it blurred. He tipped sideways, and he felt the uncontrollable urge to vomit. Colors blended together. He let go of the dazed man to clutch his aching head. His temples were throbbing again. The burning behind his eyes returned. There was a distinct fizzle—Sylvie's fire? Had she melted the *Orivellea* already? He couldn't say. Jack tried to check. When he turned to where he thought she was, however, that vile creature in the Heartstone shrieked in sudden rage.

Kill him, she said. As if he wouldn't sooner or later.

Distantly, he heard Sylvie call his name. It was followed with rapid-fire words that were too bent for him to understand. His poor attempts at deciphering them only made his head pound even more. Suddenly, Sylvie's hands were on him. Every touch was frantic and filled with heat. Then, in an abruptly clean moment of thought, Jack knew what was happening. He knew what she was trying to do. Because it had happened before.

"*Filan vahs!*" he swore, crouching into a tiny ball and shutting his eyes to the world. Her hands were on his shoulders, calling him once again. But all he could focus on was the constant, mind-blearing ringing in his ears. He couldn't tell that old man apart from Sylvie—or Sylvie apart from the voices in his head.

Her voice was deafening.

Take Silas' journal! *she* bellowed, angrier than he thought possible. What was wrong with *her*? Was *she* that offended by the man's words? **Make this scum disappear. He has done nothing to deserve my power! Nothing!**

If *she* wanted him dead, then *she* should've just let him quietly kill the man! He would've done it after—

Now! Kill him now!

So much for his wishes. Lying thing. He loathed liars.

Jack bit his lip until it broke skin. A shout cut through the haze around his mind, and he opened his eyes to find tendrils shooting out from his body to wrap themselves around the man's legs. They squeezed until they snapped. Sickening cracks filled the air. But the tendrils only squeezed more.

The man sobbed. He crawled toward the blurred figures of the slaves in the distance, begging for help that wouldn't come.

Sylvie's hands were still on him, trying to get the darkness to recede without her magic. It was a sorry attempt. But he knew she was hesitant to turn her flames on him. Jack felt it in the way she held his shoulders. Careful, yet firm. An age passed like that. Before she finally came to a decision. The wave of her magic was hotter than before. It made his blood boil, and the heat behind his eyes blistered red.

She stopped when he screamed. Loud and momentary.

Jack flinched away from her touch. He clawed at the skin on top of his ears and over his temples, as if that was where *she* resided. A rotten pot of anger bubbled in his gut. Hot poison that frothed over and begged for release. He wasn't here for *her* convenience. *She* wasn't allowed to use his body however *she* pleased. He'd be damned if he was treated like some inanimate puppet. Jack wasn't about to become another sorry imitation of those idiots *she* so easily ruined in the Drowned Tower.

He'd rather die.

"Get out of my head!" Jack yelled. "I don't care how pissed you are, get out! Get out, get out, get out!"

You must rid yourselves of him, before—

"Get the fuck out!"

For one, solitary instant, Jack was swathed in *her* presence. Then, as swift as paper fading in the rain, *she* disappeared.

The darkness lifted from his eyes, and the heavy anger along with it. He felt more than saw the tendrils retreat. They warmed his core, while simultaneously making him sick to his stomach. He folded in on himself. Jack slouched against Sylvie's frame, while the blackness writhed, wreaking havoc inside of his body in a place too deep for him to see.

Though wisps lingered along his periphery, he knew from the relieved way Sylvie looked at him that the brunt of the tendrils had receded. Gone, until they were needed again. Swift and easy. Like cobwebs brushed away by a delicate hand.

Jack tried to will away the tears of pain that spilled from his eyes, as he heaved a sigh of pure, honest relief. It was short-lived, however. Because an earsplitting crack echoed above them. The sound was followed by a dozen rolling snaps that devastated the air. They looked up to find a crevice form along the ceiling. It grew longer and deeper, spearing across an immeasurable length in an instant and showering them in sand and rubble.

Their jaws dropped in disbelief.

They both knew what was about to happen.

"Why does *everything* we enter crumble?" Jack asked.

***

Jack's body shook.

Sylvie knew immediately that she'd have to be the one to get him out. Jack was still breathing too heavily to be of any real use right now. Sylvie turned, searching for... anything.

Anything they could use to help them get away. Anything they'd regret leaving behind. But all she found was the nameless man clutching Silas' journal like his life depended on it.

That counts, Sylvie thought, as she stared at him. He couldn't move anymore. That much was obvious after a single glance. Both of his legs were twisted in impossible directions.

Above them, there was another explosion.

It shook the ceiling and dropped more rocks over them.

What's happening? Are the Nebbin trying to trap us inside?

Sylvie whirled around when the man laughed wickedly. The sound was hateful and piercing. It was shrill enough to garner anyone's attention, no matter the circumstance. But it was his smile that really caught her. His lips were stretched wide. They pushed the edges of sanity to its limits.

"I used to tell them," he began, "about the bombs I kept above their heads in case they decided to lash out. I never thought they'd end up burying me with them one day."

Sylvie pushed away from Jack.

Hands aflame, she grabbed the man's wrists. She ignored his howls as her fingers charred his skin black. Sylvie stopped only to pocket Silas' journal, before searing his arms up to his elbows. She kept going until his eyes rolled to the back of his head and he passed out. His screams died mid-way, caught in his throat like someone had squeezed it.

Sylvie remained long enough to watch his chest rise and fall a total of four times. It steadily grew weaker, and she decided that leaving him there to be crushed under the rubble was better than finishing the job. She wrinkled her nose at him in disgust. Sylvie could *feel* her magic sizzling under her skin, aching to be let out for reasons even she wasn't entirely sure of. But seeing Jack in such a state, while she sat utterly helpless...

It made her want to break something.

"Syl," Jack called, his face pained.

Sylvie reached into her robes for two flasks. She slipped one into his pocket in case they were separated, before popping open the other and pressing it to his lips.

"Drink," she ordered.

Jack didn't resist. He stood a little straighter with each gulp, and before she could object, he pulled the knife out of his forearm with a grieved groan. She ripped his sleeve in an instant, tying it around his arm as quick as her quivering fingers allowed. Sylvie muffled a shout when a slab of stone as big as her came crashing down, and with perfect aim, fell on the man's chest.

His pain came and ended in an instant. He woke, shrieking, until the walls ate up every echo, and all that remained was a puddle of blood under rock.

"Talk about divine providence," Jack commented, but she couldn't find it in herself to laugh.

"We need to go," Sylvie said, while searching for that black trail. As soon as the thought of it entered her mind, the tendrils appeared above them, leading them back the way they came.

"How convenient," Jack said, voicing her thoughts.

"Can you run?"

He still had the audacity to look annoyed.

"Can you?" she pressed.

"Who do you think you're talking to?"

No more words were exchanged between them. All of their focus was kept on running back and dodging falling gravel. Only the inner sanctum of the Pit seemed to be crumbling because as they got further away, the shaking lessened into slight tremors, and then nothing at all. But adrenaline kept them dashing toward the exit, as if they were afraid the whole mountain might fall on their heads if they stopped—just like what happened in the east.

Eight times, they stopped to warn befuddled miners about what was happening, giving them explicit orders to follow them out. Neither turned back to check if any of them did. But from the distinct lack of footsteps, it was obvious that none of them took their words seriously.

By the time they made it to the entrance—the wide, gaping hole that Jack had seen before they entered—they were both struggling for breath. Their chests rose and fell at an alarming rate. Sylvie could hardly care about the fact that she was coated in grime and sweat or that Jack favored one arm over the other because seeing the light at the end of the tunnel made her feel safe. A physical sense that washed over her entire body, from the top of her head to the tips of her toes. All from the simple assurance that the Pit wouldn't cave in, and even if it did, they'd be able to leave without the risk of sudden death.

Just as she thought it, she heard the noisy conversation of the Nebbin outside. They'd been waiting for them.

Her insides churned in distress. The magic under her skin hummed in a quiet plea to be let out. She'd felt it buzzing since the start of their run. For once, she thought she felt what Jack did whenever he told her about the enthralling voices in his head, coaxing the power from deep within his bones.

"We should head back to Yorn," Jack said, already searching for a different exit. "Before those bastards out there catch us."

Sylvie wanted to nod, to agree, to shout—*yes!*—at the top of her lungs, but then she saw one of them grab a petite slave girl by her hair. The guard's lips were warped into a perverse smile. Further off to the side, his companions beat the cheery miner they had the misfortune of encountering into a gory mess, while the others questioned them regarding their whereabouts. None of them knew. Of course none of them knew. They didn't even believe they were there in the first place.

Sylvie's arms lit up to her elbows. Her lack of control ended up burning her sleeves into ash. The sight alone was enough to make Jack halt. There was no calm to the fire that Sylvie kindled inside of her. Nothing of quietness or mercy. It was white-hot and scalding. The entire tunnel brightened with the intensity of her magic, swiftly catching the attention of the Nebbin outside.

Suddenly, everyone started moving.

The world slowed. Wind died. And Sylvie was lost in the heat of the moment.

The Nebbin approached the entrance with their weapons drawn, fully intent on investigating the disturbance, while the slaves they'd rounded backed away in sudden, collective fright. Beside her, Jack mumbled something that sounded suspiciously like a complaint about his aching arm. He was in the middle of asking her what in the world she was doing giving away their position when Sylvie—

Sylvie snapped.

Vidal,

Why is it that whenever you're involved the mess is always, always so flaming difficult to clean up? And now you want my practitioners? If I find out that this isn't for the Veld, pray that I never see your face again. My blade might very well slip and split your head.

But I'll believe you. For now.

I promise to send anyone I can spare. I don't know who might be of use to you because, as usual, you leave out all of the important bits. But I expect you to return my practitioners as soon as you're done.

Finish this quickly, Vidal, then send them back without delay. They're all good men that deserve to come home. (That includes you.)

Keep me updated.

Monet Verne née Thareen 39.27.CA
Arch Poten, Red Veld

20

The estate was eerie at night.

Dalis crept just outside of its gates. He looked behind him every now and then to see how his men fared. Fairly well, considering most weren't made for silence. It was strange for him not to see wide grins splitting their faces, but this wasn't exactly the time to smile.

He looked at Larce, gagged and bound by rope. Philip, his most trusted friend and partner, stood over his shoulder, making sure he behaved. Larce was slyer than he looked if his knowledge of them was anything to go by. They'd tried threatening him into spilling the Mistress' secret infatuation with practitioners only to come up with frightened squeals and pitiful shakes. He may have been a coward, but he was a quiet one. Still, Dalis knew that if given the chance, Larce would nick him in the back and leave him there to bleed. He had the eyes of someone that would.

But that wasn't important now. The only thing that mattered at this moment was that they weren't spotted. Dalis peered around a corner, searching for any lingering guards. He found none. His eyes drew upward instead, prepared to scale the gate. He was just about to jump when Leda grasped his shoulder.

"Are you sure this is a good idea?" she asked, concerned.

"We're raiding a place we know nothing about," Dalis said blankly. "Of course it isn't."

With that, he climbed the gate, wincing with each sound it made. His men followed close behind. They traversed down the stone path, quietly knocking out the guards and dragging their bodies into the overgrowth. For such a kingly estate, there weren't many men lingering about. Which could only mean that the bulk of them were either inside of the main building or scattered inside of the warehouses.

Dalis motioned for his men to split into groups. They made five full groups of four. The Amorphs among them quietly hid in the bushes to lookout for any errant patrollers.

Upon closer inspection, the warehouses weren't as large as he'd initially thought. Dalis peeked through a window. He cocked his head in confusion when all he saw were crates and barrels piled on top of each other. No guards. No people. No slaves. He opened the door and winced when it creaked just loud enough to sound deafening. Dalis gestured for his men to stay put, as he pushed the lid off of a large crate that sat near the door.

Empty. His lips pressed into a thin line. He looked down at his fingers and found them dark with filth. *How long have these been here?*

Dalis opened another, then five more. They were as sandy as the first. The air inside was stale and sour. Pungent enough to make him step back in disgust. The crates hadn't been opened in a long time. Perhaps since they were brought here. From the thick coat of neglect that blanketed the lids, they hadn't been touched either. Then, as if to refute his ideas, Dalis found fresh mud scuffed over a section of the floor. It circled a small, open space that was free from dust. Understanding dawned upon him, and he hurried out of the warehouse.

They place them in these when they want to haul them off, but... Dalis carefully surveyed his surroundings. *Where do they keep them hidden?* He was sure he'd heard the ring of manacles come from here during his last visit, so they must've been nearby.

In the estate? Dalis guessed. It was certainly large enough.

He searched the faces of his group and his eyes hardened when he found his prize. Dalis grabbed Larce roughly by the shoulder, startling the ugly man into yelping. It was so loud that the cloth around his mouth wasn't fully able to contain it.

Dalis' dagger was at his throat in an instant.

"Where are they?" he demanded.

Larce recoiled, but when Dalis only pressed his blade closer, drawing a thick rivulet of blood, he pointed a shaky finger at the right side of the estate. An Amorph flew over to scout the area, before beckoning them over. A short flight of stairs hidden by the foliage was there. It led into a long hallway with multiple doors. Sentries patrolled the area, while more leaned against the walls. Each stood a routine distance away. When two more Amorphs volunteered to circle the rest of the estate, they found the setup mirrored on the other side of the building.

Dalis motioned for two of the smaller, deadlier groups to back him up, then gave Philip a brief nod. A voiceless indication to lead those on the other side. Philip rolled his eyes, but went without complaint. He dragged Larce with him.

As soon as they rounded the corner, Dalis threw a cracked stone against one of the walls. It shattered upon impact. The sound echoed down into the hall. Murmurs broke the silence; a string of garbled nonsense that sounded like a mess of syllables slapped together by an angry drunk.

What language is that? Dalis wondered fleetingly. Concern was the same in every tongue, and theirs was obvious.

It wasn't long before two pairs of footsteps came bounding up. They yelled back at their noisy companions. This time, their voices were clearer—an imaginative curse, a warning not to look at their cards—all spoken in the trade tongue, but with a heavy drawl that accentuated every vowel too deeply. By the time their boots touched the grass, Dalis' men were on them in an instant.

Dalis grabbed the first from the back, then slid his blade efficiently across his throat. He left him there to gurgle. By the time he turned, the other had already been dealt with. An arrow poked out from his eye, as two practitioners slid him down as gently as possible, so as not to make too much noise.

They dragged them into the nearby bushes, piling them on top of the rest they killed, while Dalis tried to think of a plan that wouldn't get the slaves inside caught up in the bloody mess they were about to make. It would've been easier if they could blast the place with fire. Maybe even destroy the building entirely by having Philip erode the ground. But that would defeat the purpose. It was just their luck that they didn't have any wind Conjurers, and the only Elementalist and ice Conjurer they did have were with Philip, no doubt putting their powers to good use. Dalis would bet his leg that Philip took them just to annoy him.

Looks like we need to do this the old-fashioned way, Dalis thought, not even bothering to hide the scowl on his face *Great.*

He motioned for his men to get into position, while he took one of the helmets from the pile of dead guards. Dalis mumbled a polite, "I'll be taking this," in light of a prayer.

"Wes! Mathen!" one of the guards called from below. He was coming closer if his fattening shadow was any indication. "Shit and vinegar! C'mon you godforsaken sons of ten-penny whores, pick up the flaming pace! We've got a game to finish!"

Taking that as his cue, Dalis threw the helmet down the flight of stairs. It sailed through the air, before bouncing pathetically down the steps and stopping at the surprised man's feet.

There was a beat of silence; as encompassing as the noose after it had been tied. Dalis would've used it to his advantage, but the man was faster than he looked because not a moment later and his eyes were already hardening. His sword hissed as he drew it from its sheathe. No doubt the others were raising their weapons as well. Unfortunately for them, Dalis was fast, too. He slid down the steps like a ghost and shoved his dagger above the soft skin of the man's bellybutton. Twice. For good measure. Behind him, his companions poured in, hands alight with magic. It spilled from their veins and out into the open air.

The Nebbin put up a good fight, despite their shock. They swung gallantly at the Amorphs, even nicking two of them as they entered. Dalis snarled when Leda—in the form of a large hawk—was taken down by a soaring, expertly aimed arrow.

With a flash, she transformed into a wolf and scurried away

with her head bowed, only for someone to come up and slash her leg from behind. Dalis was by her side in an instant. He dropped to a crouch when the Nebbin swung at him. The man raised his sword above his head and struck downward with both hands. Dalis brought his dagger up in an unsteady block. The Nebbin was larger and stronger, but Dalis had the might of his legs and he propelled himself upward with his feet. He pressed so harshly against the floor that he thought it might crack under his weight. His free palm burned brightly in the gloom. It glowed even more when he pressed it against his chest.

Dalis' magic wasn't made for destruction, but it was enough to force the man unwillingly forward. He sagged down in sudden relaxation. The man's blade fell from his limp hands, and Dalis harshly swung his own to rip across his face. Leda had already limped off, presumably aided by another.

It was then that the Conjurers finally made their appearance. They spewed barely controlled tunnels of fire that Dalis just scarcely rolled away from. The Nebbin fell to their knees. Those that could still move their legs ran around screaming, bumping into walls, as they tried in vain to douse the flames that burned their skin. The scant few that were fortunate enough to escape, ran foolishly up the flight of stairs, where they were dealt with by the remnants of Dalis' group.

When the final scream of the last remaining guard died via an abrupt kick to the face, Dalis turned to inspect the wounded. His hands glowed fiercely. There was no time to waste. But when he saw that a number of them were already being treated, he let slip an approving smile, before clasping a few of his more idle companions on the shoulder in appreciation.

"This way," Dalis said, stopping before a door.

They hung back, hiding with their backs pressed against the wall as the door groaned like an animal before them. As soon as it opened fully, they were met with the heavy clink of chains and sharp, inconsolable sobbing. They waited a long moment, before collectively agreeing to leave their hiding space. None of them wanted to be caught by an errant guard that might've hidden inside during the fight.

The first thing they took note of once they stepped past the threshold was that the room was dark. Unbearably so. It was likely pitch black when the door was closed.

"Light," Dalis ordered when his eyes took a second too long to adjust. "Someone get me light."

A Conjurer was by his side in an instant, hastily summoning fire. Their eyes widened at the long line of prisoners caked in dirt and dressed in drab, gray rags. The prisoners recoiled at the sudden light, racing into corners and shrinking away in fright.

"Found the keys," someone said from behind him. Dalis turned to find one of his friends holding a thick iron ring with more than a dozen deceptively similar keys attached to it.

"Free them quickly," Dalis said. "Let those that want to leave go, but direct them eastward. We don't want them running straight into the Hovel, or worse, Tor. Gather the rest in the yard. We'll figure out what to do with them after."

As much as he wanted to, they couldn't let them run off wherever they pleased. Not when the nearest settlement was filled with people that worshipped the Mistress of this estate. Perhaps she gave them provisions during times of need. That was the only explanation he could think of.

"Dalis!" a voice called from down the hall, snapping him out of his stupor. "We found a few practitioners."

"Down here, too!" came another shout.

"And here!"

"Anyone from the east?" Dalis slipped out to meet them.

"We can't tell," Philip's voice suddenly rang out. Dalis found him leaning against the wall with a solemn frown marring his lips. He must've finished some time ago. "All of the practitioners are passed out and heavily injured. They've been beaten bloody. I'm having the Healers fix them as we speak. Maybe then we can get a few answers."

"Slavers are all the same," Dalis said. "I'm guessing it's another classic case of beat them if they step out of line, or maybe knock them unconscious every time they decide to use their magic. Ha! As if that ever worked on anyone."

"I doubt it was anything like that."

"Oh?"

"If they were punished for rebelling, then at least one or two of them should be alright. The younger ones especially. See a man twice your age get his leg smashed into a bloody pulp, and the fight just leaves you. And have you seen the Nebbin? All those we've come across look like spoiled babies in comparison. I doubt they all just obediently stepped inside of their cages."

"So, what? You're saying they don't deal in practitioners?"

"Exactly," Philip said. "I don't know any slaver that would want their wares missing a few... pieces."

"Pieces?"

"Fingers and toes mostly."

Dalis grimaced. "Any dead?"

Philip breathed in deeply, before nodding. "Some died from thirst, others blood loss. A few of the younger ones though... they look like they were gutted open and eaten alive by starving rats."

Dalis turned away then. He took the steps by twos, not wanting to know any more grisly details. Once he reached the top, he looked up at the sky. They still had a few hours before sunrise. They needed to finish by then.

"What now?" Philip asked, leisurely following him. "Are we finally going to raid the castle? They're likely armed and ready by now. We weren't exactly quiet down there."

"Any suggestions?"

"We could order the first and third groups to clean out the estate, then leave the others with the captives."

"Do you need me to lead one of the groups?"

"That was the idea." Philip glanced at him from the corner of his eye. "Unless you had something else in mind?"

"I wanted to take a walk with Larce."

"A walk. Right. Sounds... *friendly.*"

Dalis shrugged. "Where is he?"

"Left him with Lyss." Philip eyed him knowingly. "Take the kid with you. He's strong. You'll need the backup."

***

The *She's Disciples* was a fitting name, Dalis mused as Larce led them through hall after hall. Their muddy shoes sullied the sleek, mustard floors. The Mistress had an astounding number of men at her disposal. By the sheer amount they'd encountered as soon as they stepped inside, Dalis wouldn't be surprised if the mansion housed an entire cult.

Dalis and Lyss skillfully took out the ones they couldn't avoid, leaving those they could for the others to take care of. Their eyes lingered on the elaborate frescoes decorating the walls. They were all of various landscapes. In front of them, stood stuffed carcasses with abysmal, black eyes. It was only when they were passing a particularly long display of a majestic forest that Dalis stilled. He blinked blankly at the deer in front of him, as he recalled the conversation of the two guards he'd seen when he first came to the estate.

Think the Mistress'll stuff him?

His jaw clenched.

"What's wrong?" Lyss asked worriedly. His voice was drowned by the heavy clang of steel in the distance. It was followed by a cacophony of voices, barking orders and shouting battle cries that rapidly died on their lips. The fire outside was so large and so bright that they saw its glow spill in from a nearby window. It was nice to know that their comrades were doing a fine job of getting rid of the Mistress' men at least.

"Nothing," Dalis replied after a minute. "Remind me to burn these on my way out."

"What?" Lyss took a moment to examine the deer, before his jaw slackened in understanding. "Don't tell me, they're—"

"We need to keep moving."

Dalis shoved Larce forward. The man let out something

between a pitiful squeal and a horrified swallow, as he stumbled over his own two feet.

They walked for ages, making sharp turns and sprinting down lengthy hallways with distant ends. The mansion was bigger than either of them thought. Dalis kept his dagger pressed threateningly against Larce's back the entire time, and for an instant, he wondered if the ratty man was just leading them around in circles, waiting for a chance to escape. It's what he would do. But the doubt suffered a quick death when Larce stopped before a long, ominous hall with a large door at the far end. He pointed one wrinkly, sausage-like finger at it.

Just then, an old man rounded the corner. His arms were filled with paper and jewels and a giant staff that clattered noisily to the ground at the sight of them.

"I—No, please," he cried, though they had yet to even move. His eyes implored mercy, searching, begging for an ounce that didn't exist. But then they settled on Larce and the pleas evaporated as quickly as they'd come. "You!" he accused venomously. "You brought them here!"

"Lyss," Dalis said.

"On it."

He made to grab the old man, only to be shocked when he stepped out of the way in an impressive display of his own sprite. The old man hurriedly picked up his staff to defend himself when his feet froze.

Taking advantage of his shock, Lyss planted his hand over his mouth and froze everything from his neck up a cool blue. The ice sealed his head with an ominous *crack*. Lyss didn't waste any time. He shoved the old man against the nearest wall, shattering his brain. The shards sounded like pearls as they fell.

Larce screamed. Dalis socked him in the face to shut him up.

"Quiet," Dalis ordered. He pushed Larce forward until they reached the door. "Open it."

Larce's hand trembled violently. He squeezed his eyes shut in desperation. But Dalis didn't let him leave.

"Open the door," Dalis repeated, uncompromising.

Larce rolled on the balls of his feet as if to run, but soon fell flat on his heels, knowing what would happen to him if he tried. He took a deep breath and twisted the knob. It slid open slowly. Excruciatingly so. There was only silence as the door revealed a tiled floor and large shelves. In the middle of the room, stood the Mistress with her head cocked to the side and a furious snarl on her lips. There were no cages here. No manacles or chains. No evidence to suggest that she was the ringleader of the Disciples.

Nothing, save for the crazed look in her eyes.

She only had two guards. One was an archer that hovered behind her, the other was a spear holder that stood beside a tall bookshelf to his left. Too close for comfort.

Dalis' instincts urged him to turn and run far, far away. Self-preservation told him to return only when he wasn't walking into such an obvious trap, but his feet continued onward. As if compelled by some unknown force—his own curiosity, perhaps? He couldn't say. But his instincts were promptly damned because of it. He wasn't going to run. If he had to fight and kill this woman and every one of her sick batch of loyal followers, then so be it. He'd be doing Ferus Terria a favor as far as he was concerned.

No one spoke. But no one needed to.

The woman stepped forward. Dalis pushed Larce toward Lyss and held up his dagger. There were unsaid threats in both of their eyes. Her guards were swift to react to his sudden hostility. But by the time they drew their weapons, Dalis was already moving.

A swift arc of his blade had the spear holder to his left jumping back for better range. Fool. Dalis threw his dagger and didn't bother watching as it pierced her chest. He only dashed behind her to yank it out, red and lined with gore, before using her body to block an arrow aimed at his heart. The bolt sank deep into her, penetrating both flesh and bone. Its oiled tip clinked against the steel mesh hidden under his robes.

Well-made, that one. There was a lot of force in that shot. The archer was doubtlessly skilled. A peek around the dead woman revealed the Mistress' twisted snarl and her guard's bow pointed at his chest.

Round two.

Dalis kept the carcass upright. The perfect shield against his bolt. He gripped his blade, still dripping with fresh blood.

"My blade or your bow, whose will break skin first?"

The guard didn't speak, merely drew the string of his bow back a little further. But that was also an answer. Dalis smiled. Slow and deadly. Before he could move, however, the Mistress raised her hand high into the air. The suddenness of the action made him still in caution, but her guard wasn't so wary.

Suddenly, a volley of arrows rained down upon him.

His bolts flew through the air at an inhumane speed. They hit the dead woman's chest again and again, forcing Dalis back until he was pressed against the wall with the woman's blood dripping down upon him. The rivulets soaked into his robes like paper lost in the rain.

"Stop," the woman abruptly said, her arm still held high. Her guard ceased immediately. "Are you ready to talk or would you like to continue testing your luck?"

"Talk?" Dalis laughed, dry and humorless. He tightened his grip over his dagger's hilt. Why was she acting as if she'd cornered him? Lyss was still there, holding Larce in place and waiting to strike at his command. Distantly, he thanked Philip for reminding him to take someone along.

Dalis could either negotiate with her or just get rid of her guard and take what he wanted. It wasn't a hard decision.

"Big words," he went on, warily eyeing the bowman by her side. From the corner of his eye, he saw Lyss place his hand upon the wall, before the sound of cracking ice reverberated around them. The Mistress and her guard turned in surprise, having now only noticed his orange eyes. Ice crept forward dangerously, coating their feet and stopping right below their knees.

"What do you want?" the Mistress asked. Her voice didn't

waver. Dalis had to give her credit for that. "Why are you here? What reason could a practitioner possibly have to come here and ruin all that I've built? Who are you working for?"

There was another crack and the ice encompassed her guard completely. For the first time, she screamed. Larce yelled something unintelligible behind his gag, distracting Dalis from the woman before him. Larce scratched at the door, but his feet were frozen to the ground. Dalis quickly knocked him out with a solid blow to the head for the second time that week. He had a sinking feeling that it wouldn't be the last.

"We're asking the questions," Lyss cut in. "What have you been doing to the practitioners here?"

"Nothing!" she shouted, clawing futilely at the ice. "It was the men! The men!"

"Don't lie!" The ice grew to her hips and she screamed again.

"The men whispered things," she wailed, cradling her head with her hands. "They told me to catch them, break them, and force them to tell me their secrets."

"Secrets?"

"But they never said anything! They trusted him, didn't they?" she pointed at Larce with a crooked, accusing finger. "Yet they never told him anything! No matter how much they were beaten, they never told him their secrets! What is it?"

She whirled back and forth, crazily looking over them both. "Those magic circuits... how can animals be the only ones to have them physically implanted? I saw the crystal on the Elementalist's head! You can't fool me. That was... that was a circuit, wasn't it? Oh, I've been trying to find out how to make them. For years, I tried! Mixing blood and fingers and nails and yet... the Healers make them, don't they? I've captured dozens, but none ever knew. None ever tell."

The Mistress turned to Dalis. Her brown orbs pleaded with his blue ones. "Tell me your secret!"

As if Dalis or any other self-respecting practitioner of the Weeping Grove would ever betray the Institute.

But how did she find out about—

"She's a loon," Lyss hissed with a resentful sneer, effectively interrupting his thoughts. His expression gave nothing away. "Let's put her out of her misery."

"Practitioners from the east," Dalis intervened, before he could. His voice was a loud, assertive command that spoke little of patience. He'd give her this one chance to redeem herself. "Do you have any here?"

The Mistress scrunched up her reddened face. "Tell me—"

"Kill her."

First Adviser Sirx,

I am writing to you today to inform you that Arch Poten Cole has received your message and will take your words into consideration. A just and fitting punishment will be decided by the rest of the Potentate Union in due time.

A number of the men that practitioners Philip Rhone and Dalis Sirx have run off with are loyal members of the Red Scripts and of the Closions. The representatives of both colleges have made it abundantly clear that their men had no intention of deserting, so you must see what a… strange case this is for us. Thus, the consequences of their actions require further discussion on our end. I cannot give you any guarantees, but please rest assured that forced participation in the production of Orivellea is only for the worst of offenders. Should they return with something worthwhile to show for their absence, then their sentences will be lessened considerably.

There is no reason to expect the worst, First Adviser. The Potentate Union will contact you once they've come to a decision.

May Pernelia guide you back to those you've lost.

From the office of Aldrid Grieves,
Communications Overseer, Weeping Grove

21

The Diamond Alps never slept.

There were always classes being taught and stragglers lingering about. Amorphs cawed loudly into the night; hourly signals that annoyed Leonas to no end. Every once in a while, he'd pass an embrocologist checking on the trees or an Elder scolding an errant group of practitioners. He liked to eavesdrop when he had the time. The situation reminded him of Jack when he was young. But the way they lowered their heads in shame whenever he passed, as if afraid he'd remember their faces, was an ice-cold bucket of inconsistency.

Even as a child, Jack had displayed traces of his character. Leonas still recalled the first time Jack had raised his chin in defiance at a lecture he'd found especially boring. Needless to say, Leonas had melted. He had gushed incessantly about it to his wife, who gave the faintest of grins in return. His son was such a trying thing, though he didn't expect anything less.

That was a more peaceful time. Back when the Elders of the Zenith Council were silent in their plots, as they waited for Grand Elder Bremins to pass. Now, all they did was have their lackeys run around, securing support and bickering over the Summit's candidates. While he was glad that Cheryll had nominated him — if she didn't, then he was sure Elder Prinneus would have — he couldn't be bothered with campaigning. It infuriated his dear wife greatly, but frankly, Leonas didn't think it mattered. The Zenith Council, the Vanguard Circle, and even the three Arch Potens all knew his name, as well as his convictions. So, he didn't see a reason to convince them to look his way. They'd vote for who they wanted, regardless of what anyone else said.

His winning wouldn't change the fact that he was still a key player in the Institute's greatest assemblies. And Leonas was already tired of practitioners stalking him for an interview. He didn't want to give them another reason by actively going after an even loftier title. Not when there were already a fair few that almost lost their lives in the attempt. Those were the ones that took a shiftier approach to following him.

Leonas sighed. Even just the thought of it irritated him.

Exactly twenty-two days ago, he distinctly recalled being an unholy cross between horrified and incensed when he found that the stalker that had been trailing him for the past hour had been a boy no older than sixteen.

Leonas tended to strike first and look second. It's what kept him alive for the past three decades as a part of the Vanguard Circle. So, before he even saw the boy's face, Leonas had pressed him up against the wall with his fingers sparking a dangerous blue around his throat. He didn't attempt to suffocate him, but he might as well have. It would've certainly been less scarring. He still recalled how his nails dug so deeply into the boy's jugular that if he had just added a little more pressure, he would've broken skin. The boy would've bled all over the Alps' pristine floors, and Leonas would be labelled a murderer. As if he wasn't one already.

He remembered meeting the boy's eyes and seeing his reflection in them. His gaze was cold and wrathful after so many years. Leonas had exposed the lethality that he tried so hard to keep hidden in his day-to-day life; the one that made him such a mighty practitioner. The boy was little more than an infant in comparison. An errant lad that had suddenly realized that the man he'd been trailing after was actually a beast, wary from experience and impatient from stress. The boy couldn't even find it in himself to scream when Leonas dropped him. Quick and alarmed. Like he'd been burned.

Leonas kept guards around after that. Three, in fact. All from Cheryll's legion. Not for his safety, but for the bolder, stupider ones that somehow came to the conclusion that stalking one of the figure heads of the Vanguard Circle was a good idea.

Children, he thought, his lips curling in distaste. *Absolutely no sense of self-preservation.*

He wouldn't be surprised if some were foolish enough to follow the remnants of the Drakone family. Leonas pitied those that were. They were less forgiving and far more severe. Each of them publicly expressed their natures in ways that he could only envy. If he tried, he had no doubt that it would result in torture—the staggeringly violent sort that he was all too familiar with—and a shameful death. While he could always play things off by smiling clumsily to ease the tension after a practitioner's blunder, there'd be no one to save them from choking in embarrassment if they slipped up before a Drakone.

Some of them are more forgiving than others, Leonas conceded.

The large clock tower in the center of the square abruptly pealed, signaling midnight. Leonas sighed as he faced it. A new day with the same old topics to debate. He'd grown bored of the Council's nonsense ages ago.

Though it was no time for anyone to be awake, the noise persisted. Leonas didn't mind. He liked the clamor; silence was too eerie for his taste. He hated being able to hear the crackling wood in the hearth or the doors creaking shut. There were certain places in the Alps like that, and none of them were pleasant. The department he headed was, perhaps, the best example.

Leonas made his way to the Vanguard Circle's building. It was little more than a high-walled box that stood directly across the Zenith Council's meeting hall. Imposing as it was with its white-stone exterior, it was actually much smaller than most of the buildings in the Alps. It was also the most heavily guarded.

The Circle's symbol was emblazoned boldly across its front. Three blades piled on top of each other with their tips facing outward in three different directions. Each sword represented one of the three leaders of the Vanguard Circle. Leonas, quite frankly, believed that they were better off replacing them with hammers instead because, although his peers were undoubtedly fierce, they had stubbornness in spades. And all three of them were leagues blunter than they were anything else.

Smiling thickly at those still awake to greet him, Leonas flitted past the departments of his partners and down into the shady dungeon that made up his own.

The Department of Corrections was located in an undisturbed crypt below the building proper and could only be accessed through a hidden staircase that the Hunter Division kept a steady rotation of guards around. There were even Hunters stationed along the staircase itself; Amorphs in the form of insects that Leonas' keen eyes saw even as they tried to hide from him.

His department was more guarded than any other in the Alps. Though it wasn't because the men inside needed protecting. On the contrary, they were there to ensure that if a prisoner escaped, they'd never live to tell the tale.

As if I'd be so careless, he thought.

Leonas placed his hand upon the bronze bust of a sneering old woman, and a panel from below opened to reveal a round staircase that twisted up and out. It was silent, courtesy of the ancient enchantments placed upon it. Shifting stairwells were one of the Mentalists' more absurd designs. Leonas would've preferred *anything* else because having an entire path shift just so he could pass felt needlessly theatric.

"Stay here," Leonas said to air, blindly ordering the hidden guards that he kept with him. He doubted they could stomach what was down there, and Cheryll would maim him if she heard any more rumors about his mistreatment of them flying around.

None of them responded, though he knew they were listening because he caught a wasp veering off in fright when a muffled scream echoed along the walls. It died as soon as the stairwell moved back into place. But Leonas still frowned when he heard it. That wouldn't do. If one of the other heads had heard that, he'd be cautioned in that terribly demeaning way of theirs again. It was hard to keep up the careless act when he was infuriated. He really needed to see Vidal again. Leonas could use some pointers on how to keep his smile up for longer than anyone cared for. Hopefully, his old friend would return for the Summit.

Rounding one final corner, Leonas stopped before an iron door bolted to the walls. Another ear-piercing shriek came from within, followed by sobbing. He made a mental note to redo the enchantments on this room, before slipping his ring of keys out. He took his time finding the right one.

By the time he opened the door, the man lying flat on the stone table located in the room's center was only half-awake. Leonas seen that glassy look enough times to know that the man's pain was so great that it was now painless. Lacerations covered his body, and he was chained in thick, steel manacles framed with incantations that drained him of his magic. His face matched the scent of copper and fresh fear around them. He made for a gruesome picture, though that was hardly enough to deter Leonas. This was his job after all.

The prisoner didn't seem to register his entrance, but his interrogator had. His underling nodded in acknowledgement, before stepping away in silent concession. Leonas regarded him for a moment. Vobelle was a fairly new addition to his division. He'd been serving him for almost two years now, though he hadn't changed much. A feat, considering the kind of brutal things he had them do.

Vobelle's blue gaze was disturbed only by the scar that sealed his left eye. Behind him, stood a shaky man in Hunter's garb. The Hunter's jaw was clenched so tightly that Leonas wondered if he hated him for some reason. He might. It wouldn't be the first time Leonas had forgotten someone he'd wronged, and it wouldn't be the last.

Is he one of Cheryll's men? Leonas wondered, trying to place his face. He certainly didn't look like any of the Hunters he'd recently hand-picked for his crew, so he likely was.

Leonas needed him to get over his aversion soon because he was desperately low on men. Not many survived his rigorous training regimen. Soon, he wouldn't be allowed to just stand back and watch. Leonas smiled grimly at the thought. He only hoped Cheryll would forgive his assimilation of some of her sturdier Hunters. But somehow, he doubted it.

"Hello, Sir Assassin," Leonas said pleasantly. His jovial tone didn't keep the man from flinching deeper into his iron pedestal. When the man refused to open his eyes, Leonas poked his temple with a finger coated in sharp ice. "Look at me when I'm talking to you."

He opened his eyes. His upper lip quivered with each second that Leonas spent peering down at him.

"That's better. Now, I know this goes against your band's code, but do you think you could loosen your tongue for me?" He held his finger and thumb an inch apart. "About this much."

The assassin remained silent. His teeth grinded together in resolution, while his eyes glimmered in the sort of unexpected defiance that delighted Leonas to no end. He was tough, Leonas would give him that. Then again, he didn't expect anything less.

How long can he keep that front up?

He was dying to know.

Leonas smirked wickedly.

"Don't be like that," he urged by his ear, his red eyes shining in the dim light. "I only want to know who paid you to spy on the Elders here."

The assassin's eyes widened in shock, and Leonas showed him his teeth.

"Didn't think I knew?" he went on. "Who do you think I am? Did your benefactors say they'd pay you for each practitioner's head you take while you were here? You were a fool to think you could kill those two practitioners in the Gelid Mountains."

When he still didn't speak, Leonas leaned directly over him.

"Have you heard the stories of what happens to deserters in the Alps?" he asked. The man nodded his head mechanically, and

Leonas gave him the broadest, most rictus smile he had in his arsenal. "You know they're sent to me, yet you still choose not to speak. You're a spirited one, aren't you? Despite what you may have heard, I'm a sympathetic man. If you cooperate, then I'll show you compassion in return."

When there was still no response, Leonas frowned deeply.

He didn't stop to think. Leonas simply placed his hand over the man's wounded chest, lit it aflame, and then pressed as hard as he could. His ribs caved from the pressure. The prisoner's entire body convulsed. He struggled against his chains with the kind of desperation one only felt when death was at their heels.

Leonas heard Cheryll's Hunter retch, but it was swiftly lost to the screaming in his ears. Just as the prisoner was about to pass out, Leonas lifted his hand, granting him a brief moment of respite, before...

"Heal him," Leonas ordered.

Vobelle stepped up immediately. His hand glowed a striking blue as he placed it upon the Tipping's chest. Then, all at once, the man's wounds began to mend. The upper portion of his body raised at the sheer amount of magic forced into his veins, and he screamed in terror at the sensation. This wasn't magic used with the intention to fix or to ease. It didn't prod at the soft spots inside of him, didn't carefully seek out how to best deal with his wounds, no, this was harsh and purposely clumsy—and also one of the most effective methods of torture Leonas employed.

Before he joined the Vanguard Circle, Leonas never thought healing magic capable of crushing, of sweeping over injuries like giant tidal waves over an unsuspecting child.

But it was. Oh, it was.

And when nothing else but speed was the goal, he learned that most corners could be cut to achieve it. All Leonas needed to do was bring this man back to the brink, so that he might be a little rawer. Might be a little more able to feel the pain. After a few rounds of this, all but a select few of his prisoners usually broke enough to admit to anything. Even things they'd never done.

As soon as the Healer finished, Leonas' hands were back on him. More fire, followed by more cries and unwelcome healing. Twice this happened, with Leonas not giving the prisoner a chance to speak, and just before the third, he abruptly halted. Leonas lifted his hands up to his shoulders to show the man that he was safe. For now.

The prisoner heaved. Sobbed. Maybe even relieved himself.

Leonas turned away at that point, unsurprised to see the blood that lined his fingers. He flicked his hands, then stretched each digit out. Leonas scowled in disgust at the webs of red. His eyes lingered on the thicker lines. They looked like mucous. That was something he hadn't seen in a while. At this point, he was no longer disturbed or enamored by the sight of blood. He'd seen all aspects of it. He knew how it looked after days in a damp cell or freshly spilled over polished silver and ashen flesh. Contrary to the belief of many weary, angst-filled fighters, it didn't always look the same. It wasn't always *just* red. His hands currently sported proof of that.

No one spoke, and so, tense stillness encompassed the room. The candles were almost spent, casting a sad, disheartening glow over the Tipping's face.

Fitting, he thought. Leonas would've liked to stay for longer, but he had a meeting to attend. It wouldn't do for him to be too late, or worse, miss it completely. He was already under enough scrutiny from the Council.

Leonas turned to his subordinate.

"Leave him," he commanded. Because he clearly wasn't getting anywhere with his slow-mincing method. Vobelle needed better training. That, or a partner. He was exceptionally talented at his special brand of *'healing'* after all. "And get that Hunter cleaned up. This place already smells like a maggot's sanctuary. I don't need him adding to the stench."

"Yes, sir," Vobelle answered.

"Find Savast and Krenn after. Have them redo the charms on every room in this hall. I don't want those toppers hearing any errant screams. I'll return to finish this myself once—"

"The Lafertti Clan!" the Tipping yelled, his eyes wide and frightened at the mere thought of more.

There was a brief moment of silence, before...

"That two-bit college?" Leonas turned, deliberately slow.

"Yes!" he stammered, then choked on his own saliva. "They paid me. Sent me here to spy and said to kill who I can for a few extra gold pieces! It's true. It's all true."

"Why?"

"I don't know!" he screamed, shrinking around the neck and shoulders when Leonas' hands glowed an unholy blue. "I swear! They didn't tell me anything, but," his eyes flew helplessly around him, grasping at straws, "I did hear some of them talking about a rebellion. I—I figured it was an inside matter! A riot like the ones in the Plains!"

The light in Leonas' hands died, and he nodded his head in approval. "See? That wasn't so hard now, was it? Thank you."

"I..." he trailed off, sobbing. "I'm sorry. Please stop. No more. Please. Don't come back."

"I told you, cooperate and I'll show you compassion. I'm many things. A man of my word is one of them."

Leonas watched his dark eyes flash in relief. He'd betrayed the Tippings by speaking of his job. Leonas was somewhat disappointed because of it, but then again, principles were only as good as the will someone had to see them through.

He couldn't expect all of the Tippings to be as elite as the rumors made them out to be. Especially not such a low-standing member. Besides, those that could withstand his methods were few and far between. But perhaps he could meet someone of such caliber once the Tippings began their search to relieve themselves of this traitor. Leonas had no qualms about handing him over in exchange for a favor or two. Problem was, his talkative prisoner was still considered a deserter. And he, despite all of his other flowery titles, was still a practitioner.

So, that left him in an interesting conundrum.

But, in the end, Leonas had promised him kindness for his confession. He didn't fancy himself a liar, and he doubted a guild of assassins knew much about compassion. Particularly if the target in question was one of their own. If he handed him over, Leonas only saw more torture in his future. Maybe even worse than his. Maybe.

Coming to a decision, Leonas smiled bleakly at the man.

He did cooperate after all.

"This'll barely hurt."

***

By the time Leonas made it to the Zenith Council's hall, the meeting was already in full swing. Though, interestingly enough, Victor Sirx was waiting for him outside of its stately double doors. Even more interesting was that, despite being four inches thick, the doors did practically nothing to quiet the voices of the squabbling councilmen within.

Leonas skidded to a stop before the adviser, rubbing the back of his head and further ruining his already wild hair. He flashed Victor his signature dopey smile, then lifted an inquisitive brow when he didn't move out of his way.

"Victor," Leonas greeted with a polite nod. He couldn't very well force him to move in broad daylight. There were too many witnesses around.

The adviser opened his eyes, and they both spent a minute regarding each other. They were total opposites. Both in appearance and personality. Where Leonas was thin, Victor was portly. He had gray hair and a perfectly trimmed boxed beard. Leonas had always been approachable when he wasn't in his domain, but Victor kept himself locked away from the rest. Whenever his blue eyes narrowed, everyone knew to turn their own away. Strange, since as far as Leonas knew, the man had never raised his hand against anyone since he was appointed first adviser to the Council. Perhaps not even before then.

Maybe it was just his callous demeanor that turned people

away. Whatever it was, they were terrible judges of character. Leonas knew better. There was something admirable about the way Victor could express himself with just his eyes. His feelings were there for all to see, admire, and hate. Still, Leonas wasn't fond of the man... or of advisers in general. The cost of their counsel was seldom cheap, and Victor was much too preachy for his taste. He was frank to a fault and serious enough to dampen even his faux spirits. Victor was a good man, undoubtedly better than him, but he was galling in his own right.

"Elder Dace," Victor eventually acknowledged, complete with a gruff nod. Always so coldly polite.

"Can I help you?" Leonas asked, scrunching his eyebrows when Victor looked at him like he was daft.

"Your subordinate... the one with the burn on his arm."

"You'll have to be more specific."

"He was wispy with scars littered across his neck."

"Ahh, what about him?"

"He said you were looking for me. That it was urgent."

"Wh—oh!" Leonas exclaimed.

"Well?" Victor sighed, as if he knew this would happen.

"May I ask who you're supporting at the Summit?"

The only sign of Victor's puzzlement was a deliberate lift of his brow. He clearly didn't think Leonas cared enough about the Summit to actually search for the support he needed to win—and he was right. Leonas wasn't about to go back on his words to Cheryll, however. That was something he absolutely couldn't do.

"Forgive me, but I'd like to keep my decision to myself for a little while longer," Victor said, calculating.

Leonas deflated. His entire body slumped down in fake disappointment. "Is that so? I was hoping you'd support me."

"We've never worked together, Elder Dace."

"But we've always seen eye to eye, haven't we?"

Victor crossed his arms in distrust. "I... suppose."

Leonas was already tired of this conversation. Just because he could talk enough for ten men didn't mean he liked speaking to walls. "Actually," Leonas tacked on, "my wife was the one that decided it would be best if I found a few more supporters." He tried not to feel insulted by the sudden understanding in Victor's gaze. "She specifically mentioned you."

"Why would she do that?"

"I think it has something to do with the fact that your lovely daughter is on her way here with my son. He's protecting her apparently, seeing as she's his new Arch Poten. Cheryll found them, cleaned them up, and sent them off on the scenic route here. '*They need time to contemplate what's happened,*' she said. A true gem, my wife."

Victor stiffened at his words. Flashes of emotion flitted across his eyes, before he composed himself. When he spoke, his words were controlled and curt. "Sylvie... she's alright?"

"So my sources say." Leonas shrugged, feigning disinterest. "All reliable, I assure you. And personally, I think she's fine. She was talented enough to become the primary apprentice of Arch Poten Cephas, and she even has my son with her. Jacques can be a hammer sometimes, which can be aggravating. But at least his head is hard enough to withstand more than a few blunt hits."

Victor closed his eyes and Leonas thought he saw relief shake him. He wasn't so versed in his mannerisms to be sure.

"I see," Victor said quietly. He repeated it a second time, as if trying to make himself believe the Elder's claims. Leonas was known for lying when it suited him, but Victor doubted he'd make such a bold assertion. He'd even mentioned his son. "That is... good news. You have my thanks."

"Cheryll tells me that they have one of the Alps' treasures with them," Leonas went on.

Victor stiffened again. This time, the adviser looked him right in the eye. But Leonas was done talking. He needed to go; he was terribly late.

"That's all I wanted to say." Leonas clasped his shoulder as he passed. "I'd appreciate it if you kept this conversation between us. As a favor, I'll be sure to keep some of the... family records my wife salvaged from the Drowned Tower a secret. You don't happen to know of them, do you?"

Victor removed Leonas' hand. "What do you want?"

"To see you at the Summit." Leonas rolled his neck, getting the kinks out in preparation of the undoubtedly long meeting awaiting him. "On my side of course."

With that, Leonas slipped inside of the room, uncaring for the low growl that erupted from deep within Victor's chest or the way the door slammed shut behind him. The sound was abrupt enough to catch the reproachful stares of the councilmen.

Fifteen seconds of thick silence descended around them, to which Leonas smiled apologetically. And to his utter delight, only *two* of the Elders scoffed. Though the others did mutter something stinging that was too low for him to hear.

"You're late," came the obvious rebuke.

"I had other business to attend to," Leonas said, as he searched for the speaker. He gave up when he took in the number of frowning faces turned his way.

"More important than this meeting?" another asked.

That voice he did know. His eyes trailed to the head of the table where Roderek Drakone sat with a deliberating glower.

Leonas bowed his head sheepishly. Roderek was one of the meager few he'd lower his eyes to. To him, Roderek was the only Drakone worthy of his respect. Simply because he earned his title. Unlike his lazy brother, Dels, who sat two seats down. He was named an Elder only because of his blood.

"Apparently so," Leonas said elusively, waving his hand as if to physically move the topic aside. He took a seat in his place at Roderek's right, noting the empty spot across the table, reserved for the head of the Circle's Research Division. It seemed there was someone even busier than him at this hour. "I see Jarvis isn't here either."

"His absence doesn't excuse yours, Leonas," Roderek said.

"No, of course not. It was merely an observation. But I'm here now, so please carry on."

"You're young still." Elder Meese laughed. His appearance alone earned him the title. From his white hair to his yellow teeth, he needed help for everything. Even bending down. Why he hadn't retired yet, no one could say for certain. "We can't carry on without first filling you in on what we've already gone over."

The more impatient of the lot groaned. Leonas was sorely tempted to do the same. He smiled in preference.

"Silence!" Elder Meese yelled, red in the face. "Why, back in my day, they'd pluck out your teeth for disrespecting one of the Heads of the Vanguard Circle in such a flippant manner."

"You mean back during the First Zenith's time?" someone dangerously close to Meese mumbled. He responded with a spritely kick to his shins. "Ow! Did you just kick me, you—"

"Oh, someone get Elder Meese back in his seat."

"I will not sit here and be spoken down to by a boy thirty years my junior!"

"Quiet, old man!"

"Will you four stop acting like Veld practitioners for one minute?" Elder Seraphin, poise incarnate, spoke. Her tiny eyes were narrowed even further, as she looked at them with a critical look that she was famous among the younger practitioners for.

"What did you just say about the Veld's practitioners?" Elder Kenna—a previous Master from the south—interrupted, already half-rising.

"It's no secret that they're little more than savages, and that's on a good day."

"*Virï na sêcla den,*" Kenna spat. "Take that back, you wretch!"

The hall erupted into chaos.

"Why is it always like this when you step into meetings?" Roderek turned to Leonas, already tired of their rows.

Leonas only shrugged, just as confused.

With a quick slap of Roderek's palm over the table, all arguments ceased. They turned to find him cradling his chin in his palm, just daring them to continue.

None were foolish enough to do so.

With a disarming laugh, Leonas was the first to break the tension. "I would love to continue your previous conversation, but I've been here for a good five minutes, and I'm still lost. So, if one of you could please..." he trailed off with a cheerful grin pointed purposefully in Dels' direction.

Dels made a face in return.

Unsurprisingly, Roderek was the one to pick up where they'd left off. Already aware that another petty fight would ensue if he didn't.

"We were discussing the missing Heartstone," Roderek said. "Have you received any word from Cheryll? I spoke with her primary apprentice but learned little about what transpired."

"I have nothing to add," Leonas said. "Cheryll has a bad habit of keeping me in the dark. She didn't mention the stone in her last letter. She didn't even mention the Tower. But I suspect that the stone is at the bottom of the Zexin Sea by now."

"How can we trust those words?" Elder Seraphin cut in.

"My wife has always been loyal to the Institute," Leonas defended, his tone sinister. "Cheryll worked as a Hunter for years before being appointed captain and even developed an enhanced Demar Spell. She's shown nothing but dedication. I see no reason why you would question her."

"It's not her loyalty that concerns us," Dels said.

"Mine then? Really?" Leonas drawled. "After all I've done for the Institute? My accomplishments require their own shelf in the public archives. Not including my work for the Vanguard Circle. What more would you have of me? Shall I make public our personal letters to ease your worries? I don't suppose any of you have ever heard of privacy?"

"That's enough," Roderek cut in, scowling at the three of them. "No one's loyalty is in question."

"But after Elder Serach..." Seraphin protested. Her voice trailed into nothing when Roderek held up a hand.

"I said, *enough*," he reiterated, finality lacing his tone. "I'll send a group of Amorphs to search for the Heartstone. For now, we can safely assume that it's been lost. According to Cheryll's primary apprentice, Serach has been dealt with. She's also sent the Drowned Tower's new Arch Poten, Sylvie Sirx, along with her son, Jacques Dace, here. They should arrive soon. We need to focus on gathering the other Arch Potens before they do. It would be in our best interest to begin the Summit as soon as they arrive."

"Victor's daughter?" Elder Rocous spoke up. His friendship with the adviser was known by everyone in the Alps.

Roderek nodded, ignoring the whispers around the table. "Has there been any news regarding Monet Verne's attendance?"

"Nothing yet," came a softer voice across from him. Elder Nathaniel Borris. "But I've spoken to Arch Poten Cole. He'll be making the journey in a month's time."

"So long?"

"They've been having trouble with the Lafertti Clan. I plan to personally escort him here."

"What's going on with the Lafertti Clan?" Leonas asked, suddenly regretting the fact that he'd sent that Amorph with the too bright scarf away before.

"What isn't? They've begun pushing for the dissolution of their Potentate Union," Borris explained. "Violently, at that. And the support that they've amassed from the other colleges makes it worse. The practitioners have grown weary of answering to the seven Potens. Slavers, they call them. Some have even gone so far as to call them the second wave of Mentalists. The practitioners are tired of being forced into isolation, and Arch Poten Cole can't do much. He's gifted, but he's also young, and still in need of guidance. No one expected his master to die so early. He knows about the *Orivellea,* but wants nothing to do with them. He's left his Potens in charge of their production, along with a good deal of... miscellaneous responsibilities."

"Are they abusing their practitioners?"

"It's likely," Borris said. "With no proper leader there to guide them, those that have found their morals are speaking up. Half against the Potentate Union and half for. It isn't pretty."

"How many know about the *Orivellea*?" Leonas asked.

"Only their most talented," Borris assured. "But if they abolish the Potentate Union, I doubt they'll be able to keep their production a secret from the rest. Either they'll hold a civilized vote regarding it or turn on us for allowing something so immoral to go on for so many years."

"At least we know that Lucian will definitely vote against their continued production should they decide on the former," Rocous added. "But where does that leave us? Can we afford to make the crystals here?"

No, Leonas thought, but held his tongue.

Truthfully, he didn't see the need for such a gargantuan supply of *Orivellea* anymore. Elementalists weren't born every day, and Peose weren't handed out to anyone that wanted them. They were only available to Hunters, and even then, dozens of hoops had to be jumped through just to get a request form. Though it wasn't as if he didn't understand where they were coming from. The threat of Peose had once kept the other Institutes and leagues of protesting Nebbin in check from caution alone, so Leonas doubted his peers would willingly give them up anytime soon. But from the information he'd just received from the Tippings' assassin, it seemed that the half that stood against the Grove's Potentate Union were already beginning to rebel. Boldly, at that. But why were they after those in the Diamond Alps? To force them to comply?

A laughable notion.

The practitioners of the Alps bowed to no one.

But why was he only hearing about the Lafertti Clan? There were other colleges in the Grove. Perhaps not as old, but just as influential. Maybe even more so.

"I say we let them dissolve it," Leonas declared.

A number of the Elders turned to stare incredulously at him.

"Do you have any idea what that would mean for them?" Borris asked, affronted by his lack of concern for his home. "A civil war! Just like what happened in the Tower. All those bodies… are you really saying we should just let that happen?"

"The Tower had the added heat of breaking history then," Meese weighed in. "There are no more traditions left to break for the Grove that have not already been shattered by the generations before them."

"And really, why not just let them?" Leonas scoffed at their ill-tempered looks. "This has been a long time coming."

"A long time…" Borris rose. "Are you insane?"

"If only," Leonas shot back. "The Institutes have separate councils for a reason. We should've dissolved the Union ages ago. It was never meant to be permanent in the first place. Let those that have to live in the Grove deal with their own problems. Tell them that they'll be allowed to dissolve it only after the Summit. Not before. We can send Hunters if the Potens have a problem with that. I assume the majority are in favor of disbanding it anyway. So, if they see that we support them, then at least they'll stay off our backs once they eventually find out about how the *Orivellea* are made. A war in one Institute is better than a war between two."

"And what would the practitioners of the Veld think about that?" Dels challenged.

Leonas laughed. "They adore their Arch Poten, and even if they didn't, they're outspoken enough to stand against someone they didn't respect. But the old system works for them, so why would they even think about changing it? Peer pressure? Ha! And if, for whatever reason, they do become upset with their Union, I doubt we'd hear about it. Arch Poten Verne doesn't even bother answering our summons. Us, the governing power of Ferus Terria. What makes you think she'd request our permission to change her Institute's way of rule? For all we know, she already has. It wouldn't surprise me."

Before anyone could get another word in, Roderek cleared his throat. "We'll stop here for today," he said, ignoring their frowns. "I'm sure you all have a lot to think about. Cool your heads and sleep on it. We'll discuss this again in the morning. I trust you'll all have better solutions by then."

Some mumbled their consensus, while other nodded reluctantly. Most, however, glared wordlessly at the floor. Already lost in their thoughts.

"Dismissed," Roderek muttered, rubbing his jaw, unused to leading these meetings. He would be though. Soon.

Roderek turned to Leonas, who stood from his chair. He looked supremely pleased with himself. As always. Leonas was hiding something. He just knew it.

"I know you have duties to the Circle," Roderek said, "but don't be late again."

Leonas gave him a half-hearted salute, before ambling off. He was quickly followed by Rocous, who rested his arm good-naturedly over his shoulders as they walked.

Rocous was a well-built, albeit scruffy man with a natural charm about him. He had blond hair and piercing black eyes that were slanted sharply along the outer corners. Rocous made women swoon without even realizing it. Leonas couldn't fathom why he chose to hang around Victor, who often just grunted his way through conversations. They made for an odd pair.

"A shame about the east," Rocous said in way of greeting. "I would've liked to see the Tower one more time, before it was destroyed. But I'm glad your wife's taking the time to rebuild it. That's incredibly kind of her. Thank her for me, will you?"

"Consider it done."

"After all of this Summit business, I'm thinking about taking a trip down there to help her. Maybe even stay to start the new Assembly. They'll need leaders. Proper ones with experience. Not whatever fresh-faced, half-wit they can get their hands on."

"You want to leave the Council?"

Rocous held a finger up to his lips. "I have enough money from Roco sauce to help get them up and running again. Besides, I was raised in those dreary halls. It's only right that I help rebuild them. I don't want anyone making a mess of my home."

"Cheryll has impeccable taste, and I doubt she'll alter much."

"It's not her I'm concerned about. It's the others with her. I don't want them to turn the Tower into an underwater garden."

"That's unlikely. Although they lived there, they don't have the authority to supersede Cheryll's judgment." Leonas paused. "What's this really about, Rocous?"

"Perceptive as always." Rocous sighed. "Having your home collapse while you're away really puts things into perspective. I want to protect the Institute that raised me. That's all."

"How... sentimental of you."

"Don't you know? I'm known for that."

"I wonder if it stems from a sense of gratitude or duty."

"Both."

"Then I'll tell you now that I believe you protect the Tower well enough from here. It was a tragedy, to be sure. But one that only a select few could have prevented."

"Am I among them?"

Leonas met his gaze head-on. "No."

"How are you so certain?"

"When am I not?"

"Tell me this then, are *you* among them?"

"That's not relevant." Leonas smirked. "What's important is that *you* aren't. There was nothing you could've done, Rocous."

"You're probably right. Who am I kidding? You're *always* right. That's why that perpetually composed Borris was so intense back there. Did you see his eyes? Swords, I tell you. Sharp, gory swords. He would've made a terrifying Elementalist. I'm surprised you didn't resort to your usual tricks."

"I don't know what you mean."

"No one on the Council is daft enough to buy that ridiculous smile, Leonas."

"Really?" he questioned dryly.

"Well, some might be." Rocous laughed. "*Fhïl glin a dahanï.*"

"*Glin? Rïken?*"

"Aren't they?"

Leonas grinned in agreement. It was astonishing how easily

he could imagine the councilmen as temperamental, godforsaken goats. Instead of adding to his—*perfect*—comparison, he asked, "What do you think of all this dissolution business?"

"I'm a deathly pallid Tower boy at heart. You already know my answer," Rocous said without missing a beat. Life without a Potentate Union wasn't anything new, in fact, it was life with one that eluded him.

He dropped his arm when they reached an intersection that led into the offices of the Council's top advisers. It didn't take a genius to figure out what Rocous wanted to do.

"I suppose you want to inform Victor about his daughter."

"If you haven't already," Rocous said knowingly. "Oh, and before I forget, I'm glad your son's okay."

Leonas let slip a genuine smile. "I'm glad your goddaughter is as well."

"You knew?" Rocous rubbed the back of his neck. His entire face was red. "What am I saying? It's you. Of course you would. I haven't seen her in years. Did you know that she used to call me her father whenever I came to visit? You wouldn't believe how bothered Victor was when I told him."

Victor with any expression besides dour wasn't something Leonas could easily imagine. While he didn't say so out loud, he had a sinking feeling that Rocous saw through him because before he knew it, the Amorph was laughing.

"I'll be seeing you," Rocous said. "Oh, and try to keep better track of the time when you're down in those dungeons of yours. I have a feeling Roderek will be locking the meeting doors from now on."

"I sincerely hope so."

Rocous let out another bark of laughter, before making his way down the hall. Once he disappeared inside of a familiar room, Leonas turned to look out at the rising sun. He frowned when he realized that he hadn't gotten any sleep. Roderek kept strange hours. He hoped that the new Grand Elder would hold the Council meetings at more normal times, so he wouldn't have to skip out on his own work in order to attend them.

There was still so much left for him to do and even more to think about. But one thing was for certain—he needed to send someone to the Weeping Grove. Someone he could trust to keep their findings a secret.

Leonas grinned warmly when he saw a group of half-asleep practitioners headed off to wherever it was they needed to be at such an ungodly hour. From their conversation, he gathered that they'd be transforming into Snuff today.

A herd usually passed along the outer edges of the Alps at this time, so he assumed they'd be asked to blend in. It wouldn't be too difficult, especially for them. They were in the Alps for a reason after all. If they couldn't at least pull that off, then they didn't belong here. Then again, they might just be the cream of the crop of the Veld or the Grove. Their Amorphs were good, but not like those from the Tower.

Just as he thought it, his eyes widened to an unnatural degree, and suddenly, he knew who to send.

Leonas hummed, blatantly ignoring all of those that turned to shoot him a questioning glance. He was far too thrilled by his quick thinking to care about anyone else. Instead, he focused on the task at hand: finding his wife's primary apprentice.

Even absent, Cheryll never failed to ease his burdens.

Cheryll,

I've been pondering for ages how I might begin this letter, then I wondered if you'd bother with a response, what I'll write back if you did, and how long this would take to reach you. (Some Amorphs are just so inefficient.) You have yet to reply to my latest dispatch, so I was a tad hesitant to send another, but I couldn't help myself. I do hope that the previous one reached you without mishap and that this one does as well.

Well, allow me to start over and ask you something mundane to formally begin—How are you?

I have no idea why so many letters begin with those three words. They aren't very interesting, and I fully expect you to tell me about your troubles anyway. Perhaps it's so the sender can go off on a tangent about themselves directly after? An excuse to boast? Must people be so disgustingly selfish? But… oh, what a day. I think I've just found the secret to the art of letters! Please keep it safe. I trust you. Now that we know the reason for that mundane greeting, I need to talk about myself. It's practically a requirement now.

Things are busy. I am busy. But that's hardly new. I just attended the most cumbersome meeting I've ever attended to date. With the Zenith Council of course. Not the Circle. I quite enjoy my discussions with Roderek and Javis. Did I mention that the Council meeting was late at night? Because it was. Roderek has been leading them, so we've all been forced to match his compact schedule. He's a night owl. An awful, awful night owl. (Not that I'm any different.) While I don't care for his sleeping habits, I can't help but complain when it affects my work. My most productive hours are the ones just before dawn, and now I spend them seated around a table, arguing with sleep-deprived goats. Sleep has become a thing of fiction for me.

While I'm on the subject, I do hope you're getting enough of it. I'm sure rebuilding something as grand as the Drowned Tower is draining. Please don't be obstinate and rest when you need to.

In other news, I've spoken to Victor. He was shocked by my sudden interest in him, although pleased, too, I think. I told him about his absent daughter and had the pleasure of seeing a chink in that impenetrable armor. I wish you could've seen it. It was quite the sight. Next time.

Rocous wanted me to express his gratitude to you for rebuilding his home. He promised to return there after all of this Summit business to help you with your efforts. I was against it (and even attempted to dissuade him), but he seemed adamant. Honestly, I didn't care enough to carry the argument further. Especially not after that little spat I had with Borris.

Now, don't worry. No sparks flew between us. Like I said, the fight was a little one. Miniscule, even. Borris is worried about his colleagues in the Grove. While I don't fault him for his concern, seeing him so riled is… strange. Composure is his middle name. Though I suppose that moniker must go to another now. Borris is angry at me for speaking as bluntly as I always do. I voiced one too many opinions it seems. (I can practically see you rolling your eyes, love.) So, if you were counting on him supporting me in the upcoming Summit, I'm not sure what to say other than, he's a lost cause. Not officially of course. Only probably. Perhaps you can persuade him.

And you were right about another thing. (As you tend to be.) The cogs in Ferus Terria are moving. I don't know who started them or how they got all of that rust off, but I do know that change will come soon. The Weeping Grove is already shifting and from what I've learned—

Oh! Peaches just sashayed by! She had a rat in her mouth. I'm so proud! Look at her go. She deserves a treat for all of her hard work. I hope this means I can start feeding the birds again.

I'm sorry, love, but another demands my attention.

I'll write again soon.

Yours,
Leonas

22

Myrrh's shifting belly should have been her first clue that today would be terrible. Second, was the errant barrel of wine that had almost run her flat in the market. Third, were the noises that rang below her. Everyone was awake today. Slighted, too. But stubborn as she was, she listened to none of these omens and kept to herself, firm in her belief that she could stand against whatever came her way.

She just hadn't expected it to be Leonas Dace.

Myrrh wasn't sure how to feel about him since Roderek warned her away. But the rush of blood in her veins whenever she found herself in his presence now seemed infinitely more stressful. She could only count her lucky stars that they didn't cross paths often. Leonas was always busy doing paperwork, training recruits, and hounding the poor souls in his dungeons — or so she assumed. She didn't want to know the minute details of his work. Myrrh simply did her best to get settled in again. She picked up odd jobs from her grateful peers and checked on Ethil every now and again. Myrrh usually holed herself up in her room during the early hours of dawn, unused to doing anything after so many years spent idle in the Drowned Tower. But yesterday, she took it upon herself to request a night-long patrol. She stayed a good six hours longer than necessary, and though her muscles were stiff and her eyes were sore, it was definitely worth it.

From the position of the sun, she knew that it was long past the time for breakfast. Her stomach growled at the thought. Myrrh rubbed it, as if that might appease her hunger. It didn't.

Myrrh sighed in annoyance. Here she was, drained, sleep-deprived, and—as of the last hour—left to wait in a noisy area for her replacement. She didn't sign up for this. Myrrh didn't think it could get any worse. So, when *Leonas-flaming-Dace* appeared before her with Dwyn trailing behind him, her stomach dropped to her feet. If she wasn't so tongue-tied, she would've shouted something awful. Dwyn's snake-like grin made her skin tingle in all of the wrong ways. His useless crab clicked its pincers happily at the sight of her, as if its owner wasn't borderline psychotic.

"I've been searching for you."

Why? she almost shouted. *Have I done something wrong?*

As if seeing her inner trepidation, Leonas flashed her a pacifying grin. He didn't look any different. But she'd expected that. Myrrh prepared herself for one of his famous reprimands. It was an unhealthy mix of degrading, bitter, and psychologically scarring. She'd seen others subjected to it before. Leonas would just sit there with his narrow eyes and his too wide smile, asking scalding inquiries that made them question their self-worth. Especially when he'd rebuke each and every one of their words with a carefully placed threat.

"Did you need something?" she asked.

"I've dealt with that Tipping," he said casually.

Myrrh's eyes widened. She looked around to make sure no one had heard, only to find that all of the other patrollers had quietly fled at the sight of him. Her lips thinned at the realization that she was alone.

"Thank you, Elder Dace."

"No need to thank me. You're my wife's primary apprentice. I assure you that it wasn't done for your sake. But now that you're free from the burdens of being a target, I'd like you to help me finish what she wanted."

"Finish… what exactly?"

"Looking into the Grove's colleges," Leonas reminded her, unintentionally making her recall Roderek's words. "I'll even let you take one of my practitioners with you."

Dwyn stepped forward. The way they both smiled unnerved her to no end. Leonas was quick to notice.

"Do you know him?" he asked.

"We've worked together before," Myrrh said acidly. She suppressed the urge to sneer. "Back when he was still a Hunter."

"That moves things along. Don't mind him. Dwyn will be running under my orders. As for you, I'm sure you know best what Cheryll wants. It's a hassle to explain to others, especially since I'm not sure what exactly it is she expects from me."

Leonas was pushy. Myrrh didn't know what Cheryll saw in him. Was it the way his tongue left no room for argument? Or how his eyes made sure everyone paid attention to him? She doubted she'd ever know. She didn't want to know either.

Flexing her fingers, she settled for a firm nod.

Leonas, apparently satisfied with her answer, nodded as well. "Off you go then," he said, shooing them away. The bulky silver rings that adorned his fingers reflected the sunlight straight into her eyes. They flashed so perfectly, blinding her every time he waved, that she wondered if he was doing it on purpose.

"*Now?*" she asked. Even Dwyn turned to him in alarm.

"Why not?" Leonas countered. He looked at them like they needed a few screws tightened. "The sun is shining. If you hustle, you'll reach the edge of the Gelid Mountains by dawn."

Slave driver! Myrrh internally moaned, though her face remained the epitome of equanimity.

"But," Dwyn protested, "we haven't even packed yet."

"You have clothes on your back and magic in your veins. What else do you need?"

"Money? Food?" Myrrh threw out instantly. "Boots?"

"Oh, fine then. Get what you will, but you don't want to be here come evening," he went on. A vague smile played along the corners of his lips. "There's going to be a storm. An awful, awful storm." He took Myrrh's hands, ignoring the way she flinched at the contact. Leonas gingerly folded a thick letter in them. It had his last name scrawled hastily over the front. "You'll hand this to her, won't you? Personally? No couriers. This is important."

Her eyebrows creased in suspicion. Leonas always placed Cheryll's name in big, bold letters on his envelopes. Not their family name. Before she could voice her thoughts, he was already dropping her hands and turning away from them.

"The Council and the Grove share many secrets," Leonas said. "Dark and gritty ones. I pray you aren't too surprised by them. I'm sure you both have had your fair share of warnings about me. But do what I've asked, and I promise that you'll both be back here sooner than you might wish. Hopefully of your own free will. Because if there's one thing I've learned after all of these years as a Circle Head, it's that willing underlings work harder."

"What's happening?" they asked in unison.

Myrrh observed Dwyn from the corner of her eye, shocked by his apparent confusion. He knew much, but it seemed even he wasn't expecting Leonas' words.

Leonas placed a single finger over his lips, and in the silence, they heard the beginnings of a dozen angry shouts echo from far below them. They demanded something, though Myrrh couldn't tell what. Their voices were all tied together like incoherent fuzz. It grated on her ears. But she resisted the urge to peer down to see what was going on.

How did Leonas know she—or they apparently—had been warned about him? Why was he even telling them to leave so quickly? Myrrh wanted to stay and see what was happening. She hadn't heard this much chaos since Tiv rallied the practitioners in the east against the Assembly. Would another Institute fall? The Grove, maybe? Certainly not the Alps. Ferus Terria would burn to the ground first.

The smile on Leonas' face widened. It wasn't as dull as usual. There was too much teeth. Something was very, very wrong. Before they knew it, they both felt a sting along their ankles. Simultaneously lifting their robes, they saw the familiar marks of the Demar Spell. How long had it been since she'd been subjected to such a thing? What was he planning? Why was he doing this?

Because Cheryll asked him to? That was hardly enough reason to send Dwyn with her. Even less to keep track of her movements with a Demar Spell. She'd need to ask Dwyn about Leonas' plan once they left this place.

"What are you two waiting for?" Leonas asked.

They shared a glance, as Leonas strode away in a manner that urged them to follow. He walked to the edge of the wall, unconcerned about the trouble brewing below. Leonas pointed an enthusiastic finger at the open air before them.

"The Weeping Grove awaits!"

***

"Ethil, get up! Hurry!"

Waking up wasn't a gradual thing for Ethil. Her eyes snapped open and she hopped right out of bed. Ethil's fingers were tense and blue with magic, searching her surroundings for a threat, but all she found was Myrrh, rummaging inside of her dresser and stuffing clothes into a tiny bag. She looked through her meager belongings with a critical eye.

There was a man Ethil didn't recognize by her door. His arms were crossed and his jaw was locked with tension, as if he feared an intruder might suddenly pop in and attack them. After the events at the Tower, Ethil could hardly discount the possibility.

Picking up her tome from the nightstand, she turned to Myrrh, who immediately threw a thick robe in her face.

"Put this on," Myrrh told her.

"What?" Ethil asked, but hurriedly slipped the robe over her head regardless. "Why do I ne—what's going on?"

"Shhh!" Myrrh shushed, as she grabbed more of her things. "We're going to the Grove."

"We're *what*?"

"It was an order from Elder Dace."

Ethil stopped. The very same thought Myrrh had just forty minutes prior came to the forefront of her mind. "But isn't this what Elder Drakone warned us about?" she asked. The nameless man by the door turned curiously at that. "Is this safe?"

Myrrh waved her concern aside. She didn't know either. But Leonas had asked it of her, so it was highly unlikely.

"Does it matter?" Myrrh shot back. "We need to go."

"Of course it matters!" Ethil exclaimed, clamping her mouth shut when they both turned to glare at her. Distantly, she heard the sound of angry protests. The words rang in from her open window, but as soon as she took a step towards it, the man grabbed her elbow. "What th—who are you?"

"This is Dwyn." Myrrh smacked his forearm, forcing him to drop her. "Dwyn, Ethil."

"We should've left her," Dwyn said. "They're getting rowdy out there. I wouldn't be surprised if they already ordered a team to close the gates. I don't know how you think Corrections works, but Elder Dace will fillet me if I'm still here by sundown. I *wish* that was a figure of speech."

"You're overreacting."

"Trust me, I'm not."

"It's barely noon. The riots just started. They wouldn't put the Institute under lockdown. Not so soon."

"Lockdown?" Ethil cut in, shocked. "What do you mean lockdown? Why would the Council even consider such a thing? What's going on?"

"We'll tell you along the way, but for now we need to go."

Myrrh and Dwyn nodded at each other, both finally agreeing on something. They went to the rooftop. Ethil was puzzled to see a mess of practitioners gathered in front of the Zenith Council's meeting hall. They were shouting in *Íarre* and were practically piled on top of each other, as they banged on the walls and doors, screaming to be let in. The doors, however, were sealed tight enough that not even an ant could crawl its way through. Ethil could make out a few cool-minded practitioners doing their best to keep the peace. There were a few Masters thrown into the mix as well, discernable only by the color of their robes.

Ethil stared at her feet as she climbed. Scaling rooftops required a certain amount of dexterity that she didn't have. Her feet might as well have been sausages compared to her guides.

She paused at the thought.

Her head snapped up when she realized just how precarious her position was. Saddling along on a tilted roof, the uneven shingles were the only things that kept her from slipping down a sixty foot fall. Ethil did her best to look around her, despite the cold wind aggressively buffeting her eyes. There was one nearby building for her to jump onto. She'd passed it half a dozen times during her morning walks, but right now it seemed deceivingly far. Maybe her fear made it so. Other than that, it was all open skies. Nowhere to go, unless she was looking for a swift death.

Her foot slipped when she stepped on a loose shingle. She would've fallen right over, too, had it not been for Myrrh's grip on her arm. But Ethil was taller and heavier, and it wasn't long before Myrrh tipped with her. Through some twist of fate, Ethil managed to grab Dwyn's robes. He choked on air at the sudden weight. They would've tumbled straight down had Dwyn not managed to grab onto the edge of the icy rooftop. He held on for dear life. His shaking fingers protested against the cold.

"Well," Dwyn looked down, lightly shaking the leg Myrrh held onto. His hands were starting to go numb. "This isn't good."

"You even think about dropping me…" Myrrh let the threat hang. Her fingers tightened over Ethil's uncomfortably. "Ethil, don't you dare look down!"

Ethil gulped.

"We'll have to transform," Dwyn went on, frowning up at the skies. Dozens of birds patrolled the area.

"They'll notice right away if we fly off!" Myrrh rejected. "They're going to think we're deserting if we go now. I'd rather take my chances escaping on the ground."

"Go right ahead, but look." Dwyn gritted his teeth, as he gestured with his chin at the closing gate. Hunters were already in position around the walls. "I told you they'd lock it! We can't exactly tell them that Elder Dace sent us out. It's suspicious!"

"How do you expect us to hide a Healer in the sky?"

"I told you to leave her! This is your problem, isn't it?"

Myrrh didn't trust the smile he flashed her then. But before she could protest, a bright light blinded her and the robes she'd clutched in her hands disappeared into thin air. In its place was a large raven that cawed loudly at her, before soaring high into the distance. The crab on its back was the only thing that separated it from the unkindness that circled the sky above.

Below her, Ethil screamed as her hand slipped. Without thinking, Myrrh transformed into a large eagle. She caught Ethil with one of her talons. From the overpowering scent of blood she smelled a moment later, Myrrh realized that she clawed her arm right open. She also didn't give a damn. Myrrh had to find that stupid, sorry excuse of an Amorph that thought it was a good idea to just fly off without so much as a warning.

"There!" Ethil cried, pointing at a raven in the far distance.

Myrrh saw something blue glow beneath her. A sign that Ethil was already healing herself. She didn't allow her thoughts to linger for long, instead focusing on gliding forward. Myrrh squinted when she saw Dwyn flanked by three other Amorphs. One was crazy enough to transform into a feline mid-flight. It gnawed the living hell out of his wing. Her eyes widened when Dwyn's crab pinched the cat's ear. The top of its head froze, then with a particularly brutal smack, the cat's jaw unclenched and it fell. Dwyn's Peose seemed to know better than to mindlessly kill a practitioner because Myrrh saw that the cat hadn't been iced completely. Halfway down, the Amorph changed into a fluffy creature in order to ease its landing.

Myrrh cawed in a futile attempt to get Dwyn's attention. She got another Amorph's instead. A large, thin bird that she didn't recognize. It swooped down to pick up an Elementalist on the ground. The paralyzing fear she felt during that moment would forever be scorched into her mind. Myrrh watched in agonizing slowness as the Elementalist rode the Amorph high into the sky.

The Elementalist's hands glowed blue, and then shards of ice poured down upon them like rain. Pelting, life-threatening rain.

It pierced one of her wings.

Myrrh staggered, losing altitude. The other patrollers backed off immediately, not wanting to get caught in the crossfire. It gave Myrrh enough space to catch up with Dwyn, who had morphed into a hummingbird. Just small and fast enough to dodge the ice. His crab rode on his back like a heavy tower shield, protecting him from any errant spikes.

Oh, she hated him.

"I told you to leave the Healer," Dwyn said, as soon as she neared. The Elementalist flew somewhere above them, his eyes scanning the shower, so he knew where to blow his wind. "Look at that crazy Elementalist! Pernelia, help me. He's going to kill us! I can't believe he's actually going to kill us! I'm not a deserter!"

Myrrh craned her head back when she felt a wash of magic flow through her veins. Ethil had climbed up her large body and healed her wing. Now, if only she could do that for every new round of ice that speared her open.

"The cave!" Ethil yelled over the howling wind.

"Cave?" Dwyn was the first to ask. "What cave?"

Myrrh already knew what she was talking about. It was the small haven that they camped in before they reached the Alps. That cave had been small, but sturdy. It was hidden enough that they might be able to shake their pursuers.

Changing direction, Myrrh ignored Dwyn's confused shout, as he tried his best to follow her. Her eyes opened wide in shock when she saw what lay ahead of them—chaotic gray skies and untamable gales of snow. The bad weather settled over the area like locusts to a field.

A blizzard. Myrrh gaped. *Now? Really?*

But when she saw the practitioners behind her hold back at the sight of it, she allowed a small smile to tilt her beak in an odd way, before barreling forward.

Perfect, she thought, changing her tune.

She didn't care about the hazards hurtling through a storm

as volatile as the one ahead of them posed, only that she got away from the infinitely more dangerous practitioners giving chase.

***

Dels Drakone was dead.

And Leonas was one of the leading suspects.

Contrary to popular belief, he valued others opinions of him. Sure, he disregarded them when it suited his convenience, but he still valued them nevertheless. So, when his innocence was brought into question, he couldn't help the sting of betrayal that blossomed in his chest. Leonas had made his dislike for the fool apparent on more than one occasion, but for some of the Elders to actually blame him for his death, well, that just made all sorts of profanity dance along the tip of his tongue.

Leonas took a deep breath. He schooled his dark expression back into a smile as he exited the meeting hall in the middle of another one of their petty squabbles. Most of them were on his side. Those that weren't, however, were influential, indeed.

He felt their eyes on him as he left, insulted by his exit. Well, *he* was insulted by their conclusions. Although he couldn't say that he was surprised by them. They were always so quick to blame. Just because he told his wife's primary apprentice and one of his men to leave before the trouble started, they thoughtlessly assumed him guilty. Never mind the fact that he'd always had great intuition.

Who realized what I did anyway? Leonas stopped to look around. *Is someone watching me?*

He couldn't tell. Not with all of the shouting echoing across the courtyard. The people demanded to know what happened to a member of the infamous Drakone family and what the Council planned to do about it. They seemed angrier than Roderek with all of their whining.

So quick to forget that he was a fat, lazy fool, Leonas thought scathingly. The same Elders that criticized him also questioned Dels' right on the Council, but of course they fully supported him now that he was dead. Hypocrites. Leonas' thoughts drifted to Cheryll and the records she spoke of. *How would they react when they realize that Drakone blood isn't one of a kind after all? That there are other fragments of the First Zenith still with us now?*

Leonas headed to his office. He managed to get there with little interference. No one ever flooded the public archives. It was why he requested his office be moved there. The first thing he did when he stepped inside was open the locked cabinet where he kept Cheryll's most recent letters. Once he had those in hand, he lit the fireplace with a quick blast and then threw them in.

He didn't know how or why this happened. Oh, he could venture a guess. An accurate one, too, he bet. Someone wanted to stir things up in the Alps to force them to close the gates until all of the Arch Poten's arrived for the Summit. It was the perfect time to do so. The Alps couldn't afford to isolate themselves. Not with the Grove in such disarray. And from the Tipping he interrogated, he knew that they were already making their move.

If the practitioners in the west rose up because they thought the north ignored their calls to dissolve the Potentate Union, then they'd have a full-blown riot on their hands. Some might even die in their anger. The Grove couldn't stand against their Union without the help of the Circle's Hunters or else it might be seen as them rebelling against the Institute as a whole. And even if they did somehow win, they'd resent the Council for ignoring their pleas. Perhaps even demand a change in leadership.

At the very least, they'd stop making Orivellea.

Leonas didn't mind that one bit, but the Grove's Potens knew secrets only a select few were privy to. The Zenith Council couldn't afford to have the Grove's practitioners turn against the Potens... at least not yet. But why, oh why, was the Lafertti Clan pushing for dissolution so ardently? Did their regulars know about the crystal's production? If so, then it wouldn't be too far-fetched to believe that they conjured up a plan to use it as leverage against the Council. The Lafertti Clan's power had waned over the years. This was a perfect way to restore it to its former glory, especially if their contact in the Alps overthrew the Elders and anointed a mutual acquaintance as their new king.

But the idea alone was ludicrous enough to make him double over in laughter. Not one person came to mind when he thought of who could be mad enough to do such a thing. Their actions made no sense... not now anyway. He needed more information. Preferably sooner rather than later.

Before he could think of another reason, a fist banged on his door. It was strong enough to rattle the aged wood.

"Elder Dace!" someone called and he heard the door click as they attempted to open it. Did they really think he wouldn't lock it? "Come out. The Council is demanding that you return to the meeting hall."

For questioning, he thought sourly.

Leonas clenched his fists. Ice coated them in thick sheets. He pounded his fist on his desk in frustration. The corner of it crumbled under his strength. He was alone now. Not that it mattered. It had been this way in the beginning—when he first rose to his position on the Zenith Council—it was only right that that's how it was again at the end of it all.

Just as he thought it, the letter opener on his desk glinted in the gloom. There was an unfamiliar note under it. He tore it open savagely. Once he read the neat scrawl, his lips turned up into a thin smile and he charred the page until not even ashes remained.

Turns out, he wasn't as alone as he thought.

Leonas stepped forward. So, they wanted to question him? Fine. He'd play along. If only to figure out the mastermind behind this plan, and what in the world they thought they could achieve by framing him for something so absurd. When Leonas got his hands on them, he'd burn them alive.

By the time he opened the door, his mind had helpfully compiled a mental checklist of two dozen people that had something against him.

None of them were Tippings.

Leonas Dace,

We encountered some of your men along the Gelid Mountains.

They say you dealt with our agent deployed in the north... and that your persuasion loosened his tongue more than it should have. To succumb to interrogation tactics is a disgrace to our band, but to submit to a contract we knew nothing about is an offense grave enough to warrant death.

Rest assured that the Tippings have always treaded lightly when it comes to Institute politics, especially if it concerns the Diamond Alps directly. We're currently investigating the man's employer.

Due to the circumstances, I assume you'd like us to aid your men in their journey to the Weeping Grove? Consider it done. Our thanks for dealing with the traitor. My agents will keep you updated on the happenings in the west. I expect the same courtesy.

Regards,
Euphemia

23

Floren was plotting the best way to kill them.

Khale didn't blame him. It was strange that the others were fine with what Jorn had told them.

"Brev was an Imp," Drage had said in that assertive drawl of his. Like that one sentence explained everything. Maybe it did. As they spent more time with them, Khale quickly realized that Imps were always the first to die.

Can't move an inch without sacrificin' somethin', Khale thought bitterly. They were the gain they received in exchange for Brev. At least that's how Drage saw it. He had a strange way of looking at things. It was *simple,* for lack of a better word. Khale didn't hate that about him, quite the opposite in fact. The way Drage carried out his principles was fascinating. He had his pride and his beliefs, no matter how warped they might've been.

True to his word, Drage took them under his wing and let them do what they pleased, so long as they came back when he needed them. They participated in raids mostly, where their fighting skills could be put to use. Other times, they helped runaways or got rid of back alley scum. Though the Hellion was large, they were primarily tasked with small jobs because of how scattered they were. Drage didn't mind doing grunt work. He let the tide come and go, never once allowing the frothy waves to shake him.

During languid days when neither Khale, nor Pom wanted to step a foot outside of Brantine, Celina taught them how to prepare a ship. Celina was born for the sea. She glowed when the wind ruffled her hair and stood brightest when the tide lifted with unrest. Khale and Pom, on the other hand, simply missed being near the water. It was an easy friendship.

Jorn was easygoing as well. He'd been in the business long enough to develop the patience required for dealing with temperamental twats. He could even handle Pom, who always scowled when they came home with no news concerning Tiv. While Jorn's seemingly ceaseless patience couldn't get rid of Pom's dour mood, he was able to soften it in a way Khale only thought himself capable of doing. It was quite the sight.

Khale suddenly sighed.

He sat on a wharf overlooking the Alman Sea, letting his feet dangle above the water. If he squinted, he could see Sicin; if he flew, he could reach it. That didn't mean he would try though. Brantine's nights were unnaturally cold. He shrugged on his hood, hiding his red hair from curious urchins and money-questing whores. His features screamed, *'strange foreigner,'* and coupled with his clean clothes, he was afraid they'd think him wealthy.

Hah, me? Loaded? I sure as sin wouldn't be freezin' out here then. Khale frowned, his mood soured by his own thoughts. *Nice goin' there, Khale. Remindin' yerself how skint you are. Pernelia's feathered arse. Like my pouch ain't sad enough on a regular day.*

"There you are…" Pom said, appearing out of thin air. Before Khale could react, he dropped into a seat beside him. Pom's eyes thinned as he met Khale's gaze. "What are you doing out here? Did you even search for information about Tiv?"

"I did!" Khale defended instantly. "Yer the one that took fifty thousand years ta get back. I thought we agreed on eight hours. *Eight.* It's been ten!"

"I actually searched properly. I flew all the way to Min!"

"I flew ta Lake Kloren an' got my arse thrown out by Silas' monks." Khale showed him a blooming purple bruise on his arm. Pom could just make out the shape of a hand. "Strong grips, those monkeys. Fast, too. Caught me a second before I could transform. But they were nice enough ta tell me that no practitioners came by, y'know… right before throwin' me out on my backside in the middle of their stupid lake. With a *do-not-disturb-again* flame aimed right at my head!"

Pom tried not to laugh. He failed epically at it.

"Don't laugh! Can't you see I'm tryin' ta share my woes?" Khale said, fabulously offended. Only the grin on his face betrayed his true feelings. "That turkey's always been good at hidin' though. I'm startin' ta think we'll have keener luck if we try findin' Jack instead, yea? He's always been flashy."

"We don't even know if he made it out."

"You don't believe that." Khale rolled his eyes. "You an' I both know that maroon was born ta make war. Crumblin' Tower wouldn't've killed him even if he wanted it to."

"Yea..." Pom nodded. "You're right."

"I know I am. When're you gonna stop statin' the flamin' obvious?" Khale mocked. Pom kicked his shin and he howled in pain, before rolling dramatically on his side. He scooted away from Pom as the next words tumbled out of his mouth. "What? You kickin' me cause you can't reach the water with yer tiny legs? How's that my fault? You should learn ta vent yer frustrations in healthier ways, yea?"

Pom kicked him again.

Khale yelled girlishly when he almost fell into the water. They were both laughing now. Somewhere behind them, a half-dressed fat man stuck his head out of his window and shouted death threats to get them to quiet down, effectively waking up the rest of the neighborhood. The townspeople were quick to turn their complaints on him. The man sputtered, and suddenly, they were laughing louder. They held their stomachs, as they tried and failed to bolt from the docks.

"Waking up the entire district at four in the morning? Not even the roosters are awake. It's an unholy time," someone said from behind them. Pom and Khale calmed down enough to look at Jorn, who stood over them with his eyebrows pinched. He was more disheveled than usual. How long had he been searching for them? "This your nice deed of the day?"

"You know it." Khale smirked, not remorseful in the slight-est. "Considerate as hell, right?"

Jorn shook his head. "Drage wants you. Both of you."

They sobered immediately. Khale was the first to jump to his feet. Pom held up a hand, and he pulled him up with ease.

"He say what for?" Pom asked.

"Not to me."

Jorn led them back to the Chattering Crow. It was quiet as usual. No one was foolhardy enough to roam close to this door. The guard that stood outside smiled stiffly at them as they pass-ed, blowing hot breath into his hands. He shivered, despite the layers of cloth and leather he wore. His friends had even given him a thick, gray blanket to wrap around his shoulders. It was frayed at the edges and had more holes than Khale could count, but it was a nice gesture, regardless.

Khale found a half-empty bottle on the ground behind the guard's feet. He motioned discreetly for him to hide it, before Jorn caught him. They really needed to put a fire pit out here. Maybe then the sentries would stop drinking to keep their bellies warm. They weren't very good at hiding the evidence. While Khale didn't know many confident enough to walk into a house full of mercenaries uninvited, the few he did were powerful. The kind they couldn't afford to face inebriated.

As soon as they stepped inside, some of the men lifted their glasses to them in greeting. Drage sat at the bar, nursing a drink with Celina by his side. She leaned backwards against the coun-ter, balancing on her elbows. Celina raised her arm when she saw them. Pom ran ahead with the enthusiasm of a child, though with none of its cuteness. Khale lingered a step behind. He watched Floren out of the corner of his eye. The man was trying to death glare him six feet under. Again.

"You're here." Drage finished off his drink. "Good."

"What's up?" Pom looked around. There were noticeably less people. "Where is everyone?"

"It's four in the morning, kid. They're asleep."

"I'm amazed yer up," Khale commented. "Don't you usually sleep in til noon? A smidge early ta be drinkin' don't you think?"

"Not if you haven't slept yet. Besides," he gestured vaguely at Celina, "sleeping in wasn't an option today. She'd strangle me if I tried."

"You'd probably like it. Nasty slug."

Drage let out a bark of laughter. "You've got me there. But I'm heading out to Heathe soon. Thought you guys might like to come, since you're looking for your friend and all."

"Heathe?" Pom asked. He wore a pensive look on his face, as he tried to remember where exactly that was. Geography was never his strong suit.

"It's a few days north of here. It'll just be us four. Celina's got a sweet spot for you two. So, maybe you guys can ease Gil, too? Couldn't hurt to try, and if it turns out that he thinks your scum, then I won't have to worry about protecting you." Drage snickered, though they didn't know what he found so funny.

"Gil's my brother," Celina explained. "And he's this sweet thing's co-leader. Gil's in charge of every Imp from Aston to the Pulka Ruins. Heathe's a neutral zone."

"Why are you meeting in a neutral zone?" Pom asked.

"Me and the in-laws don't get along." Drage poured himself another glass. As if his life depended on it.

"You're married?"

"Of course not," Celina cut in. Much to Drage's amusement. He slung an arm around her shoulders, invading her personal space. Celina promptly shoved him back into his seat. "Get on with it, Drage."

"Bleeding impatient," Drage muttered, ignoring her glare. He exhaled in annoyance, and when he looked at them again his gaze was solemn and unwavering. Even the lines of his face deepened, more visible now that his smirk was gone. They could tell from the way his voice dropped that he was more than a little concerned about what was to come. "For every time Celina and I have seen eye-to-eye, Gil and I... haven't. Different ethos, you could say. I wouldn't be surprised if this was a trap. It wouldn't be the first time he's tried to off me."

"We're guards," Pom concluded.

"Don't be like that. I need help. You two want to search somewhere that isn't, well, here. We both win."

"There's always a catch," Khale said.

"None that I can see. Oh! Wait... I do remember Gil having a thing for Astonians. So, you know, watch out for that."

"No." Khale balked. "No, thank you."

"Tell that to him. Bastard doesn't listen much though."

They didn't think he was joking. There was a furious tone in his voice when he spoke of Gil. They had to wonder just what the man had done to make someone as laidback as Drage so cross just by the thought of him. They'd seen Drage fight. Swift and ruthless. Only more so when Celina was at his back. There was no telling what he'd do when you were on his bad side.

The conversation fizzled out, neither of them were interested in delving into Drage's history. Khale leaned back on the counter beside him, while Drage poured himself drink after drink. That couldn't be healthy. But Khale wasn't about to reprimand him for it. A part of him actually wanted to see Drage drunk—was it even possible? Maybe the alcohol would kill him first.

When Drage continued to ignore him, Khale watched Pom spin his dagger as he spoke to Celina about a weapons merchant that had just entered the city. Crazy dagger fanatics. He didn't see what was so special about them. Sure, it was a good weapon. But there were swords and maces and sabers, too. They were just as effective. Practitioners with weapons seemed to be more common out here than in the east. It was safer there. No open areas for them to get lost in and no raiders for them to stumble upon. Jorn was baffled when Khale had said that he didn't know how to handle anything. It still didn't stop him from giving him a knife though. Khale kept it in his boot just in case.

Wonder what Tiv would say? he mused. Tiv had never liked Nebbin. He barely liked other practitioners. Not to say that he and Pom were any better, but at least they'd learned a bit by being in the Hellion's company for so long. The Nebbin weren't much different from them. It was naïve to think they were. Though they didn't understand a thing about magic or enchantments, neither of them understood how they were able to survive without them.

It evens out, Khale mused. A content smile tilted his lips.

"What are you smiling about?" Drage abruptly asked. "Stop, or at least let me get drunk first. You're creeping me out."

"I was just thinkin' 'bout the Yova Plains," Khale lied. He let out a long whistle. "It's a whole lotta nothin', yea? Real borin'."

"You backing out on me?"

"I didn't say that. Just prepare yerself fer complaints, yea? Pom's got a mouth bigger than he is."

Neither were surprised when Pom whirled around, red in the face. His upper lip curled into a distasteful half-snarl, having heard their conversation from where he stood across the room. Amorph senses were no joke. Pom had an especially keen sense of hearing. The animalistic growl that left Pom's lips would've made lesser men piss their pants. But Celina only doubled over in laughter at the sound. Her laughter was a free and easy thing that echoed all around the room, lifting everyone's spirits.

Jorn ambled up to Pom to calm him down, before he left another hole in the ceiling. Their hideout was already falling apart. They didn't need him destroying it even more.

Drage lifted his glass to Khale. He gave him a toothy grin in return. They'd grown used to living here. It was nicer than either of them expected it'd be. But it was time for things to change again. Khale could feel it in his bones.

He only hoped that it was for the better.

***

A figure made its way through the alleyways, following after the small group of mercenaries. One of them repeatedly stumbled as he moseyed along the uneven ground. He was helped by the sole woman in their group. She chided him with an unattractive snarl, then threatened to leave him behind if he fell again. He fell two more times after that, yet she never made good on her words. The group stopped repeatedly for him to vomit. It was only after the fourth time that the man finally walked forward with wide eyes and an enthusiastic skip in his step like he hadn't been about to keel over just a minute before.

In his glee, he tossed the woman a pouch for her troubles. His eyes told her to buy whatever she wished from the market. But the woman merely opened it, looked inside, and pocketed the contents, before throwing the sack right back. It was done purely out of reflex, leading him to believe that she was used to digging through belongings and pilfering anything she deemed valuable.

The other two had hoods over their heads, shielding their faces from his view. But they spoke loud enough for him to know that they were both men. He could hear their conversation from a mile away. They were talking animatedly about… fish.

A kleptomaniac, a drunk, and two hopeless and hungry fools, he concluded. Were these really the 'extremely dangerous' people he'd been hired to watch? *This is going to be easier than I thought.*

From their direction, he could tell that they planned to leave Brantine. They were already on their way to Heathe then. It was a few days sooner than his employer expected, but that wasn't a problem. They'd just have to move up their plans.

He reeled back when the drunkard unexpectedly snapped his head in his direction. He slipped into the nearest alley and blended in with the darkness. Rather than chance a peek outside, he flattened his back against the wall and focused on keeping his breathing steady. It was too soon to come out now.

That drunkard is sharper than he looks… but not sharp enough.

When the four resumed their walk, he trailed quietly after them, purpose evident in his gait. He swore that the sound of their scuffling boots had the same ring as a pouch full of gold. Or maybe it was just the knowledge that each of their heads were worth as much.

The stranger smiled. He was going to be rich.

***

They'd reached Heathe three days ago.

It was shoddy, to say the least. Certainly poorer compared to Brantine. The streets grew filthier with each corner they turned, but that was only to be expected from a city long destitute. They passed houses made of old bricks and chipped wood, their roofs nothing more than strung thatch.

Stalls were few and far between, and each held less wares the deeper into the city they went. The town guard were a befuddled mix of alcoholics and arrogant, fat men, grown lazy from bribes. Whores settled in the street corners. They cajoled who they could with muted whispers, so that they might find enough to live another day. When desperation beckoned, very few would turn down a pocketful of coin. Especially when the only cost was a little flesh and a little soul.

The urchins didn't go near them, but they lingered. Probably hoping to rob what little the whores left with their satisfied customers before the night was through. One of the children had only two fingers; a testament to his life and the punishment he received for trying to live it. But Khale would bet ten gold pieces that the urchins were more often than not successful in their attempts. Pleased, happy men made for easy targets.

Drage chose an inn at the edge of the city. Khale inspected his room's lone window like one might inspect a piece of fruit from a dirty vendor. There was a dark alley in the back that ran in two directions and a heap of garbage directly below that Drage and Celina could fall on for a quick escape. Rats nested in the cabinets, but he didn't mind. They wouldn't be staying long... or so he thought.

Gil had sent a letter via courier with explicit instructions to meet him in a tavern three blocks away. That was two days ago, and there was still no sign of the man. Was he just that good at blending in? No, of course not. The four of them had scoured Heathe six times that first day. They would've noticed.

A trap, then? Khale thought. It certainly seemed like one.

Khale wasn't sure if the others knew, but the bartender had sold them out. He could tell from the way the tired man glanced away whenever he met his gaze. How he'd wipe his greasy hands over his apron and flash him a nervous smile when his black eyes didn't turn away. There were hardly any customers now. Only a sleeping drunk on a nearby table that clutched his half-empty mug even in slumber.

A blanket of silence settled over the room. It was different from the usual quiet that settled when people didn't want to talk. Khale knew the difference well. This one was charged and full of heat. It choked out noise. The usual patrons had probably been shooed away or, if they were smart, left of their own volition. It would be a simple thing to use the fact that the owner allowed a small band of mercenaries into his tavern as an excuse to avoid the mess about to come. Because taverns were never this empty. That was a universal truth. Although, Khale conceded, it could have just been a result of the early hour and their piss poor ale. But somehow, he doubted it. Depraved cities like this were never short on patrons.

Drage played with a coin as they waited. He idly slipped it between his fingers, while Celina checked their surroundings for the ninth time that day. Her eyes grew warier by the minute. Even Pom started fidgeting.

They do know 'bout the bartender, Khale concluded, and if their restless movements were anything to go by, they also knew that someone was coming. Khale closed his eyes and listened to what he couldn't see. *Three pairs a' footsteps outside the front. Two more from the back. Another… on the roof?*

Khale looked up, taken aback by how far they'd go. They must've paid the barkeep a great deal for him to have such an impassive gaze, while they ruined his livelihood. Speaking of the bartender, Khale watched the plump man disappear behind a door—the kitchen? That wasn't a good sign.

The fight was about to begin.

Drage seemed to understand that as well because he stood from his chair and patted the front of his pants with the air of a man that couldn't care less. The drunkard in the corner stirred awake just as Drage drew his sword. His groggy eyes surveyed their glares in confusion that disappeared as soon as the door was kicked open.

The drunkard screamed, scrambled to his feet, and then curled into a ball under the table. He was collectively ignored, as the three men Khale heard flooded inside of the room, looking every bit like the type that murdered for sport. Within the span of a breath, their swords were drawn and held high in front of them. Ready to fight. Ready to kill. Beside him, Celina and Pom drew their daggers, while Drage took to balancing his blade on his right shoulder in observation.

"Where's Gil?" Drage asked.

"Gil?" The man in front feigned ignorance, but the flash of his teeth gave him away. A thick, jagged scar ran the distance of his face. It curled with his smile.

"After going through all this trouble, after making us wait for two whole days... don't play the fool now."

"Our employer is with your friend. The angry, jumpy one. Oh, he really hates you."

Drage stiffened. His fingers tightened over the hilt of his blade. Celina cursed under her breath. And when two pairs of eyes flitted over to Khale, he knew what they wanted him to do. His hands flared for one blinding instant, before he transformed into a giant spider with long, hairy legs that padded noiselessly on the floor as he inched toward the back door. Pom shifted into a bird. He flew over the intruders' heads and soared upward to take care of the fool on the roof.

Khale pushed the back door open quickly, shocking the two men tasked to ambush them. His fangs clicked before their faces like a nightmare come to life. From their expressions, Khale knew that Floren hadn't warned them that they were practitioners. Was he trying to save money? Blunted idiot.

Shooting a web to glue them in place, his long legs extended over them, then began the tedious task of wrapping them in silk. Khale *felt* them shiver in trepidation. It filled him with a kind of predator's glee as he slowly deliberated what to do next.

The remaining men in front were stunned cold. But Drage knew better than to let them gather their wits. Using their shock to his advantage, he slashed at the one closest to him. His blade fell through the air to chop deeply into the man's collar. More guillotine that sword. There was no technique in his swing. No precisely calculated movement. Only death. The man's scream was curt and wet. A half-empty bellow that died in his throat with every extra slash.

Drage only remembered to turn when Celina parried a blow meant for his head. Celina dodged the third man just in time to land a kick on his back that sent him crashing into a table. She threw one of her daggers into his back.

Only one left.

The tip of Drage's sword flew across the floor, throwing up sparks as it went. The tip cut another jagged line into the man's face. He saw the horror in his eyes, before the man swallowed harshly, sneered, and then spat in his direction. Most of it ended up on his own clothes, but he didn't seem to notice.

Just as he opened his mouth to yell, Drage dug his sword into the soft skin of his throat. He didn't want to hear it. Drage barely registered the drunkard in the corner of the room squeak, before fainting at the gruesome sight.

Drage turned when he heard footsteps draw near. A tall shadow emerged by the door, connected to a bowman that looked green from the carnage. But his hands were quicker than his mind and Drage found himself on the other side of a bolt that looked too sharp for comfort.

"Die," the bowman said.

Before anyone could register, another man fell from the sky and landed precisely over the bowman's head. He tipped over, his arrow shooting into the ceiling. Pom jumped down a second later, stomping on the crushed man's face and bending just long enough to stick his tongue out at him. Brat.

There was a flash of light behind them and Khale emerged, whistling at their handy work. He threw a casual thumb over his shoulder. "What should I do with them?"

"They aren't dead?" Drage asked.

"Not yet."

"Leave them then." He ignored Celina's sharp glare. "Gil's long gone by now… if he was ever here to begin with."

"And Floren?" Pom asked, his voice low and threatening.

"If Gil didn't bring him, he either killed him or let him go. Probably killed him. He's an efficient bastard. Doesn't leave loose ends. I doubt he needs another Imp either."

"That idiot," Celina muttered. "He should've let it go."

"Heya," Khale cut in, raising his hand so they'd look at him. "It's three ages late an' probably worth less than a flamin' pile of Snuff shit, but we're sorry, yea? Caught yer men hangin' 'round the Mire with dead bodies at their feet, an' there we were, sweaty, moody, an' all kinds a' suspicious. We had a whole camp full a' tykes nearby after what happened out east. So, it didn't make much sense ta talk first, right, Pom?"

"Right," Pom seconded, his eyes apologetic.

They were rendered speechless when Drage looked between them like they were stupid. "Did Jorn not tell you… or," his eyes drifted to Celina, who shrugged. "Seriously? What's the point of having loud mouths in a group if you can't count on them to spill the secrets you actually want spilled?"

They stared incredulously at him.

"I hated the bloody man!" Drage wrinkled his nose at the thought of Brev. He rubbed his tongue along the inner skin of his lips, as if the mere remembrance of him left a bad aftertaste.

Khale vaguely recalled Jorn saying something about that. No one ever brought it up again. But Drage was more than happy to talk about his apparent dislike.

"He was always, *always* cutting corners and hauling men I

didn't know back to base. If that wasn't bad enough, he got all of the other Imp's in a tizzy over him. Floren was especially sore because he was Brev's lover. One of them anyway. So, I thought I'd cut him some slack by keeping my mouth shut, but ashes, was Brev a menace! Do you know how many times a week debt-collectors would come knocking on my door because of him? Too damn many. The brat owed gold to every merchant in Brantine." Drage harshly kicked a chair, releasing his pent-up frustration. "Blood and death! Just thinking about it is making me angry."

He turned back to them.

"Look, the point is, if you hadn't killed him, then I would've. So, *thank you* for saving me the trouble." Drage marched over to the bar, grabbed the nearest bottle of whiskey he found, and poured himself a much needed drink.

Pom and Khale shared an uncertain glance, before they trailed over to where he stood.

"You're thanking us..." Pom began, his voice was all kinds of astounded, "for killing him?"

"An' gettin' all sour-faced about it, too," Khale slipped in. "What? Not used ta bein' apologized to?"

"It's heartfelt, you know? We don't apologize often."

"It's practically once in a lifetime, yea? Savor it."

Drage shot them a glare.

"Oh, Drage, you big cheese stick," Celina proclaimed. "All soft and gooey inside."

She laughed boisterously behind them. Her amusement warded away the ghosts of the dead men at their feet. Celina's mirth was contagious because the two Amorphs quickly found themselves laughing right along with her.

"Oh, stuff it," Drage muttered, downing the rest of his drink.

They only laughed louder.

Olive,

Just checkin' in ta see how the kids are doin'. (Don't I sound like a worthless old man? I think I do. I'd send you a few gold pieces, but I'm skint enough ta be havin' sleep for dinner, so sorry 'bout that. You can hunt well enough anyway.) I hope yer cookin's improved. If it hasn't, don't make any a' the kids eat that stuff. Remember: hand the reigns over to Edanna. If you don't, you'll have a food poisonin' outbreak on yer hands. Just imagine all the vomit… and the stench. Creator's teeth.

Last courier I sent said he couldn't find you in the Mire. Good ta know you actually listened an' went back ta Eriam. Though the bastard ended up chargin' me double fer sendin' this. Like it's so damn difficult to climb a mountain. Flamin' highway robber.

You can send letters back ta us if you want. No scoldin's though. I'll throw 'em out. Just give 'em ta the highway robber carryin' this note. He's Nebbin, but he's trustworthy. Kind of.

Anyway, Pom's been itchy lately. Tryin' ta find information 'bout the Tower an' all that, so write somethin' good for him, yea?

Khale

***

Olivia,

How have repairs been going? Since a Hunter Captain is leading the effort, I assume everything's going well. Where are you and the others staying now? Are they safe?

On the off-chance that they find Master Orpha's body, please check if he still has his pendant. It's a Snuff's tooth. You'll know it when you see it. I'd appreciate it if you sent it to me.

If you hear anything about Tiv, send us a letter. Thanks.

Best,
Pom

24

Tiv never expected to wake again.

Though he never expected to see the familiar pool of a practitioner's robes again either. He stared quizzically at it. It was cut shorter than most, but its design was unmistakable. Forest green. It took a moment for his mind to place it.

The Weeping Grove? Tiv's eyes trailed upward, finding a pair of bright blue orbs framed by tresses so dark and unkempt he would've thought him another prisoner had he been chained. *A Healer,* he realized with no small amount of surprise. *Who?*

Definitely no one he knew.

The Healer surveyed his cell and frowned at the copious amount of blood on the floor. He glazed over the dirty tiles, the half-clean bucket, and the spreading fungus. The sight alone was enough to caution anyone against inhaling too deeply. His nose scrunched at the unpleasant smell only a stuffy room could bring. Tiv was sure the sweat and fear only added to the repugnance, but he didn't bother voicing that. His throat was scratchy and his lips were so dry that he doubted he'd have enough saliva to moisten them and talk at the same time. He should've drunken his fill last night while he had the chance. But he'd been too tired to even open his mouth then, so there was no helping it.

Behind him, the sun shined one blinding streak of light that spilled through the peculiarly open door. It was enough to tell Tiv that it was early morning and not much else.

Was this Healer here to rescue him? Or was he here to mend his wounds, so those bastards could try again? Judging from his luck so far, it was the latter. Tiv growled like a cornered animal. It turned into a wet cough halfway, and the Healer jerked around to face him. His head snapped so fast, it cracked audibly in the silence.

The Healer lifted his brows, impressed. "You're alive?"

Tiv cocked his head to the side. He ignored the pain of the stretched cut along his collar in favor of contemplating the questioning lilt in the man's voice. He didn't know how many times he'd wondered the exact same thing during his stay here. Tiv opened his mouth to speak, found that he couldn't, so he grunted his confirmation instead. The man's eyebrows rose even further, making a decent attempt to reach his hairline. If it were just a little lower, they actually might have.

"Dalis!" someone suddenly shouted, running right into his cell—he had so many visitors today—and blanching at the sight of it. He was a practitioner, too, Tiv noticed. A Conjurer with slanted eyes and a hard face. He covered his nose at the stench. "Silas' holy pyre, free me from this place. It smells like rat turds in here! What are you doing standing..." he trailed off when he saw Tiv's sorry state. "Oh, you found one, huh?"

"Did you need something?" Dalis asked.

"They finished rounding up the other captives. Some of the practitioners are waking up. Thought you might want to ask around, see if they know anyone from the Tower."

Tiv's eyes widened and he straightened in sudden shock.

"We aren't going to hurt them," Dalis said, mistaking his surprise for fear. "Or chain them either."

Dalis put his hands up and took careful, but deliberate steps toward him. He seemed disturbingly used to dealing with tortured prisoners. But, Tiv amended, if he made it this far, then he had to be. The cells here were deeper, more protected. Tiv wouldn't be surprised if he was the last they found or if they'd just blindly stumbled into this area out of pure luck.

As if just realizing something, black eyes swept the rest of the room. Tiv found the sentry usually stationed outside of his door lying prone on his side. He was soaked in a puddle of his own blood.

"Lyss," Dalis called, holding his hand out. "Water."

The Conjurer was quick to comply. He handed over a small waterskin. Leaky and filled to the brim. Dalis pressed it firmly against Tiv's cracked lips.

Tiv shuddered, humiliation burning with each greedy sip he took. It pierced his throat like broken glass. Too fast. He was drinking too fast. Though he knew it, he was still taken aback when he choked, coughing the contents all over Dalis' robes. Tiv flinched when Dalis lifted his arm, only to settle again when he reached into his robes to retrieve his personal grimoire. Tiv's keen eyes caught the dagger on his belt, but the thought was dismissed as Dalis' hands lit up.

A beautiful, brilliant blue.

"You're a practitioner," Dalis said, seemingly unconcerned about his own ruined clothes and more focused on the blood that coated what was left of his.

Dalis mumbled a soft incantation, before his hand brushed gently over his shoulder. Right over the shattered bone and the angry, purple skin. It eased the weariness in his limbs — and it was then Tiv felt it. A steady stream that swiftly became a roaring wave. It poured into his veins, fixing. Mending. *Healing.*

This wasn't the touch of an amateur. Tiv had suffered through the half-focused healing spells of the few novice Healers he knew back in the Drowned Tower, and he could tell as soon as Dalis laid his hands upon him that this was entirely different. The efficiency in which Dalis' magic spread was unlike anything he'd ever felt before. It didn't tingle like he dreamed it would. Not exactly. But it had been so long since he felt the warm loosening of his muscles that he'd forgotten what a skilled Healer's touch actually felt like.

Dalis' magic rippled under his skin. It brushed over aches

ignored for far too long and eased his pain from the inside out. Tiv felt the concentrated twine of Dalis' magic take root deep within his bones, probing, uncoiling the damaged knots. When it found what it was searching for, it surged. Past his arms, over his shoulders and the old sore spot just under his collar, even down his damaged stomach.

A profound, overwhelming convulsion rocked his core.

Tiv gasped. He squeezed his eyes shut when he could breathe again. Truly breathe. Deep, dry breaths that distended his lungs and filled him with hope—the hope of escaping this place. Dalis' magic didn't cease. It hardly even diminished. And it wasn't long before Tiv's pain lessened to a bearable ache.

"Roval!" Tiv choked, pausing to cough out a glob of leftover blood he'd been nursing in the back of his throat for the last hour. "Roval?"

"A boy. A Healer. H—He was in the cells."

They shared an uneasy glance. Lyss thought for a moment, hand on his chin, trying to sort through the eyes and faces of all those they'd freed. His eyes suddenly lit up, before dying again. When he spoke, it was careful. Very careful.

"Do you mean the boy with the... mute Elementalist?"

Tiv balked and nodded all at once at the memory of the woman. *Was she still alive? Was Roval still...*

When Lyss' eyes dipped lower, he already knew. Tiv let out a truly pitiful sound then. A cross between a helpless whine and a frustrated groan. The one eastern practitioner close enough for him to protect... and he'd failed spectacularly at it. Oh, if Master Celaris could see him now.

If Roval was gone, why was he still here? What had he been enduring all of this for? What had Rat's stories of Roval's recovery been about? Had he been lying this whole time... or did these two kill him?

Their help quickly forgotten, Tiv glared lividly at them both. The anger behind his gaze was enough to make them tense in apprehension. Good. His hands shook, and with strength he didn't know he had, he made a move to grab Dalis by the collar. But the Healer was quicker than he expected. Dalis jumped to his feet and out of Tiv's lethal grasp in one fluid motion.

"Not very grateful, are you?" Dalis remarked. He had one hand on his dagger's hilt.

"What did you two do to Roval?" Tiv yelled.

"Cool it, Morph," Lyss advised. The puddles of water and blood at his feet froze in warning. "We didn't touch any of them. The kid's corpse was already filled with maggots by the time we found him. Some sick bastard threw him in with the Elementalist. Poor woman kept herself holed up in the corner of her cell, and she still won't get out."

"Lyss!" Dalis hissed.

"What? After I took the time to open all of them, too. It's not like the keys were just lying around or held in some mutt's mouth either. Then she just—"

"What about the criminal with them?" Tiv cut in. Anger pooled in his stomach and transformed his face into something emptier. Less sympathetic. More drained. At his words, the two turned to him with a start. He saw the question form on their faces. "The greasy haired one with the slimy smile in the cell on the far end. Did you open it?"

"What did he do?" they asked simultaneously.

But before Tiv could speak, Lyss was already racing down the hall. He heard him yell something into the unknowable distance, calling more names that Tiv didn't know. Just how many of them were there? Tiv knew there had to be at least a dozen if they were able to storm such a big estate. But then again, they were practitioners. Trained ones, too. So, maybe they were just a small, elite group? Did the Grove send them? Or were they some sort of vigilante band made up of deserters? Not that it mattered. He was thankful for their help all the same. Even if the frown on his face showed otherwise.

"You're an Amorph," Dalis said, cutting through his thoughts and looking him right in the eye. There was no pity in his gaze. Only appraisal. "Why are you still here?"

Tiv's throat constricted, trapping the words. He looked contemptibly down at his chains. Dalis followed, surprise plain on his face, as he inspected the cuffs. His eyes raked over the fine lines, briefly looking at Tiv's missing fingers. Dalis scratched the dried blood lining the manacles with his nails, trying to get a better picture. The marks ran in intricate circles. Familiar, but not enough for him to recall why. Tiv didn't bother letting him stress over the cuffs design, he already knew what they were. He wasn't that much of an ingrate.

"Cuffs from the time of the Mentalists," Tiv said, watching realization break upon Dalis' face.

"Where did they get..." Dalis stopped to gape. "How long have you been here?"

Tiv didn't know. He ventured a guess. "Weeks?"

"How *many* weeks?" he went on, frantic. "You haven't been able to use your magic this whole time?"

The thought seemed to distress him more than it should have... or was that the usual reaction? Tiv vaguely recalled his own desperation when he realized what bound him, but the memory was fuzzy and distant enough that he couldn't evoke it clearly even if he tried. Now that his wounds were healed, the pain lessening to a dull throb, he felt weightless. The sting of Roval's death numbed his emotions until only weariness remained. He was tired of this place. So, so tired. Tiv wanted nothing more than to fall back into slumber, but he kept his eyes open just in case this was some kind of twisted dream conjured by his imagination. If so, he didn't want it to end just yet.

"Not answering? Well, whatever. Let's get them off of you."

Tiv jolted back in shock. But he quickly settled down again when Dalis quirked an eyebrow at him. The gravity of it all once again dawning upon him.

... They're here to save me.

Tiv twitched at how slow he was today. He always had a sharp thing to say to his captors; a snide remark that earned him an extra punch in the face. So, why was his tongue so still now? He could really use some of his sparkling wit, before Dalis thought him completely beyond reprieve.

"How should I go about this? I can't very well cut off your limbs. Unless you like stumps." Dalis laughed, but it quickly died when he saw the alarmed look on Tiv's face. "Right. Horrible, tasteless joke. Bad Dalis. Maybe we can get Lyss to freez—no, that won't work either. He'll freeze you and everything else in this room. Lyss is uncontrollable like that."

Dalis inspected the cuffs again. He eyed the miniscule keyhole with a furrowed brow. Dalis didn't trust in his ability, or lack of, to pick a lock.

"Do you know where the keys are?" Dalis tried.

"No," Tiv said brusquely. "Don't you think I would've told you by now?"

"Fair point. Hidden option number three then." Dalis poked his head out the door. He waved a hand and then the sound of footsteps reached Tiv's ears. A man came in with Rat stumbling in front of him, his shifty one-eyed gaze avoided him like the plague. "This is Philip and—"

"Rat!" Tiv yelled.

"—Larce," Dalis finished, the skin around his mouth drawn into something between a glower and a frown.

Tiv stared at Rat, appalled. The hands that had treated him so many times before were bound behind his back. An angry, yellow bruise obstructed what was left of his already hindered vision and a gag tied around his mouth kept him from shouting. The cloth was sodden with saliva. When Philip pushed him onto his knees before Tiv, Rat sobbed, begging with his tears. Tiv couldn't say what for, but he could hazard a guess.

"What are you doing?" Tiv roared.

"You know him?" Dalis asked.

"He helped me! Saved me, brought me food, fixed my wounds, *spoke* to me, and y—you gagged him? What do you think you're doing? Rat was in charge of caring for us!" Tiv wanted to bash Dalis' head against the nearest wall when his lips parted in a show of doubt. He fought futilely against the iron rings that held his chains to the wall. They rattled in protest, but didn't give. He wouldn't let them kill Rat. No. Anyone but him. Tiv coughed, unused to shouting after so long. "You don't believe me? Let him go! He's not who you think he is!"

Rat gasped against his restraints the entire time, nodding profusely at Tiv's every word, trying to back his own innocence in the matter. Tears streamed down his cheeks when Philip kicked him roughly on the side. No mercy to be found in their eyes. Rat's frail form rolled pathetically in front of Tiv.

"He's not innocent," Dalis said evenly. "He helped you to gain your trust, so you'd tell him the secret behind a practitioner's circuit. He's not some kind soul. Just another disciple."

"What are you talking about? Rat's never pressed me into answering anything! Not one! When I get out of these chains, Pernelia help me, because I'm going to rip your throat out, you two-faced little shit!"

Philip threw Dalis an uneasy glance. One that the Healer shrugged off, as he picked Rat up by the shoulders and untied his gag. Rat's immediate reaction was to shriek and sob uncontrollably. Dalis pressed his dagger to his cheek, while Philip held Rat's head back by the long strands of his hair, keeping his rotted teeth far away from Dalis' fingers.

"Where are the key to his chains?" Dalis demanded.

Rat continued to sob.

"The key," Dalis tried again in a tone far less tolerant. His blade cut a long scar over Rat's cheek, another addition to his many blemishes. Rat flinched away. Only for Dalis to shove the edge deeper.

Tiv growled at him, his magic hummed under his skin. The mere act of calling for it burned him. "Can't you see that he d—"

"In my pocket!" Rat bawled, sniveling noisily. "It's in my pocket! Please don't kill me. Please. I don't want to die!"

"And your true colors finally show," Dalis said, disgusted.

Philip reached into his tattered clothes, patting him down until he found his prize. It was a tiny thing, buried in the deepest layer of his rags. Apparently missed by the one they'd ordered to confiscate whatever belongings he had before they entered the estate. Philip might've missed it, too, had he not known what he was looking for. It was that small. Black and finely-crafted. It featured the same intricate carvings as the lock it opened.

Dalis released him, letting Rat grovel on the floor with his forehead pressed against the stone in desperation. He rapidly whispered something in a language none of them knew, but it sounded a lot like a prayer.

"Y—You had the key?" Tiv ignored the way Rat whimpered at the accusation in his voice. "You could've released me this *entire* time? How could you? After all of those things you said to me about Roval... was your helping me really just a lie?"

Rat didn't answer, only tried to squirm away. He gasped when Philip stomped on his back to halt his movements.

"Where are you from?" Dalis interrupted. "You wouldn't happen to be from the east, would you? I heard a lot of Amorphs were captured after its destruction. Judging by your current state, I'd say you're pretty tough. There's only one place in the world that trains their Amorphs to that degree, and it isn't the Alps."

Tiv's head snapped up, absolutely livid. "What's it to you?"

"You still don't trust me? Well, I can't exactly blame you. But from your reaction when Lyss brought up the Tower, I had to ask. So, are you from there or not?"

"I'm not going to tell you a thing!" Tiv spat, angry and irrational. Too much had transpired in his little world. The last time this much happened in an hour, his home was blown up. "Not after what you did to Rat!"

"You're still mad about that?" Dalis' eyes were sharper than his dagger. "Do you really trust this whining snake that much?" Dalis grimaced at the obstinate gleam in Tiv's eyes.

"You'd trust that slimy serpent over a fellow practitioner?" he went on, affronted. "Fine then. This is how we're going to play this. Philip, put the key in front of him."

"Dalis!" came Philip's instant reprimand. The scowl that decorated his lips was darker than anything Tiv had ever seen. He clearly knew what Dalis had in mind.

Partners, Tiv realized. A wordless conversation ensued between them. They brought it out into the open when neither yielded to each other's glares.

"I'm not going to do this pigheaded skink any more favors," Dalis said, adamant. "Not until he remembers who he can and can't trust."

"There are better ways to do that," Philip reasoned.

"Now is the best time to learn."

"Dalis, think. If he's from the east, then we need to ask him about the others, *not* risk his life in a mindless game of trust."

"Do you really think he'll answer anything with that kind of wavering conviction? Look at him, Phil. He looks like he'd rather attempt carrying a horse in the state he's in than believe us."

"You're insane if you think he'll trust us after this."

"This isn't for him, this is for me. I can't trust him until he proves himself."

They glared at each other for another age.

"*Fine,* you damn mule," Philip conceded. He threw the key at Tiv. It skidded to a halt in front of his knee. "But if he dies, then his death is on you."

"I'll add him to the list."

Tiv took the key with what was left of his trembling fingers. It was difficult, grasping without thumbs, but he managed as best he could. He looked up, surprised when he found Dalis watching him carefully. Dalis made sure he had a firm grasp on the key, before reaching into his robes and producing a smaller, less used dagger. It glinted dangerously in the light. Dalis dropped it in front of Rat's face, while Philip busied himself with releasing his wrists from their binds.

"If you can kill him," Dalis said, as Rat fumbled around for the dagger. "I promise to let you go. Neither me, nor my men will give chase. I'll even hand you a pouch of silver for your sodding time because as far as I'm concerned, you'd be doing us a favor. We don't need a practitioner that can't even figure out who his enemies are."

He was serious.

By the name of the First Zenith, he was serious!

Tiv sat deathly still, unable to tear his eyes away from Rat, who finally got a grip on the dagger's hilt. His one-eyed gaze was fixated on him. He clutched the knife desperately in his hands. Tiv felt sweat trickle down his brow, his eyes opened wide in disbelief at what was happening. How could they do this? How could Rat do this? The same Rat with the kind smiles and the easy grins had Dalis' knife poised to stab him, utterly uncaring for anyone but himself.

Perhaps that's how it's always been, something inside of him whispered. Tiv had just been too blinded by the joy of his company to see it.

Time slowed as Rat charged.

Tiv barely registered slipping the key into the locks around his wrists and ankles. Their jangles were lost to Rat's cry. Slips of chain fell freely onto wet stone. His shackles rang sharply against the floor, and all too suddenly, Tiv's limbs felt light enough to frighten him. He stared ahead, unseeing, uncomprehending, as the locked chasm in his body finally released.

The spill of his magic was small at first, floating narrowly up to the surface of his skin like the sun before dawn, and then it gushed out all at once. Tiv swore that the entire room brightened.

Swore, too, that the wall behind him broke to make it so.

Distantly, he heard the echo of Rat's booted feet as he took one final step before moving his arms back to stab him. The glow that took ahold of him then made Dalis and Philip shrink away. Tiv felt his bones crunch, shifting into something lighter and free. A pitch black raven swooped down.

Talons dug into Rat's extended arm, sinking through skin and sinew alike until the knife clattered to the ground. In a move done more out of reflex than conscious thought, Tiv clawed out the tender flesh of his eyelid, blinding Rat completely.

Rat howled in pain. He clutched his face in a poor attempt to stop the bleeding. Rat staggered back, right into Dalis, who stared ruthlessly down at him in aversion. He could only gasp when cold steel split his chest in two; the pain sharp for three endless moments, before it numbed. There was one, final sting as Dalis' blade slid out and Rat fell forward. He welcomed the blackness that encompassed him as the final vestiges of life left his body.

There was another flash of light.

Dalis and Philip looked up to find Tiv panting, his knees unsteady beneath him. Tiv felt as if he could pass out or violently retch at any second—and he did.

Tiv curled forward, core bent, hurling mouthfuls of bile because there was no food left inside of him to vomit. He was on his knees with tears streaming down his cheeks by the time he finished. The world spun in circles around him, and he breathed shakily until it stilled. It was only when he found some semblance of balance that he chanced looking up at his mangled hands. They were still glowing, but he didn't have the heart to force his magic back inside of his body. Not now and never again. He wanted to fly over mountains, creep through forests, and swim until he reached the bottom of the ocean.

But for now, for the moment, all he could do was look up.

Dalis and Philip stared back at him, equally mesmerized and wary. The silence that settled between them was deafening in its intensity. But no one made a move to break it.

It was only when they heard a distant, indecipherable echo that they finally snapped back to their senses.

"You probably hate me, but," Dalis held out a hand, trusting and warm, like he wasn't surrounded by flecks of blood that could so easily be mistaken for splattered paint with the amount that decorated the floors. "I'm not your enemy. Far from it in fact. I'm a Healer from the west or, if you prefer, just another worried fool searching for his sister."

There was a pause, before...

"The name's Dalis." He wiggled his fingers, urging him to take it. To grasp freedom with his own two hands. "Dalis Sirx."

Tiv's jaw slackened.

Dalis continued to wiggle his digits, pretending not to notice. "I don't bite," he assured. "So, please don't try to claw my fingers off. I like them."

Philip harshly slapped his back for the ill-timed remark. But just as Dalis retracted his hand to retaliate, Tiv grabbed it. Firm and desperate. The only salvation he had from this place.

They marveled at his unexpected hold for a brief instant, before Dalis pulled him to his feet. The Healer didn't even flinch at the feeling of so few fingers wrapped around his palm. Tiv couldn't help but respect that. Especially since he was guilty of it every morning after they were sawed off.

Tiv silently met their eyes, no more caution to be found underneath the orange and blue that greeted him. His own orbs were clouded with weariness and undue relief.

"Tiv Grovegg," he finally introduced, then tacked on, "I'm a primary apprentice from the Drowned Tower."

The grins they gave him then was liberation in physical form. Nothing and everything he imagined.

Tiv did his best to return it.

First Adviser Sirx,

We've yet to formally meet, but your son has been under my care since he was first invited to join the Red Scripts almost fifteen springtides ago. He's an extremely talented young man. Quick with a dagger and blessed in the healing arts. My primary apprentice has the fortune of calling him his friend and partner.

I was permitted to read your recent letter to Arch Poten Cole given my position, and I understand why his disappearance would be a cause for concern for you what with the recent happenings in the east. Dalis talks often about his sister. He was awfully troubled by the misfortune that befell the Drowned Tower. I apologize for not being able to stop him from leaving. But he's... stubborn. At times, unbearably so. It doesn't help that he's always so swift with his decisions. He sticks to them like dried salve on wood.

Know that I am doing everything in my power to keep the Potentate Union from branding them deserters and from exacting too harsh a sentence. They're an understanding lot... some of them anyway.

The Scripts will endure. I pray that you will as well.

May Silas light your way.

Gavin Rhone
Red Scripts Representative
Master, Weeping Grove

25

It was probably his influence, but Sylvie was out of her mind.

That was the only explanation viable to Jack, as he watched pillars of flame burst scores of men and weapons alike. She moved through the masses as if born to bend them. Jack was lost to the brilliant bursts of heat, realizing with rising horror that... so was she.

Two moved to lock him between them during his brief moment of distraction. Jack ducked under their arms, then lifted his hands to the guards covering their elbows to smother them with deadly glitters of hoarfrost. Still, it wasn't enough to slow the fire that Sylvie released not a second later. She turned with a fierce snarl, furious, with the promise of combat in her gaze, despite her inability to fully shake off the dead weight of the men at her feet. Before Jack could snap at her to stop blasting fire in his direction, more were on him, more men were dying; each time he released his magic, even more fell limp before his eyes. They faded as quickly as his stamina. His mind tore through half a dozen battle tactics faster than his conscious thought could track.

One, with a broadsword easily as tall as he was, nicked him in the thigh. Just as an arrow came soaring through the sky to stab it completely. Instinct took over then. Honed back in his days as a patroller when he and Tiv hunted deserters. But Tiv wasn't here now, and these weren't deserters trying to run.

Jack halted mid-step, unscrewing the cork of a vial with his teeth and unblinkingly downing a sour tonic he didn't remember the name of. Distantly, he thanked every embrocologist across

Ferus Terria when the gushing blood slowed. He brought his hand up just in time to summon spears of ice from the ground into the large man's chest. Jack broke the arrow embedded in his thigh with his bare hands, before whirling around to freeze the bowman's feet blue. The ice swiftly spread until only the man's head remained unfrozen, but his heart had already stopped beating by then.

Jack didn't need a mirror to know how he looked right now. He saw it in their eyes. A spent, savage beast. Grown more dangerous from strain and more violent from injury. Despite whatever his outward appearance suggested, he knew he was weakening. Jack felt the pull of his magic declining, even as he pinned another body to the ground in a shower of ice. The inconvenience of one element was tangible, and he gnashed his teeth in frustration.

Sylvie came and went along the edges of his periphery. There was fire in her hands and in her eyes, blurring the air when her magic poured from a poor woman's stomach. The stranger bowed forward into the dirt. Her mouth opened in a mindless scream, before her own comrades stampeded over her back to surround them both.

There were too many.

And they were flanked on both sides.

Enemies as far as he could see, and then some. They continuously poured in to replace each one that fell. Soon, even Sylvie was gone from his sight. Jack had no time to search for her. No time to even call her name. He could only continue fighting the hordes of Nebbin, hoping to catch sight of fire. He needed to get to her and think of an escape plan amidst this chaos. Sooner, rather than later. He doubted they'd be able to keep this up.

The only thing that kept either of them going now was the faint lullaby in the furthest reaches of their minds, urging them to keep moving. To keep fighting. The tune was scalding.

Jack's blood sang from the sound. Adrenaline burst forth in endless waves, keeping his hands alight. But that didn't change the fact that he was exhausted. The control he had over his fingers dwindled with each corpse he added to his count, until even he lost track of those that fell. There was no differentiating between man and woman. Adult or youth. The only ones before him now were enemies. Those alive and those close enough to kill.

Then, like an answer to his plea, a voice smashed through his desperation. It quieted the air around them, made screams die out and weapons still mid-swing. Rough, yet unendingly calm. It was a voice that took the air, expelled it, and made it his.

"Move, and I will gouge your eyes out."

The threat was said in the lightest manner he'd ever heard someone speak... and also the most terrifying.

Panting, Jack turned to find Vidal Verne smiling of all things. A glass smile. Fixed upon his lips so perfectly that Jack thought he might've dreamed him into existence. But of course he hadn't. Illusions could never mimic Vidal's spirit. His eyes burned with life, as red as Jack's own, and shining with the same silent promise. The anarchy didn't matter to him. The endless string of bodies were nothing more than pebbles in his path. That, perhaps, was what terrified Jack the most—Vidal's steady demeanor. He was fully prepared to make good on his declaration, despite the numbers before him.

That was when Jack saw the horde of practitioners that flanked him. They were young. Trained, but still inexperienced in any form of combat outside of the Institute. A few battle-hardened ones were thrown in between them, though many carried themselves in the same manner as someone who'd grown lazy from years of idleness would.

What sorry hovel did Vidal get them from? Jack thought scathingly. *Most are scared witless.*

... But who wouldn't be? His mind rebutted. Jack promptly crushed the thought. But not before acknowledging the fierce determination in their eyes and the snarls on their lips. *They've got resolve. Maybe that's enough. For now.*

Vidal spread his arms wide in challenge, just daring them to try his words. The smile on his lips was more daunting than the army at his back, and the Nebbin hesitated at the sight of it.

But one man, from bravery or from fear, charged. He raised his sword high above his head with a cry meant for battle, but the way he exploded into a pillar of flame was better described as slaughter. His knees gave to the pain. When he fell, his sword clattered noiselessly to the ground, silenced by corpses and his own screaming.

He crumbled before Vidal, kneeling like a reluctant sacrifice to a heinous god. Vidal's fingers dug into the skin around his sockets, tearing through flesh gone soft from heat and reaching for already melting eyes.

The sight made them all fall still.

Jack vaguely wondered where Sylvie was—could she see this? Was she all right?—but the thought disappeared as quickly as it had come. Vidal's hands suddenly spurred to life. His magic was bright enough to cover the blood that stained them, even as he squeezed his round prizes into ash. The smile on his face was, for once, nowhere to be seen. In its place was a blank expression that spoke only of malice and sleeping power. Violent squalls burst around him. As sudden and scathing as a jealous lover.

Then they charged.

And because Jack's hands still sparked, he joined them.

***

Sylvie gritted her teeth.

She was used to the sight of blood, but with the adrenaline having drained away and her exhaustion finally catching on, she couldn't help but stare at it all. It shimmered even in the dark, blending with trails of ice and fire lit upon fresh bodies that were still pink from life. It wasn't beautiful. It wasn't lovely or sad or melancholic.

It was just red.

The wound on her side blossomed with previously unfelt pain. It had some time ago. Still, she felt like it wasn't real. Like she was simply looking at things through the eyes of another. For an insane instant, she thought that maybe the body she was walking in wasn't hers. That the hordes of practitioners that suddenly came to her aid were nothing more than illusions fabricated by her hopeful imagination. Because she could still hear their screams. She could still see the glow of the Heartstone with each of her movements, burning as bright as her flames. Had *she* decided to show mercy by plunging her into this dream?

No, Sylvie thought. There was too much blood for this to be anything but reality. So much glossy red in one place. Like gory confetti exploding, painting the sky, the grass, and—

She was going to be sick.

Sylvie could already taste the bile rising in her mouth. It had such a pungent flavor, enough to overtake the spicy tang of copper and iron. Her hands moved of their own accord, finding her stomach and her throat, already knowing what to do. Her body instinctively forced her to swallow down her own petty disgust. This wasn't the time to fall into a trance. There were still men around her. Although she could hardly recognize them now.

Were they enemies, too?

Get ahold of yourself. You can't do this. Not here, not now, she told herself, hating when her mind spoke back. *Then when?*

Sylvie struggled to quiet her own subconscious.

Distantly, she registered someone calling her name. The voice cut through the ringing in her ears. It was too deep to belong to a boy, but it was also panicked enough for her to be fooled. It was such a familiar voice. One of comfort, ease, and arrogance that echoed inside of her head. It reminded her of the archives within the Drowned Tower, where her misdeeds could be buried by thoughts of smiling children and a comfortable life.

She knew that voice. She liked it. Liked the sound of her name in it even better. But then the voice stopped its calls.

Sylvie smiled. Because it wasn't an abrupt halt, but one of relieved silence. The voice had found her—and she was tired. The wound on her side bled through her clothes long ago, and the relief in that voice drew away the last vestiges of energy she had keeping her upright.

It reminded her of home.

Sylvie dipped unwillingly forward, landing straight into a puddle of red that felt like warmth and smelt like fear. She was only grateful when darkness finally greeted her.

***

The events that followed were a blur. Even to Jack.

He remembered seeing Sylvie fall forward, the sensation of his voice catching in his throat, and his feet pulling him after her. The rest of the world ceased to exist as soon as he watched her hit the ground. It was impossible to ignore the terror that surged through him then, so quick and so foreign that something deep inside of him shattered.

Jack bobbed forward as he ran, bent at the waist like a mast cracked by a sudden storm. His chest heaved from how swiftly his breaths left him. Jack's eyes clenched shut, his jaw trembled from sheer emotion, and then, without warning, he was on his knees before her. His grip on his composure long gone. He couldn't command his body. Not in the face of all that blood. There was so much. So, so much. It couldn't all be hers.

It just... *couldn't*.

His chest burned. His eyes burned. Breathing hurt. This was too much. Anymore, and he'd tear apart.

Jack vaguely recalled checking his pockets for anything that might be of use. All he found were coins and errant pieces of string. He needed a Healer.

Where in the four hells are they when I need them?

Jack checked his pockets a second time, more out of a need to move, than hope. When he only unearthed more coins, he looked around him for either a vial or a flask. It was hard to find anything amidst the string of dead bodies. But Jack didn't care what he found, so long as it was brewed by an embrocologist.

There must be something, he thought, panic rising. Desperation was his own personal brand of hell. Very old territory. He needed to get a grip. *Surely, this many people brought one…*

Beside you, she whispered in his ears.

Jack looked down at Sylvie a second time. The Heartstone glowed absurdly bright amidst the red. Although his stomach dropped at the sound of *her* voice, he couldn't find it in himself to argue. Turning, Jack searched frantically until he found a small vial peeking out from under a dead practitioner's robe.

Did Vidal bring him? he wondered. *Not that it matters now.*

Scrambling for it, Jack whispered an unintelligible string of gratitude to the dead man, before falling back on his knees next to Sylvie. He covered her wound with his hand. The warmth of her blood urged him to move faster, even as he uncorked the vial of—he didn't know. Not exactly. He wasn't an embrocologist or a Healer. But Jack did recognize the smell and the color, and he knew enough to know that the liquid inside was meant to relieve pain. If he was lucky, it might even slow the bleeding. Jack could only hope that she wasn't allergic to any of the ingredients. Giving it to her would be a big gamble, but it was infinitely more precious than whatever else he had now.

So, for the moment, it had to suffice.

Bless plants and magic and whatever else was used to create this. If this helps her, then I swear to Thelarius Merve, himself, that I'll never intentionally crush any flowers, shrubs, or any other plant ever again.

Jack made quick work of the cap, then harshly forced her mouth open in haste. To his relief, Sylvie awoke. She panicked in his arms. Her limbs flailed wildly against him in protest.

The woman inside both of their heads spoke again, but he didn't hear them. Jack was lost to the look of delirious terror in Sylvie's gaze. He didn't know how much time passed between him trying to calm her and waiting to be recognized, but eventually, he managed to catch her eye. It was only when he tilted his chin up, unyielding, that she finally relaxed against his ministrations, fully aware of who he was.

Jack didn't speak, only watched as Sylvie's eyes slipped shut. He pressed the vial to her lips. She downed everything he had to offer. Trust terrifying in its totality.

The effect of the tonic was immediate. He felt warmth return to her from where he held her and though her breaths came out slower than he liked, they were also steadier and firmer than the minute before.

Words spilled from him in a torrent of whatever language he knew. Curses and half-whispers he, himself, could hardly make out, but he had no doubt that she could hear him; that, despite his clumsy tongue, she'd know what it was he meant to say. Because it was in the way his fingers combed through her hair, the way his entire being shuddered in her presence, the way his breaths escaped in a trembling sigh—

Relief had no voice.

And then...

They were hauled off by Vidal and his men. Force fed sour potions that promised to heal and lathered with salves that made his fingers numb. Four times, Jack awoke to find himself in the back of a rickety wagon with Sylvie by his side. And four times, he was greeted by Vidal's mocking grin and an easily startled girl that peeked at the throbbing crystal under the binds wrapped around his head. He had no energy to stop her, only to observe the blush that spread across her cheeks whenever he met her eyes. She reminded him of a mouse with all of her squeaking.

What's she doing with Vidal? Jack tried to ask, found that he couldn't, then let it be. His tongue was thicker than sausages.

Their wounds were bandaged to slow the bleeding, but not to stop it completely. *No Healer*, he thought absently, before sliping back into unconsciousness.

Rest, *she* said, and because he was tired, he allowed himself to yield to *her*.

The fifth time he awoke, a stone ceiling glared back at him. Firewood cracked by his side, providing unnecessary light in an already too bright room. Despite everything, he still wasn't used to it. He wasn't used to the blinding glare of white and yellow in the dark. Flinching deeper into his terribly flat bed, he waited for his eyes to adjust, before looking around.

He was surrounded by four absurdly thin walls and the mindless chatter of practitioners. The voices, however, were deeper than he was used to. There were no children here. Their tones echoed through the halls and out into open air, filling it with ease in a way that was impossible for a tower deep under the Zexin Sea. As Jack laid there, waiting for the fog to lift from his mind, he finally realized that he wasn't in his home.

He was in the Red Veld.

The thought of blood came next, then his thirst, and finally, an arrow ripping through his thigh. Instinctively, he touched it, appreciating the lack of pain when he did. The wound was gone. Not even a scar remained. He was healed then.

Jack's eyes widened. His heart fell to his stomach in sudden realization. "Sylvie!" he shouted. Only his echo answered back.

He sprang from his bed... or tried to. The attempt only ended with him on the floor and his head pounding at an unholy pace. His hand came to rest upon his skin. The wounds were gone, but the soreness obviously remained.

"*Filan vahs*," he cursed, rubbing the back of his neck.

When the little girl he recalled from his previous awakenings unexpectedly opened the door, he turned just in time to catch her laughing at his face, bruised with the mark of uneven stone. She was a rude little thing. Nebbin, from what he could see.

Jack gathered himself enough to glare at her. The effect was immediate. She clamped her mouth shut and turned a startling shade of red, suddenly embarrassed by her own laughter.

"Where am I?" Jack asked, holding his nose. Bruised, but not broken. He wasn't that frail. Despite how he felt.

The girl looked down at her feet.

"Where's Sylvie?" he continued, undeterred.

Then the door behind her opened fully, and Vidal walked in with an easygoing smile. The crow's feet around his eyes were pinched a little tighter than usual. Jack had a sinking feeling that whatever he was going to say, he wasn't going to like it.

The little girl smiled at Jack, before running outside. Never once looking at Vidal, who gave her a reproachful look that reminded Jack of his mother. The similarity made him shudder. But when Vidal faced him again with that pleased grin back in place, the thought left him. His mother was never so free with her smiles; they'd never been so utterly terrifying either. If anything, Vidal was more like his father, which, now that he thought about it, was even worse.

It was then that Jack noticed his robes... then did a double-take. He rubbed his eyes at the fashion disaster before him. "What are you wearing?" Jack asked, before he could stop himself.

"A robe," Vidal said plainly.

"That is *not* a robe." And it wasn't. Not to him or any right-minded individual that had ever seen a set of robes before. What Vidal wore was a quilt. A rainbow quilt with puffy sleeves and clumps of cotton sewn within. Awfully at that. Even from where he was sitting, he could see the errant twists of thread dangling freely downwards.

"It is," Vidal insisted.

"It isn't."

"It—"

"Why are you wearing it?"

Vidal blinked twice. Very slowly. "To blend in of course."

With who exactly? Jack wanted to shout but held his tongue. His head was pounding.

"You need rest," Vidal told him. As if he didn't know.

Jack gathered himself, remembering what he'd been asking before Vidal had distracted him with his... tastes. He struggled to lift himself from the floor. Vidal made no move to help him. It was an unkindness he appreciated, despite whatever it may have said about Vidal's personality.

"Where's Sylvie?" Jack asked, once he was on his feet.

"Asleep." Vidal jutted his chin to a point beyond the door. "Go down the hall and up the stairs to the fourth floor. She's at the very end of the residential chambers, right across Monet's quarters. I'll send a Healer to check up on her soon."

Jack nodded his head in thanks. He made his way past him, moving with both arms against the wall to keep himself upright. Thankfully, Vidal didn't care whether he stayed in bed or not.

"Find me when she wakes," Vidal whispered, then flashed him the familiar, worn journal hidden in one of the many inner pockets of his quilt—it *wasn't* a robe.

Jack's eyes widened at the sight of it, but he made no move to take it from him. That would just end with him on the floor, possibly bleeding again. Instead, Jack gave him an incredulous look and said, "Are you really going to make me limp all around the Veld for you?"

The look Vidal shot him then said he would. Gladly, too.

"You're the one that insists on leaving your room," Vidal reasoned. "If you can make it to the door, then you can come find me. I don't coddle anyone. Unless... do you want to be coddled?"

"Do I look like I do?" Jack replied, caustic.

"That tone of yours will get you into trouble one day."

"It already has."

"The life-threatening kind."

"I know what you meant."

"Really? Seems Leonas' genes are stronger than I thought."

"Is that a bad thing?"

"Creator, no! It's a marvelous thing."

"Glad we're on the same page then," Jack said sardonically. "I'm leaving."

Vidal seized him by the shoulder before he could. "We need to discuss what happened in the Pit."

They did. But Jack couldn't be bothered with such stressful details. Not when his head felt like a blunt nail was being hammered into it. Each step made him nauseous. Still, Jack nodded. Just for the sake of making Vidal remove his hand from his shoulder, since he couldn't do so himself. Not now.

Vidal let him go without complaint, before disappearing down the hall at a pace Jack could only envy. He looked nothing like someone that just returned from a fight. Nothing like the man that silenced an entire battlefield with his voice alone.

With his head held high and his *snazzy* quilt, Vidal looked every bit the eccentric highborn he was. Talented, experienced, wealthy, and entirely too confident in his skills. The passage of time had left Vidal privy to the workings of the world. Jack resented him for it. He admired him, too, somewhere in the back of his mind where he played with the idea of becoming primary apprentice to such a man. He was sure his parents would have no problem with his choice; Vidal was capable, clever, and a few rungs higher on the political food chain.

For now, Jack amended, as his mind drifted to the freezing halls of the Alps and the contrasting warmth of his father's office.

Under Vidal's tutelage would be a good place to be. Though he'd probably have to fight tooth and nail for the position. Maybe a little begging on the side to the man, himself. But if Vidal was his Master, then he didn't think he'd mind doing those things. Perhaps the auctioneer could teach him how to live with a few of the Institute's more restricting laws. Or, more preferably, pass on his tricks about how to break them without having to deal with the consequences. Jack could use a Master that was... low on sanity. Not that he'd ever tell him that. Jack valued his life, despite some of the needless hardships he put himself through.

Like seeing Sylvie.

The walk to Sylvie's room was a vague struggle. A blurry test of endurance that went by in an instant, yet lasted a lifetime. Jack couldn't count the number of times he snarled at the worried glances of those he passed. He was always too busy stalking away. But he was sure that more than a few of the bored fools that followed him down the halls placed bets on how many times they'd hear an infuriated curse bounce back at them.

Jack passed a prayer room during his walk, and for reasons he couldn't fathom, he found himself slipping inside. He was greeted by tacky lyrics and disgruntled stares as soon as the door creaked closed behind him. The room reeked of incense and dust.

It made his nose itch. The songs made his ears bleed. And the soft light from the candles did nothing to soothe his sight; it only made him question his already failing senses.

He quickly decided that he hated this place. It wasn't much of a revelation. And even though he felt like he profaned the ground he walked on, he trudged onward.

Jack fell to his haunches in front of the smallest altar there. It was tucked away in a lonely corner of the room. A statuette of Thelarius and Pernelia stood upon it. Their figures entwined and lasting. Lovers during war, and long after. Thick vines had grown around the idol, turning it into a permanent fixture on the wall. Light flooded over it from a cave-in along the ceiling.

Like the rest of the Veld, this place was little more than ruins. A temple long abandoned by the majority of its worshippers. The pews and altars that remained were all damaged, the rest likely sold over the years. The passage of time was unnoticeable here. The world stood still, undisturbed by the sins of men. Here, walls could break and hearts could be wrenched open. There were no witnesses. Only strangers, malefactors, and sisters. Most believed they were blessed. Jack knew better. Only the damned stood by him, unable to judge. Yet, they continued to stare, unable to come to terms with the fact that a practitioner as proud as him, in a mess of weary limbs, entered their holy ground with a look that would've made a beggar tremble in pity.

It took years to properly kill pride.

Jack's disappeared in an instant.

He reached for purchase, only to grasp air, as he caught himself on his palms. Jack's forehead touched the ground in an act of pure desperation. His mind was filled with red. So much red. The stone's cool texture was a balm against the heat he felt inside of him—just waiting to burst forth—and he screamed into it, unleashing the coil of steel and unease that knotted its way around his throat. Tears prickled along the edge of his vision. His fingers dug into what must've once been a priceless rug, before the candle wax ruined it.

But the only thought that graced him now was of Thelarius and his power to turn miracles into reality. Jack wasn't a believer. Not a devoted one anyway. His faith was less stable than his temper. But here, just this once, he prayed. He spilled his hopes, and he quieted that terrible voice in his head that commanded him to do more than he thought possible. Jack reached unknowingly for salvation. From what? He wasn't certain. But by the end of it, he felt a wash of disappointment drizzle over him. He swore his pride was wailing in a corner now, banging its head against a wall, trying to wake him up.

He was already awake though... and exhausted.

The entire ordeal wasn't as eye opening as he thought it'd be. But it was enough.

It was only after his throat tore itself raw that he stood from his position. He was alone now. A blessing in and of itself. The candles were blown out. The incense gone from the tables. Even the sisters scurried away, off to sing their songs of praise somewhere he couldn't hear. If his surroundings were always this peaceful after breakdowns, then perhaps he'd do it more often.

Jack left without another look back.

After countless self-reprimands and deprecating remarks of motivation, he finally found himself standing before two double doors made of solid wood, four inches thick. He was barely able to push one open without wincing. Once he slipped inside, Jack was happy to find a chair already prepared for him to fall into. Almost as if they'd known he'd come. Perhaps they did. With the way they watched him, he couldn't discount the possibility.

The chair was positioned by the window at the far end, but the room was small enough for him to be close to everything. Jack stared at the sun through the tinted glass, burning its way ever upward. There were no clouds in sight. He wasn't particularly enthused by that. It made the room too loud, too cheerful, too... everything. He didn't think he'd ever get used to the sight of a bright sky. It pained his eyes.

It was during moments like this that he missed the Tower the most, but he'd never admit that out loud. Jack had a sneaking suspicion that Sylvie knew anyway.

Speaking of her, Jack turned to look upon her peaceful face. He exhaled a breath he hadn't known he'd been holding at the sight of her. She looked as if only a few scant hopes and subpar prayers held her together, but she was all right. Drained, yes. Vulnerable, definitely. But safe. She'd live. He knew she would.

"There's no way I'm letting you die here," he muttered. "Not after all this."

Jack observed her for a long while after that, enraptured, like she was an inconceivable shaft of light deep below ground where nothing but his demons were allowed. Words spilled from his mouth, gliding, unbidden from his lips, before he even realized he was speaking, and when she shifted to face him—so utterly relaxed in his presence—fire bloomed in his chest.

Her comfort almost made him jealous. Jack scowled in petty resentment at her ease, but it didn't last long because watching her like this calmed him. Keeping her in sight had become an odd necessity over the weeks. Because ever since their home had fallen, they'd been each other's only constant. A ground and an anchor throughout the times he needed them most. The thought of her by his side reassured him in ways he didn't think possible.

Jack's feet moved of their own accord, carrying him closer to her. Sylvie didn't stir. Not even when the chair scraped loudly against the ground, making him wince and nervously look over. He traced an aimless path along the back of her hand, taking care to hold her just hard enough to reassure himself. She had suffered so many injuries already. He'd be damned if he was the cause of another. Once he was satisfied, his hand fell back to his side.

He supposed that this was as close to home as he'd ever be. The thought stung more than he liked and the idea alone was alternately daunting and draining. But Jack was glad for it all the same. With a sigh, he closed his eyes and let sleep claim him for the sixth time.

Jack didn't dream.

***

Orange stains littered the Yovakine Plains by the time the Healer finally arrived. She knocked twice, swift and loud in the silence. It startled Jack into alertness. He knew that he was snarling something awful and that his entire form twitched in his seat at the disturbance, but he had to hand it to her because she wasn't deterred in the slightest. Though she did look helplessly at him for a moment. Almost like she pitied him. Jack furrowed his eyebrows at that, but otherwise held his tongue.

The Healer wasted no time. As soon as she stood by Sylvie's bed, her hands lit as blue as her eyes. She whispered something soft and familiar, before shimmering light burst forth from somewhere deep inside of her. Her magic was so bright it appeared as if she'd snatched the sun from twilight's grasp.

Jack was enamored by the sight. He could do nothing but gawk, caught by the bright blaze of her magic's focus. Little more than an ignorant child, ensnared by heat. The Healer's hands burned brilliantly in the darkness, lighting up all of the shadowy corners of the room in a way that reminded him of the days when he still had fire to wield, and small rooms like this couldn't contain the pressure of his flames.

A Healer's magic couldn't be underestimated. It lit even the dusty corners behind the cabinet where a rat with unnaturally large eyes scurried off into hiding.

An Amorph, Jack thought distantly. *What's it doing here? Who's it reporting to?* But his suspicions were soon dismissed in favor of searching Sylvie's face.

The change wasn't immediate. The way she roused was slow. Too slow. But with each passing second, her wounded stomach mended more and more and the ashen color that had lingered over her all morning finally began to lift. Jack thought he imagined the sudden twitch of her brow or the downward tilt of her lips, forming a pained grimace. But when she groaned, his neck audibly cracked in his sudden snap to attention.

Not a moment later, and he was on his feet, ignoring his aching limbs. He made his way toward her with a scowl that could crack glass, fueled by a flooding surge of relief so palpable that he actually choked; unable to shout the speech he'd prepared about her recklessness, her stupidity, and her utter carelessness for her own well-being.

She was a *fool.*

His mind screamed it every time he replayed her jumping head first into that fight. It reminded him too much of himself. She was supposed to be the voice of reason between them. He didn't have the patience to don such a mantle. While he knew that thinking that way was incredibly selfish of him, her sudden wild streak conflicted with his need to make sure she remained — alive and well — beside him. He couldn't reconcile the two. Jack *needed* her to keep her cool. If not for her sake, then for his.

Soon enough, the soothing wash of magic quivered, then siphoned away. Back into the arms of the kind-eyed Healer, who licked her lips, fatigued from the strain of what must've been a powerful spell. To heal Sylvie that quickly, it could only be.

"Slowly," the Healer muttered, but Jack barely heard.

Neither did Sylvie, judging from the way her eyes darted around in search — *for me*, he realized, unable to fully smother his pleasure.

"You idiot," was Jack's greeting.

His lips curled up into a furious snarl, but when her eyes met his and she had the audacity to smile, the words bent. At that precise moment, he couldn't help the pool of gladness that rocked his core. He watched as the light from the window caught in her eye. Twinkling. Hopeful. Hesitant. All of the words in his throat vanished with an inhale, and suddenly, the rest of the world no longer mattered. Perhaps it never did.

Jack cleared his throat, but when he still couldn't say what he wanted, he settled for cursing her twice in *Íarre* instead. The words exploded into the air. His tone alone was enough to silence the people he heard noisily chattering two rooms down.

Sylvie's eyebrows scrunched, slowly processing what he'd said. Jack found petty satisfaction in the knowledge that she understood his words.

"Jack," she called. Peaceful enough to be insulting.

Sylvie wanted to say more, but the words were lost to an uncontrollable cough, and she could only repeat his name again. Her voice was a mere croak. She needed water, unaware herself how thirsty she was. Her body would remind her soon though. So, he didn't bother.

"An idiot," Jack repeated, unyielding.

"I didn't hear you the first time," Sylvie said dryly.

Jack frowned. His gaze ventured to her tangled hair and how it caught inside of her collar. It couldn't be comfortable. Without thinking, he reached over to fix it, but stopped when the Healer beside them abruptly stood with an embarrassed squeal. Her chair clattered to the floor, shooting a cloud of dust all around them. She stared at them, her eyes wider than dinner plates. To them, she looked as if she'd just awoken from a long and tender fever dream. Jack's hand dropped in an instant. His train of thought utterly sidetracked at the look in her blue eyes. Her cheeks were redder than anything he'd ever seen.

Is she blushing? Jack wondered. *Creator, free me from these people. What in the world is she blushing about?*

The Healer took in their confused stares, before shaking her head and shoving a mug full of what Jack could only hope was water in Sylvie's unsuspecting hands. The woman was evidently the daydreaming type.

Sylvie stared dumbly at the mug for all of a moment, before her thirst got the better of her. The water was gone in an instant. Jack bent to dab at the trickles that fell down her chin. Despite his gentleness, his scowl was back in place and his anger was as refreshed as her throat. Jack's jaw locked in his fury. He gnashed his teeth together to stop it. The veins along his temples throbbed so much, he could feel it.

"Think before you act!" Jack suddenly chastised, his hands

white from their grip upon her sheets. If he still kept his magic, then the bed would've exploded into flames. Ice spread across its bottom instead, freezing it to the floor.

The Healer jumped, startled by the abruptness of his fury. Neither of them paid her any mind. Jack didn't bother asking her to leave. It was obvious that he wanted her to. Thankfully, the Healer got the message, having quite clearly seen his wrath.

She left a flask brimming with—an undoubtedly acrid—medicine for Sylvie, before sparing them a hesitant glance. It was clear to all of them that she wasn't fully willing to leave her patient behind with a riled Elementalist. But when Jack squared his shoulders, his Adam's apple visibly bobbing as he swallowed mouthfuls of cross relief, she knew that it would be okay to leave, despite the harsh line of his lips... maybe.

When Jack's icy glare moved to her, however, she didn't stay to rethink that decision. She scrambled outside without so much as a farewell. The door slammed noisily behind her.

"This?" Sylvie murmured once his eyes returned to her. Her voice was low and affronted. "Coming from you?"

"And what's that supposed to mean?"

"You know what it means."

"Really? Insulting me at a time like this?" Jack muttered in disbelief, his glare hardening. "Sylvie, you almost died. You have no right, absolutely none to talk about," he cut himself off with an exasperated groan, "you can't say that anymore!"

She wasn't listening, he realized. No. A part of him knew all along. It was in the way her eyes shifted to look around the room, utterly uncomprehending; the way her mouth settled into a thin frown, her eyebrows scrunched together in thought. There was a question on the tip of her tongue that clearly had nothing to do with what they were talking about. He knew her well enough by now to know that. But even when he didn't, certain sides of her had always been easier to read for him. This was one of them. It was infuriating. Especially now.

"Listen to me," he said roughly, drawing her full attention.

Finally. Good god, he was going to claw his eyes out. "You—*we* almost died, Syl. You shouldn't have rushed in. You shouldn't have blindly ran off like that or—"

"Gotten angry?" she interrupted, snarling. "You're telling me that I should've swallowed their words and let them continue what they were doing? You know that they weren't going to stop until they got answers, and you would have me—*what*? Sit back and let it happen?"

"You've always been good at that."

"Don't tell me you weren't thinking of doing the exact same thing!"

"But I didn't."

"That's the problem, isn't it?" she roared. "You pretender!"

"Pretender?" Jack echoed, genuinely stunned by the insult. It just wasn't the sort of thing someone expected to be yelled at them, and with such venom at that.

"Liar! Sham! Fraud!" she went on, red in the face. "You talk of change, yet when you see something you have the power to stop you… you don't."

"There's a difference between fighting for what you believe in and letting your temper get the better of you."

"I'm sure you know all about that."

"I do."

"How can I trust the mouth of a hypocrite? Someone who might've done the exact same thing, had I not beaten him to it."

"Why am I suddenly the idol to follow?" Jack argued. His tone was scathing enough to make her flinch. "*Vina sara vahs!* My temper doesn't excuse yours, Syl. Don't you dare try to make it."

Jack tasted blood and though he struggled to unclench his jaw, it wouldn't lift. Sylvie opened her mouth to respond, only to close it once his reasoning dawned upon her. His words sank quicker than sand. She looked down with shame on her face and in her eyes. Though there was something else there, too.

Defiance, he realized with no small amount of annoyance.

She at least looked apologetic. But that didn't mean he could just let it go. Jack needed to get the words out now because he could feel their unsettling weight deep in the pit of his stomach. He'd be damned if he allowed such a burden to fester. It wasn't even an option.

Despite his decision, the words came out weaker than he'd intended. Softer. Less scalding. More forgiving. He gritted his teeth in an attempt to make his voice sound harsher.

"You went about this wrong," he said. "Admit it. If Vidal hadn't come when he had, do you have any idea what would've happened? We would've died. We can't rely on *her* to save us from everything."

Silence now. From them both.

Jack saw the apology on her face more clearly. He scrutinized the downward tilt of her lips that spoke of regret and defense all at once. Her eyes were dimmer than he remembered them ever being. But she didn't speak, hardly even moved. Jack struggled to hear her breathe, and after a full ten minutes had passed, he wondered if maybe she'd fainted in that position. But then her entire body shot up, and for an instant, she looked absolutely livid and sorry and oh-so helpless. Jack couldn't help but stare at the mix of emotions that marred her face.

Then the moment was gone.

Sylvie slouched back against the headboard. Her entire body deflated, as she sighed in resignation and something else that he could more easily recognize—grief. Wild and naked on her face. It tore through his chest more cleanly than anything else he'd ever known. Still, she didn't speak. Neither did he.

Although he saw the apology on her lips, he squashed the urge to shake it from her. That would only get him a squawk of displeasure. Maybe even a slap across the face. Because he knew, somewhere inside of him, that if he tried to force it from her, this room would erupt in a burst of ice and fire. Neither of them had the energy for that.

Jack was tired, too. That was something Sylvie was able to realize. Because when she spoke, her voice sudden enough to startle him, the worry he heard there shook him.

"Are you alright?" she asked.

His grip tightened, unconsciously dropping the temperature in the room another five degrees. Jack caught her eye. *Stop staring,* he thought without warmth. One of his hands flew to his twisting mouth to shield it from view. His mother's words about the flaming thing came to mind a second too late.

"I'm fine," he murmured. His voice muffled by his fingers.

"That's why your hands are glowing," she said, ogling them. Jack smothered his magic. His gaze flew down to look at the traitorous veins on the back of his free hand. "You shouldn't lie."

"I wasn't," Jack told her, glaring in warning. He felt good. Well, better than before. Because Jack couldn't feel anything right now. Any physical pain that haunted him was outdone by the churning of his insides. Then, almost like an afterthought, he tacked on, "I don't."

"I know," she said, refusing to meet his gaze.

"You weren't talking about my injuries," Jack said. It wasn't a question. From the way she stared fixedly on his hands, he could only assume that she'd been referring to how exhausted he seemed. Confusing woman.

"I know that, too."

"Then don't act as if you were," he chastised with little force backing his words. "And stop staring."

"I'm sorry," she muttered then, just low enough for him to hear. It was so full of repentance and gloom that he knew it wasn't for their current conversation. She was so nauseatingly stubborn. They both were. But Jack didn't want her apology... yet, a part of him accepted it all the same.

He really hated that.

"I know," Jack said this time.

He pointedly ignored the weariness in her eyes in favor of falling back into his chair and burying his face in the sheets beside her legs like a man seeking home.

A pregnant pause followed, allowing the knotted thing in

the air between them to loosen. It was only after he lost track of the minutes that passed that he reached for the flask of medicine the Healer had left. Unscrewing it, his entire face crinkled at the horrid scent. It was like getting a whiff of old socks and death. He didn't envy her. Jack judged anyone that would.

"Drink up," he told her.

The yelp of horror that escaped her lips made him smirk. Sylvie's eyes pleaded with him to replace the cap. He almost did, too. It was that pungent. But he wasn't that sympathetic. Jack placed it carefully in her trembling hands, his eyes warning her not to purposely spill it.

"Are you trying to poison me?" she asked, staring at the goo. The sight made her insides squeeze in apprehension, and she fought to keep her breathing even. It would be the death of her. She just knew it. "I said I was sorry. Please—"

"Drink," Jack ordered, merciless, before making his way to the door. A decision he rued after one step. He fought the urge to stumble in her presence, entirely unwilling to yield to the pain riding up his torso and pressing the life from his lungs. He hid his grimace with his back.

Jack stopped only briefly to check if she braved the tonic, but instead found her staring at him with lost eyes that were too wide for his liking. Sheer surprise kept him, rather than any restraining force. His insides churned in understanding. She was watching him leave her.

Damn sap, he thought with no real strength.

"You're leaving?" she asked.

"What does it look like?"

"I need you here, Jack."

"For what?"

"Nothing." Sylvie paused. "I just... need you."

His chest heated, despite himself. "I'll be back," he assured, the words spilling out of their own volition. "I just need to call Vidal. I told him I would."

"Then I'll go with you."

Jack held his hand up when she made a valiant, but useless attempt to scramble to her feet. "No. You need rest. I already said I'd be back. I don't—"

"—lie." Sylvie waved him off. She settled down once his lips formed the words. Those magic words. So undeniably Jack, she couldn't help but let out a breath of relief. He was okay... they both were. "I know."

"Good."

Sylvie flashed him a weak smile. He awkwardly returned it. The corner of his mouth quirked up into something else entirely. But it was close enough. It made her laugh at least.

Shuffling his feet and holding his breath for a good five seconds, Jack gathered his wits, and then left like a monster would swallow him whole if he didn't. The pain of his side remained forgotten, numbed by something hot and stifling and still too new to name.

Jack's ears burned red with the possibility that maybe—just maybe—he wasn't the only one that thought of this warmth as home.

Partner,

I've officially misplaced that damned book.

I don't know if it fell out of my pack while I was creeping around those tunnels, if someone nicked it from me during that bloodbath, or if I accidentally left it in that cold room I first woke up in, but for the life of me—I can't find it! I was on a good part, too. Something about the trees surrounding the Grove. Dalis described them like giant lanterns... I held back on reading that part because I wanted to do it after we got out of that mess in the Pit. (You don't want to know.)

But now that we're out, exhausted, and stuck in this room (you don't want to know about that either) I've got nothing to do. I'm bored. My curiosity is eating away at me. Which is why I'm writing again, by the way. It's a good way to pass the time. I don't know how Sylvie considers this a stress-reliever though because just thinking about that flaming book again is making my temples throb.

Sure, I could sleep. Get the rest of the night over with in an instant. But this chair I'm on is beyond uncomfortable and a new Healer has been coming in every hour to check on Sylvie. I don't trust their eyes. They wander too much for my liking. I feel like some of the men here have never seen a woman what with their drifting gazes. Then, after all of that vital checking, they have the audacity to poke me. Me! No matter how many times I tell them that I don't need their help, they still do it. Most are pretty glare-resistant, too. I don't know how they managed that. Maybe it's a Veld thing?

I called Vidal some time ago, and he promised to drop by. But of course he hasn't... yet. What is with him and punctuality? I wonder if he does this intentionally just to get a rise out of people. I wouldn't put it past him. I don't know where Vidal's run off to, but he better come quick because the idea of giving some of these Healers frost bite is starting to sound extremely appealing to me.

Maybe I should wake Sylvie? That sounds like a good idea. Later though... when I can't bear this unending silence anymore. She looks so tired. I'll try asking one of the Healers for something to read for now.

Jack 42.27.CA

26

Monet was a sight.

Vidal, unable to properly converse with her amidst the chaos the last few days had wrought, smiled in absolute delight when he found her in her office, sipping brewed herbs that made his nose twitch. Monet didn't acknowledge him. She didn't even look up from her work, too busy scribbling a letter on fancy parchment. But he knew that she noticed his presence. How could she not? He made a grand entrance by throwing the door open and purposely letting the sound of his steps carry. He'd even shouted her name two halls down, thoroughly startling a Poten that sneered as he passed. That certainly didn't win him any approval. Not that he cared to be in the Poten's good graces.

He looked around the room, as he waited for her to finish. Her office wasn't much different from when he left six years ago to run off to Yorn. Having spent most of his time here, Vidal easily caught the minute details that had changed over the years. A cache of tonics in the corner, an extra trinket on the far side of her table, two dead plants by the window that he'd been in charge of keeping alive—small, physical proofs of his absence. There were bigger ones as well. Vidal found a mess of dusty paintings and statuettes cornered to the side, forgotten over time. The few he'd sent her over the years were in a separate pile, stacked neatly on top of each other where they could be easily accessed. But he wasn't interested in those.

Walking over, he nosed through the ones he didn't gift. A statue of some somber geezer from the Zenith Council, whose name he'd long forgotten. An amateur wooden carving of a child. The craftsman ship was poor, but the effort was there. Closer to the wall, Vidal found portraits of Amorphs he recognized only by face and an impressive painting of the Ice Crown Mountains.

Gradually, the smile on his lips fell. He was in none of the portraits she kept. Not one. It didn't bother him...

The hell it didn't.

As if sensing his unease, Monet dropped her quill with an aggravated sigh. "What," she began, voice as harsh and delightful as he remembered, "are you doing here?"

Vidal turned with open arms and twinkling eyes. "I missed you, so I came to see you."

The cold glare on her face told him that she didn't believe that. Or if she did, she didn't want to hear it. Well, he wasn't about to defend himself. Vidal knew it was true. That was enough. He strutted over to her with his ivory grin back in place and his robes floundering about him.

"Monet, my dear!" he exclaimed. "What did I do to deserve such august company?"

They stared at each other for an era, before she sighed again. Turning her head away, she muttered under her breath. "Oh, just get it over with already."

Vidal promptly wrapped her up in a hug strong enough to bruise. Monet, however, wasn't one to break so easily. Though her armor did creak loudly from the abuse. She huffed for a moment too long, and finally, almost timidly, wrapped her arms around him in an awkward embrace. It was tighter than his own. He grunted when her armguards dug uncomfortably into his sides, but he made no move to pull away. Only when he was enveloped in the familiar scent of spices and something distinctly her, did he retreat. Monet let him go without complaint.

He saw a foreign softness in her gaze that many might've missed. But he was the proud head of the Verne family—and he'd shame his ancestors if he didn't notice absolutely everything.

Very few were willing to cross his dearest wife, and those

that were, were dangerous, indeed. But he'd always been the grand exception. That was why, when he fell into the open seat across her desk with Jack and Sylvie's request on the tip of his tongue, he felt no fear. No anxiety. Nothing, but the swell of pure confidence in the fact that she'd do what he'd ask. Because he never asked for anything that didn't take her well-being into account. And, if he was being totally honest, he wasn't against talking her into attending the Summit. He knew he'd have to sooner or later. Before the Council sent someone to... escort her.

This is for Jack and Sylvie, Vidal told himself, feeling much better about the task when he did. The frown on Monet's face let him know that she knew what was coming. *Does she know about the Heartstone as well?*

There was only one way to find out.

Monet was deceptively composed as he reiterated his knowledge to her, only interrupting when she wanted clarification and bristling when he couldn't provide any. There was interest in her eyes and a flash of other emotions that were too quick for him to pick apart. He filed the look away for later contemplation. Vidal still had other things to do at the moment. All of them were important enough to tug his attention in nine different directions, but not so much that he didn't catch the way Monet rolled the corner of the paper before her. An unconscious habit she only did when she was lost in thought.

"Is that stone the reason why that Dace boy was so adamant about letting his Arch Poten peek into the Veld's archives?" she asked. "He told me they wanted access to it in exchange for their aid. I didn't think much of it then, since I thought they were like all of the rest that pass through these parts. Always searching for Conjurer secrets."

"Maybe they are," Vidal said coolly. "But the Veld's archives are a sad, sorry mess. Even I wouldn't want to be near it. Babbling treasure of the Alps be damned. And wouldn't it be embarrassing for you to show them such a decrepit place? I'm sure they're expecting so much more than a dilapidated storage closet."

"Don't insult my Institute," she said venomously.

He held his hands up in surrender. "Now that they helped, will you even allow them to go inside?"

"I never agreed to such a thing."

Vidal guffawed at the red tint that colored her cheeks at the mere thought. So, she was embarrassed about it. She did well to hide it though. He'd give her that.

"They won't be happy," Vidal told her. "But enough of that. Come. We should see them now. Jack called me two hours ago. Poor boy was hobbling down a flight of stairs, leaning on the walls for dear life by the time he found me. He snapped well and good when I told him I'd meet him back in Sylvie's room. He has an… imaginative tongue."

"What did you expect?" She sneered. "He's Cheryll's son."

"And Leonas' as well," Vidal said, thinking of his greatest friend. "That new Arch Poten he's with isn't some nameless child either. She's the daughter of First Council Adviser Victor Sirx. I know you hate Institute politics, but even you can't ignore those names. We shouldn't keep them waiting any longer."

"Oh, as if I care about their family names." Monet sneered. "They're nothing more than children with too much free time and not enough supervision. What makes you think I want to see them? Knowing Cheryll, she was the one that put them up to this in the first place."

"Regardless of their orders, it doesn't change the fact that they helped us. Their offer might've been unsolicited here, but I happily welcomed it. Not to mention, I still have questions, my dear. Many, many questions."

Vidal produced Silas' tattered journal and threw it in the space between them. It landed with a pathetic flop. Monet spared it a glance and nothing more, judging and dismissing it in that one instant. But Vidal wouldn't allow that. Not this time. He pointed an emphatic finger at the journal to make sure his obstinate wife paid attention.

"That was retrieved by Sylvie and Jack in the Pit."

"What is it?"

"The personal journal of Silas Drayr," he said, gauging her reaction. Her slack jaw didn't disappoint. "It contains letters from Thelarius Merve himself, a first-hand account of Silas' time as a member of the original Council, and the... strained relationships between each of the First Zenith."

Monet reached out, cautious, as if the journal would spontaneously combust if she grabbed it too fast. Her fingers played along its ruined edges, toying with the spotted, yellow pages. She lifted the cover with a finger and glanced at the almost illegible scrawl, before letting it fall shut again. She knew what he said was true. Vidal had no reason to lie. Monet stared at the papers that peeked out from certain pages—were those the letters?

Monet shuddered, flinching back.

Her blood turned to ice just from being in the presence of such an important piece of history. Those weren't just any letters. They were written by Thelarius Merve, himself. The man who tore the world apart, built it up again, and then disappeared without a trace. This journal was a personal documentary of the great Conjurer Silas, who was assumed to have followed in Thelarius' footsteps. One day he ruled the Veld, and the next he was simply gone from it.

Many assumptions had been made by scholars over the years about where they'd gone. A few speculated that they'd both contracted a terminal illness after the Battle of the Yovakine Plains, then went off to die together in peace. Others claimed that they killed each other in an epic duel, Conjurer versus Elementalist, only to both die from fatigue after three days of continuous war. There were a few more outrageous stories, too. A famous one was that the two had secretly loved each other. Peculiar, but not entirely dismissible. The lack of evidence kept all arguments viable. Whole novels had been written, entire anthologies compiled, and decades-long research projects undertaken in a futile attempt to prove which stories were true and which were merely hearsay. It wasn't uncommon for tall tales of dirt-poor bards to get passed on when no one had any evidence to the contrary.

There was never any proof... until now. With the true history of their deaths lost to the world, this was possibly the only accurate account of their past. If the Elders in the Alps ever got wind of their discovery, Monet would never see it again. The journal would be whisked away to a secure vault only a select few would be permitted to know the location of. Fewer, still, those it would be made available to for research. The journal would be prodded for all of its worth. Each line carefully read and reread, then reflected upon until the words were once again lost to supposition and bias.

Monet's throat constricted in unease.

"Have you read it?" she asked.

"Only a few pages." Vidal shrugged, cold and gracious. She couldn't read his eyes. "Jealousy. Adventure. Betrayal. A dozen other things contained in the scant five paragraphs I skimmed. I couldn't read more. It was too much. But both Silas and Thelarius repeatedly mention someone else. A presence... *her*."

"*Her*? Pernelia?"

Vidal shook his head. "I don't know who or what *she* is exactly. The way they refer to *her*, it's almost as if *she* isn't alive. Or they aren't sure if *she* is. I believe Jack and Sylvie would be able to tell us more. They already know more than any common practitioner should, and I've heard with my own ears their... ghostly companion."

"You mentioned that companion in your letter, too. What did you mean by that? That boy was here, in this very room, with that infuriating Dace smirk and I didn't hear a thing. Not one peep. What exactly does this companion of theirs do?"

"Points them in the right direction," he answered vaguely. Trying to get a straight answer from him was like pulling teeth. Except infinitely more difficult. "If you squint, their relationship is similar to ours. Behind every great person is another shoving them forward, yes?"

"Are you calling yourself great?" Monet scoffed. "I'm glad

you still have your sense of humor."

Vidal chuckled. He had a slight blush on his cheeks, as he rubbed the back of his head. He loved to be praised. It made no difference to him whether that praise came in the form of lies, flattery, or backhanded compliments. He even accepted sarcasm.

"Thank you," he said, pleased. "Feel free to praise me more."

"I see that you wish to suffer an early death," she threatened, dismissing his gratitude with stony composure. Barely thirty minutes, and she was already fed up with his tongue. "Shall I grant you that desire?"

Vidal grinned, brushing her threats aside with a flick of his wrist. Oh, how he missed this.

"Come now, we really should go," he urged, leaning over and pressing a painfully tender kiss against her temple. He had to stifle a laugh when her eye twitched. "Isn't it about time we had a proper exchange of information with those two?"

Monet suddenly sat up straight. Her proud figure was better than any portrait he owned. He really needed to have Rus deliver some of them. Along with a few plants to brighten up her office. It was drearier than that gray boneyard he would pass on his way to the market in Yorn, filled with weeping willows and traces of past happiness. Vidal couldn't have that.

As he thought about all of the improvements he could add to her workplace, she went back to writing. *A letter to the Zenith Council*, he realized, with no small amount of surprise. Vidal resisted the urge to bend over and read the rest of her words. Her penmanship was small and looped, and his eyesight wasn't so perfect that he could read it upside down.

After three more unsuccessful attempts, he asked, "What are you doing?"

She didn't look up. But he recognized the stubborn clench of her jaw and the distracted curve of her shoulder—all indicators that she was listening to him.

"I told you," Monet said, infuriated. "I'm not going to meet with reckless children. If you want to convene with them and exchange Ferus Terria's latest gossip, then you're free to do so."

Vidal contemplated this for a moment, deciding not to press her any further. His dear wife looked a shade too close to unsheathing Valor and making good on her previous threats. He chose his next words carefully.

"What are you writing?" he asked.

"I have to inform the Alps of my attendance in the upcoming Summit." Monet spat the words through gritted teeth. Her tone held nothing of passive surrender. It was pure reluctance and force. She was clearly only doing this because he'd requested it.

'Under duress,' as Wilhelm would say.

He never did like the old fool.

Each stroke of Monet's quill was done so grudgingly, and it showed. The ink smeared. Tiny blotches dropped here and there. She even crossed out an entire sentence. But her being who she was, she merely carried on, clearly unconcerned with what the old men in the Alps would think of such an angry-looking letter.

Watching her, Vidal smiled in joy. He relished the moment just as much as the silence that blanketed them shortly after. Those Elders were always so critical. They had been long before he decided to run off to the Veld.

She isn't good for me? Vidal thought, recalling their petty, inexcusable words from long ago. His eyes softened when Monet crossed out another phrase on her already ruined page. *Who are they to decide that? Imbeciles.*

He would have her no other way.

Vidal fell back into his seat. He smiled wide at the confused glance Monet shot him. Vidal... supposed he could let the kids rest. For now. There was no rush. Monet was with him and the rest of the Veld was quiet.

That was all that mattered.

***

The moment the soggy rag touched her skin, Sylvie shrieked like a wild animal being led to slaughter. The Healer that held the offending piece of cloth followed with her own startled shout, before falling backwards and spilling a pale of ice-cold water all over her robes.

From his spot beside her bed, Jack choked back a laugh of open amusement. But when Sylvie's caretaker parted her hair to reveal eyes filled with annoyance and promises of pain, his laughter escaped. Far louder than he meant it to. The Healer's shoulders heaved twice, before she stood with as much dignity as her appearance allowed and threw the rag at her feet. She stalked away, her robes slapping about her with every infuriated step. Jack must've been pestering her for quite some time if she reacted that badly.

"I'm sorry," Sylvie called, before the door slammed shut, leaving her with a wet floor and Jack's unholy chortles. She glared daggers at him. "You could've warned me."

"You were half-asleep," he defended, faintly insulted. Jack sank deeper into his seat, entirely unconcerned with the situation. "How was I supposed to know you'd wake up flailing?"

"It was wet and cold. *Cold.* Why would she try to wash me with ice-cold water when I'm..." her mouth slammed shut in realization. She looked at Jack, who stared at his nails like they'd suddenly become a thousand times more interesting. "You chilled it, didn't you?"

Jack lifted his hands in innocence, but the pleased look on his face suggested otherwise. "These accusations."

"They're true," she huffed, "and stop smiling."

"I'll try," he said, unsuccessfully repressing the widest one to date. "No promises though."

Sylvie wiped the lingering moisture from her forehead, not wanting to deal with him and his boredom. Jack seemed to be in an amicable mood today. More than likely because of the message the Healer in charge of her had delivered the night prior. It was from Vidal. Why he chose to have someone relay his words, rather than coming to tell them himself, neither could say. But they weren't about to go out of their way to find the man. Sylvie could hardly stand without her knees shaking in protest, and though Jack tried to hide his exhaustion, she saw how he'd pause every now and again, fingers roving along his forearm, as if he could still feel the pain of the wound.

But at least they were finished with Cheryll's little errand; it only almost cost them their lives. Was it really worth it? Sylvie grimaced when she couldn't find an answer. Although Monet would be supporting Jack's father, it still didn't guarantee his success in the Summit. It would certainly help. No one could deny that. Not to mention move things along now that the only reluctant Arch Poten finally decided to attend.

Yet, Sylvie felt like they hardly accomplished anything. Retrieving Silas' journal and ridding the world of scum aside, they were just left with more questions. One of which was the contents of the journal in question. She could only hope that Vidal would return it to them, so they could read it.

Sylvie reflexively grabbed the Heartstone, feeling an odd sense of comfort with it in her grasp. *She* hadn't spoken to them properly since her aggressive stint in the Pit. Was *she* sulking? Was that even possible? Sylvie didn't care to find out.

She blinked when Jack snapped his fingers in front of her face. His own was schooled into an impassive mask. He gestured with his head toward the door.

"Someone's coming," he told her.

On cue, the door swung open and Vidal strode in. A little girl followed closely behind him, hiding behind his legs and peeking out at them through big, brown eyes. Vidal's hands settled fondly over the girl's head. He didn't bother to introduce her. Not yet.

"I ran into your Healer down the hall," Vidal said casually. His mouth tilted up into an amused smirk. "She was wet and cursing you both. What did you two do?"

Sylvie glared at Jack, who leaned back into his seat with a self-satisfied grin. Neither spoke, but Vidal got the gist of it.

"Forget I asked," Vidal went on.

"Gladly." Jack fanned his fingers dismissively. "Where have

you been? It's been well over twelve hours since I called you."

"With my dear wife of course! We had so much to discuss."

"Why do I get the feeling that it wasn't all that important?"

"Nonsense. Our discussions are always significant." Before Jack could argue further, Vidal directed his gaze to Sylvie. He searched her for any visible injuries, then smiled pleasantly when he found none. "How are you?"

"Grand," Jack piped up. "No, even better, she's flaming fantastic! Really, how do you think she's doing?"

"I'm not sure," Vidal said in the exact same tone. "That's why I asked. I didn't know you could feel her pain, too, Jack. Do you have any other magical modifications I don't know about?"

"Sore," Sylvie interrupted, not liking where their conversation was headed. "And tired."

"That's to be expected. You both wore out your circuits. An incredibly stupid thing to do." Vidal's smile grew slicker when Jack growled. Low and beastly. It rumbled from deep within his chest. Scary kid. He could see why so many of the Nebbin from before were afraid of attacking him head on, despite their numbers. "Really though, even children know the dangers of such a thing, yet here you two are, jumping head first into a field full of livid, snarling Nebbin. When you told me that there'd be no work left for me by the time I arrived, I didn't think you were serious. How could the two of you be so reckless?"

They looked down, silent. Neither seemed partial to being lectured. Then again, who was? Their mouths were sealed shut. No apologies to be found. But, Vidal noted, simultaneously annoyed and proud, they didn't try to make excuses either. Still, if they weren't going to defend themselves, then the least they could do was apologize.

He could almost *feel* their remorse tainting the air. There was something else mixed in as well. Something dark and angry that he couldn't quite place. Had they already gone over this with each other? It was likely. Well, he wasn't about to force an apology out of them. It's not like he deserved it, and so long as they knew that they were wrong, then that was enough for him. He wasn't their nanny, and he didn't want to be.

Vidal grabbed the journal he tucked away in his robes, unsurprised to see them both suddenly come to attention. Jack pointed at it, but just as Vidal thought he'd speak, he slumped forward instead. His elbows rested on Sylvie's bed, red eyes piercing him like freshly sharpened blades. Vidal suppressed the pleased hum that threatened to erupt from his throat at the sight of it. He saw Leonas in that glare.

"I don't believe you told me the whole story," Vidal said. "But that's alright. I didn't lay down all of my cards either. Shall we do that now? Come on. Ask, before I change my mind."

Their minds worked fast. He could practically see the cogs in their heads turning, placing his words with the ones they kept filed in the back of their heads.

Vidal tried his best not to stare at the glowing stone around Sylvie's neck. It hung in the open for all to see. He wondered how they could ignore it so well. When just looking at its gleam made him want to wrap it in his fingers, pick it apart, and unravel all of its mysteries. Perhaps it was the northerner in him. Always trying to claw its way to the surface. The stone made him miss his time in the Research Division of the Circle.

Eventually, Sylvie spoke, "We met someone in the Pit. A Nebbin. He seemed to know you."

"Nathaniel Timpis," Vidal revealed, his smile fading. "He was a slave I freed long ago. Nathaniel stood by my side for years, but when my daughter, Elise, was born he… changed. Let's just say he found out a few things he shouldn't have and he requested some time off to clear his head. I let him of course. Though it wasn't as if he needed my permission in the first place. Weeks passed, and Nathaniel never returned. You have no idea how shocked I was to learn that he helped organize a group of slavers! I've been trying to get rid of him ever since. But those witless Potens never wanted to provide me the needed men. I have to thank you two for that. Those dogs couldn't let the Tower's Arch

Poten and the heir of the Dace family die handling their affairs or else they'd have a lot of important figures to answer to."

"Wait, wait, wait! Slow down. Your *daughter*?" Sylvie asked, trying to digest his words. She peeked at the little girl hiding behind his legs, but Elise only pressed herself further into Vidal's robes. She was a small thing. Easily dwarfed. "Is that her?"

Vidal nodded, as Elise screamed, "Crazy lady!"

Sylvie stared, mouth agape.

A profound silence settled around the room, broken only by Jack's sudden snickers. Which quickly turned into full-blown laughter when Elise poked her little head out and puffed her cheeks at her.

"I don't understand," Sylvie said, keeping her voice level. "How can she be your daughter when she's—"

"—Nebbin," Jack finished, serious. His eyes narrowed into slits. "She wasn't born in the Alps, was she? All the children of Elementalists are meticulously accounted for. Their mothers are watched until their term, so the newborn can have an Orive put into their heads immediately after birth."

"Spot on!" Vidal exclaimed, pushing his daughter in front of him. She resisted with all she could, but it was for naught. Vidal was bigger and stronger. Once Elise stood there, exposed to their scrutiny, she folded in on herself. Her eyes kept lifting to meet Jack's. Vidal had to raise an eyebrow at that. His fatherly instincts kicked in as soon as he saw her flustered state. But he'd have to wait to bring *that* up. For now, his free hand settled over her tiny shoulder in assurance.

"You realize that the Council could have you hanged for hiding her," Jack said.

"I'd like to see them try," Vidal said confidently. "But who would've thought that no crystal meant no power? Frankly, I always believed Elementalists were a special case. The only type of practitioner that could have two magic circuits in their heads. I see now that that was a fool's notion. An idea ingrained into me as a child and reinforced through decades of false lessons. I even ripped out the crystal from another Elementalist's head just to make sure."

They winced at the confession, but Vidal ignored them.

"And just like that," Vidal splayed his fingers wide, "*gone*. No one can have two circuits. The strain it puts on the body would kill them in a matter of days. So, Elementalists are all essentially Nebbin. I can't believe those pompous windbags in the Alps still think themselves superior, despite knowing this."

"You sound like Jack," Sylvie muttered, flabbergasted. Said man sent her a heated glare. She met it with her own.

Unbeknownst to them, Vidal's confidence faltered. He'd expected them to shout in disbelief, to stare at him with eyes wider than the saucers he used for his tea. He'd even prepared himself for a panic attack. But this... was decidedly less amusing.

After their short staring contest, desolate frowns adorned both of their faces. The kind he was well acquainted with. He'd seen it many times in the mirror when he heard something that only further confirmed the distasteful riddles in his head.

"I see you two aren't surprised," Vidal continued, halting after every other word in careful deliberation. "So, can I assume you already know that Orive crystals give Elementalists their powers? Did you read it in the journal? Did Nathaniel tell you? Or... did your parents happen to say something? The last one is a crime punishable by death, you know?"

"None of those," Sylvie said.

"Then how?" Vidal asked. His eyes drifted to Jack, then to the stone. "I noticed that you were only using ice."

Jack stiffened. "What of it?"

"Did *she* take away your powers?"

"How do you know?"

"Because of the Orive," Vidal said vaguely.

"That sick Nebbin made an Orive crystal!" Jack abruptly shouted. His voice was booming enough to send Elise into hysterics. The poor girl squeaked back in fright. But Jack was too lost in his own recollections to notice. "A large one. How did he—I thought those were only made by the Healers in the west. Aren't they imbued with magic? Isn't that how Peose," he paused, "how *we* get out powers?"

"*She* didn't tell you?"

"What?" they asked in unison, snapping their heads up in one cracking motion.

Vidal's smile reappeared. Now, that was the reaction he sought. "And here I thought the three of you were friends. Don't tell me she's ignoring you, too."

"Get on with it," Jack snapped.

"I browsed this." Vidal waved the journal around, indifferent to its flapping pages. "It has the formula for the Orive crystals in it. The very same handed down to select practitioners in the Grove by the Zenith Council. I doubt you'd like it."

Vidal threw the journal at them. The screams of every scholar in Ferus Terria rang in his ears. Or was that just Sylvie and Jack? Their yelps bounced along the walls. Both of them scrambled to grab the journal, uncaring for their sore bodies. As if landing on the fluffy bed would damage it in some way.

Sylvie reached it first. Her fingers tightly wound over the spine. Vidal openly laughed when they both sighed in relief.

"Don't laugh," Jack said, glaring. "We almost died for this."

Vidal shrugged him off with all the ease of someone who'd been doing it his entire life. Absently, he noticed Elise slip past him. Her tiny arms struggled to open the thick, wooden door. As soon as she was able to, she left without another look back. Presumably to find her mother. Vidal resisted the urge to wince when the door banged shut behind her. Focusing on them again, he waved his hands, feigning disinterest.

"I realized many things after reading that," Vidal told them. "Most, the kind that could plunge Ferus Terria into chaos. But so long as that stone remains in your keeping, then you two might be the only ones actually able to do anything about it. Tell me though, do you truly believe the past worth rehashing?"

"We wouldn't be here if we didn't," Sylvie said, resolute.

"It's good to know you're willing to endure more. You'll likely want to carry on Silas' dream after you read that journal. A word of advice though: don't take on the dreams of too many dead men or you'll be drowning in their burdens until the day you die." Vidal paused to scrutinize their expressions. "Then again, just looking at the two of you now, I can already tell that neither of your futures will carry that much peace."

"Like I want peace without freedom," Jack said.

"I like you," Vidal said bluntly. He pointed at Jack's chest, then nodded his head twice in vigorous approval. "You remind me of Leonas, but a dash more sympathetic. It's new enough for me to appreciate. Come find me when all of this is said and done. I'll make you my primary apprentice."

Jack's eyes widened. "What—"

"Don't tell me you'll actually disagree?"

"Of course not!" Jack sputtered. "But have you ever even had a primary apprentice... or even a regular one?"

"Do you think it's easy to find a non-deserter that openly despises the laws of the Institute?" Vidal gave him a once over. "Well, now that I think about it, I might have to rescind the offer should your powers not return by the time this adventure is through. I've never been fond of ice. I won't be of much us—no, I believe it's you who won't be of much use to me. That sounds right. Let's go with that instead."

Jack looked ready to snap again. Sylvie intervened before he could. "What will you do? Now that you've read Silas' journal."

"I'll go with Monet to the Alps when the time comes," Vidal said. "That's where I can make the most difference. My voice still has sway there, especially amongst the leaders of the Circle. And don't worry, so long as you bite your tongue off and choose death before ever breathing a word about my daughter, your secret, as well as the ones in that journal, are safe with me. I'm very good at keeping secrets. My pain tolerance has been tried and tested on numerous occasions. Leonas will vouch for me."

Contrary to his lighthearted tone, Vidal was serious. Sylvie didn't doubt that. His trust was well-earned, and betraying it wouldn't do them any favors.

"What will you do in the meantime?" she asked.

"For now, I have other things to occupy my time with. While the two of you have been resting in this room, Ferus Terria has continued to stir. Now that the Fetters in Aston are mostly gone, the smaller slave bands they allied with have slipped into hiding, while those that once made themselves scarce are taking advantage of their disappearance. Simply put, all of the Plains is in a panic because of us. Doesn't that just make you feel *tingly*?"

"No," Jack said. He was good at making messes, not cleaning them up. "Why are you telling us this? Don't tell me you expect us to do something about it?"

"Absolutely not!" Vidal threw his hands in the air, losing the last of whatever solemnity he had left and donning the air of an excited, overgrown child. "But don't you see? I get to hunt them to my heart's content. I resisted making a move because I wanted to get into their good graces first, so I could find Nathaniel and deal with him on my own. But I see now why they were always so hesitant about making deals with me. Perhaps sending his minions to my auctions was his way of keeping an eye on my actions? Well, no matter."

Vidal pointed outside, straight at the blinding sun.

"I assume you want to leave this place?" he went on. "You're both free to do so, though I suggest waiting for the soreness to subside first. If you don't want to wait that long, then settle for at least a few more days, so I can prepare a few poultices and maybe even my special salve. The Veld's in a tizzy now because of all the extra men. Supplies also need to be properly accounted for."

"What about our agreement?" Jack asked.

"Rest assured, it will be honored. We're going to send all of those foreign practitioners back to the Tower as soon as possible. Monet has already sent Cheryll a message, telling her to prepare for their arrival." Vidal paused just long enough to pin them with another one of his unnerving stares. "I'm going to take a wild guess and say that you'll both want to head to the Grove right after reading that journal. So, I'll tell you now that I'll inform my contacts in Curran. They'll be able to house, and more importantly, keep you two away from the Alps' watchful gaze. Think of it as advanced thanks."

"Advanced... thanks?" Jack repeated, not liking the sound of that. Gratitude from a man as capable as Vidal was never good. His heart stopped in anticipation for his next words.

"I expect you to tell me everything once you make it to the Alps." Vidal grinned. They both frowned at him, and he wondered if they did it on purpose. Probably not. Someone should really tell them that they made the same expressions so often — perhaps he might. Before they left. Just to see the looks on their faces. That sounded splendid.

With an exaggerated wave, Vidal turned to leave them to their reading. But just before he left, he spared them a final glance. The conspiratorial flash of his teeth gave away everything and nothing. "Allow me to offer one last piece of advice," he said, "make peace with whatever sleeps in that stone. Learn to play nice and consider *her* wants."

"What?" they asked, simultaneously stupefied.

"In other words, and I don't know why I even need to clarify this, but treat *her* like a lady. There are some women in this world that, when the time comes, you don't want to be on the wrong side of."

"We should just grit our teeth and let her keep leading us to wherever *she* pleases then?" Jack asked.

"Of course not. Just consider that maybe *she's* just as lost as either of you."

They raised their eyebrows at that.

"When you're alone that long, sometimes you forget how to make your way back home," Vidal said with both the patience of an elder and the confidence of a child. "So, be kind."

With that, he left.

The weight of Silas' journal rested heavily in their hands.

[The page below was torn from a separate journal, and was later addressed to Silas Drayr. His name was scrawled along the upper margin long after the entry was penned. Judging from the lack of gaps between the strokes, more expensive ink was used, though it faded just as prominently over the years.]

TO SILAS DRAYR:

I can hear her sometimes.

She lingers when I'm in trouble, blends into the scenery when I'm not. Her presence is always there, and I've felt it more often recently than I ever have before. But now that my world is changing, I finally understand why.

Ferus Terria has erupted in flames, and I'm the cause. I couldn't have done it without her. It helps that she likes to make herself useful, always asking me about my wants. I think that's how she verifies her own existence. It gives her purpose. There was a time when I physically felt monotony, and I didn't like it either. So, I can understand her in that regard, if nowhere else.

She's made herself known to Silas. My first friend and most trusted confidante. I can't even begin to fathom why. Comprehending her is beyond me. It's just one of many contrasts to the popular belief that I am capable of everything. I'm not. She knows it. Silas, too. Perhaps that's why she likes him.

Surprisingly, she isn't fond of Maurice—he'll betray me, she keeps warning—though I personally think he's a good man. Upright, noble, a true blue-blood like Pernelia. He'll be a good addition to the new council once the world settles and there are no more battles to be won. I don't know how to run the state, but I know how certain parts of it should be. Maurice… he knows more about these things. He has big ideas. Good ones. Others, not so much. But Pernelia has always been able to make him see reason. She is, perhaps, the only thing I've ever thanked the Creator for.

I miss her.

But my personal god has kept me quite occupied recently. Her whispers have become more frequent as of late. Her favorite topic is the unending darkness that once surrounded her.

'It's a cold and cruel place,' she says. 'Like used coal after the feast.'

No one cares about anything there. She told me about the places where she thrived—the flatness, the nothingness, the unending longing for light. My desperation that day interested her, wrecked the stillness around her world, and enraptured her like a siren's song.

So, she found me.

Her light. Physical and within reach. She hasn't touched anything in years—and I wonder where she's from. Where she's truly from. One day, I hope to find out. I've guessed, and the best one by far is that she's the embodiment of magic itself. My thoughts have lingered, strayed, and returned to the subject on numerous occasions, though I can't imagine actually conducting real, scientific research. I've only just learned to write. Creating theories seems too daunting a task for me to undertake. But even I know that that's just an excuse. I'm just afraid of finding something concrete. Tangible explanations would anchor her to something other than the unknown.

The last thing I want to do is limit her existence.

She's here now and that's what matters. For how long, I don't know. Perhaps until this body of mine rots. Though I'm not sure if she'll just find someone else. Another one she can trust and remain in the quiet company of. She isn't fond of the dark, I know that much.

I also know that she offered me power when I didn't have it. Came and brought me life when I was on the edge of losing the pitiful one I called my own. She yearns to change her world as much as I do. A loving being that will be the death of me. These are all facts. Yet, they're also truths that will be buried in lies, in a false history that I may or may not witness. Because there is one final truth that I've known since her introduction. The only way to ensure I keep her company until eternity ends—I must offer her my soul.

Because that's how much a wish costs in Ferus Terria.

Thelarius Merve
221 Iron Age 99

27

Tiv basked in the warmth of the sun.

He'd been doing it for days. Ever since he stepped out of that cursed mansion to find dozens of Nebbin and injured practitioners all dressed in the same rags as him. They were sprawled across the courtyard, reveling in the early morning's frigid air. They didn't care about the angry flames erupting within the castle as the western practitioners burned entire corridors filled with animal skins and priceless murals—and truthfully, neither did Tiv.

During that first day, he found Lyss with one foot on that snake-like criminal's back, waiting for him to come out and confirm the man's face. They shot a bolt through his head as soon as he did. Tiv felt a sick sort of satisfaction from that. As if he'd finally done something right after everything that happened to Roval. Just imagining what they must've put him through made Tiv's stomach lurch.

Some nights, he'd whisper apologies before he fell asleep. He was sure a few of the other practitioners heard him, but none of them made any smart remarks about his behavior. He was grateful for that. Their kindness, however, didn't keep him from waking up every time he heard the pitter patter of rain or the pealing bells that signaled midnight. More than once, he found himself shooting up from his cot, drenched in sweat and screaming at the sight of all the foliage around him.

The sight of the outside world still made his eyes sting.

Tiv didn't want to be anywhere near this mansion. But Philip told him that they were waiting for two practitioners they sent to rendezvous with a courier from the west, so they could figure out what to do with all of the new practitioners they rescued. Tiv couldn't argue with that. But he still wasn't happy about it, and he used every chance he got to fly through the skies. The feel of the wind beneath his wings was as familiar as the shape of his own name. Familiarity, however, didn't stop him from almost passing out. Twice. Philip berated him thoroughly for that.

Dalis still hadn't asked about his sister. Not that Tiv knew where Sylvie was or if she even managed to escape. But Tiv had a feeling Dalis didn't want to hear his answer, afraid he'd say something he wasn't yet ready for. That was perfectly fine with him. Tiv didn't want to have to tell him that they saved him for nothing; that the last thing he'd heard about Sylvie was that she was in the deepest part of the Tower when it fell; that she was with his partner and they were both probably...

On the third night of camping outside of the mansion, Tiv used the final hours of darkness to find the origin of those bells. He didn't have to search for long. They tolled long enough for him to find it on his first try.

The sound came from a dirty white tower near the back of the estate. The path was obscured by a broken wagon. Inside, was a creaky wooden chair and a shattered lantern. There was a forgotten helmet that sat conspicuously before a winding staircase which led all the way to the top. The copious amounts of dust told him that the bells rang on their own, controlled by a mechanism he didn't know how to operate. It sat just to the right of them. Innocent and unfeeling.

Tiv crushed it with a barrage of badly aimed punches.

Creator, he hated those bells.

When he came back down with his bandages stained red with blood, Dalis took one look at him and slapped him over the head with his tome. He was nothing like Sylvie. The bastard even left him to bleed for a good twenty minutes before healing him. Needless to say, Tiv never tried anything that foolish again.

By the fourth day, most of the prisoners were sent on their way. They were each given a small satchel with food and water. Those too injured to leave were meticulously tended to by the Healers that Dalis had with him. There weren't many. But with time, they were able to mend everyone's wounds. Even that tongue-less Elementalist was healed. Sometimes he'd catch her staring at her glowing hands in wonder, as if she couldn't believe her magic was real.

Tiv hesitated approaching her, caught between wanting to ask about Roval and wondering if she'd only turn her head away because his words were a reminder of her own inability to speak. But during their fifth day stranded there, Tiv found the courage to walk up to her. Albeit, in the form of a black dog, but who could blame him? She had the most menacing glare he'd ever seen... and he grew up with Jacques Dace.

From the way her eyes widened, the Elementalist recognized him. Tiv wasn't exactly sure how she managed that because he was positive that his appearance didn't give anything away. He'd mimicked the form perfectly. Tiv didn't bother asking though, opting instead to silently keep her company until the sound of rattling gates made every capable practitioner in the area turn their heads in apprehension. Absently, he noticed her hands ignite. There was nothing of quiescence in her flames. They burned all the way up to her elbows. But she forced them back under her skin when Dalis walked up to the newcomers with open arms and a smile.

"It's about time," Dalis said loudly. "What kept you?"

Before the two practitioners could even speak, Dalis nicked the scroll from their hands. He glanced at the wax seal on it and frowned, before ripping it open. The parchment flapped audibly in the breeze.

Tiv found himself transforming back to his normal self and walking up to their little group to sneak a peek. But by the time he got there, Dalis was already rolling the scroll back up and tossing it at Philip across the yard. Dalis was clearly concerned by its contents because he began pacing around the two panting men like a caged tiger.

"What's wrong?" Tiv asked.

Dalis blinked, as if only now seeing him. Tiv was about to ask again when Philip came up to them. He threw the scroll right at Dalis' head.

"Philip, you damn—"

"The Council has approved the dissolution of the Grove's Potentate Union," Philip interrupted. He ignored his huffing partner in favor of meeting Tiv's gaze.

"Oh... wait, what?" Tiv asked dumbly. He held up a hand to stall him, then breathed in as much air as his lungs could hold, but the news still refused to sink. "I didn't even know the Grove had problems with their Potens. What do they want to do? Create an Assembly like the Tower?"

"I suppose you could say that. Perhaps that's what they'll publicly announce, too. But the Grove doesn't want a body of Masters, they want the leaders of the colleges to take control. It's about time, too. The colleges have worked as sovereign units within the Grove for the last two ages, and their leaders have amassed a lot of support over the years. The representatives even have the right to prevent their practitioners from attending classes or accepting offers of apprenticeship."

"I didn't realize they had so much power," Tiv said, amazed.

"It's unofficial. The only thing they can't do is send their practitioners out for private jobs, which leaves all of the formal control to the Potentate Union. It's a lot of bureaucratic nonsense and everyone knows it. The representatives have been pushing for the Union's abolition for years. While the Alps might've finally yielded, they did so under the condition that the Grove maintains its current order until the end of the Summit."

"What will happen until then?"

"The Grove will likely begin preparing for a change in leadership. Delegating tasks, seeing who's in charge of what. Equally dividing responsibilities is more difficult than it sounds.

I'm sure Arch Poten Cole will remain on the final assembly as its official representative for meetings in the north, much like the Tower's Assembly. But more than that, I don't know."

"Isn't that a good thing?" Tiv pointed at Dalis. The Healer was extremely upset, and it showed. "What's wrong with him?"

"It's complicated." Philip chose his next words carefully. "Some of the colleges know things that the others don't."

"What kind of things?"

"The sort that should never be revealed. If they are, then certain... work might be refused. The few that do know about it are already refus—" Philip cut himself off with a vigorous shake of his head. "Look, this declaration basically means that we have to return if we don't want to be officially labelled deserters. Dalis and I, most of us here actually, are part of the same college. The Red Scripts. We all esca—left without permission."

"All of you just left?" Tiv gaped. "And they let you?"

"Oh, they tried to stop us. Much good it did them. But now that something this big has passed, we're all needed back in the Grove. Especially me." Philip pointed at himself. "I'm the primary apprentice of the Red Scripts' representative."

"Then—"

Tiv was cut off by Dalis.

The Healer grabbed him by the shoulders with a grip strong enough to shatter bone. Tiv didn't flinch, but he might as well have. He stood frozen under Dalis' wild, blue gaze. There was a question in his eyes, skipping along the tip of his tongue. Dalis bit his lips, trying to give it voice but even after waiting an entire minute, it still refused to come. Though, when it came down to it, his hesitation hardly even mattered because Tiv already knew what he wanted to ask.

"I don't know where Sylvie is," Tiv watched him stiffen, "but she was in the Assembly's Tower when it exploded. On one of the deeper floors."

"How do you know that?" Dalis asked. Quiet and hoarse.

"Because she," he swallowed, "she was with my partner."

Dalis' grip loosened.

For a moment, he looked as if he was going to crumble to the ground and shed the gathered tears in his eyes. Ready to lose his mind and scream at the cruel, cruel world. He breathed instead. Deep and gathering. Tiv saw a cloud of numbness take ahold of him, before he turned his back on them.

A mute war waged within him. Each battle fought by his mind's denial and his acceptance of the inevitable. The latter was winning now. Philip clasped his shoulder in reassurance. Dalis didn't ease, but he did find the courage to murmur a disgruntled, "*I know,*" to his friend. His voice was filled with both emptiness and resolve. Tiv didn't think that was possible. But it was. Oh, it was. And it made him shiver in admiration.

Dalis collected himself. Another deep breath and he was already turning to address the practitioners all staring at them.

"My sister may well be dead," Dalis said just loud enough for them to hear. He didn't stutter; he was quite proud of that. "But that doesn't change the fact that I came with the intention of helping each and every one of you. It's only right that I suffer the consequences of those that want to continue. I wish we all could, but the Grove needs us back, and the crime for not returning is being labelled a deserter. That affects us all. Philip and I won't make this decision on our own. You should all decide for yourselves whether or not you'll return to the Grove or come along with me to continue searching for your family and friends."

Dalis shot Philip a pleading look. Philip quickly stepped up and lifted his hand, taking over for him.

"I want to find my cousin," Philip began, "but it looks like I have to return. I can't let the Red Scripts fall behind the other colleges because of my own selfishness. All those in favor of returning to the Grove with me, raise your hands."

They collectively glanced at each other, mumbling amongst themselves and deciding what to do. Their indecision didn't last long, however. They were silenced by Lyss, who half-heartedly raised his hand. He looked bored. Sleepy, almost, as he stared impassively at all of those that turned to him.

"I don't know about the rest of you knobs," Lyss began, before pointing straight at Dalis, "but I'm not going to force him to desert because I decided to skip my duties. I don't fancy the thought of not knowing where my family is either. But after I find them where would I return to?"

A profound silenced washed over them. Slowly, one by one, they all raised their hands.

"Looks like we're all going back then." Philip heaved a sigh of relief as he leaned on Dalis' shoulder. "That's great. I don't think I'd be able to handle having to hunt you down and kill you after all this."

"As if you have what it takes," Dalis said, shoving him aside.

"That hurts," Philip said, flipping Dalis off when he walked somberly away. He watched him go for a moment, before raising his hands and splaying his fingers out in a wide, boom motion. "Now that that's out of the way. Where are the fire Conjurers?"

Tiv jumped in excitement. Because at long last, they'd be leaving. He didn't care where they'd be going. He didn't even know if he'd stick with them all the way back to the Grove. Tiv just wanted to get away from this place.

As the Conjurers gathered around Philip, Tiv watched in barely restrained glee. Behind him, the sun floated high into the sky, giving his sickly pallor life. He'd dreamed of this moment for the past four nights. Fantasized about it for even more.

Today, they'd finally burn this awful mansion down.

He was going to relish every second of it.

***

"Disappeared? What do you mean they disappeared?"

Khale and Pom stumbled back at Drage's sudden roar, while the others in the bar turned to stare curiously at them.

Drage stood above his toppled seat, gazing intensely at the young messenger that quivered in his boots. Khale felt bad for the kid. He looked about ready to piss himself. His hands were shaking so bad that when he tucked them under his armpits, the chains on his leathers started rattling.

Celina was by Drage's side in an instant. She nudged the man in the stomach with a strong elbow until he backed off.

"That's what I heard in Tor," the boy said, shrinking away. From his accent, Khale knew immediately that he was Astonian. "A big army a' practitioners from the Veld went an' got rid a' the Nebbin campin' out at the Pit. An' I saw a big fire down across the marshes on my way back, so I reckon their army might've gone an' snagged the Disciples, too."

"Two big players..." Drage trailed off, replaying the boy's words in his head. He didn't think the Veld had that many men at their disposal. Clearly, he was wrong. "What happened to their leaders?"

"Dead most likely," Celina cut in.

Drage turned to her. "That's two heads of the Fetters gone from the table. Just like that! A few days and poof! Is the Veld out to eliminate them? I didn't think—"

"Is this really a problem?"

"No!" Drage stepped back when he realized he'd shouted. He ran his fingers through his hair, trying to gather his wits. "I just never expected them to act so quickly. I didn't even know there were still that many practitioners left in the Veld. They'll be going after smaller groups now. We aren't slavers, but I don't... I don't know how far they'll go to purge us from the Plains."

"I'll stop you right there, pigeon," Khale said, patting Drage on the shoulder.

"Did you just call me a pigeon?"

"Don't sweat the little things," Khale dismissed. "Fact is—"

"You did call me a pigeon, you little shit."

"Fact is," Khale repeated, shooting him an annoyed glance, "the Institute's never had problems with mercenaries. *Never.* If they did, then I sure as sin wouldn't've joined yer little band, yea? I'm a real stickler fer the rules or ain't that obvious?"

"Here, here," Pom chimed.

"Wonder what made 'em move so suddenly though." Khale turned to the boy, who looked much more comfortable now that Drage had eased back into his usual slouch. "You don't happen ta know, do you?"

The boy straightened again at his sudden attention. "All I heard was that some beefy, fifteen-foot, four-armed Elementalist was leadin' 'em."

"What?" Khale sputtered. "Yer jokin'."

"I wish."

"Pom." Khale turned, enunciating every syllable. "We *have* ta see that."

"And what? Bring these two along for the ride?" Pom asked. "I don't think so."

"Why not? Fer all we know Tiv might be there, an' if they're so worried 'bout what the Veld's up to, then they can hash their troubles out with that monster Elementalist." Khale snickered, before pinning Drage and Celina with an expectant gaze. "What do you say? It won't be that bad, I swear. An' if those skinks try anythin' I'll be sure ta fly you two right out. I'm reliable like that."

"You're crazy," Drage dismissed. "I'd rather wait here."

"With cups of hosed down piss?" Khale asked, skeptical. He ignored the bartender's sudden glare. "C'mon! You said you'd help us find Tiv, yea?"

"About that, why are you looking for him anyway? Is he really that special?"

"Nah, he's a cracked wishbone." Khale shrugged. "Good friend though. We don't have too many of those left. Never did really. There was this unspoken hierarchy in the Tower that most of us followed. I'm not all that proud of it now, but back then I was. Tiv an' his partner, Jack, were the only ones in our... class that we really got on with. Dented pair a' walnuts, them."

"They're gone now," Pom added, forlorn. "I don't know if Jack managed to escape, but he's always been a survivor. Tiv though. Him, we actually managed to leave the Tower with. He was captured right under our noses."

"Dragged off ta who knows where. I'll be honest, I actually want ta head ta the Veld since the kid says they got rid of slavers. A lot of 'em, too. I don't wanna think 'bout Tiv bein' captured by animals like that, but it's possible, yea? If we want ta find him, then the Veld's the place ta start lookin'. I just thought you two'd like ta meet him is all."

"And if the practitioners in the Veld are anything like the ones from the Tower, then they could stand to meet some good Nebbin."

"Especially ones that can knock 'em down a few pegs, yea?" Stiff silence followed their words.

Drage and Celina glanced at each other. Their lips tipped down into uncomfortable frowns. Drage rubbed the back of his neck in contemplation. He didn't think for long because in the next moment, he threw back his head and downed the rest of his drink. Celina did the same.

They banged their cups on the table, shattering the glass.

The bartender wasn't glaring anymore. He was downright furious, breathing in and out through his flared nostrils. Khale's feet turned toward the door, prepared to run, as the bartender grabbed an empty bottle from behind the counter. He was going to break it over their heads. Khale just knew it.

"You two really know how to make a guy feel terrible, you know that?" Drage said, drawing Khale's attention away from the bartender.

He slammed a wad of cash on the counter, and Khale let out a relieved breath when the bartender dropped the bottle. The fat man nodded obligingly, the wrinkles on his forehead easing up a bit in approval. Though he still kept the bottle close. Disturbingly close. Crazy old man.

"Oh, just admit it," Celina said, as she rested her weight on his side. "You want to go."

Drage failed to hide his smirk. "I do. But if they start pointing those glowing fingers in my direction, I'm leaving."

"You'd probably like it."

"I knew it!" Khale yelled, horrified. "I *knew* you were starin' at me whenever I used my powers. I could feel it. All slimy an' seductive an' interested. Gah!"

"Don't flatter yourself, you damn Astonian."

They all turned when Pom lit one hand up. He waved it wildly back and forth. None of them cared about the way the others in the bar gawked or how the bartender reached for the empty bottle again.

"Oh," Pom's mouth formed the letter. He blinked twice in amazement. "You really did look."

"For the love of…" Drage trailed off.

He nicked the empty bottle from the stunned bartender's hands and turned to his three grinning companions. They held their hands up in surrender. But he wasn't going to let them off so easily.

She was right. As always. I should've known.

And now I'm left with the options of maintaining what I can of her and stopping Maurice. It honestly isn't much of a choice.

I would give my life to see her continue living, even if it was back in that darkness she so hates. Perhaps that's why I'm doing this. Giving up everything I've known and worked for. But it's alright. I hold no regrets. No ill will. I know I'm not suited for this job anyway. A former slave leading a nation? Laughable.

Pernelia and Silas will handle things in my stead, and if not, their children will. Maurice must be stopped. His methods are merciless and entirely too unforgiving for a being that did nothing but aid in the abolishment of slavery. His way of thinking is traditional, and really, I should've seen this coming.

Stupid. Stupid. Stupid.

~~Is he trying to find a way to make himself an Elementalist or have his purist ideals finally shattered all common sense?~~

Maurice believes her to be a worthy sacrifice for his cause. He wants more Elementalists. But why? Is it to make the country stronger? Only time and cooperation will do so. Is it so he can finally rid the world of Nebbin and give everyone the power of magic? An earnest goal, but this kind of power shouldn't be in the hands of so many. It will disrupt the current order of practitioners within the Institute and breed a class of elites. The power of Elementalists will only divide the world. Again.

But Maurice has already begun. The crystals have already been embedded into the new generation. How many have died because of it, I wonder? No, I don't even want to know the answer.

For all that I've come to know so far, it appears as though I haven't learned much at all. My speculations are becoming more and more like those of a madman. I cannot afford to lose what little is left of my reason.

I must finish this, before I do.

[The letters below were penned on separate pages, though they've all been wrapped together with the same twine. They bear yellow and brown-toned spots where droplets of water ruined the parchment. The frantic penmanship suggests tears.]

PERNELIA:

I'm sorry.

I don't know what I can do to make sure you're aware of my feelings. Is it enough to say 'I love you?' I want you to know... I need you to know because I'll be going ahead. I've let you down many times, and I pray that this is the last. I've never liked upsetting you, despite my long record of doing so.

Live well and find happiness where you can. Find someone that can bring you peace because I won't be around to do so. Just know that there's nothing I find more peaceful than being with you. Our days together and the love we shared are my everything.

Thank you.

That's not enough. Not nearly.

SILAS:

My dearest friend, you've given me stories to tell and allowed me the privilege of standing by your side, despite my history. But the time has come for me to disappear. Don't bother searching for me, tell no one of where I've gone, and try not to divide the lands any more than they already have been. Please. I've asked so many things of you over the years, and I know that they've all been burdensome, but I promise that this will be the last.

Because the time has come for me to go. This is something I must do. Rest assured, however, that I will endure. I will live to see more sunrises and sunsets. Because, when it comes down to it, that's all I've ever really wanted. At least this time I'll have a reason other than my own selfish desires to keep on doing so.

Today, I choose, as my rights allow, to fulfill my end of our sacred deal. There was a time I thought I'd die a quiet disappointment to myself and even to the Mentalists that bought me. I believed I would never be able to choose anything of my own volition. But that ended a long time ago, and I have her to thank for it.

You taught me many things, Silas. The best of them is to stand by those that need me the most.

She needs me.

Farewell.

Thelarius Merve
106.11.OA

28

Sylvie crouched before a basin of warm water.

She wiped down her arms, careful not to wet the bandages around her shoulders. Her body was still sore from the fight, but she was glad to be free from any angry bruises and open wounds. Now, if she could just go out and make a few topical salves to numb her pain, then she'd at least be able to get out of bed without wincing. But everyone, including Jack, seemed adamant about keeping her confined to her room.

"Rest," they insisted. Like she didn't know her own limits.

They claimed that the Institute was too busy for her to be walking around, but she just didn't understand the reasoning behind their words. The Veld was the second largest Institute out of the four, and the largest edifice in the entire Yovakine Plains. Surely, there were places free of people. Somewhere other than her room, where she wouldn't be in the way. But when Vidal came in and told her the exact same thing, she stopped asking. He'd mastered the art of terrifying smiles to the point where she dreaded the thought of even looking at his face.

As Sylvie dug through their dishearteningly flat packs for fresh clothes, she thought of what they'd read in Silas' journal. It was a lot of information to take in, yet all her mind could settle on was how *right* Vidal had been about them. He was able to predict where they'd want to go and what they'd want to do after reading Silas' words. Frightening, for someone that had only known them for a handful of days. Vidal knew how they ticked, and that unnerved her in ways she couldn't adequately express.

Sylvie wanted to go to the Grove. It was where Maurice ruled up until his death and where *Orivellea* were made. But the more selfish part of her wanted to go simply because that's where her brother stayed. Sylvie hadn't spoken to Dalis in months. They were out of contact long before the Tower fell, both too busy leading their own lives to sit down and pen a letter. She hadn't even considered sending him one after the incident, too afraid he'd tell their father about where she'd gone. Sylvie didn't want her father whisking her away. Because she knew, without a sliver of doubt, that that's exactly what he'd do once he found out where she was. No questions. No excuses. His word was law.

Many words could be used to describe Victor Sirx, but as far as she was concerned, the first on that list would always be—worrywart. Unyielding, was a close second. But this was different. Sylvie couldn't just bow her head in acquiescence and go to the Alps. Not yet. She and Jack still had so much to do.

Will it ever end? she wondered.

Truthfully, Sylvie didn't even know what they were doing anymore. They recuperated in the Veld, letting the hours press on like they had all of the time in the world to waste. Sylvie felt as if she was just fumbling along, writing down tasks given to her by other people, then striking each one off after completion.

Right now, they were playing in the palm of *her* hand, running around Ferus Terria to sort through the scraps of information that *she* threw at them.

Sylvie sighed.

There was no used dwelling on it now. Her knees were beginning to ache from crouching too long, and Jack would surely be against her trying to figure it all out on her own. He hated it when she *needlessly* mulled over things that involved them both, or so he always claimed. She had a feeling that he just had an intensely specific dislike for her worrying over him, rather than having an actual problem with being excluded from her personal deliberations regarding their situation.

She smiled at the realization. Typical Jack.

Sylvie sifted through the small pile of clothes in their packs. Her brow pinched in sudden exasperation as she picked out three random sets of robes. All of their threads were bare at the edges. She was certain one had a cowl at one point because there was a large tear all along its back. What was once an inner pocket had become a hole the length of her arm. It was torn all the way to the upper sleeve, and she found herself staring at it for longer than necessary. How in the world could Jack have done such a thing without her noticing?

She couldn't deny that she was slightly impressed by his ability to somehow ruin all of his robes and act as if they were perfectly fine. Nevertheless, she couldn't just let him keep doing this. They couldn't afford to waste money on new clothes each time they went to the market, neither could they keep grabbing improperly fitted ones from the drawers of whoever happened to be kind enough to offer them a few sets.

Sylvie looked up at the hook on the back of the door, where Jack's cloak hung. Exhausted, she took whatever linen shirts he had left and tossed it up onto the hook to join it, unable to muster any particular concern when two of them landed on the floor instead.

"Look," Sylvie began, stepping back into her room with his torn robes. She made sure to kill all traces of amusement in her eyes and put on her best grumpy face. "I don't know what you did to these, but they're beyond repair. Do you have something against clothes, Jack? Or is your magic just that volatile? It better have been your magic because if you tell me that you had a hissy fit and ran your knife through these, then we're going to have a problem. How did you manage to ruin these so flaming qui—"

Both her tongue and her steps grinded to a halt when she noticed Jack's silence. No smart remarks. Not even an irate sigh. More than enough to worry a girl.

Her words took a moment to settle inside of the room, before they were replaced by the boisterous laughter of two boys down the hall and an old woman shushing them. Further away, a group of men sparred. The clang of steel meeting steel echoed through the open window to caress her ears. A murder of crows—Amorphs, Sylvie suspected—cawed noisily in the unknowable distance. They were louder than usual in the silence.

And through it all, Jack just... slept.

The hour was at that peculiar time between too early for a nap and too late to still be in bed. But there he was, comfortably curled on his side on top of the velvet throw. One of his arms was outstretched, while the other was pillowed under his head.

Tranquil, save for the steady rise and fall of his chest.

She'd never seen him so still.

His breaths were quiet and even. He wasn't a noisy sleeper. Yet, in that moment, the soft sound of his exhales were loud enough for her to hear, despite the noise outside. It was strange how even while asleep, his presence was still so immense.

"You took my spot," she muttered, alternately resentful and resigned. Sylvie wasn't angry at him. Not really. It was a subdued sort of anger. The kind one felt when yielding to something they weren't entirely against in the first place. "If you were tired, you should've gone to your room. Or you could've said something. When did you stop voicing things?"

Jack didn't wake, only stretched his leg suddenly, pulled in a deeper breath, and then relaxed again.

His comfort was almost offensive.

If she threw his robes at him, would he wake up, livid and glaring? Would his magic burst forth from his body and cover bed and floor alike in webbed frost? Without a doubt. Was it worth it though? When she saw his head tilt comfortably to the side, she knew that it wasn't. Nothing was.

"Fine then," Sylvie conceded.

She dropped his ruined robes by the foot of the bed where they belonged. As quietly as she could, she closed the creaky windows and drew the threadbare curtains. They didn't hiss as she slid them into place. She was quite proud of that. But looking at them did make her realize that her room was in dire need of repairs. She'd have to bring it up to Arch Poten Verne when she got the chance. Perhaps the Veld could afford to do it now that they had more men at their disposal.

With her limbs still too tender and aching from movement, Sylvie all but fell into Jack's previously occupied seat. She let the silence take root around them, opting instead to observe his face. No tension. No lines. Just peace.

When he showed no signs of waking, her eyes roamed the rest of him. She found bandages peeking out at her from the opening of his too large robes. They were cut wide and pooled low. Fashioned more for a surly Amorph than a lean Elementalist. Sylvie reached out to fiddle with the edge, to see the extent of his injury—why hadn't someone healed it yet?—but her hand fell just as quickly.

Of course he was healed.

They wouldn't fix her, then leave him to suffer with his wounds. Even if he could be infuriatingly cocky when he was in pristine condition. The likelier conclusion was that he just didn't bother removing the bandages on account of how sore he was.

She frowned at the thought.

Sylvie curled a loose strand of his hair around her finger. Thick, dark, and in dire need of a trim. His hair was insultingly soft for someone that didn't give a damn. She knew he washed it with whatever he had on hand, which was often just water. Sylvie needed to ask his secret. Later. Before they left. After he awoke. Or some hour in between. There was no rush. Time passed deceptively slow here, and they were here to rest.

Sylvie paused when Jack stirred into wakefulness. Slow at first, then all at once. He blinked hazily up at her, not quite sure what was going on. But then his eyes sharpened into something more familiar. For a moment, she thought that he'd be upset. That he'd tell her off because leaning over people while they slept was creepy. Because he was Jack—a biting ice cube of a man that always, *always* found something to antagonize over. Emotionally useless in front of others when it came to anything but fury. But this was different. This was soft and tender and breakable.

He hummed. Spent and low.

"I took your spot," Jack murmured, knowing.

His voice was floppier than she'd ever heard, and he was very still. Sylvie barely saw the rise and fall of his chest. Jack's eyes were shadowed by exhaustion as he looked up at her. How hadn't she noticed before? She could blame it on his belligerent tone or the fact that they had so much on their minds after everything that happened. She could even blame it on the stone. But none of those reasons were true.

She lacked awareness. It was as simple as that.

"You did," Sylvie finally said. "It's okay though."

"Want to share?"

Her jaw slackened at the offer. But his eyes fell shut again, unconcerned for whether or not she accepted. He'd sleep either way. Sylvie frowned at his inattention. If they were ambushed right now, he'd die. Without a doubt.

Jack waited, patient only because of his comfort. There was a ghost of a smile on his lips that disarmed her in ways he would never know. The rhythmic tap of his fingers over his chest was the lone sign of his wakefulness. Sylvie observed it steadily lose life. It wasn't long before he barely lifted one.

"There's no room," Sylvie objected eventually. She rose from her seat regardless.

"There's plenty of room," Jack refuted.

She hummed in reluctant agreement. There was no use arguing with the truth. She didn't want to either.

Sylvie braced one hand beside him. Distantly, she thought that maybe the chair would be more comfortable. That Jack was probably delirious from—*something*. That he'd be properly angry at her tomorrow for even accepting the offer. He'd wake up, groggy and unsure, before shouting curses until her ears bled and they both fell off of the bed and groaned from the pain.

She also didn't give a damn.

If her strength wasn't flagging, Sylvie told herself, if his presence wasn't so warm or comforting or such a stark reminder of things past and yet to come—it was though. It was.

And though the beds in the Veld were made smaller than most, made more for function rather than comfort, against all odds, they fit. They arranged themselves precisely so that no hands or feet hung uncomfortably off the side and no sore spots were pressed too roughly against.

She could feel Jack breathe.

"See?" he said, pleased. The smugness in his tone was drowned by a torpid yawn.

Sylvie didn't bother opening her eyes. "I don't."

Jack's response was a curt sound between a purr and a groan. It rumbled from deep within his chest. He inhaled, and there was barely enough space for even the rise of his chest between them.

They had to leave soon; had to go off to the west, where undoubtedly more answers awaited. More problems, too. But none of that mattered now. The only thing that Sylvie cared about in that moment was Jack's voice, and how important it was that he never stopped speaking.

Folded in his arms, it was easy for her to see how someone could be so utterly enraptured by another. Sylvie knew that if the world diminished to only this, to his satisfied exhale, enveloping her in warmth and fire and an emotion still too fledgling to name, then she could be happy. Irrevocably so. It would be easy to leave mediocre things like responsibility and duty behind. To leave it to those more capable; to those more willing.

She resisted the urge to groan in comfort. No use stroking his ego. Sylvie was content to just lay there. The minutes pressed on, until only the vague flashes of candlelight behind her eyelids kept her awake. As she continued to drift between the realms of perception, she heard the indulgent sigh of her name. It was low enough to ignore, but heated enough to startle her into wakefulness. She blinked, alarmed, when Jack said something her ears failed to catch. He seemed to understand that she didn't hear him because he repeated it. But his voice was lost to air a second time.

"Syl," Jack called mulishly. He pinched her side until she cracked one eye open. "Are you listening to me?"

"No."

"Of course," he muttered, slighted. "I asked you if there was anything you wanted."

His words were startling enough to warrant both of her eyes open. If she was on the fence about it before, then now she was certain that something was wrong with him.

"Something I want?" Sylvie repeated.

"Because *she* hasn't thought to ask in a while. Considerate of me, don't you think?"

Why he'd even be curious about such a thing was a question for the ages. Sylvie considered telling him to take better care of his clothes, but decided against it. Merciless as he was, she had no doubt that he'd shove her right off of the bed. If he was feeling particularly vindictive, he might even freeze the ground just before she landed.

"Next time," she began, finally answering him, "I want to control my temper better."

"You sound like me." Jack laughed, rich and strong and vital. It was a good sound. The walls shook with it. "And no, that's not a bad thing."

"It's a terrible thing."

Jack sighed. She felt his breath fan over her forehead, but he didn't retort. Instead, his questing fingers pressed against her neck. They followed the chain resting there.

Is he looking for the stone? she wondered. *What for?*

Sylvie was curious, but not enough to break the spell of silence. So, she let him be. Her eyelids were drooping again anyway. Nothing could steal her from the pull of sleep, not even the icy pads of his fingers finding their prize and grasping tight enough to shatter any normal rock.

If the being inside stirred, Sylvie didn't notice.

All that mattered now were his digits threading through her hair, massaging her scalp. Jack whispered something, but the words were gone as soon as they left his lips.

Noise disappeared first, followed by scent and her already blurring vision. Colors bent into darkness, and darkness into something all-encompassing rather than the usual plaintive nothingness to be scared of and stared at. There were no tendrils or unknown paths behind her lids. Touch was the last to go. She felt the heaviness of her limbs fade into air. The sensation of his body's solid heat enveloping her washed away with the rest of the world, and the electricity she'd first felt when he invited her to join him eased into sleepy comfort.

There was still so much for them to do, and yet, Sylvie's final, conscious thought, before slipping into protected slumber filled her with warmth she didn't think possible.

Fifty-four days since they'd lost their home.

It felt like years. Like seconds stretched into eternity. But it was funny how the picture of home shifted into something else entirely in her mind. Because in that wonderful moment between worlds, where she was safe and treasured beyond reason, she could say with certainty that she'd finally found a new one.

It was time to stop counting.

The following pages have been creased and flattened so many times that the spine opens to them out of habit now. Noticeable flaps of varying sizes are folded haphazardly along the outer corners, and like skin knitted into a battle scar, some are so ancient that the sheets no longer return to their intended positions. Scribbled amidst entries are tiny, hapless scrawls of mundane worries. As if somewhere between recalling memories and reliving emotions, the writer might forget to sign the clinic's requisition for more herbs or to feed the birds before noon. From some of the later notes, it was a frequent occurrence, despite how boldly the reminders were underlined.

There are other entries as well. Many of them, in fact. Written in codes and dialects older than present knowledge. But none so important as the ones here, marked with slips of paper that bear the words: *'Read this'* in Vidal Verne's elegant script.

<u>*77 Iron Age 96*</u>

I met the strangest man today.

A practitioner that believed himself Nebbin all of his life. I didn't even think that was possible. Could someone really be so out of touch with reality? There's a first for everything, I suppose. And Thelarius is unlike any Conjurer I've seen. He's able to harness the power of all the elements. I saw him produce magic strong enough to rival that of any of the great Mentalists. Past and present. Yet, for reasons I can scarcely fathom, he can't control his damnable fingers. Honestly, I should be referring to them as sausages at this point.

Thelarius has mastered gracelessness in its entirety. I'm afraid he's more akin to a child-genius that has yet to realize how great he truly is than to an adult practitioner brimming with raw skill. Everything surprises him. I don't doubt it was because of his time spent as a slave. I'll watch over him for now. I think I'll teach him how to read. Writing can come after—or perhaps during? I've never taught someone how to be literate. This will be an interesting challenge.

But still, damn these Mentalists and their senseless system. Once I become head, I'll change it all. I swear it.

304 Iron Age 97

Thelarius isn't the fastest learner, though he isn't the slowest either. He has the trade alphabet mostly memorized, and is immensely proud of the fact. I wonder if I can begin teaching him other languages as well. But I don't want to confuse him, so perhaps I'll hold off on it for now. Maybe we can create our own secret code? It would help if we could communicate without having to worry about eavesdroppers. We could make it from a mix of symbols that he's comfortable with.

Oh, I'm getting excited just thinking about it.

Even if he isn't particularly gifted in academics, he's a natural with his magic. The idiot was able to conjure flames close to mine after only a few days of practice. I envy him for that, but at the same time, I don't as well. Is that strange? I think so.

If properly trained, Thelarius will become a force to be reckoned with. He'll far exceed me and any of the other Mentalists for that matter. I just know it. But for now, we've opted to keep his magic a secret. I think it's for the best. Thankfully, so does he. I'm glad to see he has some sense at least.

In other news, he's finally stopped looking at me like I'm hiding some awful demon of pure torment under all this skin. He's stopped addressing me so formally, too.

Amity soothes the soul.

[A list of complex words beginning with the letters: *s* and *v* fill the next three pages. Some are circled.]

154 Iron Age 98

Thelarius accidentally slipped up in front of someone from the Melandeer family! Showed their heiress and her Healer friend not one, not two, but three elements. Three! They stared at him like he was some sort of golden Snuff! And who could blame them?

I can't get their interested eyes out of my head. I doubt this'll end well. Maurice and Pernelia, were their names. I'm writing it here as evidence, so I'll know who to look for if Thelarius' secret gets out and he's dragged to the Mentalists in one of the stricter Institute's.

Creator, help me. I feel like an old, humorless man right now. What will I do if my hair starts to turn gray? I've only seen 26 winters! That's too early for my hair to lose its lavish shine!

Perhaps I can enchant it?

Hmm…

[Followed by labelled sketches of plants known for their leaf extracts.]

<u>216 Iron Age 99</u>

It wasn't my imagination.

I heard a voice, and Thelarius confirmed it.

He claims it made him a practitioner. What nonsense. But what reason would he have to lie? I saw his shackles. I taught him how to read for Elder Bindrow's sake! Then again, why would that thing even choose to come to him?

What's the point of all this?

I need to lie down. The world is going to split tomorrow. I can sort these thoughts out after. If I'm still alive that is.

Alaina, guide me back home to you.

<u>499 Iron Age 99 – 01 Oak Age 01</u>

He did it.

Thelarius triumphed over the Mentalists. With her help. With ours, too, or so he says. I'm flattered. Truly. But with or without us, I firmly believe he would've been perfectly capable of doing this. All of it. Everything. Given, it may not have been as fun without my stellar jokes, and he would have never met Pernelia, but… I've lost the point of this.

Things really will change now.

I suppose it's already beginning. Maurice has already taken steps to change the age. Thelarius suggested the "Bright Age". Why he chose

'Bright,' I'd rather not know. I have a feeling it's very sappy. Maurice and Pernelia snubbed it of course. They voted to keep the tradition of physical things. Some customs are good, they say. Even I can't deny that. They chose 'Oak' instead. Sturdy, but not unbreakable. Just the kind of mindset Ferus Terria needs. They even changed how we write it out on documents—OA. Just another thing I'll have to get used to, I suppose. I never anticipated this much change in my lifetime.

I wonder what the next age will be and what it might bring. Well, there's certainly no rush. Five hundred days to a year, and one hundred years to an age. I will let my grandchildren fret over the name.

(Though I did like the sound of Bright.)

[Flecks of water and ink ruined the notes written between the margins.]

<u>05.04.OA</u>

These constant meetings are giving me headaches. I was meant to bathe things in fire and spark the blazes of war, not preside over arguing farmers and squabbling houses. Never in my wildest dreams did I think about becoming a councilman, and I know Thelarius feels the same.

I'd like to talk to him about all of this. But I don't know where he's been hiding recently. Perhaps I can lure him out with a game of cards. Maybe even convince him to bet some of his riches. It sounds enticing enough—for me anyway.

I'm sure they can survive without us for a few hours. Personally, I think they'll be better off. Pernelia and Maurice thrive in this type of environment. They're noblemen to the core, and for that reason alone, I don't think we'll ever truly see eye-to-eye. I just don't understand the appeal of it all.

The Thareen family has been especially aggravating lately. How many times must I refuse their offers of marriage, before they get the point? Flames! I already have a wife. A very crabby one at that, thanks to them. Alaina's always angry at me nowadays, and with the baby on the way, her ire has only worsened.

Oh, speaking of the baby, I need to ask Thelarius about becoming the little tyke's godfather. I have a feeling he's going to refuse though. He gets this wistful, self-deprecating look in his eye whenever he thinks about children. 'Fatherhood doesn't suit me,' he says. Nonsense.

Perhaps I should do him a favor first. Something to butter him up. He does want to tell the others about 'her.' Really, he's too honest for his own good.

I have a bad feeling about this, but if it's what he wants, then I'll support him (and help myself in the process.)

<u>18.08.OA</u>

Maurice has chartered aid from the Pulka scholars.

They're a parliament of reclusive researchers that rejected society in favor of their own pursuits... or so every single mentor I've had since I was a child has told me. I've never actually seen one of them until now, but lo and behold, there they sat in circles around the common room, sipping tea and discussing gemstones of all things. Like the rest of Ferus Terria didn't believe them myths.

I'll have to ask how Maurice found the time—and the resources— to bring them here; and why he did, too. To advise us, perhaps? I hope not. I don't like them. They're scrawny and haughty and have these maddeningly curious eyes. Way, way too fanciful for my taste. I'm actually disappointed. I feel like a little boy that just realized dragons no longer exist because humanity is full of rotten buffoons.

But... Ferus Terria needs men like that now.

Maybe I should retire and become a hermit.

[Illegible scribbles and half-finished diagrams follow.]

<u>442.10.OA</u>

Ever since Maurice produced the Orivellea and did the impossible by creating Peose, Thelarius has become extra prickly. He won't tell anyone why though, and Maurice isn't any help either. Flaming blue-

blood is good at keeping his mouth shut that's for sure. But it's surreal for me to realize that Thelarius is so unhappy with him and not know the cause. He used to tell me everything. While they've always just barely gotten along, I've never seen Thelarius go out of his way to offend the man. I wonder what happened between them.

The war room is suffocating enough without them adding to the tension. Pernelia is engrossed in her work, but I'm sure she noticed it, too. I'll have to ask her opinion. Perhaps she can order them to reconcile. She's always been good at that. Terrifying woman. What they see in her, I'll never know. I don't want to either.

Though I am curious about Maurice and his army of weeds. How did they come up with the recipe for that crystal? Even if it's still considered experimental, the fact that it can grant a few animals the gift of magic is amazing—it even has me wondering about its potential. Maybe I should find out more about it?

Oh, I can feel my magic tingling in approval at the idea. This hasn't happened since the last age! It's good to know that I haven't seen all this world has to offer. I've missed getting excited over new things. I intend to look into this matter immediately. But first, I really need to sign those documents, before the pile becomes anymore ungodly than it already is. Just looking at it is menacing.

Alaina is going to yell at me again.

Fantastic.

106.11.OA

I found the recipe... and I regret ever finding it.

Why didn't Thelarius tell me what was going on when the crystal was first made? Shame? Regret? Or did he just want to deal with it on his own? I would've gladly roasted that bastard Maurice into oblivion. With or without his approval. ~~Maybe that's what he was afraid of.~~

I can't believe he sealed parts of 'her' away. I didn't even think that was possible. My hands are still shaking from the mere thought of all of the corpses they must've used to create a solid place to hold her essence... is that why so many practitioners and Nebbin have been disappearing recently? That's vile! Atrocious! I can't even express—

This isn't what I created the Demar Spell for!

How could Maurice turn a precautionary measure for departing practitioners into… this? What's more, how was he able to concentrate her essence into the, no, there's no use dwelling over it now. It was a mistake to tell the others about her. He's using those crystals to create more Elementalists. Those dreadful Peose were only the beginning.

But why is he—

I need to find Thelarius.

107.11.OA

Thelarius is gone.

How could I let this happen? How could I just let him—

He's left me with this mess of a country. Always passing along the hard jobs. Then he has the gall to leave a letter telling me not to search for him? Idiot. As if anyone can stop me. Or Maurice for that matter. That demented Healer has locked Pernelia away in a place beyond my reach. She's surrounded by Peose and practitioners and…

I can't do this! Not alone.

Where are you Thelarius? How could you just leave without me? Without a word to anyone? I would've followed you regardless of the danger. I would've always, always followed. I hope it's not too late. I'm going now, regardless of that stupid letter. I had to say goodbye to my wife and son, but I can rest easy knowing they're safe.

I'm on my way to the Pit in Aston. Perhaps his birthplace will hold the secret. If not to him, then to her.

143.11.OA

I've been stranded in the Pit for days. My magic circuit is going to give soon. There are so many Peose here. Just how many did Maurice send? Well, it doesn't matter. Not anymore. I've found what I came for.

Thelarius definitely passed through here. He left tracks. Deliberate ones. He isn't careless enough to leave any obvious signs of his presence by accident. Did he know I would come then? Some of the walls were carved with his thoughts in our code, so he must have.

He claims that she'll come for him. That she'll find him because he's currently waiting with a piece of her. I can venture a guess as to what that means, but I'm still sore at him for failing to mention where he was waiting. If he's going to reach out to me, why must he remain so damn elusive? (Though I suppose vague words are better than none at all.)

I never realized that she had one, singular conscience though. And what in the Creator's name does that final bit he wrote about that piece of her keeping him bound mean? I don't understand any of it. But I don't need to. As his guardian, I know what I have to do.

I'm exhausted, and it'll alert them of my presence, but these walls needs to disappear.

Now.

147.11.OA

I can hear them. They're close.

With death so near, I wonder why the only noises ringing in my ears are that of my crying son. I'm going delirious, surely. This is no time to bereave. I need food. I need water. I need to leave this place.

Perhaps it's my famished mind playing tricks on me again, but I think I understand what Thelarius meant now. A little too late of course. Nevertheless, I'm happy to have known something was amiss rather than spend my days blind to it all. I'll leave my journal here in the hopes that one day, someone can reveal the truth. The one I wasn't able to. Hopefully it isn't too late.

If you're still there and have yet to tire of the mindless prattles of a once very important Conjurer, then hear me now:

The strongest of practitioners are nothing more than Nebbin. An artificial class bred from ill intentions. Human Peose, if you will. To the one reading this, I can only pray that those atrocious creatures still aren't around. I've enclosed within this journal the recipe of the Orive crystals. As you may have already surmised from my previous entries, pieces of 'her' are sealed within. I cannot explain to you what she is or from whence she came, but know this, she exists... and she is powerful beyond imagine. She is tied only because her consciousness has been separated from the pieces of her that Maurice sealed and stripped away. Only the "head," so to speak, is needed for the parts to strive and multiply. I don't know how he singled her out and separated her, but what's done is done.

The Orivellea are crafted from the bodies of those that can contain her, or in other words, us. Nebbin mostly, but, oh, when those awful crystals are powered by the bodies of dead practitioners, you wouldn't believe the kind of effect they —

I know this may not make much sense.

Truthfully, I feel like a fool just writing it, but even if I was insane, I still wouldn't have done what he did. So, please believe me when I write that Maurice operated behind our backs. I knew nothing of this, and I can vouch for my oldest friend as well.

Now, I can only pray that the world becomes what we envisioned. A place for Nebbin and practitioner to peacefully co-exist. A place where everyone has the freedom to choose and live how they please. Shackles be damned. I want to see the Demar Spell used for its intended purpose. Not to trap, but to provide assurance for the younger generation that might feel threatened in a world they've never been allowed to roam; assurance to those that seek extra security, while the Nebbin resolve their anger at their fathers for their unholy ways.

Perhaps the world I dream of is nothing but an idealist's fantasy. But I've seen the impossible happen again and again during my time by Thelarius Merve. Another miracle certainly isn't out of the question.

Not when he's still here to make it happen.

01 Bright Age 01

Thelarius is alive.